THE

BEST MAN

D0828649

THE BEST MAN

BRENDA JACKSON

CINDI LOUIS

FELICIA MASON

KAYLA PERRIN

St. Martin's Paperbacks

NOTE: If you purchased this book without a cover you should be aware that this book is stolen property. It was reported as "unsold and destroyed" to the publisher, and neither the author nor the publisher has received any payment for this "stripped book."

THE BEST MAN

"Strictly Business" copyright © 2003 by Brenda Streater Jackson.
"Catch Me If You Can!" copyright © 2003 by Cynthia Louis.
"Promises and Vows" copyright © 2003 by Felicia L. Mason.
"Kidnapped!" copyright © 2003 by Kayla Perrin.

All rights reserved. No part of this book may be used or reproduced in any manner whatsoever without written permission except in the case of brief quotations embodied in critical articles or reviews. For information address St. Martin's Press, 175 Fifth Avenue, New York, NY 10010.

ISBN: 0-312-98218-6

Printed in the United States of America

St. Martin's Paperbacks edition / February 2003

St. Martin's Paperbacks are published by St. Martin's Press, 175 Fifth Avenue, New York, NY 10010.

10 9 8 7 6 5 4 3 2 1

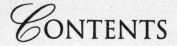ONTENTS

STRICTLY BUSINESS

BRENDA JACKSON

ACKNOWLEDGMENTS

To my husband and biggest supporter, Gerald Jackson, Sr.

To my niece, Regina Renee Franklin. You are one special young lady.

To all my avid readers who love the Madaris family and their friends. This one is especially for you.

And to my Heavenly Father, who makes all things possible.

A man who refuses to admit his mistakes can never be successful. But if he confesses and forsakes them, he gets another chance.

—Proverbs 28:13 (*The Living Bible*)

PROLOGUE

MITCHELL Farrell was man enough to admit he had made a few mistakes in his lifetime. But he had absolutely no intentions of making the same mistakes twice. With a determined smile he snapped his seat belt in place and settled into the flight that would take him to Houston.

Never in his life had he been so determined to achieve a goal—a goal some would think was impossible with all the obstacles he faced. But he was a man with a plan.

A plan to get his wife back.

As his private jet cleared the Los Angeles runway and tilted its wings toward Texas, he settled back in his seat and remembered the first time he had seen Regina Grant on the campus of Texas Southern University seven years ago; the mere sight of her had taken his breath away. It hadn't been like him to fall hard and fast, but against her he hadn't stood a chance. No other woman had taken such hold of his mind and body like she had. She completely captured his heart.

During his teenage years he had grown up dirt poor, so he'd been determined to one day have wealth and power at his fingertips, determined that nothing and no one would get in his way of achieving that, especially a woman. He had pretty much kept that resolve until his final year in grad school, when he had met Gina. She had been in her senior year of college. He had been lost the first time they'd made eye contact. That day she'd become as basic to him as breathing.

For the longest while he'd thought he could simply add her to the list of things he wanted in life, which was why he had married her less than a year later. He soon realized that marriage to Gina was more of a challenge than he'd anticipated. He could not get her to understand the driving force of his need to make it to the top at the cost of everything else—including the baby she desperately wanted. Their marriage hadn't worked out, and after four years it had ended. That was a huge mistake. He should never have let that happen.

He had been a fool to let her walk out of his life, an even bigger fool to have placed more emphasis and importance on making it to the top than holding their marriage together. And the main reason he'd walked away so easily was that the amount of love he'd felt for her had disturbed him. He had never counted on loving any woman so intensely that it made him lose his focus.

It had taken him two lonely years after their divorce to accept just how much he had loved her and that success was nothing without her. He wanted and needed her back in his life. For him the tragedy of September 11, 2001, served as a blunt reminder that you could be here one day and gone the next, and that when you left this world you couldn't take anything with you, especially not the material things you had worked hard to accumulate.

He had been in New York that day for a meeting at the World Trade Center with a business associate and friend, Tom Swank. But a phone call that morning from his office in Los Angeles had delayed him at his hotel. Quite frankly, that phone call had saved his life—but nothing had saved Tom's. That had been his first wake-up call to reexamine who he was and what he was. In the end he'd decided he didn't like himself very much. At thirty-five he'd realized that his priorities were screwed up and knew he had to take whatever measures necessary to get them back in order.

He was no longer the workaholic he used to be; no longer endlessly driven by success. The only thing that drove him now was the tremendous task he faced of convincing Gina to give him another chance. And if given that chance, he would give her every damn thing she had ever asked for:

the honeymoon they'd never gotten around to taking, the baby she'd always wanted and more time for them to spend together since he'd always been constantly on the go. A part of him refused to believe it was too late, that things were completely over between them.

So he was headed to Houston with a plan. And it was a plan he intended to make work, by any means necessary.

CHAPTER 1

THERE were certain things that a woman just couldn't forget.

For instance, she could not forget the time she progressed from girl into womanhood; the time she began wearing her first bra; the time she had her first date; the first time she fell in love and the first time she had made love.

Gina was reminded of the latter two as she sat across from the man who had played an instrumental role in both: her ex-husband, Mitch Farrell. She tried to concentrate on what he was saying and not on the memories invading her mind. Memories of naked bodies and silken sheets; memories of lovemaking sessions that had seemed to last forever, and orgasms of the highest intensity that had no endings.

Seeing Mitch again reminded her of all those things. It also reminded her of pain still lingering deep within, and was a rude awakening that even two years after their divorce, he was not yet out of her system, not fully out of her heart. That thought made her rather uncomfortable.

"What about it, Gina?" Mitch asked softly after taking a leisurely sip of his wine, interrupting her thoughts. The eyes that met his were curious yet reserved.

They sat at a corner table in Sisters, a well-known restaurant in downtown Houston. On weekends it was usually filled to capacity, but tonight—a weeknight—the amount of people dining was a good number: not too many to be considered crowded and not too few to be considered cozy. The atmosphere was relaxing, comfortable and tranquil.

"Why me, Mitch? Why have you come to me with such a generous offer?" she finally asked him, her brows knit.

He smiled before his gaze shifted to the magazine in front of him, having expected her question. "I think the answer to that is obvious. That piece you did on Jake Madaris and Diamond Swain was outstanding and says it all."

She smiled. "Thank you."

When wealthy rancher Jake Madaris and movie actress Diamond Swain had announced to the world they were married, and had been for nearly two years, everyone had wanted their story. It had been Gina Grant Farrell, a twenty-eight-year-old freelance writer and family friend of the Madaris family, whom the couple had gotten to do the exclusive interview and write the article. Before then, Gina had done a number of jobs for various publications but the piece on Jake and Diamond for *People* magazine had brought her skill as a journalist into the national spotlight.

"And you know how I am when it comes to my privacy, Gina," he continued. "You know me better than anyone, and I think it's time people knew the real Mitch Farrell as well. I want you to be the one to tell my story because I know you'll be fair and objective."

Gina inhaled slowly. Yes, she did know him and at one time she'd felt she had known him better than anyone. But that had been before the demise of their marriage. After that she'd wondered if she'd really known him at all. She silently admitted there were times when she thought there were things about his past that he refused to share with her. But the one thing she did know was that Mitch wasn't the cold, hard, self-made millionaire the media made him out to be. He was fast becoming one of the largest land developers in the country, and everyone wanted to know all they could about the elusive, wealthy divorcé who'd made his mark in real estate.

"People might think I'd be *less* objective since we *were* once married," she finally said.

"Or they may think that since we were married you would have the inside scoop if there were any. I want my story told, Gina, so people can stop speculating."

Again she was surprised. The Mitch she knew wouldn't have cared what anyone thought. She had been a journalist long enough to know that people liked reading whatever they could get their hands on about the rich and famous—regardless of whether the information was true. "The speculation may not stop, Mitch. It may only increase."

"I know, but I want to put it in writing once and for all that I live a very normal and very dull life that doesn't include a different woman in my bed every night."

Gina took a sip of her wine. She was glad to hear that. Although she hadn't wanted to believe what she'd read in the newspapers and tabloids, the thought that he had become a womanizer had bothered her more than it should have.

She sighed as she placed her wineglass down. There was a lot to consider. She had thought about him a lot over the past few weeks after hearing he had returned to Houston on business. He had moved to California within months after their divorce.

He had come to town to discuss a business deal with Madaris Enterprises, a company formed by the Madaris brothers—Justin, Dex and Clayton—to fulfill their dream: to build an exclusive office park that would house the fifteen-story Madaris Building as well as a cluster of upscale shops. She had been surprised to get a call from Mitch yesterday, inviting her to dinner to discuss a business proposition. The last time they had seen or spoken to each other had been at her brother Trevor's wedding reception almost a year ago. She knew Trevor and Mitch had stayed in contact over the past two years.

Her mind went back to the offer he'd made. She knew any journalist would jump at the chance to do an exclusive with Mitch. He was a man who seldom did interviews. But not only was he willing to do one, he wanted her to be part of it.

And that was the crux of her problem. That was the reason she felt so tense. There was no way she could spend any amount of time with him and not remember what they had once meant to each other. Although they had agreed to remain friends after their divorce, all it took was for her to look at him to know that even after all this time she was still attracted to him. He was still handsome, sexy and masculine, with eyes so compelling they not only penetrated your soul but had the ability to draw you in. Even now when he looked at her, his eyes went almost black. They were just that intense, dark and magnetic.

She sighed deeply. The effect Mitch still had on her was startling and played havoc on her raw nerve endings. He could still make her body ache in certain places. The interview would take a good week to complete if she did it in stages like the one she'd done on Jake and Diamond. How would she survive Mitch Farrell for an entire week?

"Where will the interview take place?" she asked, breaking the silence between them and trying not to notice his hands. They were hands that used to give her hours upon hours of earth-shattering pleasure. Of all the things they used to disagree about while married, sex was never an issue; the both of them had had overpassionate hormones. The main reason they had decided to go ahead and marry so soon after they'd met was that they had found it hard to keep their overheated sexuality under control. It was during those times in his arms, while they were able to bring each other to a second orgasm while still trembling from the effects of the first, that she'd felt so much an integral part of him. Even now, a part of her body tingled from thinking about how they used to make love all night long.

"My ranch."

Gina raised an arched brow when she realized he had answered her question. "Your ranch? In Los Angeles?"

He gave her a smile that had the ability to actually reach out and touch her, which was bad timing after just having thoughts of them making love. "No, the one here in Houston," he murmured softly.

She stared at him through the lingering fog of his words, confused. "You own a ranch here in Houston?"

He knew that information had surprised her. "Yes. Actually it's a few miles out, a hundred acres of land in Fresno. I bought it six months ago. Are you familiar with the area?"

Gina nodded in stunned shock. Yes, she was familiar with the area. It was a beautiful section that was far enough away from the hustle and bustle of downtown Houston but close enough by way of the interstate. The land, rich in dark

Texas soil with large oak trees and lush green grass, was beautiful and scenic. She knew Trevor and his wife Corinthians were thinking about buying land in the area to build a new home.

"How are your parents, Gina? I understand they're back together."

Gina refused to let him smoothly change subjects especially after the bomb he'd just dropped. "Yes, after nearly twenty years Mom and Dad are back together and are ecstatic about being grandparents," she said, thinking about her three-month-old nephew. Then, without missing a beat, she asked, frowning, "Why did you buy a ranch in Fresno, Mitch?"

He met her gaze. "Because I'm moving back here."

She frowned some more. "Why?"

Rather than tell her the truth, the absolute truth, Mitch decided to give her the watered-down version. "I miss Texas, Gina. Houston especially. Although I was born in Beaumont, I consider Houston my home since I spent the majority of my time growing up here. Is it so unusual for someone to want to return home?"

She considered his question thoughtfully before responding. "No, but you used to hate Houston because of the things you didn't want to remember." They were things he had never shared with her. "Is it easier to come back now that you've gotten everything you wanted in life?"

A part of Mitch knew that now was not the time to tell her he hadn't gotten everything since he didn't have her. Nor was it the time to tell her that he'd found out the hard way he had never been satisfied. The more he had obtained, the greedier he had become. But in the end he'd realized material possessions and success weren't everything. Having someone you loved and someone who loved you were. And he did love the beautiful woman sitting across from him. He loved everything about her. He loved the way she wore her hair now, an abundance of shoulder-length, precision-cut layers. And he loved her full lips, the high cheekbones on her cocoa-colored complexion and the dark brown eyes that conveyed sensuality and allurement all rolled into one.

"No, that's not the reason, Gina," he said as the corners of his lips lifted in a smile. "I guess you can say that I've come back to find myself. That's one of the reasons I want you to do the article. Talking about it, getting it out with someone I trust will help. That's one mistake I regret making while married to you. I didn't openly communicate with you as I should have."

Gina said nothing for a long time. This was definitely not the same Mitch. He might look the same but his views had definitely changed. What he had just confessed was true. He hadn't openly communicated with her because he'd been too busy making it to the top. Being successful and having money and power were all that had mattered. He had wanted those things more than he had wanted her. What had bothered her most about their breakup was how easily he had walked away from their marriage without putting up a fight.

"I need to think about it, Mitch."

"That's fine but I'd like to know something within a week if possible."

She nodded and glanced at the magazine that was still in front of him. A week was plenty of time for her to really think things through. "All right. I'll let you know something by then."

She then looked up at him and again got caught up in the way he was looking at her. His gaze was touching her; she could feel it through the clothes she was wearing. The deep penetration of his eyes was hot. She let the scope of her vision run lightly over his face, everywhere except the deepness of his dark eyes. She took in the rich chocolate coloring of his skin, the sharp cheekbones, the jutting chin with its dimpled cleft, the full lips. She inhaled deeply when she felt deep sexual awareness and knew she had to make sure his offer was just what it was. She could not fill her head with illusions that it was more than that. For a moment she tried reading his thoughts; but as usual his expression was unreadable.

"This interview is strictly business, right, Mitch?" she decided to ask.

Mitch lifted his wineglass and met her stare before taking a sip. "Yes, Gina, this is strictly business," he said smoothly. He then tipped the wineglass to his lips and while the cool wine slipped down his throat he thought, *Strictly* unfinished *business.*

CHAPTER 2

GINA heard her phone ring the minute she walked into her home. Locking the door behind her, she quickly crossed the room to answer it. "Hello?"

"How did things go tonight?"

Gina smiled upon hearing her sister-in-law's voice. The woman her brother had married almost a year ago had become the sister she'd never had. With only a three-year difference in their ages, she and Corinthians had quickly formed a bond that was priceless.

Easing onto the sofa, Gina pulled off her earrings and adjusted the phone to a more comfortable position. "They went okay, I imagine, given the fact that I sat across from Mitch hot and bothered the entire time. Isn't that pathetic?"

"No," Corinthians answered softly, not trying to mask the smile in her voice. "Considering that you still love him, I don't think it's pathetic at all."

Gina released a long, deep sigh. "I never said I still loved Mitch."

"You didn't have to. I heard love in your voice the first time you told me about him. And if you'll recall, you were rather upset that Trevor had invited him to our wedding reception."

Gina sighed, remembering that time. "Only because we'd been divorced less than a year and I didn't think I was ready to see him again."

"But you did see him and you survived."

"Yes, but just barely. And now that he's back makes it harder, especially since he mentioned tonight that he's moving back to Houston and wants me to do an exclusive interview with him."

"That's a generous offer. Are you going to do it?"

"I don't know. Financially, it's a great opportunity since a lot of magazines are just dying to get their hands on his story, but I don't know if I could handle being around him long enough to do it."

"If he's moving back to Houston you'll be around him anyway, won't you? The two of you are bound to run into each other occasionally."

"I can deal with occasional sightings. What he's proposing is for me to do the interview at his ranch. A good solid interview will take a week to complete, especially with the angle I plan to use. I can't imagine spending a week alone with him, Corinthians."

"Where's his ranch?"

"He bought one in Fresno."

"Umm, then there's a good possibility we might become neighbors. Trevor and I put a down payment on some land in Fresno today. We hope to start building sometime next year."

Gina smiled, happy for the brother she thought would never marry. Not only did he have a wife he loved completely, but he also had a son he simply adored. Not wanting to talk about Mitch any longer, at least not any more tonight, she changed the subject. "And how is my darling nephew?"

Corinthians laughed. "Right now he's in his father's arms watching a football game. Trask is here and he's explaining the rules of the game to Rio."

Gina shook her head grinning. Trask Maxwell, a family friend and former professional football player, was still considered the greatest running back in NFL history. "Does Trask really believe a three-month-old baby can understand football?"

"Evidently he does since he's been at it since the game started. Surprisingly, Rio doesn't seemed the least bored and is still awake." Corinthians sighed happily. "Of all my accomplishments I think having Rio is the greatest. He's such a wonderful baby."

Gina shifted slightly in her seat as old tinges of longings rose up within her. Since Trevor had been older than her by ten years, she had spent her adolescent years wanting her parents—who'd separated when she was six years old—to get back together if for no other reason than to give her a baby sister or brother. And when that hadn't happened, she had grown up looking forward to the day she would marry and have a child of her own. While married to Mitch she had wanted his baby more than anything, but he had staunchly refused to talk about her going off the Pill.

"Gina?"

"Yes?"

"Don't worry. Things will work out. I believe there's a reason Mitch is moving back to Houston."

"There is. He wants to find himself."

"Oh? And where do you fit into all of this?"

"I don't fit anywhere."

"What about the interview he wants you to do?"

Gina released a deep, lingering breath as she remembered Mitch's words. "The interview is strictly business."

"What are you smiling about?" a deep, masculine voice asked from across the table.

Mitch quickly wiped the smile from his face as he looked into the curious gaze of Trevor Grant, the man who had once been his brother-in-law and who, if Mitch succeeded with his plan, would one day again hold that same connection. He had awakened that morning with a smile on his face after a night spent having hot, vividly sensual dreams about Gina. And now it was close to noontime and he was still smiling. He doubted Trevor would want to know the real reason for his jovial expression. After all, Gina was the man's sister.

"No reason," he muttered, looking down at his watch. He then glanced around the restaurant. "What time will the Madarises get here?"

"Soon enough. They had to swing by the airport and

pick up Justin, which is just as well since it gives us time to talk."

Mitch allowed himself a minute before reluctantly looking at Trevor. He had an idea just what Trevor wanted to talk to him about but decided to play dumb. "Talk about what?"

"Gina."

Mitch leaned forward and placed his hand on the table. "What about Gina?"

"I want to know what your intentions are, Mitch."

Mitch shrugged. "What makes you think I have any?"

"Mainly because I know the two of you went out to dinner last night and just a few minutes ago you had that same stupid-looking smile on your face that I sometimes get on mine when I'm thinking about Corinthians."

Mitch angled his head. "And you assume my thoughts were on Gina?"

"Weren't they?"

Mitch pulled his gaze away from Trevor knowing the truth was in his eyes. Feeling agitated that he was under cross-examination, he answered, "Yes."

"Then I want to know what your intentions are."

Mitch frowned as he tossed down the scotch, flinching slightly as it burned his throat, and then signaled for a refill. "You're not her father, Trevor," he said angrily after he'd gotten his second drink.

Trevor's expression hardened. "No, I'm her brother but if you'd prefer I could get my father to ask the question."

Mitch tossed down another swig of scotch. That was the last thing he needed, he thought grimly, feeling the hot liquid settle firmly in his stomach. Maurice Grant was a hard man to deal with when it came to his daughter. Mitch still remembered the day he had asked for Gina's hand in marriage. It had been like asking for a piece of the Red Sea. He had to all but prove his worthiness. Both Mr. and Mrs. Grant had felt he and Gina were rushing things and should wait at least another year before considering marriage. But Mitch wouldn't hear of it. He had wanted Gina and since she had been determined to remain a virgin until marriage, he'd had no intentions of waiting another year. There were only so many cold showers a body could take.

Mitch leaned back in his chair, closed his eyes and rubbed his temple. Dear heavens, he didn't need this. Especially not now. "Why are you giving me grief, Trevor?"

"Because I don't want to see Gina get hurt again, dammit."

Mitch opened his eyes and met the hard, cold-steel ones of Trevor Grant. He stared at his ex-brother-in-law without flinching, something most men wouldn't be able to do. "I made a mistake, man. I love Gina. I always have and I always will."

"Then why did you let her go?"

Mitch winced at the hardness he heard in Trevor's voice. He couldn't help but remember how he had lost his parents before his sixth birthday and how after that he had gone to live with the grandmother he'd adored until she had died when he'd turned ten. The three people he had loved the most had left him. After that, for two solid years he had been tossed from one relative to another, never fitting in with any of them and never feeling completely loved. From the age of twelve until he had graduated from high school, he had lived in the worst kind of poverty, when he'd been sent to live with an alcoholic uncle. The man used the money the state gave him each month for his nephew's care on booze and women. There had been many nights that Mitch had gone to bed hungry, and many days he had gone to school wearing the same clothes he had worn the day before. He had made a solemn vow then never to depend on anyone being there for him and do whatever he could to never live in poverty again.

"I let her go mainly because I was too stupid to appreciate what I had and too afraid to completely give my heart to anyone again," he said softly.

Trevor leaned toward him; from the look in his eyes Mitch knew the explanation he'd just given hadn't been good enough. But Mitch refused to be more specific. He owed Gina an explanation before giving it to anyone else.

"I always liked you, Mitch," Trevor said in a tone of voice that indicated he was not taking the conversation lightly. "Mainly because deep down in my gut I felt you loved my sister senseless, although things didn't work out between the two of you for whatever reason. She got her life back together after you left and I don't particularly relish the thought of you returning to town messing it back up again. I'd rather you conclude this business with the Madarises as quickly as possible, and go back to California."

Mitch kept his anger in check. After all, Trevor was only trying to protect Gina. "I won't hurt her, Trevor."

"You did once," Trevor accused.

"Yes, but everyone is entitled to make mistakes—just like everyone is entitled to a second chance." He met Trevor's stare. "And I'm asking that you give me that. Both Gina and I made mistakes in our marriage, and we both gave in to the divorce too easily. When push came to shove we forgot about the vows we'd made that said *for better or for worse*. We should have stayed together and worked things out, but we didn't."

"And now?"

The two men stared at each other for a long moment before Mitch finally said in a throaty whisper as something sharp and blunt swirled around his heart, "And now the main reason I've moved back to Houston is to get my wife back. I love her, Trevor, and I hope I can convince her that I've changed and to give me another chance. These two years without her have shown me just how wrong my priorities were. She was the best thing to ever happen to me and in my own selfish and self-centered way, I put my wants and needs before hers. I'm ready to do whatever I have to do to regain her love." Mitch saw belief, then acceptance, in Trevor's dark eyes.

"So," Trevor said as he leaned back in his chair and took a sip of his drink. "I imagine you must have a plan because you're definitely going to need one."

Mitch nodded. "Yes, I got a plan."

"And you think it's going to work?"

Mitch nodded again. "I pray to God that it does."

Trevor gave him a slow smile and said, "I pray to God that it does, too."

• • •

Six days after Mitch's offer Gina still hadn't made a decision. She had spent most of that time collecting all the recent articles about him she could. Most of them had been sketchy, including the one that had appeared in *Newsweek* four months ago, when Mitch had made news as the first Democratic African-American appointed by a Republican president to serve on a committee for land acquisition and development.

She was proud of all the accomplishments Mitch had made in his life. A part of her knew she and Mitch had wanted different things while they had been married: He had wanted his career and she had wanted his baby. And neither had been willing to compromise. The only place they had compromised had been in the bedroom, giving in to each other's demands, wants and desires.

She stood and walked over to the window. She had converted an empty bedroom into an office where she did most of her writing. Presently, she was working on a piece for *Ebony* magazine for Black History Month.

Without realizing she was doing it, Gina gently touched the windowpane. She remembered a day that was very similar to this one, when she had stood by a window and watched as Mitch had loaded the last of his things into the car. It had been the last day they had spent together under the same roof as man and wife.

She would never forget the day she had asked Mitch for a divorce. She slowly removed her hand from the window and placed it on her waist as her mind relived that day.

"What do you mean you want a divorce?" Mitch paused from placing the folders in his briefcase long enough to ask.

"I mean just what I said, Mitch. I'm going to file for a divorce. We no longer have a marriage. You spend more time at the office than you do here. We never spend any time together and I'm tired of it."

He slammed his briefcase shut. "You're tired of it! How in the hell are we supposed to eat around here? How are the bills supposed to be paid? Most women would want their husbands working hard each and every day to take care of those things. They sure as hell wouldn't be standing around whining about it."

She shook her head. "You just don't see it, do you?"

"All I see is a woman used to being pampered by her father and brother who now wants to be pampered by her husband. Well, I think there are more important things to do than spend my time pampering you, like putting food on the table and making sure that we keep a roof over our heads. That's why I work as hard as I do, Gina, so we can have those things we want. I want you taken care of."

"No, that's not it, Mitch. And it's not like I don't have a job, because I do. You work as hard as you do for your own satisfaction. I want a husband who will spend time with me; a person who is my friend as well as my lover. I don't have to have a husband with a prestigious career and a well-thought-of position, or someone making over a hundred thousand a year. All I want is someone who I can talk to, someone I can see and spend time with."

Tears filled her eyes. "You don't love me, Mitch. You love whatever it is you're trying to achieve. We have different goals in life; different needs and different dreams. I don't need the huge mansion on the hill, the Mercedes in the driveway or the bank account that's overflowing with money. All I need is a husband who loves me."

"I do love you, Gina."

"No, you don't, Mitch. At least you don't love me as much as I love you and I can't take it any longer. Just give me a divorce so I can get on with my life and you can get on with yours. And I hope that the two of us can remain friends."

She had waited, had hoped and prayed that he would cross the room and take her into his arms and tell her that he did love her as much as she loved him, and that he didn't want a divorce . . . but he never did. Instead he just stood there looking at her for a long moment before walking over to the closet to begin packing his things. An hour later he had walked out the door without looking back.

Gina blinked when the sound of a car horn broke into her thoughts. She drew a deep, shuddering breath and slowly

went back to her desk. Anything and everything that she and
Mitch had ever shared was now in the past. They had been
divorced for almost two years and the only thing they now
shared was friendship . . . and possibly a business deal if she
agreed to it. He had asked that she give him an answer within
a week and time was running out. She hadn't seen or heard
from him since that night but knew he was still in town, and
could only assume he was staying out at his ranch. She gazed
at the piece of paper he had given her at dinner that night,
which contained the phone number where he could be
reached. Before she could change her mind she picked up
the phone and began dialing.

"Hello."

Gina felt every muscle in her stomach constrict at the
sound of Mitch's voice. She thought it was everything a male
voice should be—deep, throaty and seductive. She couldn't
help remembering that same voice whispering sensuous and
sexy words in her ears while he made love to her. She closed
her eyes briefly as the impact of those memories swept over
her like a warm silken caress.

"Hello."

She blinked her eyes, coming back into awareness when
she realized she hadn't responded to his first greeting. "Hello,
Mitch. This is Gina."

Mitch silently sighed and allowed himself a moment of
profound thanks. At least she had called. When days had
passed and he hadn't heard from her, he had gotten worried
that maybe she would not accept his offer. Even now he still
wasn't sure that she would. "Yes, Gina?" he asked softly.

"About your offer for me to do the interview."

He swallowed hard and tried not to sound too anxious.
"Yes, what about it? Are you interested?"

Mitch's gut twisted at the brief pause . . . and then she
said, "Yes, I'm interested. I would love to do it and want to
thank you for giving me the opportunity."

Mitch felt the tension in his shoulders ease and let out
a deep, ragged breath of relief . . . and of thanks. "It's my
pleasure, Gina," he said huskily. *And*, he thought, *I can guar-
antee you that in the end it will be your pleasure as well.
You can count on it.*

CHAPTER 3

GINA was still having misgivings about accepting Mitch's offer when she drove down the long driveway leading to his ranch house. A frown marred her features when just ahead she saw what she thought to be the most dilapidated looking structure she had ever seen. It resembled an old worn-down farmhouse more than a ranch house.

She blinked twice, thinking she must be seeing things. Surely this building wasn't the ranch house Mitch had purchased. Apparently so, she thought a few seconds later when he got out of a black Durango SUV in front of the house when she brought her car to a stop. She blinked again. He was wearing jeans. Other than that calendar he had posed for last year, she could count on her right hand the number of times she had seen him in something other than business attire. He'd always stressed that a person should always dress for success, so even while lounging around the house he'd worn casual designer slacks and shirts, a totally different look from the well-worn jeans he was sporting now. She couldn't help but appreciate the well-put-together male body, a definite eye-catching look. It was the kind of look that could distract a woman something awful. She shifted her attention to his face and caught her breath at the same time that her heart stuttered. The dark shadow covering his chin, along with the well-worn jeans, made him look like a desperado from yesteryear.

A very handsome desperado at that.

"Good morning, Gina." He greeted her with warm brown eyes and a heart-stopping smile as he opened the car door for her.

"Good morning, Mitch. Are you sure today is a good time to start?" she asked, trying not to concentrate on the deep huskiness she heard in his voice.

"Yeah, I'm sure. We can get started just as soon as I get your opinion of the place."

Gina walked around the side of the car and took a good look at the building that was supposed to be a ranch house. Up close it was worse than she'd thought.

"Well, what do you think?" he asked, coming to stand next to her.

She tried to focus on his question and not on him standing so close beside her. Once again it was beginning to bother her that after nearly two years, he still had the ability to stir her physically. "Well, I guess it has potential," she finally responded. "But it depends on what you plan to do with it."

He smiled. Gina had always been blatantly honest; almost too much at times. "I plan to live here," he said softly.

"You're going to tear it down and rebuild?"

Mitch chuckled. "No, I plan to remodel."

Gina glanced back at the huge house that was barely standing. He had to be kidding. And she told him so.

"No, I'm not kidding. Believe it or not the structure of this place is still good. I've hired a really good team of professionals to assist me in restoring it to how it used to look."

She couldn't help but find that idea amusing. "Back in the eighteen hundreds?"

Mitch shook his head, grinning. "No, not quite that far back; but I have plans for this place. It will take me a while but I hope to have it livable within a year."

"That will take a lot of time and work."

"I have the time and will enjoy doing the work."

Surprise showed in Gina's face. "You won't be working?" she asked, then clarified by saying, "Your regular job as CEO of your corporation?"

"Yes, I'll still be working. In fact I'm meeting with the Madarises again later today. But I no longer spend all my time working my regular job, Gina. I have a couple of young executives for that. That gives me the time to do some of the things that I enjoy doing."

"Well, that's a switch," she said before she could stop herself. "I remember a time when all you did was work." *And never made time for yourself or for me*, she thought bitterly.

"Yes, I know. And I hate that I did that when I think of all that I lost in trying to be successful."

Gina actually heard regret in his voice but a part of her hardened. Too bad he hadn't realized that two years ago. It would have spared her a lot of heartache and pain. He'd been so quick and eager to make a marriage commitment with her but hadn't been so quick and eager to do what it took to make their marriage work. In the beginning a part of her had understood his need to do what was necessary to make it to the top. But she could not understand nor accept the degree in which he had done so. First there had been the countless hours of overtime that would extend into the weekends. Then, when he had made operations manager and later operations vice president, there were the business trips that carried him from one part of the country to another. He literally thrived on the hustle and bustle of the business world, and more times than not he was packed and ready to fly out, destination unknown, at a moment's notice. It became a norm for her to come home from work and find a note letting her know he was gone again.

Gina sighed. There was no reason to waste time thinking about their past. The only reason she was here was to talk to him about the interview. But still, she couldn't help glancing around and asking, "So, where are you staying? At a hotel in town?"

"No, I'm staying in that trailer over there through the trees."

Gina looked where his fingers pointed and saw a trailer very much like one of those usually stationed on a construction site, only it was a tad larger. "You're staying in that?" she asked disbelievingly.

"Sure. It has a bath, bed and a small kitchen. Everything I need."

Gina knew he could afford a hotel room if he wanted one, so that couldn't be the issue. "Why are you staying out here instead of at a hotel?" she couldn't help asking.

He smiled. "I like it here. It's so quiet and peaceful. Out here I'm attuned with nature, my surroundings and with myself. I think this is the perfect place to be." He met her inquisitive gaze. "This used to be my grandmother's home."

Gina sucked in her breath, shocked at his revelation. "But . . . but I thought you were born and raised in Beaumont."

"I was. My father was born in this house. He moved to Beaumont when he met and married my mother, and that's where I was born and lived until they were killed. Then I moved here with Gramma Eleanor when I was six."

He smiled warmly upon remembering that time in his life. "She was everything a grandmother should be and I loved her dearly. Together, she and I spent many hours walking this land, taking care of her gardens and farm animals. My life was the happiest until I turned ten. That's the year she got sick and died."

Gina swallowed upon hearing the pain in his voice. He had never shared this part of his life with her. She'd known his childhood had been less than grand, but he'd never shared any intimate details like he was doing now. "Where did you go after your grandmother died?"

"To an aunt and uncle who took great pains to let me know I was a charity case. And because of their attitudes, I rebelled and got into all kinds of trouble. As punishment they sent me to live with my Uncle Jasper."

She nodded. He *had* shared stories with her about his Uncle Jasper. "He's the one who had a drinking problem, right?"

"Yeah, he's the one," he said angrily through his teeth.

Gina knew his anger was not directed at her but was the result of lingering memories he had of the man who had tormented his life during his teen years. She glanced around the property again, now seeing it through different eyes and accepting it for what it really was. This was the place Mitch had been most happy during his childhood. This was the place that had brought him the most joy.

"Did you inherit this place after your grandmother died?" she asked. If he had, he had never mentioned it during the time they'd been married.

"No, my father had a brother and when Gramma Eleanor died this place automatically went to him. As you can see he had no use for it and over the years let it run itself down. It was only recently that I was able to negotiate a deal to buy it from my aunt when my uncle passed."

She stared at him, dumbfounded. Aunt? Uncle? He had never, ever mentioned that he had any relatives. In fact, she remembered distinctly asking him about any when she had made out wedding invitations and he'd told her there were none. Evidently he'd not grown up close to them.

Gina suddenly felt rattled. She had learned more about Mitch in the past few minutes than she'd known in the entire four years they had been married. There had been certain things he'd never discussed with her. His family, or lack of one, had been one of those topics he'd avoided. A part of her was surprised at the depth of what he'd revealed.

"So, where do we start?"

His words were casual, soft-spoken, yet they had the effect of something hot and luscious, snapping Gina back to the moment. And the tone, all sexy and sensuous, sank right into her bones. "Where do we start what?"

He gave her a crooked grin. "The interview."

Realizing that her thoughts had gone off in another direction, one that had a tingling settling in her midsection, she quickly reeled them back in. "How about if we agree on the questions I want to ask you?"

"You can ask me anything, Gina."

"Well, yeah, but I'm sure there are some things you'd want to avoid sharing with the world. Things you hold sacred that you want kept private."

"Like our marriage?"

She lifted her chin. "I said things *you* hold sacred, Mitch. Our marriage was never one of them."

There was a sudden quietness. The only sounds that could be heard were those of insects buzzing about and the distant sound of water flowing through a nearby stream. The smile on his face was gone, replaced by something close to misery. If that were the case, then the saying that misery loved company was true because she was right there with him. For two people who had once loved each other deeply, they had made a complete mess of things.

"I did hold our marriage sacred, Gina," he finally said softly. "Maybe not as much as I should have, but I did. I want very little said about our marriage in this article. There's no reason letting the entire world know what a complete fool I was in letting you go."

"Dammit, Mitch," Gina said, staring up at him and feeling the sudden threat of tears in her throat. How dare he say something so bold, that he realized he'd made a mistake in letting her go? A part of her was glad he did recognize it, but then another part knew the realization had come two years too late.

"Why, Mitch? Why are you saying these things? And why now? Why are you being so repentant?"

His expression went from misery to regret. "Because I am. I'm fully aware of what I lost the day you divorced me. I'm also aware that too much damage was done for any type of repair. I've accepted that, Gina. But that doesn't keep me from acknowledging just how wrong I was and what mistakes I made."

Gina took a breath, full of emotions. He hadn't been the only one who had made mistakes. She had to admit that she had made a number as well. She had gone into their marriage thinking it would be simple and easy. After all, they loved each other and love would certainly be enough; however, the first time she saw that it wasn't enough had been difficult for her to handle.

She sighed. Rehashing the past was a waste of time. Their marriage was over. There was no way they could ever go back. She knew it and hoped that he knew it as well. She decided to ask him to make sure. "You do know that we can never go back, don't you, Mitch?"

He sighed deeply. "Yes, Gina, I know it and I've accepted it. But we can be friends, can't we?"

"We've always been friends, Mitch, even when we weren't in touch. My parents were separated for over twenty years and remained friends because of Trevor and me. And although we didn't have any children together I see no reason to become enemies just because we decided we could no longer live together as man and wife. Things between us just didn't work out and we moved on. End of story."

Mitch knew that this wasn't the end of the story. It was just the beginning. He hadn't been completely truthful with Gina just now when he'd said that he had accepted the fact that they could never go back. He had every intention of winning her back, and he knew it meant patience on his part. Patience had never been one of his strong points, but some-how, someway, he would pull this off. He had to. First, he would strengthen their friendship and then go from there.

He glanced down at his watch. "How about if we decide on those interview questions over lunch?"

"Lunch?"

He smiled. "Yes. I can still fix a mean grilled cheese sandwich if you're interested. And I just might be able to find a few lemons to squeeze while I'm at it. You've always loved my lemonade."

Gina smiled. That was no joke. For the first year of their marriage they had lived on Mitch's grilled cheese sand-wiches, lemonade and love.

Love.

They had been so much in love that first year, she thought. Then things had changed after he'd gotten that pro-motion he'd always wanted. "I'd love a sandwich and lem-onade."

"Come on, then. My modest kitchen awaits you."

He held his hand out to her. She hesitated a brief mo-ment before placing her hand in his. Immediately the touch of his hand on hers made her shiver although the Texas sun was hot and shining bright in the July sky.

Mitch felt her tremor and looked at her. "Are you okay, Gina?"

She nodded that she was okay. However, a part of her doubted she would ever truly be okay again now that Mitch Farrell was back in town.

CHAPTER 4

GINA sat on a stool at the kitchen bar and watched Mitch. He was standing at the stove with his back to her, grilling their cheese sandwiches. One word that readily came to mind as she continued to watch him was sensuous. He was such a sensuous-looking man.

She had thought that very thing each and every time they'd made love. At twenty-two she had come to him a virgin; and on their wedding night he had slowly, yet completely, introduced her to all the wonders of a woman and man coming together in love, meshing their minds, bodies and hearts in a way that took her breath away. In bed, in his arms, there was no right and wrong. Whatever they'd felt comfortable in doing and exploring was all right. Sometimes their lovemaking would be slow and easy. At other times he would take her with an urgency of passion so fierce, so demanding and so frenzied, the effects would last for days, nights, even weeks. While in his arms nothing else mattered; not their problems, differences or the inner turmoil that plagued their marriage. Whenever he filled her the only thing that mattered was him, and the sensations and ecstasy he was able to share with her.

He would know just where to kiss her, just where to touch her and just what parts of her to concentrate on to bring her the greatest degree of pleasure. The bed was the only place she had truly felt as one with him, mainly because it was during those times that she knew—without a doubt—

that she had his complete attention. Those were the only times when his job and career had played second to her.

She sighed deeply and decided to switch her thoughts. It didn't help matters when she glanced around. The inside of the trailer was cozy. Too cozy. The furnishings were nice for a trailer, especially the bed she had seen on her way to the bathroom to wash her hands. She had tried not to stare, but she couldn't help thinking about all the wicked and wanton things that could be done in that bed with Mitch.

"Gina?"

She blinked, realizing Mitch had turned around and said something to her. Their gazes met and a pulsing heat began gathering low in her body, spreading in a hot, sensuous rush to all parts of her. She wanted him, she silently admitted. Desire was flitting too fast and furious throughout her to *not* admit it. For nearly two solid years the thought of being with a man had never entered her mind, mainly because she hadn't been ready to indulge in any type of a serious relationship with anyone. But now her senses were on full alert. Mitch was too close and too overwhelming for them not to be. Even from across the room she could smell his aftershave—a deep, male, potent scent. Her fingers itched to touch him, her tongue yearned to taste him and her body hungered to have him.

When he repeated her name she blinked, bringing both her breathing and mind under control; or at least trying to. "I'm sorry, I wasn't listening. What did you say?"

He stared at her and she hoped and prayed he hadn't figured out what she'd been thinking.

"I said I ran into Corinthians yesterday at the mall. It was the first time I had seen her since the wedding reception, and just from the brief conversation we had I can tell she's an awesome person. I can see how Trevor fell in love with her."

Gina smiled, remembering both Trevor and Corinthians' tale of how they had hated each other in the beginning, although neither would say exactly how they had met or why they had disliked each other so. It evidently was a secret they shared. "Yes, Corinthians is a sweetheart."

"Trevor is a lucky man."

Gina nodded, thinking that was definitely true; the good thing about it was that her brother knew just how lucky he was and never took his wife for granted. He worked hard but when work time was over he knew how to come home and take care of business. He knew how to balance both work and home life, which was something Mitch never could figure out how to do.

"Don't, Gina."

Gina lifted her gaze and looked directly into Mitch's eyes. "Don't what?"

"Don't remember the bad times."

She swallowed and wondered how he'd known what she'd been thinking. She slowly eased off the stool when he walked toward her, suddenly feeling cornered when he came to stand in front of her.

"There *were* good times in our marriage, weren't there? The memories aren't all bad, are they, Gina?" he asked in an almost whisper, as he gently gripped her upper arms.

Touching her again was a huge mistake. The moment he did so, she gasped as sensations that had been left on hold for two years suddenly rushed straight from the top of her head to the bottom of her feet, making her fully aware of every inch of him and herself as well. Just from his touch, she felt like a woman for the first time in two years.

A woman who ached for the man who used to be her mate.

A shiver of passion aroused her and she knew Mitch felt it. Their gazes held for the longest moment. Then slowly, deliberately, he lowered his head toward hers. A part of her demanded that she step back but she couldn't. The only thing she could do was stand there while he claimed her mouth slowly, tenderly and thoroughly.

Heat, in various degrees, inflamed her when he slid his tongue between her lips. She took the time to feast on him, to taste him as he sought out her tongue, which she readily gave to him. Her body knew exactly what to expect. It knew what it wanted and just what it was going to get. A deep ache grew inside of her and began spreading to all parts of her body. Mitch made kissing an art form and today he was at his best.

He drew her closer and tightened his hold on her. The lower parts of their bodies touched and she could feel his hard erection through his jeans. It was such a familiar and a missed feeling that she immediately reacted and widened her legs to cradle him between them. Blood pounded fast and furious in her veins at the thought that after all this time she still affected him as much as he affected her.

Mitch heard a moan. He wasn't sure if it had come from him or Gina, but neither did he care. Right now she was where he wanted her to be: in his arms while he kissed her with all the feelings of a man in love. He was lost. Totally and completely out of control . . . and evidently out of patience. He hadn't meant to kiss her this way so soon. But when he'd looked across the room and saw her watching him, he couldn't help himself. Some things just didn't change, and their deep attraction for each other seemed to be one of them.

Knowing he had to bring them up for air sometime, Mitch slowly broke off the kiss. Then he bent to brush a soft kiss over her lips, wanting to taste her again, even if it was a quick taste.

"That kiss was inevitable," he said quietly, his voice a soft, smooth murmur. "Just like it's inevitable for us to do it again."

He leaned over and closed his mouth completely over hers once more, absorbing the minty flavor right out of her mouth. He hadn't realized just how much he had hungered for her taste until now. And he could tell from the way she returned his kiss that she had hungered for his as well.

It was Gina who finally regained control of the situation and returned back to reality. Breaking her mouth free of his, she placed her hands on his chest and pushed out of his arms. She inhaled a deep breath and released it. He was right. The kiss was inevitable. At least the first one had been. But not the second, and had she not pulled back there would have been a third. Possibly even a fourth. She and Mitch had always been spontaneous combustion just waiting to ignite. But that was no excuse—those days were supposed to be long gone . . . in the past.

She forced her gaze up to Mitch. He was looking at her

and saying nothing. Just looking at her. "This was supposed to be business," she said softly, not knowing what else to say. At the moment all other words escaped her.

"It is."

She frowned. "Two people conducting business don't carry on the way we just did, Mitch."

He eyed her with a ferocity that made heat skitter down her spine. "They could if they wanted to."

Gina sighed as she continued to pull herself together. Mitch wasn't helping matters. "Maybe we ought to lay down some ground rules."

And maybe we ought to just lay down, he thought as he continued to watch her. *Mmmm . . . that had numerous possibilities.* Knowing he had to smooth her over before her feathers got ruffled any further and she decided to call off the interview, he said, "Like I said, the kiss was inevitable, Gina, considering our history." He smiled apologetically. "I got carried away. I promise to control myself in the future."

Knowing he hadn't indulged in the kiss-a-thon by himself, she smiled wryly and said, "Same here. I promise to control myself in the future, too."

He hoped not. He'd always liked her out of control. "Go ahead and sit back down," he said, nodding toward the stool. "Lunch is almost ready. Or instead of sitting you can help by getting a couple of glasses out of the cabinet and filling them with ice for the lemonade. They're in the cabinet over the sink."

She chuckled at his request. "That sounds easy enough."

He shook his head, grinning as he remembered she was definitely not a whiz in the kitchen. But then her capabilities in the bedroom had more than made up for it. "It *is* easy enough."

He watched as she sashayed around him and walked over to the cabinet to take out the glasses. In the pair of slacks she was wearing, her backside seemed to have gotten a bit curvier since the last time he had checked it out. He smiled. He couldn't wait for the chance to check it out again. He could imagine undressing her, removing every stitch of clothing that covered her, then pulling her to him—skin to skin.

He groaned silently, knowing it was time to move on to the next phase of his plan. He just hoped Gina was ready for it. He knew that he definitely was. Slowly, methodically, he intended to break down every barrier she had erected. In the end he was going to have her so dizzy with passion, so saturated in desire and so full of need that she wouldn't be able to think straight.

And he intended to make sure that happened as quickly as possible.

CHAPTER 5

"ARE you sure you're fine with the interview questions, Mitch?"

Mitch watched Gina as she placed her writing pad back into her briefcase. After lunch she had immediately developed a strictly business manner. It was one she figured would not be swayed. Boy, did he have news for her.

"Yes, I'm sure," he said, taking another sip of his lemonade. At this point he would be satisfied with just about anything that would provide a chance for them to spend an ample amount of time together. "Now that we have that covered, how about me showing you around?" he said, standing.

She glanced up at him. "All right. But when can we officially get together for the interview?"

Mitch glanced at his watch. He was meeting the Madarises in a few hours. What he needed was to begin breaking down her defenses on her own turf.

"How about if I drop by your place later tonight?" He watched her reaction to his suggestion and could just imagine the wheels that had suddenly begun turning in her head.

"My place?"

"Yes."

"Later tonight?"

"Yes. From what you said earlier it will take approximately a week to finish up the interview. Right?"

"Yes."

"Then we'll need to meet every free chance I get. Unfortunately, getting things off the ground for the construction of the Madaris Building will take up a lot of my time this week."

Gina nodded, understanding the predicament he was in. He probably hadn't counted on it taking her an entire week to do an interview. "All right. Stopping by my place tonight will be fine. What about around seven?"

"Nine o'clock would be better. I have a meeting already scheduled for seven."

She frowned; nine at night was awfully late for them to do business, but she did want to start on the interview. "Okay, nine o'clock will be fine."

Mitch nodded, pleased with himself. "Now, come on and let me show you around. I especially want you to see the places I most enjoyed as a child."

Gina's heart began beating rapidly as she got to her feet. She was eager to see anything that was part of Mitch's past; a past he'd always been reluctant to share with her. "I'd like that."

With his hand on Gina's back, Mitch guided her around his property, sharing with her tidbits of his childhood and how much fun he'd had while living with his grandmother. They came to a stop when they reached a huge pond. Earlier that morning there had been a light drizzle so the ground was still damp. The air smelled of earth and pine and was stirred by a gentle summer breeze.

"You loved your grandmother very much, didn't you?" Gina asked after he'd shared yet another fond memory with her.

He smiled. "Loved, admired and respected. My grandfather died in the early years of their marriage, but through hard work and dedication she was able to hold on to the ranch with only two young sons for help. And even when those sons later decided ranching wasn't for them, she continued to hold on to the ranch, hiring out seasonal workers and depending on her neighbors only when she really needed to."

He picked up a twig and tossed it into the pond. "When I arrived here I was still mourning the loss of my parents. In time she made my hurt go away; and as I continued to live here, a part of me knew that I'd be the one who would stay and be the rancher. I loved and enjoyed everything about this place just that much. I felt I had everything I needed right here and had no intentions of ever leaving."

Gina nodded, wondering what had happened in his life to make him change his mind. She knew the time he'd spent with various family members after his grandmother's death had had a lot to do with it, especially the time he'd spent with his Uncle Jasper. Had there been something else, too? Something he had never shared with her?

"This has always been my favorite spot and it seems fitting that I bring my favorite girl here."

Gina's pulse raced at what he'd said. "Your *favorite* girl?"

He tilted his head back and smiled at her surprised expression. "Yes. You were the first woman I'd gotten serious about during my four years of college and two years of grad school. I had almost made it to the finish line free of any serious involvement with a woman, and then one day I bumped into you coming out of class and wham, my life hasn't been the same since."

Neither had hers, Gina thought as she shook her head, smiling and remembering that day. Mitch Farrell had not only bumped into her that day, he had literally rocked her world. He had shaken it and in a short space of time he'd had it revolving out of control. But still, for him to claim nearly two years after their divorce that she was still his favorite girl was a bit much.

"What about all those other women I read about in the magazines and newspapers whom you've been involved with? Surely, they rate much higher on the scale than I do."

Of all the things that could have happened just then, Gina hadn't expected—nor was she prepared—for Mitch to suddenly whirl her around to face him in such a way that brought them chest to chest, and made her tip her head back to see him. She'd barely had time to register what he'd done when she noticed the darkening of his eyes and the firm set of his jaw. When she did, her stomach curled and her nipples tightened. He wasn't smiling, which indicated the intensity of his thoughts; she knew whatever he was about to say was serious.

"I evidently need to make something absolutely clear, Regina Farrell. Divorce or no divorce, no woman rates higher in my life than you do. You're the woman I chose to be my wife, but you were more than that. You were my best friend and my most loyal supporter. And no matter who I may have dated after our divorce, you're the only one I've ever wanted with unadulterated, relentless and endless passion and never-ending and undying love."

Gina's heart thumped so hard in her chest that it hurt. *Never-ending and undying love?* Was he saying what she thought he was saying? She shook her head. *No, he doesn't mean it. At least not the way it sounded*, she thought. *Especially not after all this time. There is no way.*

She sighed deeply. A part of her knew Mitch still loved her; it was the same kind of love she had for him. You couldn't fall madly in love with someone and then expect that love to go away with a mere divorce. A part of her still loved him and cared for him—as someone who had once been a special part of her life, nothing more than that. And she figured that for him it was probably the same. She was the only woman he had ever taken the time from his busy schedule to pursue. And he had done so relentlessly until he had broken down all her barriers, except for one. He had not gotten her to change her mind about them sleeping together before marriage, not that he had tried. Once she had told him of her intentions to wait, he had respected her wishes. But that hadn't stopped things from almost getting out of hand a few times when they had been alone at his apartment. However, he'd always been able to regain control and bring things to an end before they'd gone too far.

The declaration he'd just made about how he felt about her rendered her speechless, and before she could say anything he glanced down at his watch. "It's time for us to start heading back if I'm to meet the Madarises on time."

Gina nodded, glad for the change in subject. "So how are things going with the plans for the Madaris Building?" she asked as they began walking back toward the area where their vehicles were parked.

"What Justin, Dex and Clayton plan to build is awesome. It's been a dream of theirs for a while and I'm glad to see them move forward with it. And I definitely appreciate them letting me be a part of it."

Gina nodded. "Who will be the builders?"

Mitch chuckled. "I think that was decided before the first piece of land was purchased. Madaris Construction Company will be the ones handling things. They plan to keep it all in the family. At first I thought it was too large an undertaking for two such young men, but Justin, Dex and Clayton felt comfortable in letting their young cousins do the work. After meeting them I can see why. Those two guys have good heads on their shoulders and there's no doubt in my mind they will do a fantastic job."

Gina smiled. The cousins Mitch was referring to were the twenty-seven-year-old twins, Blade and Slade Madaris. Originally, the construction company had been owned by the twins' grandfather and father, Milton Madaris Senior and Junior. Milton Sr. had long ago retired; Milton Jr. had recently decided to take early retirement and travel a bit and turned over the running of the operation to his offspring. Already Blade and Slade were making a name for themselves and had been awarded a number of building contracts.

When they reached her car Mitch opened the door for her. After she slid in he leaned down and reached across her and snapped the seatbelt in place. She appreciated his thoughtfulness. "Thanks, Mitch."

"You're welcome." He had to hold back from adding, *I now know the importance of taking care of what's mine*. He was still leaning down and at that angle he was staring straight at her mouth. His gut clenched and he suddenly felt sweat form on his forehead. His control was good, but not good enough to resist moving in just a bit closer to taste her one more time.

He gazed into her eyes and saw the exact moment she realized his intent. He heard her breath catch and heard her gentle sigh. Then he saw her automatically part her lips for him. With such an invitation, whether intentional or not, he leaned closer and stroked his tongue past her parted lips and right into her mouth. Her tongue was there, waiting on his.

Sweet, moist, delicious. He wanted to devour her but knew that now was not the time. He had to move cautiously since he didn't want to do anything that would make her want to call off tonight's meeting.

So after tasting her thoroughly for a heart-stopping minute, he retreated and slowly, reluctantly, eased his tongue out of her mouth. "Tonight," he said in a husky whisper. "I'll see you later tonight. At around nine."

Gina swallowed. Mitch's voice was rich with promise. A part of her wanted to tell him that tonight was off, since it appeared that she couldn't trust herself around him. In her book he was the epitome of everything sexual. He was vital, strong and all male. Definitely all male. Even now she could feel moisture gathering between her legs just thinking about just how male he was. Somehow and in some way she had to emotionally distance herself from Mitch before . . .

She didn't want to think about what might happen if she didn't. Every bone in her body was beginning to turn to mush at the very thought. "Mitch?"

"Yes?"

"About tonight."

"Yes, what about it?"

"Ahh. . . ." She tried to speak but couldn't. Never before had she felt at such a loss for words. The only other time she had been this aware of a man had been her first encounter with Mitch. His very presence had taken her by storm, just like he was doing now. But still, she intended to keep things strictly business between them, even if it killed her . . . which, from the way things looked, it just might. "Nothing," she said softly. "I'll see you later tonight."

Stella Grant glanced across the table at her daughter. Papadeaux was their favorite place for dinner; Gina just loved their seafood. But she couldn't help noticing that Gina had barely touched her food. "Are you are all right, Gina?"

Gina lifted her head and met her mother's concerned gaze. "I met with Mitch today." She knew that about said it all. Of all people, her mother knew just what Mitch Farrell had meant to her at one time. Her mother also knew how much the breakup of their marriage had hurt her.

"So you have decided to do the interview?"

"Yes."

"Why?"

Gina sighed. She hadn't heard censorship in her mother's voice, just blatant, outright concern. When it came to her children, Stella Grant was a fierce protector. But then, on the other hand, she had always allowed them to make decisions for themselves. Gina and her mother had always had a close relationship. Nothing had changed.

"The reason I decided to do it is because it's a good career move for me that will also pay well when some magazine buys it. But I also have an ulterior motive for doing it. While I'm interviewing Mitch, I'm hoping that I can find out some things about him. In fact, I already have," she said softly, thinking about what he'd shared with her about his parents and grandmother. Each time she conversed with him she learned more and more about the man she had once been married to.

"But those are things you should have learned when the two of you were married."

"True, but there was never any time since Mitch spent most of his time working. The only time we communicated was in . . ." Gina cleared her throat upon deciding that no matter how close they were, she had no intentions of sharing intimate details of her marriage with her mother. Besides, she was more than sure her mother got the picture.

"So, where will all this lead?" Stella asked, concerned.

"I really don't know, Mom. All I'm hoping to get out of this is one fabulous article. Both Mitch and I keep stressing this is strictly business, yet . . ." She sighed, about to go there again. Why were she and Mitch such passionate, oversensuous people? It seemed the only thing they used to do with their free time was make love, think of making love or plan to make love.

"Gina?"

She blinked upon realizing her mother had spoken to her. "Yes?"

"What you do with Mitch is your business. I just want you to be careful."

Gina nodded. "Careful that my heart doesn't get broken again."

Stella nodded. "Yes, that, too. But I was really thinking about being careful that you don't end up pregnant."

"Mother!"

Stella waved off Gina's tone of indignation. "I want you to hear me out, Regina Renee Grant Farrell. I've been where you are now, remember? Your father and I were separated for nearly twenty years and during that time I still loved him something fierce. Around Maurice I knew how it felt to be a woman mainly because he was the one who made me into a woman." She smiled. "There were times when he would come and pick you and Trevor up for the weekend, and I had to fight to hold back from throwing myself at him. While I always maintained control, there were times I literally climbed the walls after he left because I had wanted and needed him just that bad." She looked at Gina pointedly and added, "I know all about wants and needs, young lady."

Stella reached across the table. "I know children oftentimes can't imagine their parents as passionate and sensuous beings, but they are. You and Trevor wouldn't be here if Maurice and I weren't. I know firsthand how it is for a woman who's been without love and passion for a while. You haven't seriously dated anyone since your divorce. It's a wonder you aren't pulling your hair out about now. And although you've never mentioned it to me it was no deep, dark secret that you and Mitch had a rather active sex life."

Gina raised a brow. "And how do you know that?"

Stella chuckled. "Because each and every time I phoned to chat the two of you were in bed, getting in bed or getting out of bed. And let's not forget those unexpected visits when I would interrupt the two of you . . . doing things."

"Okay, Mom. I get the picture."

"No, dear, I really don't think you do, at least not the one I'm painting. What I'm talking about, Gina, is sexual needs. What kept me from losing it when those sexual needs hit were you and Trevor. The two of you kept me busy and helped to occupy my mind. You don't have a diversion."

"I have my work," Gina said, wondering if her mother

had somehow been privy to the recent dreams she'd been having about Mitch.

Stella smiled. "Yes, but now your work includes Mitch. You run the risk of mixing work with pleasure."

"Things are strictly business between us."

"Yeah, right. If you believe that then you probably still believe there's a Santa Claus. Get real, Gina. It's been almost two years. Take my advice and play it safe. Before going home stop by the nearest convenience store and get a pack of condoms since you're no longer on the Pill."

Gina leaned back in her chair, not believing the conversation she was having with her mother. "Trust me, Mom. I won't need condoms or any other type of birth control. I've never indulged in casual sex and I won't start now."

Stella smiled. "There's nothing casual about sleeping with an ex-husband, trust me. In fact, it's probably one of the most serious things you can do. The effects of it can possibly leave you in a way you aren't prepared for. Emotionally and physically. You would be sleeping with someone you definitely know, someone you once loved and someone who still has a part of your heart—even if it's a very small part. And last but not least, he is someone who's the very person who taught you everything you know in the bedroom; every itty-bitty little detail and then some."

Gina could feel her face flush. "Ahh, can we change the subject please?"

"If that's what you want."

"Yes, that's what I want."

"All right. But remember my warning as well as my suggestion."

With her head lowered Gina slowly resumed eating her food. She could feel her insides heat up at the thought of every itty-bitty little detail Mitch had taught her. He had been thorough, absolute, consummate and outright perfect. In her heart and mind she believed that even if she slept with more than a hundred men, none would ever compare to the way Mitchell Cameron Farrell made love. He'd had other faults but in the bedroom he had reigned supreme in her book. Just thinking about him made her . . .

No, she wouldn't go there . . . again. She had to believe

that she was still in control of her mind and body and that her mother was wrong. Casual sex was casual sex no matter who your partner was. And as long as she believed that, she didn't have a thing to worry about.

At least she hoped and prayed that she didn't.

CHAPTER 6

"FORGIVE us for boring you, Mitch."

Mitch snapped his head around and looked into four pairs of grinning eyes. He shrugged. "Sorry, guys."

Justin Madaris smiled. "Hey, don't apologize. We've all been there. In fact, we're still there."

Mitch raised a brow. "Where?"

"In love."

Mitch smiled, not really caring that the four men he had joined for drinks at the conclusion of their business meeting had figured things out. "And just what gave me away?"

"Your mood," Justin said easily.

Dex Madaris spoke next. "It was the way you keep looking at your watch."

Clayton Madaris then added, "For me it was the fact that you mentioned three times since we got here that you have a business meeting with Gina at her place tonight at nine."

Mitch's gaze then moved to Trevor to see just what he had to say. "For me it was that silly-looking smile you still have on your face."

"Oh." Mitch chuckled and took another sip of his drink. When he absently checked his watch again a few minutes later, the other men began laughing. And he couldn't help but join them. He had met the Madaris brothers through Trevor after he had become engaged to Gina. The Grants and the Madarises had grown up in the same neighborhood and were a rather close-knit group.

Deciding to change the subject about his love life, he turned to Clayton. A few months back a demented escaped convict had run Clayton over when he was leaving his office one day. The hit-and-run had been intended for Clayton's wife, Syneda. He had pushed her out of the way and taken the impact himself.

"I'm glad to see you're out and about and back to your old self again, Clayton," Mitch said seriously.

Clayton smiled. "Thanks. And you know what they say, you can't keep a good man down."

Mitch nodded then asked Clayton and Dex how their wives were doing. Syneda and Dex's wife, Caitlin, were both expecting. Mitch was suddenly reminded of the times that Gina had asked him for a baby, and how he'd flatly refused her with the excuse that he wasn't ready to become a father. But now, if given the chance, he would gladly give her fifty babies if that were what she wanted. The thought of becoming a father didn't bother him like it used to. In fact he actually relished the idea of having a son or a daughter if Gina was his child's mother. He could imagine a little girl who was a replica of her mother.

"You got that silly smile on your face again, Mitch."

Mitch took another sip of his drink and rolled his eyes at Trevor. "You know, I could be thinking about all the money I'm going to make off this deal."

Trevor nodded. "Yeah, that could explain the smile, but it doesn't explain why you're looking at your watch every ten minutes." He crossed his arms over his chest and gave Mitch a hard stare. "Now tell me again the reason you're meeting with Gina this late at night."

Dex chuckled. "Leave him alone, Trev. There's nothing wrong with a man who admits to making a mistake and then goes about trying to make things right."

"And you think he plans to meet with Gina, *this late at night*, to make things right?"

Evidently Trevor's question raised some serious doubt in the other men's minds; they suddenly eyed Mitch suspiciously. "Hey, guys, back off. What's going on with me and Gina is our business," Mitch said in an irritated tone. Jeez! It was bad enough he'd felt the need to defend himself to

Trevor a few days ago, but now the Madaris brothers were trying to give him grief, too. It was a known fact that they considered Gina as one of their sisters.

"Okay, we'll back off for now," Dex said slowly. "Like I said, there's nothing wrong with a man who admits to making a mistake and tries making things right. Just don't think about making the same mistake twice."

Mitch knew that of the three brothers, Dex was the one he had to worry about. He meant what he said and said what he meant. "Trust me. I don't plan on making the same mistake with Gina."

Evidently satisfied that enough had been said, Clayton Madaris decided to change the subject. "Has anyone noticed that Blade has just as many women as I did when I was his age?"

Justin raised his eyes to the ceiling. "And you think that's something to brag about?"

Clayton smiled. "Hey, it's good to know there's another Madaris out there keeping the ladies happy."

Dex frowned. "Oh, is that what he's supposed to be doing?"

"You bet. If he keeps it up he'll be the one to inherit that case of condoms I've been keeping in my closet, since I won't be needing them anymore."

Mitch chuckled. It was common knowledge that Clayton was Houston's number-one womanizer during his bachelor days. Also, it had been rumored that he'd kept a case of condoms in his closet. Evidently it had been more truth than rumor. Hearing Clayton mention condoms made Mitch wonder if Gina was still on the Pill. He decided not to take any chances—he'd stop by the convenience store on the way over to her place.

He looked at his watch again. The time was close enough for him. "I hate to leave but I got to run," he said, standing and tossing a few bills on the table.

"Maybe the four of us should go over to Gina's place with you."

Mitch frowned at Trevor's suggestion. "Don't even think about it." He then turned and hurriedly walked out of the restaurant.

• • •

Gina paced restlessly about her house after checking the clock for the umpteenth time. Was Mitch still coming over? Was he on his way? Why was she so anxious to see him? She had interviewed a dozen people, so what made him any different?

She sighed, knowing the answer to that one. None of them had been a man she had slept with before.

She looked down at the outfit she had chosen to wear for tonight's meeting; a skirt and blouse and there was nothing provocative or tempting about either item. She wanted to set the mood for what their meeting was—strictly business. In fact, instead of them sitting in the living room she had decided to conduct the interview in her office. At no time did she want Mitch to think this was a social call.

Thinking that the lighting in her living room appeared too seductive, she quickly crossed the room and switched on another lamp. The last thing she wanted or needed was for Mitch to get any ideas. They had kissed three times already that day and the last thing she wanted was a repeat performance. Heaven help her if she got one, so she figured the best way to handle the situation was to start out letting him know what she expected and what she would not tolerate.

She took a deep breath when she heard the sound of the doorbell. Taking another large gulp of air for good measure, she slowly crossed the room to the door and glanced out the peephole.

Gina sighed resignedly as she opened the door; she immediately knew she had made a mistake in agreeing to this late-night meeting. When his gaze met hers she felt all the things she had felt the first time they had met.

Sexual chemistry. Instant attraction. Animal lust.

And it certainly didn't help matters that he was now clean-shaven and dressed in a designer business suit that gave him a suave, elegant and professional appearance. There was an aura of masculine strength in the tall, powerfully built body standing across from her. This was the Mitch Farrell she knew and was used to. He looked nothing like the Mitch who had resembled a desperado earlier that day.

The porch light reflected confidence and an air of sensuality that almost took Gina's breath away. Mitch held her gaze with the compelling force of his. She nervously licked her bottom lip and immediately knew it had been a mistake when his gaze shifted to her mouth, then seconds later snarled hers again.

Finally he spoke. "May I come in?"

Gina tried to ignore the tiny flitters of pulsing heat racing through her body at the sound of his voice, deep and husky. She stepped back. "Yes, of course."

She inhaled deeply when he entered. He was bringing into her house the scent of a man. Her throat felt tight and her insides burned hotter with the masculine aroma. It was earthy, sensuous and all Mitch. Tension pricked at her nerve endings and she wondered how she would survive being in his presence in such close quarters. She drew a steadying breath, determined to get through it.

Closing the door, she watched him glance around her living room and noted a variety of expressions that crossed his face, admiration and appreciation among them.

"You have a beautiful home, Gina."

"Thanks." It was slightly larger than the one the two of them had shared. She had always wanted for them to get a bigger house so they could start a family, but he'd kept making excuses as to why they couldn't.

"Since the time is already far spent," she said, heading straight into business, not wanting her thoughts to dwell in the past, "we may as well get started. I plan to conduct the interview in my office."

He raised a surprised brow. "Your office?"

"Yes. I thought it would be appropriate since this *is* a business meeting."

He nodded smiling. "That's true, but do I get the offer of something to drink first?"

"Sure, what would you like? I have cola, tea, fruit juice, water, wine . . ."

"A glass of wine will be fine."

"All right. I'll be back in a minute."

Mitch watched as she walked away and looked at the sensuous body he knew so well from head to toe. He inwardly grinned. If Gina thought tonight would be strictly business she had another thought coming. Oh, sure, things were bound to start off that way, but he planned a totally different ending to the night—and he was determined to make it so. He'd known it the moment she had opened the door. She looked beautiful and he knew that although she probably had not done anything to deliberately get him aroused, just seeing her had effectively done that.

While she was in the kitchen getting his wine, he decided to check out the layout of her home. Specifically, he wanted to know the location of her bedroom. He made a quiet and quick assessment and returned to the living room a few moments before Gina appeared carrying a wineglass.

"Here you are," she said, walking over and handing it to him.

"Aren't you going to join me?"

"No. I prefer not to drink while conducting business."

He nodded. "Oh, I see. Well, in that case, I don't want to take up any more of your time than I have to. So let's get started."

"Thanks, I appreciate it, Mitch."

"Don't mention it. Like I told you that first night at dinner, I want the article done right and I know you'll do that."

She led him across the living room into her office. Again she watched him glance around and saw his satisfied expression. "This is nice. I bet you spend a lot of time in here."

"Only when I have to do a lot of typing and research. I seldom do interviews at home. In fact, you're my first."

"Again?" he asked, turning to her and smiling over the rim of his wineglass. "I was also the first man to ever make love to you. The first guy to ever make you . . ."

Come. A jab of desire went through Gina at the memory. Although he hadn't finished the sentence it had been very easy for her to supply the missing word. Her body, which was already heated inside, began burning hotter with all the memories.

Deciding not to make a comment, she cleared her throat and said, "You can sit in that chair, Mitch." With trembling fingers she picked a sheet of paper up off her desk. "Here's a copy of the questions I plan to ask tonight. As you can see, there are only six so you won't be here that long. And to help things run smoothly, I will tape this session. Is that all right with you?"

"Yes, that's fine. When will you get around to asking the other questions?" he asked, accepting the paper she handed him. He knew she had at least twenty questions to ask him for the interview.

"Later this week when your schedule permits. Tomorrow I will replay your responses and work on tonight's segment. For the next group of questions I'd prefer if we were at your ranch. I think a change of location for each session will enhance the interview."

Mitch nodded. "You believe that technique is better than asking all the questions in one session and be done with it?" he asked, not that he was complaining. He liked the thought of spending a lot of time with her.

"Yes, I think so," Gina answered, taking the chair behind her desk. "This way neither the interviewer nor the interviewee gets tired and fizzles out. I want you to relax and be yourself. And I want you to be open and honest with me."

"Thanks. I intend to." He glanced down at the questions. All six involved his love life.

Seeing his curious expression Gina said quickly, "I thought it would be best if we go ahead and cover these questions first. There are a lot of women who have been fantasizing about you ever since you did that calendar." She decided not to add that she was one of them.

"It was for charity."

"I know, and from what I understand the sales were phenomenal. I'm sure the relief fund for the September eleventh tragedy appreciates you and the other men who participated."

Mitch removed his coat and tie, taking her up on her suggestion that he relax and be himself. Gina leaned back in her chair and crossed her legs to fight the heat forming between them as she watched him. He had such a wonderful body. No wonder the women had gone bonkers when he had appeared in the calendar as Mr. February. Dressed in a pair of tight-fitting jeans and an open shirt that had revealed his beautiful chest, he had definitely been a lot of women's flavor for the month. She had been totally surprised when a friend from college had mailed her a copy of the calendar. The Mitch Gina knew would not have done such a pose, no matter the cause, and she wondered why he'd done it.

Curiosity got the best of her and she found herself asking, "Why did you do it?"

"Do what?" he asked as he eased down in the chair.

"The calendar."

Mitch glanced down at the sheet he held in his hand. "That's not an interview question," he said, smiling.

"No, it's not. I just want to satisfy my own curiosity."

"Like I said, it was for charity," he replied, looking directly into her eyes. But knowing that she knew him better than anyone, he added, "And also for Tom."

"Tom?"

"Yes, Tom Swank, a business associate of mine and also a good friend. He was in the World Trade Center when it went down."

Gina heard the pain in his voice. "I'm sorry, Mitch."

Mitch nodded, accepting her words of regret. "Tom and I had a meeting that morning."

Gina sat up straight in her chair. "You were in New York that day?"

"Yes. And I was to meet with Tom at eight but a phone call from my office delayed me. It also saved my life."

"Oh, Mitch," Gina said as a lump formed deep in her throat. She shivered at the thought that Mitch could have been one of the victims and thanked God that he hadn't been. And her heart went out for Tom Swank's family. "Was Tom married?"

"Yes, and he had a six-year-old son. That's when I began examining my life. I thought it was so fortunate that Tom had had a child that he had spent time with; a child who would carry on his legacy. It made me realize what I didn't have."

"I always wanted to give you a child, Mitch, but you didn't want one," Gina said, her voice rising slightly.

"I know," he responded quietly. "But that was then. If

I could turn back the hands of time I would get you pregnant in a heartbeat."

Their eyes held. Neither spoke. Both knew they could not turn back the hands of time even if they wanted to.

"Ah, I suggest we go ahead and get started," Gina said, clearing her throat and reaching across her desk to turn on the tape recorder. It was time to move on. "Rumors have been circulating for the past three months that you're having an affair with model Lori Brasco. Is it true?"

"There's no affair. Lori and I are nothing more than friends who share the same interests."

A good reporter would ask just what those interests were, but Gina decided she really didn't want to know. "What about your alleged affair with department store heiress Nicole Lane?"

"Nicole and I dated a few times but that's it," he said as he casually undid the top button on his shirt. Then the second. And the third.

Gina tried not to notice what he was doing but found she was watching him anyway. She swallowed and forced her vision back down to the paper in front of her. "Do you ever plan to remarry?"

"Yes."

Gina's head snapped up, surprised he had answered so quickly and with such conviction. "You think you're good husband material?" she asked curtly. That question was also not on the paper.

"Now that I've learned from my past mistakes, yes."

Gina sighed. The interview was going badly. She wasn't asking the questions she should be asking and was asking some she shouldn't. "And what have you learned, Mitch?"

He smiled. It was a beautiful, rich smile but at the same time it was serious. He stared at her for the longest moment before replying. "I've learned not to ever take a wife for granted again. I also learned that success is just a level of achievement, but a wife is a gift, a beautiful gift to be loved and cherished. She's not a possession to be picked up and played with on a rainy day . . . or made love to when the urge to do so strikes you. I've also learned that although it's a very enjoyable part, there's more to a marriage than sex.

And I've learned to appreciate the good times in a marriage, as well as the bad. But more importantly, I've learned to appreciate a wife."

Gina's throat was so thick she could barely swallow. She was supposed to remain neutral, unattached and unbiased, but she was doing a poor job of it. "And what brought on this stunning revelation?"

Mitch held her stare when he said, "Losing my wife, the woman I had loved more than life itself. I had two years to analyze what went wrong with my marriage and what I could have done to make things right. In the end I acknowledged all the mistakes I had made and didn't like myself very much, so it became crystal clear why in the end she didn't like me either."

Gina fought the tears that clouded her eyes and waited a few minutes before asking softly, "Does your wife know that?"

"She does now."

Dragging her eyes from his, Gina fumbled with the paper on her desk. "If you plan to remarry, do you have someone in mind?"

"Yes."

A part of Gina's heart felt crushed with that one single word. She should be happy for him, glad that he had realized the importance of taking care of a wife properly, but she felt saddened that someone else would reap the benefit of that lesson. All she could think was that another woman would wear the name of Mrs. Mitchell C. Farrell.

When seconds ticked by and Gina didn't say anything, Mitch asked, "Aren't you going to ask me who she is, Gina?"

Gina slowly lifted her gaze to his. Hurt and anger filled her eyes. "Why would I want to know that?"

"For the interview."

That single statement made her remember that she was indeed supposed to be conducting an interview with him. She swallowed tightly. "All right. Who is she? Who is the woman you want to marry? I'm sure there are a lot of women who would want to know."

She watched Mitch stand. Then she watched him slowly walk over to her desk. She tried to concentrate on him and not the bare chest revealed by his unbuttoned dress shirt. When he reached her desk she tilted her head back to look up at him. With him standing over her, she was acutely aware of everything about him. He was looking down at her, drawing her in and making her feel cornered, restrained and desired. There was a hot look in his eyes. One she recognized and had come to know well during the time they were married. The question that suddenly crossed her mind was: How could he want her *that* much but intend to marry someone else?

"How, Mitch?" She voiced the question before she realized she had spoken, but she knew he clearly understood what she was asking. When he reached out and touched her chin with his finger, every nerve ending within her body ignited with heat, which flooded her face at the same time it flooded the area between her legs.

"I would think the answer to your question would be obvious, Gina. *You* are the woman I want to marry."

CHAPTER 7

IT took Gina a minute to find her voice, then she exclaimed, "Marry!"

"Maybe the proper word should be remarry." Mitch couldn't help but appreciate the shocked look on Gina's face. It was priceless. She stared up at him with eyes so filled with astonishment he was tempted to kiss the look right off her face. Satisfied he had finally made his intentions clear, he crossed his arms over his chest and waited for the rest of her reaction.

She shook her head as if to clear it, making her hair tumble carelessly around her face before taking her hand and smoothing it back in place. He immediately felt aroused. That simple act was too sexy for his peace of mind. As he continued to look at her, he saw he had successfully boggled her mind and squelched further speech. Then all too soon she got it back.

"You can't really mean that!" she said, coming to her feet, which forced him to take a step back.

"And why can't I?"

"Because it makes no sense, Mitch. Until you came to town last week, I had not seen or heard from you since . . . since . . ."

"Trevor's wedding," he supplied easily.

"Yes, Trevor's wedding and that was almost a year ago."

"And your point is?"

She stared at him for a long moment thinking her point

should have been obvious. "My point is that we don't have a relationship, Mitch. Other than having been married once we no longer share a connection. After our divorce you went your way and I went mine. Although we remained friends, you didn't call me on the holidays, I didn't call you. You didn't send me *I'm thinking of you* cards and I didn't send you any either. In other words, you and I have not shared a life, a thought, a concern or interest for almost two years, and for you to—"

"There wasn't a day that went by that I didn't think of you, Gina."

She glared at him. "Oh, is that right? I'm sure that will probably come as quite a surprise to all those women you have dated since our divorce."

"They meant nothing."

She frowned, her eyes narrowing. "And you expect me to believe that?"

"Yes, I see no reason why you shouldn't," he replied, meeting her glare with one of his own. "I loved you, Gina. I loved you with all my heart. That kind of love can't be turned off with a divorce."

"You didn't love me, Mitch, not really. You loved your work. You desired me and you wanted me."

Mitch looked at her and got the uneasy feeling that she actually believed what she was saying. "That's not true, Gina."

"It is true," she said venomously.

"If you believe that, then I'll have to prove otherwise."

"I don't think you can."

He saw serious doubt in her eyes and took a step toward her, capturing her in his arms. "The hell I can't," he muttered moments before kissing her with purpose. He opened his mouth fully over hers, effectively absorbing her gasp of surprise and her breath of existence. His tongue slipped inside— tasting deeply, exploring thoroughly and claiming completely. He heard her soft moan of protest and deliberately ignored it when she wrapped her arms around his neck and returned the kiss with equal intensity.

The kisses they had shared earlier that day were nothing compared to this. The sexual hunger that had been clawing at him since his return to Houston had taken over his mind and body. He could still remember the first time he had kissed her, the first time he had exploded inside of her and the first time she had screamed out his name in a torrential climax. Those sensuous memories of the past invaded his thoughts and combined with the pleasures of the present, hammering away at the last thread of control he had.

Her hips were moving instinctively against him as he kissed her with an all-consuming hunger. They fitted together perfectly, just as always. Desire flared between them and he knew she was as out of control as he was. No matter what she said or thought, Mitch knew that for him this was love. Love of the purest and richest kind. No other woman had ever made him feel this way.

Only Gina could make him want to give her the sun and the moon and not settle for giving her anything less. Only Gina could make him appreciate being a man because he knew he had her as his woman. And only Gina could make him want to stay locked inside her body—real deep and extremely tight—for the rest of his life.

He eased his hand under her blouse wanting to touch her everywhere and deciding to start with her breasts. He had always loved the feel of them in his hands, especially the feel of her nipples hardening from the caressing brushes of his fingertips. He knew just what type of bra she was wearing—one made of lace with a front closure. He sucked in a ragged breath when he unsnapped it easily, then traced a path with his fingers over her delicate skin.

"Mitch!"

His name was a whimpering sound on her lips. Without responding he leaned forward and gently captured a nipple between his teeth, then began laving it with the relentless stroke of his tongue. First one breast and then the other received his hot attention. He glanced upward and saw her eyes flutter close as another sound, this one a sweet, delectable groan, escaped her lips. When she looked like she was about to swoon, he pulled his mouth from her breast long enough to lift her so she could wrap her legs around his waist.

Walking over to the chair, he settled her in his lap and kissed her lips again with such urgency that she responded in kind. It was as if he wanted to eat her mouth up, frantic for the taste of her and almost delirious with desire for yet something else. His fingers skimmed her leg moving upward to her thigh. Pushing her skirt aside he sought out bare flesh. He drew in a deep breath when his fingers inched higher. The feel of her electrified every nerve ending in his body and caused additional heat to flood his bloodstream. Two years had been a long time without this, he thought, wanting with every part of his being to bury himself deep inside of her.

His hand came in contact with silky panties and he slowly, methodically, skimmed his fingers over the soft material seeking the easiest opening to slip underneath. He found it and heard her soft gasp when he touched bare skin. Her flesh felt soft, smooth and delicate. Wet.

He cupped his palm over that area between her legs that he had branded his on their wedding night, feeling the heat of it at the exact same time that he felt a shiver touch her body in response to him touching her so intimately.

She tilted her head back and looked at him through glazed eyes. It had been a long time since he had seen that look, and he suddenly realized just how much he had missed it, had missed her, had wanted her and needed her. Having her in his arms this way and knowing just how much he loved her, he bent his head to hers and kissed her deeply. At the same time his hand shifted the lower part of her body to accommodate the fingers he'd slipped inside of her. He felt the jolt of her body against him but continued to kiss her as his fingers penetrated her beyond the satiny folds of her flesh.

"Mitch!" She freed her mouth from his and her face dropped forward on his chest.

He heard the desperation in her voice. He also heard the urgency. "What do you want, Gina?" he asked, whispering the words in her ear as his fingers continued to intimately caress her. "Tell me what you want, baby."

She slowly lifted her head from his chest. Her gaze was heated but he knew his eyes were just as smoldering. "You. Inside me. Now!"

Sweat dampened Mitch's forehead at her words. But he

wasn't ready to put an end to his torment or hers. "No, sweet-heart, not yet."

Not yet? Mitch's words whirled around in Gina's head. The urge to mate with him was so strong she didn't want to wait. Her mother had been right. Her body knew this man and it wanted and needed him in the worst possible way. It was letting her know that two years had been a long time. Tonight it had no shame, just outright greed. It wanted it all and was too desperate to offer any type of resistance, not that she wanted to anyway. There was nothing casual about this, nor was this something she could walk away from. Her body and all the elements within it were reacting to the only man it had known, wanted and loved.

She couldn't help wondering why he was torturing her. Why didn't he give her what she wanted and obviously needed? She bit down as the heated movement of his fingers inside of her continued to arouse her beyond comprehension, escalating her desire.

Leaning forward she kissed his mouth, his throat and the part of his bare chest exposed through his shirt. If she was going to be tormented then so was he. Her tongue glided over him, licking his salty dark skin. She reached up and undid the rest of the buttons on his shirt, wanting to expand the area where she could taste him.

She heard his groan and sharp intake of breath when her tongue came into contact with his nipples. She could feel him straining beneath her, his erection fully grown and hard. She lifted herself off him just a bit and reached down to unzip his pants. Sticking her hand into the opening, she heard his tortured groan and felt his stomach tense when she slipped her fingers beneath the waistband of his briefs to take control of the part of him that she wanted. He felt big, pow-erful and hot in her hand. *Oh, so hot and hard.*

"Let go," he growled in her ear in a voice that was fast losing it. She had begun stroking him just the way he had taught her; the way that gave him immense pleasure.

"I'll let go of you when you let go of me," she an-nounced flippantly.

Instead of letting her go, he arched his back and worked his fingers deeper inside of her. He looked up at her to see the play of emotions on her face. He felt her hand tremble, but she did not let go of him. In fact she met his smoldering gaze and continued what she was doing. Her fingers were working their magic on him, very gently and very thoroughly, smoothing his flesh all the way down and up again. When an explosive curse broke forth from his lips she smiled naughtily and with an arrogance that could only match his own asked softly, "You want to take a bet on how long you'll last, Mitch Farrell?"

He frowned. She knew she was pushing him to the limit and was enjoying every damn hellacious minute of it. "No, I don't want to bet," he rasped, barely able to think straight. He had taught her the art of seduction too well.

"Then give me what I want, Mitch. Now! No more games." She softly whispered her command blatantly clear in his ear.

"Okay, you've convinced me," he said huskily and stood with her in his arms and quickly headed toward her bedroom.

"If I didn't know better, I'd swear you've been here before."

He laughed and looked down at her. "I have. In your dreams."

She shook her head, grinning. "You're kind of sure of yourself, aren't you, Mitch?"

"Do you deny it?"

He placed her on the bed and stepped back. His eyes were dark and hot as he looked at her, waiting for her to answer him. "Do you deny it?" he repeated.

Gina inhaled deeply. He stood before her with his shirt unbuttoned, revealing the most gorgeous chest any man could possibly possess. And due to her brazen handiwork, his pants were unzipped, with the most proud male part of him unashamedly exposed. She thought he was the most virile man she'd ever seen. And he was right. She remembered the dreams she'd had of him just last night, not to mention the ones she'd had occasionally over the past two years. He had been in this bedroom with her before—right in her dreams.

"No, Mitch, I don't deny it."

The thought that she had dreamed about him brought a

sexy smile to Mitch's lips. "Well, baby, I'm about to make your dreams come true," he said silkily, slowly removing the belt from his pants.

Gina reclined in bed and watched him strip, definitely enjoying the show. She had always thought he had one hell of an incredible body and seeing it again only reaffirmed her belief. He was hard and muscular in all the right places; his shoulders were broad and his hips narrow. And she didn't want to even concentrate on his thighs. They were Herculean thighs. Strong, solid and built. She remembered all too well the feel of those thighs rubbing against hers while he pumped relentlessly into her, bringing her body pleasure beyond measure.

"Now it's your turn to take everything off."

She met his gaze and slowly slid out of bed. "You sure you want to watch this?" she asked, grinning. "It might bore you."

"I doubt that," he said, taking his turn reclining on the bed to watch her.

Trying to drag things out for as long as she could, just to torment Mitch some more, slowly, ever so slowly, Gina removed her skirt. Her blouse followed and then the bra that was half off anyway.

"You are perfect, Gina."

She smiled over at him. "Full of compliments, you, Mr. Farrell?"

He returned her smile. "Among other things." He slid off the bed and stood. "Come here, Gina."

Not hesitating, she walked over to him and took the hand he held out to her. He picked her up in his arms and placed her on the bed. "I don't want to use this until the last possible moment, Gina," he said raspily, displaying the condom he held in his hand. "Is that all right with you?"

Gina remembered her mother's words. There would still be a risk if he waited until the last possible moment to put the condom on. She looked at that part of him, large and hard before her. They had never used a condom when making love since she had always been on the Pill. One of the pleasures she had always gotten while making love to him was the feel of him exploding inside of her while her inner muscles gripped him, and squeezed out of him everything she could get and then some. But still . . .

"Are you sure about that, Mitch? What if . . ."

"What if I forget? What if I lose control and don't want to stop and take the time to put it on? What if I'm buried inside of you so deep I don't want to come out?" He paused a moment, then said huskily, "And what if I'm driven beyond reason to make you pregnant?"

Gina wasn't sure just how long she stood there, unable to speak. Then she regained her wits. "But you don't want children. You didn't want them while we were married so why would you possibly want them now that we're divorced?"

Mitch slowly shook his head. Evidently she still didn't buy into his theory that they wouldn't be divorced for long. He had every intention of remarrying her, baby or no baby. She belonged to him and would always belong to him. He loved her and would spend the rest of his life proving that to her if he had to. "But what if I was that driven, Gina?"

Gina drew in a deep breath as she thought about what he was saying. The only thing she'd ever known Mitch to be driven to do was to be successful. Although he hadn't relished the idea of them having a child, she had always believed that he would have made a good father. A hard-working one but a good father nonetheless. And she had always wanted a child, which hadn't changed. But she had never thought about being a single mother. Although her parents had been separated while she was growing up, both had played major parts in her life. Her father had always been there for her, just like her mother. She'd had a close relationship with the both of them. She hadn't missed out on having a father figure in her life just because her parents had not lived under the same roof. However, a part of her had always wanted her parents to get back together because for some reason she'd felt they had still loved each other. Even as a child she had felt love between them, even if they hadn't. But, as her mother had explained one day when she had been old enough to understand, it was not a matter of simply kissing and making up. There had been too much hurt and pain for that.

Gina couldn't help but wonder if Mitch understood that the same held true for them. They couldn't kiss and make up. Nor could they make love and make up either. Although she had every intention of making love to him tonight, as far as she was concerned their situation had not changed. At least not enough to rebuild what had been torn down.

"Gina?"

Mitch regained her attention. She fully understood what he was asking, and more specifically, what he was insinuating. Had it been a night where she was not filled with profound need, she would have thought a different way. Her mother had forewarned her about long-denied sexual needs; and tonight Gina wanted and needed Mitch in the most intimate and elemental way. It was the way a woman was meant to want a man. That meant she would have her night with him and her morning, and possibly another day and night, maybe several. But sooner or later he would realize, just like she did, that what they shared was physical. Emotionally, he didn't stand a chance with her because she would not allow him to invade her heart a second time.

Fully understanding her position, even if he didn't, she slowly walked over to him, naked as the day she was born into the world. So was he. Standing on tiptoe she placed her arms around his neck and brought her body close to his, skin-to-skin, flesh-to-flesh and sensuality-to-sensuality. "If I get pregnant, Mitch, I'll deal with it. I've always wanted a child, anyway."

"And what role will I get to play?"

"The only role you can play. The father."

Mitch nodded. In time he would establish the role he would play in her life as well—her husband. But right now, tonight, he wanted to give her a taste of that role, a sampling she would not forget. He slid his arm around her waist and drew her even closer to his body. Now they were bone-to-bone, hip-to-hip.

He slowly walked her backward to the bed, and when they couldn't go any farther, he eased her down on the bed with him the same moment he took her mouth into his, kissing her wildly as he splayed his hand across her hip and thigh, and sought out the area between her legs.

A fierce rush of sexual need flooded Gina and she could barely get breath into her lungs. Mitch was touching her, tormenting her and branding her and she was helpless in his arms. Then the next instant he was hovering above her. Ready for him, she widened her legs and lifted her hips the moment he drove his hardness into her.

He felt huge and was inside of her so deep she thought he must have gotten bigger since the last time they had done this. Her body felt tight around him. Tight and incredibly feminine. She groaned deep within her throat when he shifted their bodies and lifted her even more into the cradle of his while buried deep inside of her.

The position he had placed her in forced her to look at him. After wrapping her legs around his waist, he braced his hands on either side of her head and stared down at her without moving.

"I love you, Gina."

His words, spoken like a soft caress, penetrated her mind and made her insides quiver. But a part of her refused to accept his declaration. She knew it was lust and not love that was talking.

"No, you don't love me. You love *this*."

"I love *you*."

"No, you love this. Admit it."

He held her gaze for the longest time before saying, "Yes, I love *this* but only because *this* is a part of you. But I love this, too," he said, pressing a kiss to her nose. "And this," he said, kissing an area just above her right eyebrow. "And I'm plumb crazy about this," he said, gently brushing a kiss to her mouth. "There isn't an area on you that I don't love, mainly because I love you, Gina. So damn much."

And then he began moving, slowly, making sure she felt every stroke he made into her body. On and on, back and forth, in and out he moved, rocking into her and setting off shock waves of pleasure throughout both of their bodies.

The sound of Gina's moans increased as she became delirious in desire to the point where she could barely speak. He heard her draw a deep gasping breath with every stroke he made, just as dazed and overcome with passion as he was. His gentle strokes turned into deep thrusts and he fought back his intense need to explode inside of her.

When he felt himself losing control he reached for the condom he had placed on the nightstand next to the bed and ripped it open, intent on pulling out of her and putting it on. But that was before he felt her body quivering uncontrollably as she surrendered to her own release.

"Mitch!"

Her legs tightened around him and his body automatically detonated at the feel of her internal muscles clenching him. He began pumping into her, flooding her insides with enough semen to produce fifty babies.

When the both of them were completely spent and their bodies had begun melting down through a sweltering haze of sensations, Mitch pulled Gina closer into his arms and whispered "I love you" one last time before pulling the covers over their naked bodies and giving in to sleep.

The ringing of the telephone woke Mitch. Disoriented, he glanced around the room, saw it was barely daylight outside, then remembered where he was and who he was with. The sensuous smell of the woman sleeping in his arms was a welcoming reminder.

Without thinking he reached over and picked up the phone before it could ring again. "Hello."

"Good morning, Mitchell."

Ah, hell, Mitch thought, closing his eyes. *Why on earth had he answered the phone?* He slowly reopened his eyes. "Hello, Mrs. Grant."

There was a soft chuckle. "Somehow I just knew you would be there."

Mitch decided not to ask how she'd known. "Gina is asleep," he decided to tell her as a way to hurry up and end the conversation. He could just imagine what Gina's mother thought with him answering the phone this time of morning. And what was so bad, everything she thought was probably true. He and Gina had done a number of wild and wicked things throughout most of the night.

"Please wake Gina up. I need to talk with her."

He started to tell her Gina was probably too tired to talk, but decided that wouldn't be the wisest thing to do. He didn't want to make waves with the woman who would soon be his mother-in-law again; someone he could definitely use as an ally. Shifting positions in the bed, he gently nudged Gina. She looked at him sleepily and before she could say anything he quickly handed her the phone.

Confused, sluggish and still very drowsy, Gina yawned as she spoke into the receiver. "Ahhh, hello . . . ?"

"And what were you saying just yesterday about things being *strictly business* between you and Mitchell, Regina Renee? If anything, it seems whatever you two are working on is *strictly pleasure*."

Gina quickly sat straight up in bed. "Mom!"

CHAPTER 8

MITCH lay with his hands behind his head as he watched Gina talk on the phone to her mother. He couldn't take his eyes off of her. She was an extraordinarily beautiful woman.

The sheet had fallen past her waist, leaving the top part of her bare. Deep in conversation, she didn't bother to cover herself. His gaze feasted on her breasts, firm, squeezably soft and a perfect fit for his hands. His heated vision then blazed a trail lower to the curve of her small waist and the flatness of her belly.

He felt his body become aroused as he continued to watch her, wondering how much longer she would be on the phone. He could tell from her expression that whatever her mother was saying, she wasn't too happy about it. He watched her move the phone to the other ear and waited for the time when he could claim her attention. He wasn't in any hurry since he didn't plan to leave her bed anytime soon.

Finally, she glanced over at him. Her cheeks tinted when she saw he lay uncovered, unashamedly exhibiting a full erection. She tried looking away but a few seconds later her gaze returned to him. He smiled when she unconsciously began licking her lips.

"Uhh, Mom, I have to go. Yes, I'll tell Mitch, but the decision will be his." Gina inhaled deeply as she continued to look at him. "Tell Daddy that I love him, too. Good-bye." Taking another deep breath she handed Mitch the phone and watched as he placed it back in the cradle without shifting positions.

"You'll tell me what?" he asked, his voice low and intimate, as he reached up and touched her shoulders. He immediately felt a shiver race through her.

"Dinner," she said, barely getting the word out. She felt herself melting from his touch and the heated look in his eyes.

"What about dinner?"

When she felt his hand move lower toward her breasts, she had to think hard for an answer. "They want you to come to dinner."

"They who?"

A long breath staggered from her lungs when Mitch touched her breasts, slowly caressing one nipple and then the other. His touch felt so good she found herself closing her eyes to . . .

"They who, Gina?"

She reopened them and looked at him. He had shifted positions and was now close to her face. She quickly sucked in a gulp of air when his hand moved lower, to her stomach. How on earth did he expect her to concentrate while touching her this way? "My parents. They want me to bring you to dinner tonight. Can you?"

Mitch gently massaged her stomach. He couldn't help wondering if perhaps he had gotten her pregnant last night, and if even now his child was taking shape and forming into a life inside her womb. That very thought made him want her even more. He leaned up closer to her ear, tasting her right beneath it with the tip of his tongue, before moving to her mouth. "Can I what?"

"Can you come?"

He chuckled against her lips. "After last night how can you even ask such a thing? Yeah, I can come, plenty of times. In fact I'm about ready to come now."

"Mitch," she whispered, her voice straining, her body blazing hot. "Don't misinterpret the question. Mom and Dad want you to come with me to dinner tonight at their place. But you don't have to."

"Thank you," he said, placing butterfly kisses around

her mouth and chin. "For letting me know that I don't have to, but I don't mind going."

Gina swallowed. With the way he was kissing her and touching her, overwhelming desire was clouding her mind. "You sure?"

"About what?" he murmured as he traced kisses from her mouth to her shoulders.

"Dinner at my parents' place." Gina was wondering how long she would last before finally going up in flames when he slipped his hand beneath the sheet and found her hot and wet. Her body jolted to awareness when his finger intimately checked her for readiness.

"The only thing I'm sure about," he said, gently easing her on her back, "is that I want to make love to you again."

Moments later, when his body entered hers, the only thing Gina could think was—*Good answer, good answer.*

The interstate into Fresno wasn't the least bit crowded, Gina noticed as Mitch drove them to his ranch. After they had made love once, then twice, they had showered together. He had invited her back to his place, saying she could interview him on the way there. So she had, although it was hard thinking about business when the two of them had had so much pleasure the night before and that morning.

"So, now that you've gotten chummy with our president, does that mean you will be changing political parties?"

Mitch chuckled, trying to recall if that particular question had been on the list. "No. I plan to remain a Democrat until the day I die and the president knows that. Appointing me to that position showed he cares more about what the real issues are than party affiliations."

Gina nodded. "Do you have to travel to Washington often?"

"I did in the beginning. But now the committee only meets twice a year unless there are some major concerns."

That piqued Gina's interest. "Have there been a number of major concerns?"

Mitch smiled over at her when he finally pulled up in front of the ranch house and brought his Durango to a stop. "I know for a fact that that wasn't an interview question,

Gina. And I don't think the president or the other committee members would appreciate me telling any secrets."

Gina grinned as she unfastened her seat belt. "I'm not *that* kind of reporter, Mitch."

He raised a dark brow at her. "Any reporter is *that* kind of reporter once they get wind of what they think is a news-breaking story. Come on, you can finish asking me your questions later. I need to talk to that group over there."

The "group" he was referring to were the contractors he'd hired to completely renovate the ranch house. She smiled when she saw it was the twins, Blade and Slade Madaris. Throwing up her hand, she waved to them as she headed for the trailer. They were a year younger than she was, and she remembered the times the three of them often played together as kids while growing up along with the twins' cousin, Luke Madaris.

Once inside the trailer she glanced around. Mitch had to be one of the neatest men she knew. Everything was in place. When they were married he had nearly driven her crazy with his fetish for being tidy. She smiled. She felt better today than she had in a long time.

Half an hour later, without looking over her shoulder Gina said, "Lunch is ready," as she stood on tiptoe to take some plates out of the cabinet.

"Can I take a chance and eat it and live?"

She turned around with a frown on her face. "I'll have you know, Mitch Farrell, that I've learned to cook."

Mitch leaned against the closed trailer door with his arms crossed over his chest looking skeptical. "Since when?"

Gina smiled. "Since I no longer had you to do it for me," she said, remembering how Mitch enjoyed doing all the cooking. Even those times when he had put in long days at the office, he would get up at the crack of dawn and prepare a four-course meal for dinner before going to work. The only thing she did in the kitchen was to go get a plate.

"Besides," she added, placing bowls and cups on the kitchen table. "You can't go wrong with a can of Campbell's soup and a box of saltine crackers."

Mitch shook his head, smiling. "No, I guess you can't.

Give me a second to wash my hands and I'll join you."

"All right."

By the time he returned Gina had set the table. "I didn't want us to eat anything heavy to ruin dinner. Knowing Mom she's probably preparing a feast. Trevor, Corinthians and the baby are coming to dinner, too."

Mitch slipped into the chair opposite Gina. For the second time in less than twenty-four hours they had shared a meal together. Yesterday he had prepared lunch for her and today she had prepared lunch for him. He could actually count on his fingers the number of times they had shared a meal together while married. Usually he was so late coming in from work that by the time he got home she would have eaten and gone to bed.

Bed.

Now that was where they had spent most of their time together. No matter how late it had been when he got home, once he went to bed, Gina would willingly come into his arms.

"Now for the next question."

He looked up after saying his grace to see her pull out her writing pad and pencil. He also noted she had the tape recorder sitting on the side. He frowned. "I didn't know this would be a working lunch."

Gina grinned at him. "So now you know. I thought if we got through most of the questions, we wouldn't have to spend our time later tonight discussing them."

A smile tilted the corners of his lips. He knew exactly what he wanted them to do later tonight. "That's a good point."

She laughed. "Yeah, I thought you would agree." She flipped through the pages to find the questions she wanted to ask him. "Now then, what drove you to become successful?"

She could tell the question bothered him, judging from the way he looked when she asked it. "Mitch?" Some sort of struggle was taking place inside of him but she didn't understand why. "Mitch, why does that question bother you? It was on the list."

"Yes, I know, but I wasn't prepared for it yet."

"Surely, you've been asked that before?" she countered.

He stared at her for the longest moment before saying, "No, I haven't ever been asked that. Mainly because no one knows how hard I worked to become successful. And no one knows how I let it become an obsession. I was truly what you'd call a workaholic. I became addicted to work the same way a person becomes addicted to drugs or alcohol. Do you know by the time we got a divorce, I was working well over eighty hours a week?"

Gina shook her head. She hadn't known he'd been working *that* many hours, although she'd known he had been working quite a lot.

"Well, I was. The only time I wasn't thinking about work was when I was making love to you. You were the only distraction I had, Gina."

"But why, Mitch? Why were you driven so?"

He sighed deeply. He wasn't ready to share with her how it was to be a child and go to bed every night hungry. Sometimes the hunger pains were so bad you couldn't function in class the next day. Then you had to deal with teachers who thought you weren't paying attention because you were slow, when in truth you were so hungry you couldn't think straight. The only thing that had kept him going, that had kept him from giving up, was his determination to one day never be hungry and never be thought of as slow again. He had vowed to work hard, study hard and be successful. There had been nothing wrong with that goal—except somehow he had taken it to the extreme.

He began talking, hoping that Gina would understand without his having to tell her everything. "For the longest time I had convinced myself that the reason I did it was because of what I went through while living with my uncle. I've often told you what a miser he was. I promised myself that I would grow up and become successful and I wouldn't go without anything. And I guess that was partly true. But somewhere along the line I lost focus. Somewhere along the line I began working in order to live and living in order to work. Work became the center of my life, and while other things were important to me, work became number one."

Gina nodded. He wasn't telling her anything she didn't

already know. She had realized long before she had finally asked for a divorce that she had been relegated to the bottom of his list.

"So to answer your question, Gina," he said, reclaiming her attention, "I guess you can say that I was first driven because I somehow believed that I *had* to be successful. In my mind not being successful meant being a failure. Then when I married you I knew I had a tough act to follow with your father. Although he didn't live with you and your mother and Trevor, he still was able to provide for you. I considered you as high maintenance. Although you didn't ask for much, I knew you were used to having nice things and I wanted to continue to provide you with those things."

"But I had a job, Mitch. I worked every day and had money."

"Yes, but I felt that as your husband *I* was supposed to take care of you and provide you with the things you needed and wanted. I was determined to take care of you, and in order to do that it meant I had to work hard and move up in my career. At some point I became unable to separate work and play. Other than sex, work was what energized me."

"And what about now, Mitch?" she asked softly, wanting to know; needing to know. "What energizes you now?"

He smiled across the table at her. "You. With you I'd rather play than work."

"Why now and not before?"

"Because I've changed and I've allowed my priorities to change. And because I've been so damn miserable without you in my life, Gina."

She wanted to believe him. She wanted to believe that he was no longer working himself to death and that his life was more manageable now than it had been when they were married. She wanted to believe all of that, but a part of her was afraid to. The last thing she wanted was a repeat performance of pain in her life. "When you finish eating, how about if we take a walk and I can complete the list of questions I have for today?"

Mitch nodded. He knew that she was deliberately bringing the interview to an end for now. She didn't want to accept that workaholism was a disease just like alcoholism and that people could become bona fide workaholics. One day he would tell her how he had met Ivan Spears, a successful banker, at a gym, and how Ivan, a former workaholic himself, had talked him into attending with him a Workaholics Anonymous meeting. Ivan had organized a group of men and women—all African-Americans—who were in the same predicament as him. After several meetings they had helped each other realize that, as African-Americans, they shared the belief that giving one hundred percent in the corporate workplace wasn't enough. They had to give one hundred and fifty percent or even more to reach the same success level as their white counterparts. Being supportive of each other had helped. And although they couldn't change the way corporate America operated, at least they knew what they had to do to recover from workaholism.

"Mitch?"

He smiled across the table, bringing his thoughts back to her suggestion. "All right. After lunch we'll go for a walk."

CHAPTER 9

"YOUR father still doesn't believe in sugar-coating his words, I see," Mitch said as he opened the door to Gina's house. They were just returning from dinner at her parents'.

Gina smiled. Considering everything, she thought the evening had gone rather well. At least Mitch was still alive and in good health. After their divorce her father had claimed that he would do bodily harm to Mitch if he ever came within five feet of her again. He had behaved himself at Trevor's wedding reception, and had even tolerated the two of them dancing together, but only because at the time he and her mother had reconciled after a twenty-year separation and had been too busy acting like newlyweds themselves to worry about her.

"Dad is Dad, I doubt he'll ever change, Mitch. I'm sure Mom told him that you spent the night, and he's still over-protective where I'm concerned."

Mitch nodded, thinking that was an understatement. However, he had to admit that during his and Gina's marriage, Maurice Grant had never meddled in their affairs. Once he had turned his daughter over to Mitch's care as her husband, that had been that. But Mitch knew he had let the man down. He had promised to love, honor and cherish Gina and he hadn't always done that. He had loved her with every breath in his body; he also felt he had honored her as well. But he had been sorely lacking with the cherishing part. He had been too busy working long and extended hours to cherish anything. He now regretted every minute he had stayed late at the office instead of going home and spending time with her.

"It's strange seeing your parents together that way," he said, following Gina into her kitchen.

A smile curled her lips as she began making a pot of coffee, remembering how openly affectionate her parents were to each other. "I know. It takes some getting used to. Dad loves Mom and she loves him. Too bad they had all those wasted years when they could have been together."

Mitch nodded. "Yeah, but they're together now and that's what's important."

"You're right and they just love being grandparents. Did you see how they carried on over Rio?" She laughed. "That baby is going to be spoiled rotten."

Mitch chuckled. "Hey, you were doing a pretty good job spoiling him yourself tonight, Aunt Gina. For a while I thought he was glued to your arms."

Gina leaned against the counter knowing that was true. It seemed that every time she held Rio, the desire for a child of her own pierced her heart. He was such a good baby, a beautiful and precious baby who would grow up in his parents' deep love and protection.

"You've gotten quiet, Gina. What are you thinking about?"

She looked up at Mitch and decided to be honest with him. "I was thinking about Rio and how each and every time I hold him I wish I had a child of my own. I've always wanted a baby."

Mitch looked into her eyes and knew he had disappointed her in that department, too. He distinctly remembered the number of times she had asked, almost begged, for them to start a family and how he had refused her on the grounds that he wasn't ready to become a father. He had to be sure he could successfully provide for a child before agreeing to bring one into the world. He hadn't realized until now just how wrong and selfish he had been to withhold from her the very thing that would have made her happy.

With a deep ragged sigh, he reached out and pulled her into his arms. "I'm sorry, Gina."

"For what?" she asked, liking the feel of being held by him, pressed so close to his strong body. His chest felt wonderful against her chin.

"For all those times you asked me for a baby and I refused to give you one."

A tiny, sad smile touched Gina's lips. "That's all right, I understand."

Mitch looked down at her. "Do you, Gina? Do you really understand? I don't think so because I've yet to give you a reason to understand. And now I think it's time that I do."

Gina saw the intense look on his face and knew whatever he had to tell her would be serious. "All right." She nodded. "Give me a second to pour us a cup of coffee and then we can sit at the table and talk."

"Okay."

A few minutes later they were settled in chairs at her kitchen table. She said nothing as she waited for Mitch to begin speaking.

"I never told you everything about my Uncle Jasper. I know I told you he had a drinking problem and that he was stingy, but I never went into the extent of emotional abuse that I had to deal with, too. He wanted me to believe that I was dumb, worthless and no good, and he spent every day that I lived with him telling me that. Most of the time he didn't feed me. For a while I had to eat scraps anywhere I could find them to survive. Other times I went hungry."

Gina was appalled. "Weren't there agencies around that were supposed to check to make sure you were getting the proper care?"

"Yeah, I suppose there were. But I figured I somehow had fallen through the cracks. Once I ran away, and when I was returned to him, he gave me the beating of my life. In fact it almost ended my life it was so severe. The check he was getting every month was what enabled him to buy his booze and his women, and he wasn't about to let me get away."

"Oh, Mitch."

He sat across from her and saw the deep emotions in her face and the mistiness that appeared in her eyes. She was sad because of what had happened to him. Reaching across the table, he captured her hand in his. "Don't be sad for me, Gina, because I survived. Every night that I went to bed hungry and every day that I went to school ashamed of how I looked made me that much more determined to grow up and make something of myself. I tried so hard, but at times it seemed that no matter how much I studied and tried to do well in school, I couldn't. I would sit in class so hungry that I couldn't concentrate. But I did finish school, and the following day—without taking anything with me—I left Uncle Jasper's house and vowed never to return."

"Good for you."

Mitch smiled. "Yeah, I thought it was good for me but I still found things hard. But I had a determination that no amount of starvation had gotten rid of. I was determined to be successful, no matter what it took. I applied for a loan to go to college and worked two jobs while attending classes, and I kept those same two jobs when I went on to grad school. I had also made up in my mind never to become involved with anyone until I had accomplished all my goals. I read every motivational, rags-to-riches book I could get my hands on, and in the end I knew what I had to do. I had to work hard and use my brains."

Gina's heart went out to Mitch for all he had endured. Now she finally understood why he had been so obsessed with making it to the top, why he had been so driven to be successful. She then remembered what he had told her earlier that day. "You really did become a workaholic, didn't you?"

"Yes." He was glad she finally comprehended things. "I also became a perfectionist. Everything had to be perfect and timed correctly. The reason I couldn't think about us having a child was because in my mind the timing wasn't right."

She nodded and looked at him. "What about marrying me? Had the time been right for that?"

He released her hand and smoothed his fingers across her bare arm before saying, "No, the timing was all wrong. I hadn't counted on falling in love with you, Gina. But you came into my life and I couldn't get you out. And for the first time I became obsessed with something else other than making it to the top. I knew somehow and some way I had to have you and still be successful, and I really thought it would work."

"But it didn't."

He chuckled. "It sure as hell didn't. From the beginning you demanded my time, more time than I had ever given anyone. And I found myself liking it. I enjoyed being in bed with you more than I enjoyed attending some seminar about how to succeed in life. I found myself watching the clock every day at work, counting down the hours, minutes and the seconds when I could leave the office to go home and be with you. I used to sit in board meetings and remember how it had been the night before to slip inside your body and reach an orgasm with your name on my lips." He smiled. "I had it pretty bad."

Gina swallowed the lump in her throat as she remembered the first year of their marriage when Mitch had given her so much attention and so much love. "When did you realize that?" she asked softly.

"When my boss called me into his office and said that I didn't seem as focused as I once had been, and wasn't as sharp and dedicated as I used to be. He thought that maybe something was wrong at home. I was too obtuse to tell him that it was just the opposite and that everything was right at home—my wife was wonderful and my life was happy and I had found a way to balance both work and home. Instead, in my mind I took his words to be synonymous with what my uncle used to say about me. And a part of me was determined to prove him wrong. So I began working harder and staying at the office later."

He drew a long breath before continuing. "That meant putting you second and my career first. That also meant not giving in to anything I thought would set us back. I had my eye on a house in McGregor Park. It had always been my dream to live there."

Gina nodded. McGregor Park was a very old, established and exclusive area of Houston where the well-to-do lived. "If you felt I was a threat to your career plans, why didn't you just divorce me, Mitch?" she asked, seeing and now understanding the extent of what he'd been going through.

"Because as much as I wanted to be successful, and as

much as I wanted all those goals I had been determined to achieve, I loved you and couldn't give you up. I had convinced myself that in time I would be able to handle both you and work. It hadn't dawned on me then that a workaholic is never satisfied. They constantly take personal inventory and come up with other things to aspire to and they buy in to the belief that more money will solve all the problems in their life."

He was silent for a brief moment before saying, "After our divorce I realized the mistakes I had made. I had never really given our marriage a chance to work because of the way I was."

He sighed deeply. "I joined Workaholics Anonymous and met other men and women like myself who were suffering from the same affliction. My group consisted of African-Americans who knew that the issues we face in corporate America aren't faced by our white counterparts. We have helped each other tremendously, most of us have since recovered and have found that balance between work and family."

He captured her hand in his again. "I love you, Gina. I know it's a lot to ask, but I'd like you to give us another chance."

Another chance? Gina felt battered from her emotions, she could barely think straight. "Mitch, I don't know. I need time to think. You shared a lot with me tonight. Most were things you should have shared with me long ago. Then I could have been more supportive and understanding. But I don't know if we can put the past behind us."

"We can at least try, can't we? I don't expect you to make a decision tonight, Gina, or even this week or this month. All I want is for you to agree to let me back into your life. I want to see you, be with you, as a friend and a lover. I want you to give me the opportunity to make things up to you, to wipe the slate clean and start fresh. I want to have the chance to prove that I do love you and that I have always loved you and that I will always love you. Will you agree to at least giving me a chance, Gina?"

She sat still; unsure of herself and the situation Mitch had placed her in. She looked down at their joined hands.

He wanted them to establish a relationship; a very serious and exclusive relationship. He wanted to be her friend and her lover. But what happened if things between them didn't work out? What if . . .

"Gina?"

She slowly lifted her gaze, suddenly ensnarled in the imposing silence that filled the room and the heat that flowed from his eyes to hers. This was the man who had taught her everything she knew about the physical aspects of love. He was the man who had provided so much for her while they were married.

She sighed deeply. As much as she didn't want to admit it, she loved him and wished she had been stronger and had fought harder for him and their marriage. But she had to wonder if love would be enough. It hadn't been the last time, and she didn't think she could go through that again. But a part of her was willing to do what he asked and give him—give them—another chance. They were sleeping together again anyway, and she didn't see that coming to an end any time soon—especially when her body wanted him something fierce. She might as well have a relationship with him because like she had told her mother, she had never been into casual sex, and without a relationship, that's what sleeping with him would become: casual, a way to appease her sexual hunger. And he meant more to her than just a bed partner.

"All right, Mitch," she finally said. "We'll date and do the relationship thing. But if things don't work out the way we think they should, then we should bring things to an end, before either of us gets hurt. Agreed?"

He looked from her face to their joined hands and then back to her face again. He gave a satisfied nod and said, "Agreed."

CHAPTER 10

DURING the following weeks, Mitch and Gina settled into a nice, satisfying routine. She had finished the interview and had given him the rough copy to read and approve. He had told her he had been impressed with what she had written. The article would satisfy the masses' curiosity but at the same time keep his privacy—and his secrets—intact.

Work had started on the ranch house and she was astonished with the results. Retaining the structure of the original house, the Madaris Construction Company was fulfilling Mitch's dream of returning his grandmother's home to the place he remembered and loved.

Their relationship blossomed more every day and on occasion, they would dine with her parents. She had explained her and Mitch's relationship to her family and had been adamant that they understood that just because they were together as a couple did not necessarily mean that they would remarry. At the present what they were trying to do was build a solid relationship, one that could and would withstand anything, especially the pressures of marriage.

She found that she and Mitch were communicating more. She also found herself included in a number of his business decisions, and he often asked her advice and opinions on a lot of issues. They spent every night together, either at her place or his, and Gina had to admit that she was the happiest she had been in a long time.

"You're glowing, Gina."

Gina smiled as she looked up and met Corinthians' smile. The two of them had decided to do lunch together at Sisters since her mother had eagerly volunteered to keep Rio. "Am I?"

Corinthians arched a dark brow and returned Gina's smile. "Yes, you are. In fact you are glowing all over the place." She tilted her head to study her. "You have a certain look about you. It's a happy and a serene look, a satisfied look. I would say Mitch definitely agrees with you."

Gina chuckled. "Thanks, I think I'll keep him around."

Corinthians' smile widened. "Does that mean the two of you have finally decided to remarry?"

Gina frowned. "No, it means just what I said: I think I will keep him around."

Corinthians placed her menu aside and leaned back in her chair. "And how long before you decide to make a decision on your future with him?"

"There's no rush."

"Maybe not for you, but it's obvious that Mitch would remarry you in a heartbeat if you gave the word. What are you afraid of?"

"I'm not afraid of anything."

"Aren't you?"

Gina hesitated for a long moment before finally deciding to be honest with Corinthians. She loved Mitch. She had known that before she had agreed to his offer of giving them another chance. But he was back to working again. Although he was now the boss and made his own hours, a part of her got nervous each and every time he got involved in some business deal. Although he had been doing a good job balancing his time with her and whatever business he needed to take care of, she was afraid he would again find she wasn't enough and would go back to being the workaholic that he used to be.

"Yes," she said softly. "I'm afraid."

"Of loving him?"

"No, I'm afraid of him not loving me, the way I want and need to be loved. I don't think I could handle playing second fiddle to his job again."

Corinthians chuckled. "Honey, I doubt very seriously

that you ever will. Everyone can see that you, and only you, have Mitch Farrell's complete attention. Remember that night last week when the two of you were over to our place? He couldn't keep his eyes off you and when he got that call on his beeper, he didn't leave. He stayed right there."

Gina nodded, remembering. "But it shouldn't have bothered me if he *had* left. There will be times when he'll get an unexpected business call and have to take off. I should be at a point in our relationship where I'm fine with it and don't feel threatened."

"Then why do you feel threatened?"

"Because I lost the number-one spot in his life before."

Corinthians reached across the table and captured Gina's hand and squeezed it gently. "I believe Mitch knows the mistake he made doing that and regrets it, Gina. In my heart I believe he doesn't plan on doing it again. But I don't think you're being fair to him. He's trying so hard to make things up to you and still you're remembering the past and holding it against him. At some point you have to forgive him and believe in a future for the two of you. It's going to be up to you, Gina, to put things behind you and move on."

Gina tilted her head to the side and studied her sister-in-law. "Sounds like you're speaking from experience, Corinthians."

A gentle smile touched the corners of Corinthians' mouth. "I am. Your brother and I couldn't stand each other. For nearly three years after we first met we could barely tolerate the sight of each other, and being in the same room for any length of time was a total nightmare."

"Wow," Gina whispered softly, finding that hard to believe.

Corinthians' smile widened. "Believe it or not, but things were just that bad. And only because neither of us would let go of the past, which had a lot to do with how we first met."

Gina nodded. As usual her curiosity was piqued but she knew Corinthians wasn't ready to divulge the details of that quite yet. "So, when did the two of you put things behind you and move on?"

Corinthians chuckled. "Not until my father intervened

and sat us down and talked to us. I guess you can say he forced us to see the light and we're so thankful that he did. It was only then I discovered that Trevor loved me and he discovered that I loved him. But I would advise you not to wait for anyone to intervene in your case, Gina. It's going to be up to you to do it. And if you love Mitch as much as I believe you do, then you will."

Gina was still remembering the conversation with Corinthians while taking her shower later that night. Coming out of the bathroom she glanced across the room at the clock. Mitch had called a couple of hours ago and said he would be detained for a while because he was at the trailer waiting on an important business call.

She tried not to think about the fact that his job was keeping him from her. She went into the living room and decided to find something to watch on television. An hour later, after having watched a program she'd found interesting, she turned off the set and went into the kitchen.

The table was still set for the dinner she had prepared for them and she could feel herself getting angry and annoyed. *How dare Mitch do this to me?* She had just opened the refrigerator to start putting the food away when the phone rang. She quickly picked it up. "Hello."

"Hey, baby, sorry I was delayed. I just finished that business call I told you about. Unfortunately, it took longer than I expected. I'm about to leave. I'll be there in half an hour."

"Don't bother."

"What?"

"I said, don't bother. I'm ready for bed."

"So?"

"So, I'm ready for bed. I went to the trouble of cooking you dinner tonight thinking you'd be coming here when you said that you were and now everything is cold."

"Dinner? Oh, I'm sorry, honey, I didn't know. Why didn't you tell me?"

"It was supposed to be a surprise."

"And I ruined it. I'm sorry you're upset."

"Yeah, well, I should have learned my lesson by now,

don't you think? It's not the first time your job came before me."

There was silence on the phone, and then Mitch spoke. "I'm on my way, Gina, and your butt better still be up when I get there." Gina could tell from the tone of his voice that what she'd said had really angered him.

"My butt . . . how dare—" She stopped speaking when she heard him hang up the phone on her. She became furious. "I can't believe he had the nerve to do that! Oh, just wait until he gets here. I will *definitely* tell him a thing or two! I don't care if I never see him again. Just wait!"

Gina was still fuming half an hour later when she heard Mitch's car outside. She barely gave him time to knock before snatching the door open. "How dare you say such a thing to me, Mitch Farrell!"

"And how dare you say such a thing to me, Gina!" he said, coming into the house and slamming the door shut behind him. "You are spoiled and selfish!"

"I am not spoiled and selfish!"

"Yes, you are. Case in point: Last Monday, you were supposed to meet me at Sisters for dinner at six. You got there at seven-thirty. Did I get upset?"

She glared at him. "No, because I called and told you I was running behind and would be late."

He began pacing the floor to walk off his anger. "And then last Wednesday, you were supposed to meet me at the ranch at four, but you didn't get there until six."

"Yes, well, I got detained. I got a business call at the last minute from a publisher interested in me doing an article for their magazine. I told you that."

"Yes, you did, and I understood, didn't I?"

"Yes."

"Then why can't you afford me the same courtesy, respect and trust? I called to let you know I was waiting on an important business call and would be a little late. Granted, time went a little beyond what I had expected, but still, I would think being a businessperson yourself that you would have understood. Instead, you got royally and I do mean royally pissed and decided to throw things up in my face about my past deeds. I thought we had gotten beyond all of that. Haven't I proven to you over the past five weeks that you mean everything to me and that I love you? So I'm going to ask you again, Gina. Why can't you afford me the same courtesy, respect and trust that I give to you?"

When she didn't answer immediately, he walked over to her and stood in front of her. The eyes that glared at her were livid. The corded muscles in his neck were straining, his jaw was clenched hard and his nostrils were flaring. "Why can't you, dammit?"

Gina glared back up at him, not knowing what to say. So she told him the truth. "Because you're right," she said softly, breaking eye contact with him and looking down at her hands. She took a deep breath and met his gaze again. "I am spoiled and selfish." Feeling tears sting her eyes she added, "But when it comes to you, I can't help it. I want you all to myself, Mitch. I had to share you the last time and won't share you that way again." A tear slid down her cheek and she wiped it away.

Mitch swallowed his anger as he looked at her. He saw her hurt and tears, but more importantly, he saw her uncertainty. Four years of playing second fiddle to his job had really done a number on her. It would take time and patience for her to feel she had regained that number-one spot in his life.

He reached out and smoothed a few strands of hair out of her face and leaned down and stroked his tongue across her lips. "Oh, baby," he murmured softly against her mouth, nibbling gently on her lips. "Don't you know that you will never share me again? Work is work. You are you. I know where to draw the line now. I had that pretty well figured out before I returned to Houston. You are the most important thing in my life, Gina. Please believe that." Then he kissed her, his tongue thrusting deep in her mouth, making them both groan.

Kissed out of her mind, Gina felt herself drowning as Mitch sucked the very air from her lungs. She wasn't sure if she would ever breathe again, but if she had to die, then this was just the way to go. His tongue, hot, intimate and delicious, was inside her mouth mating with hers and sending pleasure waves to all parts of her body, making it ache.

He broke off the kiss and framed her face with his hands. "I love you, Gina. I love *you*."

She closed her eyes and felt herself being lifted into big strong arms. She knew exactly where he was taking her and could barely wait to get there. She reopened her eyes when she felt him place her on the bed. He stood back and for a few minutes he simply stared at her. And then she saw what he had wanted her to see all along. It was there, clearly in his features—especially his eyes. He loved her. He had always loved her and he would always love her.

"Oh, Mitch." She reached out her hand to him and he took it and joined her in bed. With agonizing slowness he removed her gown and then removed his own clothes. As usual he placed a condom on the nightstand next to the bed. He had yet to use one of them, she thought. For a man who used to believe in doing everything at the right time, he hadn't been able to pull himself out of her to put a condom on. But the thought that they had been taking a risk each and every time they'd made love hadn't bothered her. Nor had it seemed to bother him. After each lovemaking session, they would promise themselves that they would get it right the next time; however, they never did. And something deep inside Gina told her that they never would.

First he began tormenting her breasts with his mouth and fingers, and pretty soon she was thrashing about in the bed, begging and pleading for him to stop, to continue, to hurry up . . . whatever.

Then his fingers, slowly and deliberately, began blazing trails over her body for his mouth to follow. No part of her was left untouched and untasted as desire cascaded over her. Tension was building everywhere, causing every inch of her to throb out of control.

"Now, Mitch!"

"Not yet."

Not yet! What does he plan to do? Torture me to death? "Mitch, please, now!"

He ignored her plea and continued what he was doing, sending the most incredible pleasures racing through her body. She curved her hands around his shoulders to stop him from pushing her over the edge and out of control but it was a waste of her time and effort. He was deliberately driving her insane.

"Mitch!"

It was then and only then that he parted her legs, lifted her hips and entered her, filling her completely and sending a bolt of heat through the most intimate part of her body. He then set the pace, withdrawing slowly and reentering, over and over again, each time going deeper and deeper. Her entire body began trembling from the impact of the sensuous rhythm he had established. Excruciating pleasure shattered her mind as he increased his pace, faster and faster, and adjusted his body to go deeper and deeper. When the explosion came, it was like a torpedo hitting the both of them hard and at the same time, sending them whirling into a space that was void of anything and everything but the two of them. It was an experience so emotional and tender, they clung to each other, soaring together beyond the stars and the moon and then slowly returning to earth and reality.

But not for long.

Mitch suddenly felt fully rejuvenated; the need to have her again rammed into him. He began pumping vigorously into her, over and over, relentlessly.

"Mitch!"

When the second orgasm came crashing down on them both, so soon behind the last, they both screamed out at the top of their lungs as they soared to heights so high, swift and powerful, they thought death would surely follow.

They lay for a long moment in each other's arms, not saying anything, still in awe at what they had just shared. Finally, Mitch spoke when he saw the unused condom on the nightstand. "We goofed again, baby." He then thought about their bodies' double explosion and added, "Big time."

She smiled as she snuggled close to him. "Don't worry about it. We'll get it right one day."

"I may have gotten you pregnant tonight. You were real hot inside both times, and I filled you up pretty good."

Gina smiled. She had always appreciated the fact that she and Mitch had been able to talk candidly and frankly to each other in the bedroom. That sort of sexual communication only enhanced the sensuality they shared. "Don't worry about it. I didn't get pregnant tonight," she whispered, turning in his arms and looking at him.

"You sound pretty sure of that."

She leaned over and softly kissed his lips. "Trust me, I am."

He lifted a brow, wondering if she had gone on the Pill or if she had used some other type of birth control and had failed to tell him about it. "How can you be so sure?"

She met his gaze and a smile tilted each corner of her lips. "Because a woman can't get pregnant when she's already pregnant."

Gina saw his forehead bunch as he tried figuring out just what she meant. Then she saw the crinkle of happiness that immediately appeared in his eyes and the grin that suddenly shone on his mouth. "You're having a baby?" he asked in awe, barely able to contain his happiness and excitement.

"That's what the doctor said this morning."

"Why didn't you tell me?"

"I had planned to. Tonight. That was the reason for the surprise dinner."

Mitch pulled her into his arms. "Oh, sweetheart, I can't believe it. A baby. We're going to have a baby."

She nodded and wrapped her arms around him. "Are you happy about it, Mitch? I mean, are you truly, really happy?"

He leaned down and gently kissed her lips. "Yes, I am truly, really happy."

She leaned back in his arms, contented with his answer. "I hope you know what this means."

Mitch shook his head smiling. "No, what does this means?"

"It means, Mr. Farrell, that as soon as it can be arranged, you'll have to make me Mrs. Mitchell Farrell all over again."

He pulled her closer to him. "And it will be my pleasure. You've always been Mrs. Mitchell Farrell, Gina. In my heart you were always my wife."

"Oh, Mitch, I love you so much."

He leaned over and kissed her, thanking God for giving

him this second chance with her, and believing in his heart that this was how things were meant to be. They were supposed to be together, and this time he was going to make sure it lasted forever.

EPILOGUE

A month later

ONLY family and close friends were invited to witness the marriage between Mitch and Gina. Corinthians' father, the Reverend Nathan Avery, had been more than delighted to perform the ceremony. Trevor had happily served as Mitch's best man and Corinthians had been Gina's matron of honor.

They hadn't told anyone about the baby, deciding to keep it their secret for a while. As Gina glanced around at the number of pregnant women in the room, she knew when the time came she would be in good company.

Syneda, Clayton's wife, was due to have her baby in a few months and Jake's wife, Diamond, was not far behind. Then there was Dex's wife Caitlin, who had recently found out with an ultrasound that they were having a son. Last, but definitely not least, was Nettie, the owner of Sisters, who was married to Ashton Sinclair, one of Trevor's best friends. Everyone was excited with the news that Nettie was having triplets, all boys.

Gina glanced across the room at Mitch and smiled. He was talking to her brother and just looking at him sent heated desire racing down her spine. She couldn't wait for them to be alone later.

"You look absolutely radiant."

She smiled when Corinthians' compliment snagged her

attention. "Thanks, and I feel radiant as well as very happy. Today has been a very special day."

Corinthians chuckled softly. "The first of many more to come."

Gina's smile widened when she thought of what her future had in store. "Yes, the first of many more to come, and I appreciate everyone who came to celebrate our joyous occasion."

Corinthians took a sip of her punch, then said, "Speaking of joyous occasions, I wonder what's wrong with Alex? He seems bothered about something."

Gina glanced across the room at the man Corinthians was talking about, Alex Maxwell. He was Trask's brother and a close friend of the Grant and Madaris families. Her smooth forehead furrowed. "I don't know but it looks like he's glaring at Christy Madaris."

"Hmm-mm, I think you're right," Corinthians said as her gaze followed Alex's and lit on the beautiful young woman with vibrant red hair who had arrived moments ago and was circling the room. Christy was the Madaris brothers' baby sister and when it came to Christy, the brothers were overprotective.

Gina shook her head smiling. "I can't believe how Christy has grown up and just to think that she'll be graduating from college next spring. I can remember when she was a teenager who had a big-time crush on Alex. I'd often wondered if she would grow out of it and apparently she has."

Corinthians nodded as she glanced back across the room to Alex. He was still glaring at Christy. She remembered a time Trevor wore a similar expression when he looked at her. A slight smile touched her lips and she wondered if perhaps history was about to repeat itself.

'So, you pulled it off, I see," Trevor said to Mitch, smiling as he glanced across the room to where his sister stood talking to his wife. He could tell from the smile on Gina's face just how happy she was.

Mitch chuckled. "Did you think for one minute that I wouldn't?"

Trevor grinned. "No. That night I talked to you, you were pretty damn determined. I'm glad you're back in the family, Mitch."

"And I'm glad to be back." He glanced across the room to where his father-in-law was standing talking to Reverend Avery. "Excuse me, Trevor, there's something I need to take care of."

He walked over to the two men. "Excuse me, Reverend Avery, but I would like to speak with Mr. Grant privately for a second."

Nathan Avery smiled. "Sure thing, son. We were discussing our grandson there. I'll check out those little sandwiches Stella just put out."

When Mitch found himself alone with Gina's father at first it was hard for him to gather up his thoughts. And it didn't help matters that Maurice Grant was looking at him through those dark eyes of his that reminded Mitch so much of Trevor when he wasn't too pleased about something.

Mitch cleared his throat. "There was a reason I didn't ask for Gina's hand in marriage this time, sir."

"Oh? Were you afraid I wouldn't give it to you a second time?" Maurice Grant said, unsmiling.

Mitch shook his head. "No, I felt it wasn't needed. You had given it to me once and a part of me felt you knew I was doing the right thing by getting her back."

"And have you done the right thing, Mitch?"

"Yes, sir, I have. I love your daughter very much."

Maurice didn't say anything for a long moment. Then he let out a deep sigh. "I know you do. I've always known how you felt and I was fairly certain we hadn't seen the last of you, although Gina was pretty convinced we had. So, I really wasn't surprised when you showed back up in Houston."

"You weren't?"

"No." The older man let out an amused chuckle. "In fact, I had expected you sooner."

"I had a lot of issues to resolve."

"And have you?"

"Yes, sir."

"Good. My daughter loves you very much, but I guess you know that."

"Yes, sir, I know that."

"And I guess I don't have to tell you that I expect you to make her happy."

Mitch shook his head, smiling. "No, sir, you don't have to tell me that."

"Good." He extended his hand out to Mitch. "I'm glad to have you back in the family, son, and I know in my heart that you are the *best* man for her. You are the *only* man for her."

A lump formed in Mitch's throat. It had been important to him to regain this man's trust and confidence. "Thank you."

"Mitch?"

Mitch turned toward the soft, ultra-sexy voice and smiled when he saw Gina. "Yes, sweetheart?"

She glanced from him to her father, then back to him again. Concern showed in her eyes. "Is everything all right?"

He chuckled. "Yes, everything is fine. Come here, Mrs. Farrell."

She closed the distance between them and walked straight into his opened arms. He held her tight and close to his heart. Tonight they would leave on a trip to the U.S. Virgin Islands, St. Thomas and St. Croix, for a four-week honeymoon. Two weeks for the honeymoon they'd never had the first time around and the other two for this marriage.

From now on everything between them would be *strictly pleasure*.

CATCH ME
IF YOU CAN!

CINDI LOUIS

To my brother, Donnell Lavalais, and my cousin, Mitchell Lewis, who are real fathers, real men.

And the Hotties.

ACKNOWLEDGMENTS

Thanks to: Jerry Crimiel and Wes Sivley for the information on the Air Force and FBI. And my editor, Monique Patterson, the best thing since sliced bread and caller ID.

PROLOGUE

LONZELL Jenkins dropped the key three times before he was able to open the hotel room. They had talked about this moment for years, and now that it was here he was more nervous than a one-legged frog in rush-hour traffic. He just wanted everything to be perfect for them. He loved her more than life itself and he wanted her to know he loved her—mind, body, and soul. They had managed to keep their relationship a secret all the while they were in Lovebug, which was hard to do in such a small town. Now, they were out from under the watchful eye of the hometown people and could do whatever they wanted. "We're here," he said to his ladylove, Leesa Fairchild, as he pushed the door open and let her walk in before him.

The sweet aroma of coconut greeted Leesa as she walked into the room. She took in everything; from the small, round table and two chairs that sat in the right-hand corner to the big, beautiful picture that hung above a king-size bed covered with a green-and-cream floral spread. There was a clock radio on the nightstand, and also a lamp that gave a soft glow to the room. There was a nineteen-inch TV on the dresser. Leesa closed her eyes; she wanted to remember this moment forever.

"Do you like the room?" Lonzell asked, bringing in her suitcase.

"Oh, Lonzell, this is very nice," she said, turning around to make sure she didn't miss anything. Lonzell had gone all-out to make her first time wonderful. "I love it, the coconut candles are nice."

Lonzell put her suitcase on the rack that was in the corner by the closet. "I'm glad you like it. I know coconut is your favorite and I wanted to make this as special for you too," he said, walking over and taking her hand. "Come, sit down and let's talk."

Leesa didn't move.

"What's wrong?" he asked with concern.

"I-I thought we . . . we were going to . . . you know," she said, shyly tilting her head toward the bed.

Lonzell smiled. "Baby, we will, but right now, I just want to hold you. It's been a long time since I've been able to do that."

He was right, it had been a long time: with him at Officer Training School at Lackland Air Force Base in San Antonio, Texas, and her at Florida State University, it made it hard for them to be together. "Okay," she finally said.

They had talked for more than two hours. Now they were in the bed and he was rubbing some warm coconut-scented oil down her bare, smooth chocolate body. "How does that feel?" he asked.

"Mmmm . . . nice," she answered in a mere whisper.

"Good," he said, massaging her lower back. "Turn over, baby." Lonzell kissed his way up her body.

Leesa did as he asked of her.

Their eyes held. Lonzell sucked in his breath as his mind took a photocopy of the black beauty that lay before him. She was perfect in every way. Her shiny, coal-black, waist-length hair fanned out over the white pillowcase. Her eyes were the color of a black velvet sky, sparkling like the stars on a clear July night. Her high cheekbones were a gift from her Indian ancestors. And that cute little nose, it was straight and thin, but not too thin. Lonzell's eyes moved down a fraction to her lips, lips that were full and covered with a hint of an earth-toned lipstick.

Then she flashed one of her sweet smiles at him. Lonzell thought he would lose it right then and there. Even with braces she could still turn him into putty.

"Is something wrong?" Leesa asked as she watched his chest rise and fall.

Not knowing if he could use his voice, he answered in a mere whisper. "No, I just want to look at you. You're so beautiful."

She gave him that smile again. Lonzell didn't know which was melting the fastest: him or the coconut-scented candles that he had lit throughout the room. He continued his visual journey down her small body, then back up again, only to stop at her firm breasts. Not being able to resist any longer he covered them with his large hands. Closing his eyes, he moaned. They felt just like he remembered—soft. . . . They fit his hands perfectly, full and ripe for the picking—his picking.

Taking the small buds between thumb and forefinger he massaged them as if she were the clay, and he were the potter.

Lonzell couldn't stand it any longer. He had to taste her or he would surely die. He moved his hand from her left breast and replaced it with his mouth, letting out a soft moan. She was just that sweet. Whoever came up with the saying "The blacker the berry the sweeter the juice" had not lied. He was intoxicated by the nectar of this black beauty. He flicked his tongue over the rock-hard bud, and was pleased when Leesa purred and gasped for air. He wanted her to enjoy the things he planned to do to her as much as he would.

With his mouth, he paid just as much attention to the other bud before he kissed his way down her body, stopping only to make love to her belly button with his tongue. He had to hold her down when her lower body lifted off the mattress. Raising his head, Lonzell reached across Leesa for the coconut oil that sat in a warmer on the nightstand. Smiling down at her, he said, "Hold on, baby, we're just getting started."

Just getting started! Leesa said to herself. She didn't know it could be this romantic. Sure, she had read all the romance books, but this was real and according to her best friend Tara Collins they should have been through fifteen minutes after they had walked into the room. That wasn't the case with her and Lonzell. Fifteen minutes had been up for some time now.

They had been here for hours and the only thing they had done was talk and take off their clothes—well, Lonzell still had on his Air Force pants. Which was all right with Leesa because his big, strong, wonderful hands were all she could handle right now. She closed her eyes as she felt them on her right thigh working their way down her leg.

Leesa's breath caught in her throat. She opened her eyes to see the top of Lonzell's head as he sucked on her toes. He kissed her feet and moved slowly up her legs, thighs, stopping at her triangle center. With very little coaxing he parted her thighs and tasted her.

"Huh! Oh! Mmm . . ." was all she could muster.

Lonzell loved her until he felt her body lose control. He kissed his way back up her warm body and looked at her eyes, eyes the color of black gold. He had so much desire for her that if he didn't have her soon he would explode. "Did you like that?" he asked, kissing her sweet lips.

Leesa nodded with a smile.

"I've always wanted to do that to you," he murmured, kissing her neck and going back down her body.

Leesa was so out of it by the way he was making her feel that she hadn't noticed he was now totally nude until her eyes got stuck on the part of his body that let her know he was more than ready to join them as one. As he stood, the light from the candles silhouetted his golden-bronze skin. His biceps and triceps were huge, as was his chest. Her eyes traveled down his body past his six-pack stomach and his firm thighs, but what she loved to look at most on his body was his bowlegs.

She loved him so much it hurt. Her mouth formed a perfect O as she got a full view of his tight, firm, bounce-a-quarter-off-it rear as he walked away from the bed. Leesa knew this wasn't the place or time to be thinking about Ida Jean Jenkins, but she knew the woman would shit a brick if she knew her son was here with her. Leesa knew that, because her skin had been darkened by nature's sun, Ida Jean didn't want her son with her, but love had no color and that was something Ida Jean would just have to learn. Leesa also had a feeling that Ida Jean didn't like her for other reasons, but she couldn't put her finger on it. Pushing his mother out of her head and out of their room, she said softly, "I love you, Lonzell."

"And I love you, Leesa. Never forget that," he whispered, lighting a few more candles.

At that very moment she wanted to touch him in the way that he had touched her.

As if reading her mind he walked back over to the bed and climbed in beside her.

Leesa brought her left hand to his face to touch the small scar over his left cheek. When he was only three years old, he had picked one of the blisters from a bad case of chicken pox.

People who didn't know him thought he was a lion, but she knew he was a big old cub and wouldn't hurt anyone. Knowing that, she felt bold enough to gently push him back on the bed and straddle his waist.

Lonzell drew in extra air when her body touched his. "W-what do you think you are doing?" he asked in a voice he didn't know was his own.

Leaning forward, only inches from his mouth, she answered, "I read. I know what men like for women to do to them."

He couldn't stand it anymore, he had to touch her. Stroking her back, he said, "Oh, yeah? What do men like?"

"This . . ." she said as her mouth found his. Leesa could feel his body's reaction to the heart-stopping kiss. "And this . . ." she said, nibbling his earlobe, then placing her tongue in his ear.

"And this . . ." she whispered, placing small, wet kisses down his chest. She continued down his body until she reached his manhood. With a steady left hand, she wrapped her fingers around his hardness and began to move her hand up and down in slow motion; at the same time she brought her head down, only letting the tip of her tongue touch him, tasting him.

Lonzell gasped for air as if he had been underwater too long.

"Did I do something wrong?" she asked, alarmed, moving her head and hand away from him, thinking she was holding him too tight.

"No!" Lonzell said in a voice filled with want. "You are doing it right." He took her hand and brought it back to his manhood. "Don't stop. I like the way you love me."

With no coercing, Leesa began to show Lonzell just how much she did love him.

Lonzell knew it wouldn't be long before he lost control as he watched his shaft disappear into Leesa's mouth over and over again. He didn't want their first time to end that way so, with one smooth movement, he gently pulled her up and flipped her on her back. "I want to read what you have been reading. My books don't have anything like *this* in them," he said softly against her lips.

Leesa was shocked as to how she had ended up under Lonzell so fast. She had to blink twice before she could answer him. "W-what's that?" she finally said.

"Love," he answered, taking her mouth. They kissed long and hard as if their lives depended on it. Leesa opened her mouth as his tongue pushed against her lips.

Lonzell drank her in. He had kissed her enough times that he had mastered how not to hurt their mouths because of her braces. Releasing her mouth, he planted tiny kisses down her body. As his left hand roamed over her body, his right hand came to rest at her patch of curls. Skillfully, he entered two fingers into her moist body. Leesa gasped and stiffened.

Lonzell could feel she was ready for him, but she was still afraid. "Don't worry, baby, we'll go slow. I won't hurt you, I promise," he said, as he removed his fingers from her hot wetness. He kissed her again as he let his index finger tease the ripe little bud of her center. Leesa began to relax again and enjoy the pleasure he was giving her, as he whispered softly in her ear. "I won't make love to you until you are fully ready. I'll never do anything to hurt you, Leesa, I promise. I love you so very much."

Leesa heard his words, but her mind was in never-never land trying to control her shaking body for a second time. From reading those romance novels she knew what was happening to her and *Lord*, it was so much better than the book.

Somewhere in the far distance she heard Lonzell say, "Let it go, baby. I'm right here with you."

It was all the encouragement she needed as she called out his name and shredded into a million pieces.

Lonzell's kisses brought her back to this side of heaven. When Leesa opened her eyes the first thing she saw was Lonzell's dancing eyes. "Now, was that better than the book?" he asked with a smile.

"Oh, yes, so much better," she answered in a shy voice.

"Good."

Leesa could feel his iron member against her thigh and knew he was more than ready to join the two of them together. Without taking her eyes off his handsome face she moved her right hand to the part of his body that made him all man and covered it. "I want you to make love to me now," she said as she gently stroked him.

Lonzell covered her hand with his. She was driving him out of his mind. He said in a husky voice, "Baby, you have to stop, so I can protect you."

She watched him as he tore open a small foil package he had gotten off the nightstand earlier and covered his male organ. Within seconds, he was between her legs.

"Are you sure, Leesa?"

In a sweet whisper she said without hesitation, "Yes, I'm sure."

Lonzell then positioned himself over her body, putting his weight on his upper arms. "I love you, Leesa," he said, looking into her eyes as he pushed his way into her body. She gasped at the flare of pain. Lonzell held himself still, allowing her body time to adjust to his size. She was so small that he didn't want to hurt her any more than necessary.

The pain didn't last long, but it did bring water to her eyes. Leesa felt her eyes burn as the tears ran into her hairline.

Lonzell knew something was wrong the minute she closed her eyes. "Leesa, baby, talk to me. I'm sorry. We'll stop right now."

Leesa opened her eyes again as the pain began to subside. "I'm okay," she answered in a mere whisper.

"Are you sure, my luv?" Lonzell asked.

"Yes," she uttered as he tried to leave her body. "I want you to make love to me. It was just a little pain, but I'm okay now."

Lonzell wasn't sure. Hell, she was only the third woman he had been with and the first two had been older and not virgins. "Okay. I just don't want to hurt you any more."

"You won't," she assured him, moving her body under his. "Love me, Lonzell."

Kissing her moist face he moved slowly inside of her. Soon Leesa caught on to the age-old dance of lovemaking. The more he loved her, the more she loved him back. The harder he thrust inside of her, the more she wanted him. They had become as one. Lonzell slid his hands under her bottom, pulling her closer to him as he pushed deeper and deeper into her valley, all the while telling her how she made him feel.

Leesa cried out in pure pleasure. Lonzell was right behind her as he called out her name, taking them to paradise.

As they lay in the afterglow of their lovemaking, Lonzell lifted his upper body off of her and said, "I'm sorry I hurt you."

"It didn't hurt that bad." She touched his chest.

Searching her eyes to see if there were any regrets, he found none. "I love you, Leesa. I promise it won't hurt like that ever again."

Leesa smiled at him. "I know."

They were still joined together and Lonzell didn't want to leave her body because it was so warm—too warm. Not wanting to signal to Leesa that something might be wrong, he eased from her body and looked down as he lay beside her. His worst fear was becoming a reality. The condom had indeed broken.

God, how was he going to tell Leesa this? They had been so careful all this time. The night was so perfect; he had wanted their first time to be so perfect—now he had to tell her something that would just kill the mood, but she had to know that they had had no protection. She trusted him. He had heard of this happening to other people—but he never thought it would happen to him and Leesa.

They had their life all planned out. He was on a thirty-day leave before reporting to the Kun San Air Base in Korea for the next two years to work in law enforcement. This was Leesa's last year of college and she wanted to start her own company. Sure, they had talked about getting married and having children, but not like this.

Leesa could tell something was wrong because of the way Lonzell was breathing. "Lonzell, what's wrong? You're scaring me." She rose off the pillow, pulling the sheet over her moist body.

Pulling her tightly into his arms, he whispered, "It broke. Leesa, it broke."

Leesa pulled away from him and looked at him in disbelief. "No. This can't be happening. We were so careful. How? When? What are we going to do?"

Leesa fired question after question at him, knowing he would have the answers. *It broke! It broke!* was all she could hear in her mind. What was she going to do? She had already taken a year off because she hadn't been able to handle losing both her parents the day after her high school graduation. Thank God the university had been willing to hold her scholarship for a year. Now this!

Her mother and father were counting on her to finish college. She just knew her parents were in heaven looking down on her—shocked—and trying to find a way back to earth to ask her if she had lost her mind. What was going to happen now? God! What had she done?

"What if I'm pregnant?" She knew it was a question neither one of them wanted to be true, but it could happen. "What's going to happen to us? What about me finishing school? You're just starting your career in the Air Force. What are we going to do, Lonzell?" she asked again, this time unable to hold back the tears.

Lonzell pulled her closer to him. "We will get through this. We're jumping to conclusions. It's just this one time. Everything will be all right," he said, trying to convince himself more so than Leesa. He knew it only took one time to make a baby. "No matter what, Leesa, I'll always be here for you. I promise."

Leesa pulled back but not away from him as she said,

"Lonzell, how are you going to be here for me when you'll be in Korea? I'm supposed to graduate in December."

"Come here, baby," he said, pulling her back into his arms and kissing her hairline. "Look, I'm going to be here another week with you, then I'm going to Lovebug to visit my mama. You know you can catch me there."

"Please! You know your mother can't stand the air I breathe. Call her house!" Leesa wiped her tears away.

"She's not like that, Leesa, really. I'll make sure she knows I'm waiting to hear from you; besides, I have your dorm number."

"I know that, but remember I'm moving out of the dorm and into an apartment with Tara next month. And you'll already be gone," she cried.

"Don't you worry, baby, I'll find you. Once I'm in Korea and get my living quarters, I'll call my mother with my address and phone number. She'll give it to you."

"Besides, I don't see why you can't get your own apartment. I told you I'd pay for it," Lonzell said, wiping her tears away with the pad of his right thumb. "You know that my grandparents set up a trust fund for me the day I was born, and I haven't touched the money."

"Lonnie, I don't want your money, I never have. Anyway, my parents left me a nice little nest egg. Besides, I like the idea of rooming with Tara, she is my best friend."

"Don't worry," he said again. "We'll get through this—together. I promise."

Leesa heard his word, but deep in her heart she knew things would never be the same between them again.

CHAPTER 1

Four years later

LEESA opened the doors of the Guiding Star Baptist Church. She and Miles took a seat on the next-to-last pew. Her mind took a trip down wonderland as she wondered about her parents' wedding day. Whenever they spoke of their special day, her mother would get that faraway look in her eyes, and her father would grin from ear to ear.

She loved to hear the story of how her father's family came from miles away to witness his marriage to a dark-skinned African American woman.

"Mommy," Miles said to bring her back to the present.

"Yes, sweetheart."

"You got some gum?" Miles asked, as he got off the pew and stood facing her, with his back on the pew in front of them.

"Yes, I do, but you can't have any more."

"Why not?" he asked, while leaning towards her, looking her directly in the face. "I'm not gonna swallow it—this time."

"No gum, Miles, no gum!" she said softy, but firmly, giving him a kiss on the nose.

Miles gave her his best sad face, even his bottom lip poked out. He put his head down and climbed back on the seat and leaned his head into Leesa's right side.

Leesa let a small sigh pass through her lips. Miles knew

how to push the right buttons to get his way with her. And today was no different. She looked into her small handbag and found a piece of candy. "You have to keep it in your mouth, so you won't mess up your clothes," she said, unwrapping the candy and giving it to him.

Miles took the candy and popped it into his mouth. "I love you, Mommy," he said, still leaning on her, and swinging his little feet as the sweet juice captured his tastebuds.

"I love you too," she said, patting him on the leg.

Leesa listened to Miles as he sang one of his favorite nursery rhymes, before her mind slipped back to her parents—right up to the day they were killed. They were on their way home from their date. It was something they had done every Saturday night for as long as she could remember. The police officer said they had died fast—so did the nineteen-year-old boy who'd lost control of his car while speeding.

"Mommy, why the wedding is taking so long?" Miles asked his mother for the twentieth time.

"Sweetheart, it's not taking long. It's just not time for it to start. Remember, we got to the church early just in case Mr. Bruce wanted to take some pictures of you before the wedding," Leesa said to the boy, who was looking more and more like his father every day. She could see Lonzell Jenkins in her son in ways no one else could, like his lips, his hands, and for sure his bowlegs.

"But Mr. Bruce already took pictures of me a *long* time ago. Now I'm ready to go to the wedding," Miles said, looking up at his mother, waiting for her to tell him it was time.

"Miles, please. It's not going to be that much longer." Leesa knew it was going to be a long day and she just wanted it to be over with. She wished now she had told Bruce that Miles couldn't be in his wedding, but how do you tell the mayor of Lovebug you didn't want your child to be in his wedding?

True, she had brought Miles in early to have some pictures taken, but the real reason she wanted to get to the church before it got too crowded was that she needed to be prayed up by the time she saw Lonzell Jenkins.

It had been years since she had seen him, and if she could have had her way, she'd keep it that way; but Miles was at the age where he wanted to be around men and recently had begun to ask questions about his father. So, she had swallowed her pride—which was a bitter pill because Lonzell had hurt her deeply, by swearing on a pledge of love that he would be there for her, but hadn't been—and for the sake of their son she would make peace. Today, Miles would meet his father face-to-face and she would stand back and let the chips fall where they may.

"Hey, Ms. Leesa," a young voice said nipping into her thoughts.

"Oh, hi, Tammy," she said, turning to look at the girl who was standing in front of her.

"Ms. Nadia said could you please come and see if you can get the bloodstain off of Ms. DeLisa's dress?"

"What! Come on, Miles, sweetheart," Leesa said, already up and taking Miles by the hand. "What happened?"

"She was trying to open an envelope and got a paper cut, some of the blood dripped on her wedding dress, and now she's freaking out."

"Is it time for the wedding now, Mommy?"

"No, sweetheart, Mommy is going to help Ms. DeLisa and I want you to stand right outside this door like a big boy, okay?"

"Then we going to the wedding?"

"Yes."

"Oh boy! Oh boy!" He jumped up and down as Leesa opened the door to the choir room, which the bride and her bridesmaid were using.

"I'll be right back." Leesa then threatened, "Don't move!"

Lonzell had gotten into town too late last night to make the wedding rehearsal and dinner. It had been four years—well, two years, really, but that didn't count because he had only been here for three days before he'd left to go to Tallahassee in search of Leesa.

That successful search had turned out to be a heartbreaking fiasco, forcing Lonzell to go back to Korea and extend his time for another two years. Now, for the first time in his life, he wanted to be anywhere but in Lovebug. Too many memories, good and bad, and that was why he was only going to stay a few days before heading back to Quantico, Virginia.

Although he had been up for captain in the air force, he had decided instead to resign and take a job with the FBI because of his background in computers and law enforcement. He had already found a house in Virginia and was scheduled to close on it within two weeks. Going on with his life was the best move for all.

Lonzell had just stepped out of the pastor's study, talking with Reverend Hatch, when he heard a child sniffling. As he turned the corner, sure enough, a little boy stood at the choir room door, crying.

The child looked at Lonzell as he moved toward him.

Lonzell hunched to the child's level before he said, "Hey, buddy, why the long face?"

The child studied Lonzell for a few moments before he uttered, "My mommy is in there with a bunch of girls and she won't let me in. And I'm ready to go to the wedding," he added, looking down at his white shoes. Lonzell looked at the closed door, then back at the child, smiling at the little boy, who looked to be about three or four years old. "Well, I can take you if you like."

The child looked up before he said, "My mommy said I can't go with strangers."

"Your mommy is right and a very smart lady," Lonzell said as he touched the young boy's little pug nose.

The little boy giggled and said, "No, she not no lady, she just my mommy."

Lonzell laughed. "Okay, buddy, she's your mommy. What's your name?"

The little boy slapped his right hand up on his forehead and said, "I can't tell you that. Don't you watch Barney?"

Smart kid, Lonzell said to himself as he looked the child over, wondering why he seemed so familiar. Maybe he knew his parents. Sure, it had been a long time since he'd spent any time with the good people of Lovebug, but his mother kept him abreast on what went on in his hometown. Maybe the child was from the bride's side of the family ... still, he looked like someone he knew very well, but who?

Lonzell looked at the child once again and thought if he didn't know better, the child could have been his. But of course he had no children. No matter what people thought of military men, he kept *his* lieutenant under lock and key and had no plans to release any soldiers anytime soon. He had had unprotected sex once—and that was because the condom had broken. Thank God, nothing had happened that one night long ago. He couldn't wait to see the parents because he and the child had the same nose, eye shape, and—what was so funny—the boy was also bowlegged. *Wow*, he thought, smiling.

"We have on the same clothes. Did your mommy buy that?" the little boy asked, touching Lonzell's tux.

Lonzell didn't answer at first. He was thinking about his mother, Ida Jean Jenkins, who would be here any minute. They were still close, but something in her had changed. For some reason she had not wanted him to come to the church this morning to talk to Bruce. Truth be told, he just wanted to know how did he find a nice girl from Froghop, Mississippi, to marry him? Ida Jean had told him all he was going to do was stand next to the groom and there was no need for him to get up early when he had gotten in so late.

"No, my mommy didn't buy it this time." Lonzell snapped his fingers. "Hey, I know someone who knows us both," he said.

"Who?"

"Mr. Bruce."

"You know Mr. Bruce?" the child said with huge brown eyes. "He said I can stand next to him in the wedding."

"Really?"

"Mm-hmm. And guess a-what?"

"What's that?" Lonzell asked, never taking his eyes off the child.

"I get to carry the rings on a pillow."

"Well, all right, my man. Give me five," Lonzell said, holding his hand out.

The child didn't disappoint him as he slapped his hand in Lonzell's.

"Now, are we friends?"

"Yes."

"So, if I tell you my name will you tell me yours?"

"My name is Miles. What's your name?"

"My name is Lonzell, and it's nice to meet you, Miles."

"I have to go to the bathroom."

"Sure, I can take you, it's just two doors down."

"Okay."

Lonzell stood to his full six-foot-two height and led Miles to the men's room.

"Please, DeLisa, stop crying! It's not that bad," Leesa said, wiping at the red spot that was now almost gone. Leesa had moved back to Lovebug seven months ago because she had gotten homesick and missed the small-town setting. She had started her own company, LM Services, as a "Vendor Relations Specialist"—she found service providers for three large department stores. It was good money, but it required her to work crazy hours. Which was okay because she worked from home or anywhere else she could get on the Internet.

"Can someone check on Miles? He's too quiet out there." Leesa gave DeLisa's dress another wipe with a sample of a new cleaning solution for hard-to-get-out stains a prospective client had given her. From the looks of it, she would definitely be using them as one of her vendors.

"I'll go check on him," one of the bridesmaids said, walking to the door.

"Okay, little buddy, I'll see you later. You wait right here for your mommy, okay?"

"Okay."

Just as Lonzell turned and walked off, the door opened and the bridesmaid said, "Hey, Miles, your mom will be out real soon, okay?"

"I want to go with my friend."

"Who?" The woman looked down the hall at a man's wide back. "Is that Darius?" she asked, more to herself than to Miles.

"Him, my friend." Miles pointed down the hall to where Lonzell had stopped to talk to some people.

"Hold on. Let me ask your mom."

Miles looked at the closed door and took off down the hall to where Lonzell was standing.

"Hey, Leesa, Miles wants to go with Big Mama Shirley's grandson, Darius, who's standing down the hall."

"Okay, tell him he can go, and I'll come and get him before the wedding."

The woman opened the door again. "Okay, Miles—" Miles was nowhere to be seen. "Miles?" she called down the hall.

Miles stepped around Lonzell and yelled, "I'm right here."

"Come here, little boy!" she said in a firm voice.

Miles looked up at Lonzell and said, "I be right back, okay?" Not waiting for Lonzell to answer, Miles took off running.

Now standing in front of the woman, he said, grinning, "Ma'am."

"Your mom said you can go and she will come and get you before the wedding."

"Oh boy!" he said and took off running again. "Hey, my friend. Hey, wait for me."

Lonzell was just turning the corner when he heard Miles. Crouching toward Miles with both hands on his knees, Lonzell spoke gently. "Hey, buddy, does your mommy know you're down here?"

"Yes, sir. She say she come get me for the wedding."

Ring.

"LM Services, this is Leesa."

"Hi, Leesa, this is John at the call center."

"Oh, hi, John. What can I do for you?" Leesa said as she closed the choir room door and walked outside the building so she could hear better.

"I have a work order for one of the JC Penney stores. Work order is 12—"

"I'm sorry, John, what is it? I'm not at home," she said, cutting him off.

"The glass in one of the front doors is broken."

"Oh, just send that to Glass & More Glass. Vendor number 26589."

"Okay, will do. Thanks, Leesa."

"Anytime, John."

Leesa felt bad handing her son off to Darius. If his own father had thought enough of him, maybe things could have been different, but no, he preferred to send a check once a month and think that would be all right. Well, it wasn't and she was sick and tired of his attitude about Miles. Like now, he could be here helping with Miles, but of course he had yet to show up. And he was the best man. He was a *best*, all right, but it wasn't a man. "No more Ms. Nice Lady. I didn't make him by myself and I'm not going to raise him by myself." She spoke out loud as she headed back into the church, never noticing Ida Jean Jenkins walking up behind her.

CHAPTER 2

LONZELL stood next to his best friend, Bruce Woodmen, as he watched the nine bridesmaids, two maids of honor, and one matron of honor walk down the aisle. All were dressed in lima bean–green ruffled dresses and matching shoes. Now, true, he wasn't the fashion police, but he felt they all should be arrested for those dresses. *What in God's green earth made DeLisa pick that color for her wedding?* Thank God he was wearing all white like the groom.

Lonzell smiled as the children came down the aisle; two little girls exchanged baskets, never dropping the flowers on the white rug. Then it was Miles' turn. He walked slowly, his head down, watching the rings as they sparkled on the white lace pillow that he carried in both hands.

A very soft-spoken woman said, "Hold your head up, honey."

The little boy turned to the back of the church and said, "Look, Mommy, I don't drop them."

Laughter filled the church as Miles made his way down the aisle to stand next to Bruce and Lonzell.

Lonzell thought the voice came from the bride's side and he wanted to see who had told Miles to hold his head up, but he couldn't see a thing because everyone was now standing for the bride to make her grand entrance.

The music had changed and a sigh went up and rippled over the heads of those closest to the beautiful woman. She was a vision in heavy beaded satin, white lace, and netting.

Every woman in the crowd immediately had tears in her eyes; every man, thoughts he'd never confess. She was downright gorgeous.

Leesa looked as the bride took her place next to her knight in shining armor. She could feel the burning of the tears in the back of her eyes—not for the bride, but for her son as he looked up at his father. She watched father and son standing there. Her heart was breaking as she wondered how he could be so cruel to his own flesh and blood.

Miles only wanted what any little boy wanted, to be loved by his father. So, why was Lonzell denying his child the opportunity to know him?

Everyone had just taken a seat when Leesa's cell phone began to vibrate in her hand. She looked around before she started to stand and looked dead into Ida Jean Jenkins' eyes. If looks could kill, she would be one dead lady right about now. But Leesa didn't let Ida Jean shake her one bit as she eased out of the last pew and walked out the door.

Leesa was barely out of the church before the cell phone vibrated again. "LM Services, this is Leesa."

"Hi, Leesa, this is Amy, from the call center."

"Hi, Amy, how can I help you?"

"I need a plumber for one of the Giant Super Stores. The main pipe has burst and water is everywhere. The plumber we have in the system can't get to the store until Monday."

"What city and state is the store in?" Leesa asked, knowing this was going to take some time and that she was probably going to have to leave the wedding.

"Dallas, Texas."

"Okay, Amy, I think I have someone I can send out, but I need to get home first."

"Oh, you're not home?"

"No, I'm at a wedding, but I'm only twenty minutes from home."

"I'm sorry," the lady said sincerely.

"Oh, no, it's okay. It's part of the job. I'll talk to you soon."

"Okay, Leesa."

Leesa pushed the END button. "Great! Just great," she

murmured as she looked in her small handbag for her keys.

"Baby, what are you doing out here in this heat?" an older woman asked as she walked down the three steps and over to Leesa.

"Hi, Mama Shirley, I was just on my way to find you," Leesa said, looking up at the older woman who had been heaven-sent when her parents died and even more so when she'd moved back to Lovebug. Mama Shirley never asked any questions about Miles, but Leesa knew deep down in her soul that Mama Shirley *and* most of the good people of Lovebug knew Lonzell was Miles' father. And after they read the wedding program, the rest of them would know because "Miles Jenkins" was in there big as day, which was just fine with her because she had nothing to hide.

"Well, baby, you found me, what you got to ask me?" Mama Shirley said, in her heavy Southern accent.

"I have to go to work and I wanted to know if you would drop Miles home after the wedding."

"Sure, baby, but why can't he go to the reception? You know he's no trouble."

"It's not that, Mama Shirley. I don't know how long this is going to take and Miles can be a handful on some days. I thought it would be best if you drop him home."

"Child! Stop that foolishness. You must've forgot I'm the woman who gave birth to nine children, grandmother of twenty-one, and great-grandmother of three. Miles ain't no more of a handful than the ones running around my house every day," Mama Shirley said as she put her hands on her ample hips.

Leesa knew she couldn't win this one, so she just said, "Thank you, Mama Shirley. I'll meet you at the reception."

With a nod of her head, Mama Shirley said, "Good. Go do your job. Miles will be just fine. Now, I'm going back into this here church before I pass out from this heat. It's so hot it feels like Satan is throwing a block party—out here, mind you."

Leesa laughed as she walked to her car.

Once Leesa got home she went straight to her contact list of plumbers. On the fifth try, she found a plumber willing to go out, do the job, and be paid on a net thirty. After she got him set up in her system, she called Carmen, asking her to set the vendor up and fax over the work order. It didn't take as long as she thought it would. Leesa started to go back to the wedding, but it would be over shortly, so she decided to just meet Miles at the reception.

Leesa stepped into the civic center and just as she had expected, the whole town had come out to celebrate the wedding of the mayor. The waiters were circulating with their silver trays, which held glasses of champagne. There was a wet bar on the other side of the hall that had soda, juices, and, of course, the hard liquor.

Leesa looked around to see if Mama Shirley and Miles had made it from the church, but there was no sign of them.

"Charmaine," Leesa called to a young girl passing by.

"Yes, ma'am."

"Did Big Mama bring Miles with her?"

"No, ma'am."

"W-who did he come with?" Leesa asked, trying not to sound nervous.

"He got in the car with Lonzell. They should be here soon, because they were right behind Big Mama," Charmaine said, looking toward the door. "Look, there they are."

Goose bumps sprang up on Leesa's arms. She sensed a change in the people around her. The air seemed electrified.

Leesa couldn't have stopped her heart from beating in double time if she'd wanted to. It was as if two strong hands touched her shoulders and made her turn around to face the door.

Standing there in the doorway was the one and only Lonzell Jenkins and her son—their son—on his shoulders.

Her mouth went dry. If such a thing were possible, Lonzell was more handsome than four years earlier. There he was, all decked down in his white Hugo Boss tuxedo, all smiles as if he were the poster child for father of the year. She wondered how many more people knew Miles was his son? Oh, yes, she had heard people talking behind her back when they didn't think she could hear them. Like today as she had entered the church, she overheard Sister Betty Mae tell Sister Tate that Miles looked a lot like Lonzell, but how could that be when Lonzell had just gotten back from over-seas?

Well, if she didn't do something, the ones that didn't know would know real soon, for they would be able to see what she saw every day.

Lonzell smiled as they came through the doorway. He knew he had to find Miles' mother before she called the police on him for kidnapping her child. If he were ever to have kids, he would love to have a son like Miles. He was well-mannered and very smart for three and a half years old. That's what Miles had told him when they were in the back of the church before the wedding started.

"Mommy, Mommy," Miles cried out over Lonzell's head.

"Where's your mommy, buddy?"

"There."

Lonzell looked in the direction that Miles was pointing. When he saw who the child's mother was, Lonzell felt as if he had been hit by a dump truck. It just couldn't be. Not after four years. But it was: Leesa Fairchild. Gone was the long, black silky hair that had stopped at her waist. It now rested on her shoulders and curled upward. She had also gained about thirty pounds, which looked good—damn good—on her, considering she had only weighed a hundred pounds in college.

"Mommy," Miles said, nipping into his thoughts again.

Leesa was close enough now to say, "Sweetheart, use your inside voice."

The braces are also gone, he thought.

"Okay, Mommy," Miles said in a softer tone.

Like two live wires moving across a rain-slick county road, Leesa and Lonzell's gazes met and sparked, jolting Lonzell all the way down to his white leather Stacy Adams shoes. He swallowed hard against the knot of sudden anxiety in his throat, but his gaze never wavered as reality hit him: The child he held was his own son.

A marathon of questions ran though his head. There were so many feelings they made him dizzy. He had to take

Miles off his shoulders, afraid he would pass out and hurt the child—his child.

It took every ounce of his military training to appear calm and keep a straight face for the crowd of people that watched their every move. So, he was Miles' missing-in-action father, but it wasn't by choice. Why hadn't she told him about his son?

"Mommy, this is my new friend," Miles said, smiling up at Lonzell.

Leesa looked up at Lonzell, then back at Miles before she said, *"Your friend?"*

"Mm-hmm. Mr. Lon . . . Lonz . . . Lonzell."

Leesa was so hot about what Miles had just told her, that if someone had placed a piece of coal in her hands right then, she would have given them a diamond in return. "Sweetheart, why don't you go see Big Mama and ask her to get you some juice? Mommy is going to talk to your friend for a little while."

"Okay, Mommy." To Lonzell, he said, "Bye-bye."

Lonzell picked Miles up again and in a voice he didn't recognize asked, "Can I have a hug?"

Miles nodded and hugged him.

Lonzell hugged his child and thought about all the hugs he had missed over his short life. He didn't want to put him down, but he and Leesa had some things to talk about and they couldn't wait. So, he put Miles down.

As soon as his little feet were on the floor, Miles took off running.

When Miles was out of range Leesa turned to Lonzell and lit into him. "That was cute. *You* deserve an Oscar for that role, but before you start thanking your supporting cast, can I see you outside for a minute?" she said, already heading toward the double glass doors that led into the flower garden.

"You bet your sweet ass, you can. I don't know what kind of childish game you're playing, Leesa, but I am not the one. How dare you keep my child from me?" Lonzell barked as he followed her out the door.

Leesa wasn't outside a hot second before she turned around and bumped into his wide chest. Fire. That's what it felt like. If hell was anything like this, she wasn't going.

Even her blood seemed to simmer at his touch. What was happening to her? All the old feelings that should have died a long time ago were back. Her body came alive like there was no waiting in line at the DMV.

Finally able to find her voice, she uttered, "I suggest you take some of that bass out of your voice when speaking to me." That said, she moved out of his reach.

Lonzell just looked at her, because if he had been paying attention to her quick move and not to the way her hips moved under the white linen dress, he would have known she had stopped. But it was too late. They had touched and he too could feel the fire that moved from his body to hers. Just her touch smoldered his skin through his suit.

"I'll take it out when you tell me what the hell is going on here. Why did you keep my son from me? He is mine, isn't he?"

That hurt—deeply. Leesa wanted to cry and run away to mend her broken heart, but she couldn't do either right now. Batting her eyelids several times so the tears wouldn't fall, and placing a Band-Aid over her broken heart, she snarled, "Yes! Miles is your son. Don't give me that bull, Lonzell. You knew about Miles from day one. Just as soon as I found out I was pregnant, I did exactly what you told me. I called your mother.

"Now you're here playing daddy after all this time. What? Did you think your money and gifts would be enough to make us go away? Well, let me tell you something, Mr. Let's-travel-all-over-the-world, Miles don't need your money or your gifts. Don't you know children spell gifts T-I-M-E? All their little hearts want is your time. Something you don't have *time* for." With that said she started to turn and leave him standing there looking stuck on stupid, but his bark made her stop in her tracks.

"What the hell are you talking about? You never called me. You just up and left, without a trace. And what money? I never sent you any money, not that I wouldn't have; he is my son and my responsibility too. I'm not here to play daddy, I'm here to be a daddy. Do you know how many black boys are without a father or male role models in their young lives?" Not waiting for her answer, he went on. "Well, let me tell you. Millions! I'll be damned if I'll walk around helping other kids and not do anything for my own child. You got me messed up!" he said in a low but lethal voice.

"Yeah, Lonzell, I know there are millions of boys *and* girls out there without role models." Leesa knew that tone. She also knew he was doing all he could to hold on to his control. "Look, why don't you ask your mother?"

"Don't you think I did that already?" he said, lowering his voice as people passed by them. "Why did you come back here today, Leesa? Of all days, why today to tell me about my son? And how did you get Bruce to have Miles in his wedding?"

Leesa frowned. "Come back! I live here, Lonzell. I've been back for seven months. Did—"

"That's a lie. My mother would have told me if you were back here that long."

"Well, I guess there's a lot of things your mother didn't tell you. I told you how she felt about me a long time ago."

"My mother has nothing to do with this. Maybe you talked to the housekeeper and she didn't give me the message. I know my mother, she wouldn't keep something like this from me."

Open your eyes! she wanted to scream at him, but only said, "Okay, Lonzell, *whatever* you think. But I know I spoke with your mother. I told her I needed to reach you—"

"Lonzell."

Leesa didn't have to turn to see who was calling Lonzell; she knew the seed of Satan's voice anywhere. Ida Jean Jenkins.

"Lonzell, darling, what are you doing standing outside in this heat? You know if you stand out here too long you're going to burn and get as black as—oh, hello, Leesa," Ida Jean said, holding her right hand over her eyes, keeping the sun out of them as she and a young woman walked up.

"Not now, Mother," Lonzell said tightly, never taking his eyes off of Leesa.

"Lonzell, I'd like you to meet Candice Andrews. She's new to our fine town," Ida Jean said, not caring that he and Leesa were having a conversation.

"Not now, Mother!"

"Oh, darling, at least you could say hello to Candice, she'll be here for a few days. Maybe you can show—"

"Nice to meet you, Candice." Lonzell looked at the woman and continued, "This is Leesa Fairchild, and I'm talking to her now, so if you two will excuse us."

"Leesa won't mind. Would you, honey?" Ida Jean asked as she pulled a handkerchief from her handbag and wiped her upper lip.

Leesa looked over at the young woman, who was very pretty—and if she were a shade lighter, would be the color of cream. "No."

"Yes she would, Mother, and so would I," Lonzell said, looking from his mother to Leesa.

Leesa had had enough of Ida Jean. "Look—" the running of footsteps made Leesa turn around.

"Leesa! Come quick, it's Miles, he's having a hard time breathing," Bruce said as he gave Lonzell a disgusted look.

"Oh, God, no!" Leesa cried as she ran toward the building. Lonzell was right behind her.

CHAPTER 3

LEESA paced the emergency room like a caged tiger, ready to strike at any second. She and Lonzell had rushed Miles to the hospital after the medicine for his asthma didn't work.

"Miss," the tall, thin nurse called to Leesa.

"Yes." She rushed to the desk. "Is there some word on my son?"

"I'm sorry, ma'am, I don't know. I just need you to fill out some forms and I'll need to see your insurance card."

"Could you please see about my child, his name is Miles, we brought him in a few minutes ago," Leesa cried as she looked for her insurance card.

"Sure, ma'am."

"Oh, no!"

"What? What's wrong?" Lonzell asked, standing behind her.

"I-I don't have anything in this purse but my keys, cell phone, and license."

"Well, we're going to need some type of payment to-day—" the nurse began.

"Fine," Lonzell said, slapping a platinum American Express card on the counter. "Get what you need off of that."

The nurse took the card and turned to type something into the computer. "I still need her to fill out the forms."

Lonzell had learned a long time ago not to show fear or too much emotion, but today had taken its toll on him. First he had learned he had a son, now that same son was fighting to breathe on his own. Picking up the clipboard with his right hand, he touched Leesa on the arm with his left. "Let's sit down and fill out the forms. I'm sure the doctor will come and talk to us soon."

All the fight in her was gone. Leesa didn't protest when Lonzell led her to a row of chairs. Maybe it was too much for Miles. Maybe she should have said no to Bruce when he asked if Miles could be in the wedding. "This is all my fault. Oh, God, please let him be all right. He's all I have in this world." Holding her head in her hands, Leesa cried harder.

For the first time Lonzell noticed that some of the people from the wedding were there, and they were staring at them. Without giving it another thought, he pulled Leesa to his wide chest. "It's not your fault. He's going to be just fine."

Leesa let him comfort her; she even took the handkerchief he offered to wipe her eyes and blow her nose. "Thank you." Leaning away from him she added, "I'll pay you the money back just as soon as I get home."

Lonzell's jaws tightened—he couldn't believe his ears. "Didn't you say Miles is my son?"

"Yes, but—"

"Let it go, Leesa—for now. We can talk about payment later." Holding up the clipboard, he went on, "I filled out as much as I could. I don't know his birthday or—"

"His last name is Jenkins, not Fairchild," she said, cutting him off when she saw he had put her last name for Miles.

Lonzell looked at her as if he had never seen her before in his life. "Leesa, what the—"

"Mr. and Mrs. Jenkins, I'm Doctor Grant. I'd like to talk to you about your son . . ."

"I told you that was his son," Sister Betty Mae said in a loud whisper.

"Well, his mama said he didn't have no children. Now, who you gonna believe?" Sister Tate asked, with her head turned to the side so no one would think she was talking about people.

"Well, this program tells it all." Sister Betty Mae pointed to Miles' name. "Besides, you know good and well, Ida Jean can lie through her teeth. And you know how proud of that boy she is. She ain't gonna have nobody looking down on her boy."

"Maybe she kept the child away from him because of Ida Jean. I know they fooled around in high school because I caught them one day."

"Rose Tate, you just a liar, I told you that. It was in my home economics class; Leesa was staying after school to finish a dress she was making."

Betty Mae taught Home Economics, while Rose Tate taught English at Lovebug High. They both said this would be their last year teaching.

"Ah, shit! It don't matter what they did in high school, they done made this baby and now they walking around like we too dumb to know they did it," Sister Tate said, turning her back to her good friend of sixty years.

"You two need to get you some business."

"What are you talking about, Shirley?" Betty Mae asked with her lip turned up.

"Yeah," Rose chimed in, as she looked Shirley up and down. "Who died and made you the queen?"

"Nobody died and made me queen, but you two are talking loud enough that the dead can hear you. Leesa and Lonzell are right around the corner, and I'm sure they can hear you too."

"What's the big secret? Everyone knows how they got the child," Betty Mae said, hitting her hand on the arm of the chair.

"Just, nobody talked about it," Rose said, looking down the hospital hall.

"Just listen to you two old bats." Shirley looked at them both and went on, "You must've forgot I know you both. We grew up together. I know what you did in Lovebug too."

"W-what are you talking about?" Rose asked nervously.

"I seen you many a night, or should I say *morning*, climbing into your bedroom window after Bubby would park his old red truck down the street so nobody would see it in front of your house that time of morning."

"So, what are you trying to say, Shirley? I had a boyfriend and you didn't?" Rose asked sharply.

"No, Rose, what *I'm* saying is, there were only two things open that time of the morning, one being Mr. Sam's gas station and the other being your legs."

"Why, you—"

"It takes one to know one."

"Hee, hee. She got up on that one, Rose." Betty Mae laughed as she slapped her right knee.

"Betty Mae, I don't know why you find all this so funny, you just remember I know how many children you're supposed to have," Shirley snapped.

Betty Mae closed her mouth so tight that it made her lips a thin line that matched her narrow eyes. "Look, Shirley, just because you had all them there children, don't go talking my business. I did what I thought was best." Her eyes were already misted. "You make like she's one of your children," she said flatly.

"In a way she is. I told Ruth and Running Wolf if anything should happen to them, I would look after Leesa as if she was one of my own." Shirley looked at the two women she'd called friends for so many years. "And if it means putting you two in your place, so be it. I'm not going to stand by while you try to put that child down because she had a baby."

The room was so quiet you could hear a mouse walking on cotton.

"Now, I'm going back to check on Miles, so if you want, you can talk about me, but remember you need to sweep around your own front door before you try to sweep around mine." Shirley turned and walked around the corner, leaving Sister Betty Mae and Sister Tate with their mouths open and looking stuck on stupid.

It was after two in the morning when Lonzell carried Miles into Leesa's house. Miles was knocked out. They had to give him a shot to stop the wheezing and a prescription for Albuterol, which was a new type of inhaler. The doctor told them to make sure Miles took it slow the next few days. And that was what Lonzell planned to do. Everything else would just have to wait.

"Which way?"

"Straight down the hall," she whispered.

Lonzell placed the sleeping child in the bed as Leesa turned on the light. She moved around the room with so much grace that it amazed Lonzell. She didn't make a sound as she opened and closed drawers. He looked around the room; it was done in a soft white and slate blue. On the wall were pictures of airplanes in all sizes. On the chest of drawers were airplanes and cars—even the lamp was an airplane.

"Here, let me put his pj's on." Moving toward the bed, she told Lonzell, "I can do it."

"No. I want to help."

They put on Miles' pj's in silence. Once they were finished, Leesa went to kiss Miles, who opened his eyes.

"Mommy."

"Yes, sweetheart, Mommy is right here."

"Where's my friend?"

"I'm right here, buddy." Lonzell moved to the foot of the bed. "You get some rest, okay."

"Can my buddy stay with me tonight, Mommy?"

Leesa didn't know what to say. She didn't want Lonzell to stay, but she didn't want to upset her sick child. Did Lonzell want to stay?

"Yeah, buddy, I'll stay with you tonight," he said as if reading Leesa's thoughts, "and to—"

"Okay, he can stay with you tonight." Leesa cut him off because she didn't want him making any promises to their child he couldn't keep—like he had with her.

Miles yawned and closed his eyes. "Mommy."

"Yes, baby."

"Are you going to call Auntie Tara to tell her I'm sick again?"

"Yes, sweetheart, I'll call her later, and let you talk."

"And Uncle James," he said with a yawn.

"I'll call them both and you can talk to them at the same time," Leesa said as she felt Lonzell's eyes on her. "Okay, sweetheart?"

Miles didn't answer because he was fast asleep again.

Lonzell looked at the sleeping child, then back at Leesa, "Who the hell is James?"

"Tara Collins speaking."

"Tara! Where were you all weekend?"

"Leesa?"

"I got to pour you some tea. You are not going to believe this."

"Leesa, is that you?"

"Yes, who else would be calling you at work on a Monday talking about pouring tea?" Leesa said.

"Do I need a small teacup or do I need a big pitcher?"

"Get a big pitcher, maybe two."

"Wait, let me close my office door," Tara said as she got up and closed the door to her office, which overlooked downtown Mobile, Alabama. She really didn't know how she and Leesa had come up with the phrase "pouring tea" when they had to tell each other some news, but it had been around for years. And no matter who was pouring the tea, it was always good. "Okay, get to pouring."

"Guess what I did this past weekend?"

"Took Miles to the movies and met a man who wants to be your love slave?"

"Not even close. I had the pleasure of spending my Saturday afternoon and Sunday with the one and only Lonzell Jenkins."

"Girl, no. Well, just slap me and call me silly," Tara said as she put her left elbow on the pecan wood desk. "Now, how did that happen?"

"Well, you know Miles was in Bruce's wedding."

"Yeah."

"Well, what I didn't tell you was Lonzell is Bruce's best friend and he was the best man."

"Why, you little let's-keep-a-secret-from-our-best-friend," she said jokingly.

Leesa laughed for the first time in two days. "I really meant to tell you, but I got so bent out of shape knowing he was going to be there. I tried not to think about it. Sorry."

"Yeah, right. Anyway, what happened? Did he tell you why he hadn't been by to see Miles—or you, for that matter?"

"That's just it, he said he didn't know anything about Miles. I know he's lying."

There was no response on the other end.

"Tara? Are you there?"

"Yeah, I'm here."

"Well, say something."

"You might not like it."

"It won't be the first time. So, say what's on your mind."

"I think he is telling the truth."

"What?" she said in disbelief.

"Think about it, Leesa. You two dated most of high school—secretly, which is hard to do in a small town like Lovebug. Then you both go away to Florida State University, him first, you three years later. You two waited until your senior year to sleep together. So, when he said he didn't know about Miles, I think he really didn't."

"Tara, I can't believe you're taking his side on this. You know how many times I called Lonzell, then ended up on your sofa crying my eyes out over him. And what about the address she gave me? He never wrote me back, not once."

"You know I would never take sides on this matter. I just think you should really hear him out on this one. Didn't you say his mother was the wicked witch of the south? Maybe she didn't tell him you called. Maybe she gave you the wrong address and phone number. Leesa, think before you react—the witch is his mother."

"How can I forget?"

"Was she at the wedding?"

"Yes, and she kept giving me the evil eye. Then when Lonzell and I were outside talking she was there too, with some girl she wanted Lonzell to meet. I was just about to tell her a piece of my mind, but Miles got sick and we had to take him to the hospital."

"Hospital! Is he okay?" Tara asked with concern.

"Yes, he's fine now. It was his asthma, Tara, I have never been so scared in my life. He had never had one that bad."

"How bad was it?"

"They had to give him a shot to stop the wheezing."

"Poor baby. You tell him his godmother sends him lots

and lots of hugs and kisses. And to look for a surprise later today."

Leesa laughed as she said, "You are spoiling him."

"That's my job," Tara replied sweetly.

"If you hold on, I'll go and get him, and you can tell him yourself."

"Where is he?"

"Standing outside with Lonzell."

"Lonzell is over there? What are you doing on the phone with me?"

"It's not what you think. He's talking to Bruce, and Miles is sitting on his shoulders. Hold on."

"Wait!"

"Yes."

"What is Bruce doing there? Didn't he just get married?"

"Yeah, but he wanted to check on Miles before they left for the Bahamas."

"What's his wife like?"

"Oh, DeLisa is—"

"De-who? Girl, what kind of name is that? Where is she from?" Tara asked as she tried to suppress a giggle.

"Froghop, Mississippi," Leesa said through tears from laughing so hard.

"Froghop! Where in the hell is that?"

"About fifty miles from Jackson."

"Girl, she need not tell anyone she is from Froghop, Mississippi—oh, but then again, she did move to Lovebug, Texas," Tara said, now laughing just as hard.

"Well, excuse me for not living in the big city of Mobile, Alabama, like you. I happen to like it here, thank you very much."

"I'm sorry, girl, I'm not making fun of small towns, but where do they get those names from? Now, you were saying."

"I was telling you that DeLisa is really nice and she seems to fit right in."

"That's nice. Now are you going to go and get my godchild?"

"Hold on."

"You are supposed to be my boy. Why didn't you tell me about"—Lonzell looked over his shoulder to make sure Leesa and Miles were out of hearing range—"Miles being my son?"

"Man, I tried to tell you about Miles for years. Every time I said Leesa's name you got ticked off. You told me to squash it," Bruce said, hitting his right fist into his open left hand. "And that's what I did."

"How many people do you think know?"

"Come on, man, this is Lovebug. People who didn't know knew Saturday night." Bruce held his hands up. "And that's about ten."

If that was the case, his mother *did* know about Miles and she *had* kept it from him. He needed to talk to her, but that would have to wait because she was in Paris for the next few weeks.

"Look, man, you and Leesa need to squash whatever is keeping you two apart." Bruce tried to get him to see where he was coming from. "You know, I'm your boy and all, but, Lonzell, this isn't about you and Leesa. It's Miles' right to know his father."

"What about the guy I saw her with?" Lonzell asked as if Bruce had the answer.

"Did you ask her about him?"

"No, but Miles said something the other night that made me think it must have been pretty serious: she has Miles calling him *Uncle James*. And when I asked her about it she said he was a good friend," he voiced sourly.

"I think it could have been the *way* you asked her. Ask her again, you won't regret it. It's time."

CHAPTER 4

LONZELL didn't want to fight with Leesa anymore. In truth he still loved her, but could he trust her? She had never lied to him about anything before, but she wouldn't talk about this guy named James. Over the last week they had talked about everything but James. He hadn't told her that he would be leaving in two days. He wondered if she would let Miles visit him.

"I start a new job in a few weeks."

Leesa's heart skipped a beat. "Really, where is it?"

"Virginia."

"What!"

"Virginia," he said again.

Ring.

"I have to get this." She was glad to get the call. She wasn't ready to hear Lonzell say he was going to be leaving. "LM Services, this is Leesa."

"Hi, Leesa, this is Nolan. I have an urgent work order."

"Okay, what is it?"

"One of the Shoes and More Shoes stores can't lock their doors. A key is broken off in it."

"You can send it to Pop-a-lock, vender number 21215."

"Will do, thanks, Leesa."

"Anytime, Nolan, 'bye." Leesa ended the call and turned back to Lonzell. "I'm sorry, but I'm on call twenty-four hours a day, seven days a week."

"That's okay, but what do you do?"

"Let's say you go into one of your favorite stores and the lights are going on and off for no reason. Or you feel water dripping on your head," she began.

"Okay."

"Well, you tell a store manager and he calls it in to the call center. If the call center already has someone set up in the system they call that person; if not, they call me and I have to find a new service provider."

"And you can do all that from your home computer?" he asked, very impressed with her job.

"I can work from anywhere, just as long as I can hook up to the Internet."

"There's something I wanted to talk to you about."

"Okay. What's that?" she asked, crossing her legs and sitting back on the green love seat.

"I'd like for you and Miles to come and visit me in Virginia," Lonzell said. He was seated in the matching chair, his arms resting on his thighs, hands clasped. "I don't know where this is going to go, Leesa, but I do want to know my son, and I want him to know about me."

"For how long?"

"How long do I want you to be there or how long do I want to know Miles?"

"Both." Her eyes never left his.

"You can stay as long as you like. As for Miles, I want to tell him I'm his father."

"It's too soon."

"Maybe when you come to visit, we could tell him then?"

"Maybe."

"Come on, Leesa, meet me halfway on this. I told you I didn't know."

"I just don't want my child—"

"He's my child too."

He was right. They had to be friends for Miles' sake. "I can't get away right now."

"That's fine. You just tell me when and I'll meet you at the airport."

"I think it will be better if I just rent a car while we're there."

"Fine, Leesa, whatever you want."

It was the end of August before Leesa had packed four bags, mostly Miles' clothes, and headed for Dallas/Fort Worth International Airport. Once they landed in Virginia, she rented a car; once she had Miles buckled in the car seat in the back, she got in the car, said a short prayer, and headed down the highway. The whole idea of the trip made her nervous, but she was doing it for their son.

Leesa had no trouble finding Lonzell's house in the outskirts of Quantico. The homes were beautiful. They each had a different color of brick. Lonzell's was a rich red and it only made the house more appealing to the eye.

Leesa pulled around back like Lonzell had told her. As she turned the car off, the garage door opened and Lonzell walked toward them. She licked her lips as she lightly passed her left hand on and under her chin to make sure she wasn't drooling.

Leesa had forgotten just how fine Lonzell was; but seeing him now with no shirt on, showing off his washboard stomach, and in jeans that hugged him all the way down his bowlegs made her remember all too well: The man was *fine*.

"Mommy, that's my buddy," Miles stated, cutting into her thoughts as he tried to get out of his car seat.

"Yes, it is, sweetheart," Leesa answered as she opened her door.

Lonzell had already opened the back door and was taking Miles out by the time she walked around the car.

"Hey, buddy," Lonzell said, happily taking Miles out of the car seat and giving him a hug, then tickling him. "How are you?"

"Fine." He giggled.

Leesa had to catch her breath. It was uncanny. Ray Charles could see that Miles was Lonzell's child. And the whole town of Lovebug knew too. They just didn't gossip in front of her and Miles like big-city folks would.

"Did you have any problems finding the house?" Lonzell asked Leesa.

"No. Your directions were adequate," she replied. Their

eyes held for a few moments before she looked away.

"Let's go inside, it's too hot out here," he said, walking toward the garage. "I'll get the bags later."

Leesa nodded and walked behind him and Miles. Which was a huge mistake; she couldn't keep her eyes off his nice backside. She also wondered if she could still bounce a quarter off it. *Okay, Miss Not-had-a-man-in-four-years. Don't do anything crazy,* her mind chastised. The cool air startled her. Leesa realized she was now inside the house, but how? Talk about following the leader.

"Wow!" Miles said, looking around the huge living room. Leesa was just as taken. The room was beautiful. She knew it had been professionally done. The décor was exquisite. The furniture was all cherry wood with vivid colors of hunter green, navy blue, and cream. There was a fireplace, which only enhanced the room.

"You have a nice home," she managed to say, while keeping a close eye on Miles. To him this was a toy store and he was ready to go shopping.

"Let me show you your rooms and later I'll give you a tour," he said, but what he really wanted to do was take her in his arms and kiss her senseless. She was just as beautiful today, standing there in a turquoise sleeveless dress and matching mules on her feet, as she'd been the day they made love. Call him a fool, but he still loved her.

Maybe things will work themselves out, she thought. "I'd like that," she said to him. *Just as much as I still love you,* she thought.

It was after two when Lonzell gave Leesa the grand tour of the house. It was a nice size. Three bedrooms, two and a half baths, formal living and dining rooms, and his office, which he would share with her. The next stop was down to the basement gym, which had everything in there—even a small refrigerator. They finished the tour in the kitchen, where they sat as Lonzell poured them some sweet tea.

"I was thinking maybe we can put some turkey patties on the grill. I mean, if that's all right with you?"

Leesa took a sip of the tea before she said, "That's fine with me. I'm sure Miles will like that. He likes hamburgers, well, turkey burgers." She knew she was rambling, but he made her more nervous than a virgin at a prison rodeo.

Lonzell could tell she was nervous—hell, he was too. They had a lot to talk about. He was glad Miles was taking a nap. That had been a task all by itself. After Miles had seen his room, all he had wanted to do was play with his new toys.

"Oh, I have some papers for you to sign. Let me get them now," Lonzell said, walking out of the kitchen.

Papers? What papers? Leesa questioned herself. They'd never talked about anything, let alone her signing any papers.

"Here we go," Lonzell said, taking a seat next to her. "I put Miles on my insurance, here's your card for him. Also, I had my attorney draw up a new will, leaving eighty percent of everything I own to Miles. This is the amount I should be paying in child support. If it's okay with you, you just have to sign the papers. Or you can get your attorney to look everything over before you sign," he said, handing her the pen.

Leesa looked the papers over, then she looked at the amount of money Lonzell wanted to pay her. "Why so much?" she asked, not taking the pen from him. "You never paid this much before."

"Because, based on my income, that's the percentage I should be paying." He dropped the pen on the table.

"But I have a job, and I do very well," she said, ignoring what he said.

"Leesa, this isn't about what you or I think, it's about our son," he said, picking the pen back up, only to toss it back on the table.

She took the papers and folded them up. "I'd like to read these later."

"Fine," he said as his jaws tightened. "I want to tell him that I'm his father."

"When?"

"Today. I don't want to wait any longer." Holding his head down, he went on, "I've missed so much already."

He was right. *They* had missed so much. Maybe Tara knew what she was talking about. Maybe, just maybe he *hadn't* known about Miles. "Today is a good day to tell

Miles you're his father, but I'm warning you—don't hurt my child—".

"He's my child too," Lonzell said tightly.

"I know that," she snapped, "but you can't be running in and out of his life. Being a father is a full-time job."

"Are you saying I got you pregnant and walked away?" he hissed through clenched teeth, trying to hold on to his temper.

"All I know is you never came back. Maybe you weren't ready to be a father. Maybe you thought you were too young to take on so much responsibility—"

"Responsibility!" he barked, pushing away from the table. Lonzell stood and paced the large kitchen like a black panther ready to attack anything or anyone in his path. "How can you sit there and say that? The night we came together, sure, we used protection, but it broke, making the risk even higher of us conceiving a child. Don't you think I know that? How dare you fix your mouth to say I didn't want the responsibility. If you think that way, you never loved me as you once said."

"Never loved *you!* Oh yes, I loved you. I loved you so much I lived on your broken promises for three and half years." Leesa's voice filled with grief as the banks of water ran freely from her eyes. She also stood and walked over to Lonzell as she continued, "I loved you so much I didn't even want to date. Can you say the same? I never let another man touch me. I haven't been with anyone else. Can you say the same? Can you say the *same?*"

Lonzell didn't answer. He knew he couldn't say the same. Too many willing women overseas to turn down—not that he slept around, but there had been some one-night stands along the way. Nothing he was proud of.

"So don't tell me I didn't love you, Lonzell. Don't you dare!" she cried as her small fists beat his chest.

Lonzell didn't move as Leesa hit him. He knew she was hurting. He'd broken his promise. He should have been there for her. Even if he didn't know she was carrying his child. What went so wrong? He gently pulled her to him. "I'm sorry. I'm so very sorry. I never meant to hurt you, Leesa," he said, wrapping his arms around her, holding her close as his own tears fell into her hair.

Leesa freed her hands from being sandwiched between them and wrapped her arms around him. They held each other and wept as if they were on a raft riding out a storm. And they were—the storm of life.

Later that night, Leesa turned the kitchen light off and headed upstairs. The day had taken its toll on her. All she wanted to do was go to bed, but she and Lonzell still had to tell Miles that Lonzell was his father.

"Where's my mommy?" Miles asked as Lonzell helped him with his pajamas.

"I'm right here, sweetheart," she said, sticking her head in the bathroom.

"Mommy," he squealed, running to her.

Leesa braced herself because Miles was coming at her full speed.

"Don't run, s—Miles," Lonzell said softly, but firmly.

"Yes, sir," he answered, now walking to his mother.

"Hi, sweetheart"—she kissed him on both cheeks—"how was your bath?"

"Fun." He laughed. "Mr. Lonzell is funny just like you, Mommy."

Leesa looked up to find Lonzell watching them. She could see he really loved Miles and she knew it was time. "Sweetheart, Mr. Lonzell and I want to tell you something, but first let's get your prayers said and you into bed."

Lonzell led them into Miles' room. He turned on the lamp and turned down the bed.

Miles said his prayers and hopped into bed. "Okay, I'm ready," he said brightly.

Lonzell and Leesa sat on the side of the bed. Leesa started, "Miles, do you remember where Mommy told you your daddy was?"

"In the air force," he said, looking from Leesa to Lonzell.

"That's right, sweetheart. What else did Mommy say about your daddy?" Leesa asked their son softly.

"That he loved me very much and would come and visit

me one day," Miles replied as his eyes moved from Lonzell to Leesa again.

"Well, your buddy, Mr. Lonzell, is your father," she said, and her voice cracked.

"Ah man! Ah man!" Miles yelled as he tossed the covers off his small body and gave his father a big hug. Still holding on to Lonzell, he said, "Now we can move our house in your house." He turned and looked at Leesa. "Can't we, Mommy?"

"We can talk about it later." Her eyes were moist. "Right now it's your bedtime."

Covering his eyes with his hands, Miles laughed. "I'm not sleepy."

Lonzell tickled him. "Tell you what, why don't I read you a story, then you go to sleep."

Miles took his hands from his eyes and asked, "Can I call you Daddy?"

Lonzell ran his hand over Miles' head. "Yes, son, you can call me Daddy," Lonzell said loudly.

"Daddy, I want to sleep in your bed."

Lonzell looked at Leesa for approval.

She nodded.

He thanked her with his eyes, before picking Miles up. "Let's get one of your books Mommy brought with you."

Leesa was already going to Miles' suitcase to retrieve one of the books. She knew from now on she would have to share Miles with his father. It would be hard. But still she was happy for her son—and for the man she loved.

CHAPTER 5

LONZELL was just about to step into his office when he heard his name.

"Lonzell, hold up a minute."

Lonzell turned to see an older man and very attractive woman walking down the hall.

"Welcome aboard, Lonzell. I'm Gregg Milton, one of the program managers," he said, extending his right hand.

"Nice to meet you, sir," Lonzell replied, shaking the man's hand.

"I've heard a lot of good things about you, Lonzell."

Lonzell had only been an FBI agent for a month, but in that short time he had helped crack one of their biggest cases. "Thank you."

"Oh, I'm sorry, where are my manners?" Gregg said as he looked at the young woman. "This is Marcella Hurst, she's on the blue team."

"Hello, nice to meet you," Lonzell said, shaking her hand.

"Likewise," Marcella said as her brain went into overdrive. *Nice face, nice body, nice smile. No ring on his left finger and no tan line as if one had been there. And last time I passed by his office there were no pictures of kids or girlfriend. Yeah, baby! It's time to reel him on in.* "So, have you had the chance to do any sightseeing?" she asked, giving him her best cover-girl smile.

"A little, but I plan to see more this weekend."

Steady, girl, steady. "Well, if you like, I'd love to be your tour guide."

"Oh, yes, Marcella is a great organizer," Gregg voiced, giving her praise. "She's the one responsible for all our activities away from work."

"Thank you, Mr. Milton, I am a team player," she said, giving him a light punch in his left arm.

"I'm sure you are, Marcella, but we'll be okay. Thank you anyway."

We! Who are we? "Oh, I guess Penny with the welcoming committee beat me to it, huh?"

"Oh, no, nothing like that, my son and his mother will be flying up, and I'm going to take them to the State Fair," Lonzell said, as he walked into his office and got a picture off his desk. "I just got this yesterday."

Gregg and Marcella looked at the picture.

"Nice looking family there, Lonzell. Hope you three have a good time," Gregg said, before looking at this watch. "I'd better go, or I'll late for my meeting. Marcella, are you going?"

Might as well, this one is already hooked, and reeled in. "Yes, I hope you guys have a good time too," she said to Lonzell. "I'm ready when you are," she turned to Gregg, hoping he couldn't tell she was torn-up from the floor up, and all she wanted to do was throw up. She had made a fool of herself—again.

"Goodbye, Lonzell. I know I'll be seeing you around," Gregg said as he fell into step with Marcella.

"See you later, sir." Lonzell walked back into his office. He placed the picture back on his desk and smiled. Showing off his family wasn't something he did, but he could see where Marcella was heading with the "tour guide" thing. He had seen that look in too many women's eyes before. She was going in for the kill, until he showed her the picture of Leesa and Miles.

"Look, Mommy!" Miles yelled out as he and Lonzell went around in the small roller coaster—for the fifth time.

"Hi, sweetheart." Leesa waved at them. Lonzell had

thought it would be a good idea to take Miles to the state fair while they were in Virginia.

The ride came to a stop and Lonzell helped Miles off, and they walked over to where Leesa was standing with all the stuffed animals Lonzell had won for her and Miles. There was no way they could take all of them on the plane.

"Hi," Lonzell said with a smile while holding Miles in his arms.

"Hi. Where to now?"

"I think there are some boats on the other side, we can take him to ride them."

"Okay." Leesa picked up two big stuffed animals, giving one to Lonzell and one to Miles, then she picked up the other two and the small ones. "Let's go."

For the next two and a half hours Lonzell, Leesa, and Miles rode so many rides and ate so many different foods they stopped counting. Miles was getting cranky—he hadn't had a nap all day and it was now after eight o'clock at night. They were ready to go.

The drive home was quiet; Miles was asleep before they were on the main road.

"I think he'll sleep through the night," Lonzell said, taking a fast look at Miles.

"Yeah, I think he will too. He had a good time."

After a few minutes Lonzell said, "I did too, thank you."

"So did I," Leesa said as she held her hand out.

No words were needed, as Lonzell took her hand and entwined it with his.

Leesa watched as Lonzell carried Miles to his room and gently laid him down on the bed. She took off shoes, socks, and jeans, but Miles never stirred. Leesa could feel tension in the room. No words were needed, just the thought of Lonzell making love to her made her nipples tingle.

"I'll get the stuffed animals out of the car tomorrow," he whispered.

Leesa nodded.

Lonzell kissed Miles' forehead before getting up.

Leesa also kissed Miles as Lonzell took her hand. "Let's talk." Once they were downstairs, Lonzell pulled her into his arms and kissed her. Softly at first, brushing his lips against hers like a butterfly on a sweet flower. His tongue stroked hers; his hands began to roam over her body. When she wrapped her arms around his neck, he deepened the kiss.

"I want you," he mouthed, caressing her breast.

Leesa moaned as her hands found the belt on his jeans. Her fingers worked fast to undo the buckle, then to unzip the jeans. Lonzell forgot he needed to breathe in order to live, but when she touched him, his knees almost gave way.

He picked her up, never taking his mouth from hers. Leesa wrapped her legs around his waist while he walked them to the sofa.

It didn't take them any time to get out of their clothes, then Lonzell slipped his head between her legs.

Leesa let out a soft cry as his mouth touched her hidden garden. It didn't take long for Lonzell to make her body explode.

Lonzell kissed his way up her body and mumbled, "I've missed you, so much."

"I've missed you too, Lonnie," she said, breathless. "Where is it?"

"What?" he said, his hands still wandering over her body.

"The protection."

Lonzell froze. He had forgotten about the protection. It had been a while for him and he never thought to have some on hand. He hadn't had the desire for a woman for the past fourteen months—not until Leesa walked back into his life.

"Lonzell," Leesa called, cutting into his thoughts.

"I don't have any."

"You don't have any?" she asked, sitting up. "Lonzell, I want to make love to you, but not without protection. We already have one child—"

"I know. I know," he said, falling back on the sofa. "It wasn't supposed to happen like this. But being with you lately, I just . . . wanted you so bad, I lost my head."

They sat in complete silence for what seemed like hours before Leesa stood and reached for his hand.

Taking her hand, he looked up at her and asked, "Where are we going?"

"Nowhere. Lie down."

Lonzell did as she asked.

Leesa kneeled down over him and took his member in her hot hands and stroked him. She did it over and over again, driving him crazy. "I'll be right back," she said, rising and walking into the kitchen. She took an orange from the fruit bowl on the island. She looked in one of the drawers and took a small knife out and cut the orange in half. After putting the knife in the sink, she took both halves back to the living room.

Lonzell lay on the floor spread-eagle, with his soldier at attention. His breathing was heavy. Leesa was driving him out of his mind with her touches, and if she didn't stop, he was going to explode, like no tomorrow.

"Close your eyes," Leesa said in a husky voice, standing over him.

"Lee—"

"Shh . . . we don't need protection—this time." Lonzell didn't argue; he just closed his eyes as she had asked of him.

Leesa grabbed a pillow from the sofa to use as a cushion as she kneeled beside him. Leaning over his hard member, she only let the tip of her tongue touch him.

"Ah . . . sh . . ." he moaned.

Raising her head, she uttered, "You have to be quiet or I'll stop. Miles is upstairs sleeping," she warned.

His breathing rough, Lonzell nodded. Leesa repeated the action again, but this time she covered all of him. Then she moved her head slowly until only the tip of him was in her mouth.

Lonzell slipped his fist into his mouth to muffle his moans. He didn't know how much more of this he could take. Leesa then moved between his legs and said, "Open your eyes."

Lonzell did and looked at her. He was shocked because if he lived to be a hundred, he would never forget what was happening to him now. There between his legs was Leesa, holding him between her breasts as the top of his member disappeared between her lips.

"Ah . . . baby . . . ooh . . . yeah . . ."

When Leesa realized he wasn't going to last much longer, she stopped. "Not yet, baby." Kissing her way up his body backward until she was above his head, she took one half of the orange and began to squeeze the juice over the upper part of his body. Then she kissed his forehead, eyelids, nose, and then his mouth. She released his mouth only to squeeze some of the juice into it. Leesa then took his mouth again as their tongues entwined and feasted on the sweet nectar.

Leesa pulled her mouth away and continued down his body, leaving them both wild with need. Lonzell had never been kissed like this before. He loved the things Leesa was doing to him, but he wanted to touch her as well. So, as she kissed his nipples and her breast touched his lips, he grabbed it and sucked the hard bud.

Now it was Leesa's turn to lose control. She moaned at the feel of his hot, wet tongue on her nipple. She reached and grabbed his member.

Lonzell then released her and she continued down south on him, stopping only to pick up the other half of the orange. Just as she squeezed the orange juice on his member, he pulled her wet core back to his mouth and covered her.

Leesa called out his name before she covered him.

They teased each other for over an hour before Leesa's body shook into an orgasm. A few moments later he joined her. They made sweet orange marmalade love, until the sun came up.

Leesa pulled her hair into an updo. It was already Friday; Lonzell should be at the house any minute. She had missed him more than he would ever know. It had been two weeks since they had last seen each other. They took turns visiting, now he was going to be here for the weekend. Then in a few weeks she and Miles would spend a week or so with him.

Whenever she and Miles went to visit Lonzell, he always insisted that he pay for Miles' plane ticket. It had been an issue for her, but after Lonzell explained it was the least he could do and would she please let him, Leesa stepped back and let Lonzell have at it.

Now that she had hired another person, she didn't have

to work every weekend. Lonzell said he had talked to his mother about the wrong address and phone number she had given Leesa, but of course she denied everything.

Leesa looked at herself again; a smile pulled at her lips as she thought about Ida Jean being fit to be tied when Lonzell told her he wouldn't take a blood test to prove Miles was his son.

"Mommy, why we have on our church clothes?" Miles asked, looking at himself in the mirror, smiling.

"Your daddy is taking us out to dinner."

"In our church clothes?" He wrinkled his nose before opening up his mouth and looking down his reflection's throat.

"Sweetheart, please sit your bottom in the chair before you fall," Leesa said, taking him off her dresser.

"I not gone fall, I'm a big boy," he voiced, climbing on her bed.

"Miles—" Leesa said just as someone knocked on the door.

"I'll get it, I'll get it," Miles cried as he jumped off the bed and ran to the door.

"No, sweetheart, Mommy will get it."

"Why?"

"Remember, Mommy said only people tall enough to see through the peek hole can answer the door," Leesa said, pointing at the small object on the door.

"If you pick me up, I can see too."

Leesa had to laugh. He did have a point. "Okay, sweetheart, but Mommy will look after you."

She picked him up and let Miles look. "That's my daddy, that's my daddy!" he cheered. "Open the door, Mommy. That's my daddy—you see him?"

"Oh, yes, I see him," Leesa voiced more to herself than to Miles as she opened the door and screen door.

"Hi," Lonzell said after he found his voice. Leesa was beautiful standing there in a black dress that showed off all her curves.

"Hi, yourself," she said, taking him all in. He was wearing a dark blue Hugo Boss suit and chalk white shirt with a two-tone blue silk tie. The man was *fine*.

"Daddy, guess a what?" Miles said, looking up at his father as he stood between them.

Lonzell hunched down so Miles could turn right into his arms. "Hey, buddy, where is my hug?" he asked, holding Miles as if his life depended on it.

Miles gave Lonzell a big hug before he said, "You making me lose my air."

Lonzell and Leesa both laughed.

"Sorry, buddy. I just missed you," Lonzell said in a hoarse voice.

"Guess a what?"

"What?" he asked, touching Miles' little nose.

"We all got on our church clothes."

Lonzell looked up at Leesa for understanding.

"Yes, sweetheart, we all are dressed up, because Daddy is taking us to dinner. Remember?" she stated, looking over at Lonzell with a smile of her own.

Lonzell laughed as he stood and asked her if they were ready to go.

She nodded and they walked out of the house together . . . like a real family.

Thirty minutes later they were taking their seats in La-Houston's, a five-star restaurant. The lights were low and it was very cozy. They were seated and the hostess promised to return with their drinks.

Lonzell and Leesa made small talk to keep Miles entertained as their food was being prepared. But once their meal was placed in front of them, Miles only looked at the big hamburger.

"Sweetheart, what's wrong?" Leesa asked, rubbing his back.

"I just want a hamburger," he stated.

"Son, that is a hamburger," Lonzell said, placing his fork on the table.

Miles frowned and shook his head. "It's too big." Looking at his parents he went on, "I want to go to Mickey D's."

Lonzell looked at his son and could see where the child would think the burger was too big. Hell, he wasn't thinking; he just wanted to take them out to a nice place to eat. This would have been a nice place for him and Leesa to go to, but not with a three-year-old child. He looked over at Leesa and smiled. "I guess we're going to Mickey D's," he said, looking for their waiter so he could get the check.

CHAPTER 6

"LONZELL," Leesa called as she entered the house with the keys he had given to her. She had to take the rental car back because the "service soon" light had come on, and she didn't want to take any chances with Miles in the car.

"Down here."

Leesa tossed the keys on the kitchen table and picked up an orange from the fruit basket, but put it back down as she headed down the stairs to the weight room.

Lonzell was bench-pressing when she walked to the door. Leesa didn't say anything. She just watched as he lifted the weights with ease. Her heart fluttered as her eyes roamed over his beautiful body. The only clothing he had on was a pair of black biking shorts that showed everything, and she did mean *everything*. The last time they were together came back to mind. Lonzell had had to call a cleaning company to get the juice stains out of the light tan carpet.

Leesa closed her eyes as her mind screamed, *Think!* She tried to concentrate on anything other then Lonzell, but it was a lost cause.

Letting out a deep sigh she said, "God help me, this isn't working." Her eyes opened and she looked dead at Lonzell.

"I remember the last time you said words like that," he said, wiping his face with a towel. "I also remember it didn't work."

"Lonzell, please. Where is Miles?"

"I'm just making conversation," he said, getting up and

walking toward her. "He's upstairs taking a nap."

"Oh, how long has he been asleep?"

"Not long, but long enough to where we have the place to ourselves," he said, now standing in front of her.

Leesa found it very hard to breathe with him standing so close with nothing on but his shorts. With much will power, Leesa moved out of his space—not because she wanted to, but because she had to. She still loved Lonzell, but she wasn't going to be a fool again.

"Actually, I was going to take a nap myself."

"Why?"

"Lonzell," she said, taking a seat on the bench, "you know the only reason why I'm here is because of Miles. Let's not pretend anything more."

"Pretend? Pretend what, Leesa? Pretend we couldn't get enough of each other, or should we pretend Miles wasn't made from our love? Oh, I know, why don't we pretend you don't want me as much as I want you right now?" Lonzell never raised his voice from a mere whisper.

"What!" she said, coming to her feet.

Lonzell shook his head and smiled. "Come on, let's talk about this."

"I remember the last time we were going to talk," Leesa said, looking up at him.

He laughed. "No, really, I want to talk to you."

"Lonzell—"

"No, let me say this, please," he said, cutting her off.

She nodded.

"I know I was short with you on the phone the other night, but when I tried to call you and you weren't there I got worried. I didn't know what to think."

"I'm sorry. Miles had a small asthma attack. Besides, you had just gotten to work."

"Let me tell you something," he said, taking both her hands in his, "and I want you to understand this. A job can come and go, but my life as Miles' father doesn't end until the day I close my eyes in death."

If she didn't love him already, at that very moment she would have. "Okay. I won't keep anything from you when it comes to Miles."

"Thank you."

Looking up at him, she said, "You're welcome."

Lonzell straddled the bench and gently put his arms around her, pulling her in to his warm body. He said, kissing the top of her head, "I know I can't make up for the past, but I'm here now and I plan on staying. Please, just let me show you."

Leesa nodded. "All right, but don't just show me, show your son," she said in a mere whisper.

"I will show *our* son how much you two really do mean to me." At that very moment Lonzell knew he didn't want to live without them in his life, and he wouldn't. "You'll see," he said, staring at her as if suddenly he saw something that he hadn't seen before.

She watched as his face came closer. Looking into his eyes, she could see the flicker of light in them. Leesa felt his warm breath fan across her face. His firm lips touched hers, tentatively. A dull ache throbbed deep within her.

He drew back to look at her again. They stared into each other's eyes. Then his gaze traveled down her body and back up again, stopping at her breasts where her shirt had molded itself to her. Under his gaze, her breasts seemed to take on a mind of their own; they became heavier and more sensitive. Her nipples hardened into little pebbles, and she knew he could see their shape. She cursed herself for not wearing a bra. Her face grew warm with awareness.

He softly touched the side of her face. "Ah, Leesa, my sweet, sweet Leesa," he said in a soft crooning voice.

She was afraid to move but she wanted to touch him as well. Slowly, she lifted one hand toward him. He made a small gasp when she touched his face. He turned his mouth to kiss her exploring fingers. The sensation that shot through her was exquisite, almost mind-blowing.

He moved closer and kissed her again. His mouth was moving slowly across hers, molding and loving it.

Without thinking, she opened her mouth under his. Her tongue found its way into his mouth. The silky, smooth yet rough texture was just like she remembered.

He let her tongue move to meet his. Their tongues touched and circled as if they were going to slow dance. He groaned deep in his throat and pressed his mouth harder upon hers in a kiss that became more demanding. He drew her tongue into his mouth again to taste her sweet nectar, just as she tasted him.

She was aware of a deepening hunger that made her press closer to him.

He ran his hand down her throat to her collarbone and across to her shoulder. His large, hot palm moved from her shoulder and covered her right breast. It seemed to burn her through the fabric of her shirt. She gasped into his mouth at the incredible sensation that streaked through her, beginning at the core between her thighs. She moved closer to him, if that was possible.

When he broke the kiss, they were both breathless. "I-I got protection this time," Lonzell said, kissing his way down her dark chocolate neck.

Breathless, she uttered, "Are you going to make love to me right here in the weight room?"

"Well, my plan is to start here and work our way to my bed," he said, pulling her top over her head. "If that's okay with you." With that said he covered her left breast with his mouth.

Leesa let out a small cry. "Yes . . . oh yes," she said as her arms slipped around his neck and held on. She arched against him, feeling her lower belly warm under his touch. Somewhere deep inside she could feel the heat igniting a delicious sense of anticipation. By the time he'd kissed her other breast she was overcome with yearning.

Before Leesa knew what was happening, her green jean skirt and yellow panties were on the floor and Lonzell was standing and lifting her up over his head in such a manner that her thighs parted and rested on his big shoulders and her hidden treasure was only a centimeter from his mouth.

"You're mine, Leesa," he said as his tongue flicked the tiny bud of her center.

"Ah . . . Oh . . ." Leesa cried as she held on to his head and crossed her legs at the ankles.

It was like music to Lonzell's ears as he made love to her, drinking her sweet nectar.

"Oh, that feels sooo goood, Lonzell. Yesss, ohhhh,

yesss!" Leesa moaned. Lonzell bit softly with his lips at her bud, careful not to hurt her, but trying to increase the level of her pleasure—and he did: just then her body shook and she cried out his name. "Lonzell, oooh . . . Lonzell." Leesa gasped, trying to catch her breath as Lonzell kissed her back to this side of the world. He lowered her back down to the bench.

"I'm going to make love to you like this is our first time," he said, kissing her nipples.

Leesa was still getting her breathing under control when she said, "Make love to me, Lonzell."

Removing his shorts, Lonzell sat behind Leesa on the bench pulling her into his arms. He kissed the back of her neck as his hands roamed over her body. "I just want to touch you. It feels like—forever. I missed you," he whispered in her ear.

Leesa loved the way it felt to be in his big strong arms again. She felt safe; she felt love. "I missed you too," she confessed, kissing his arms as they wrapped around her.

"Turn around, baby."

Leesa did as he asked.

A new volt of energy passed through Lonzell's iron member as she turned to straddle him and her wet core touched him. He knew she felt it too.

"You always knew how to get a rise out of me," he murmured, kissing her lips softly.

Leesa's unsteady hands gripped his iron member and began to slowly stroke him. "Is this okay?" she asked, holding him with one hand now.

"Heaven," was all he could mumble.

Lonzell slipped his hands from her breasts and let them travel down her body until they came to rest at her hot, wet core, where he made sweet love to her again, taking her over the edge. He slipped his hands from her core and found her breasts. He moved against her mouth as his thumbs located the stone-hard nipples. His mouth left hers and closed over one eager nipple.

Leesa continued to stroke him as she inclined her head back, giving him better access to his desired target.

Lonzell palmed her right breast as his left hand traveled

down her anatomy, cupping her again; she sighed openly. A moment later he inserted two fingers inside her, giving her pleasure that was so intense she thought she would cry.

"You're wet, Leesa," he said, never taking his mouth from her breast.

Eyes closed, she nodded.

His fingers dipped farther into her, and she gasped aloud as they explored her body. Pulling them out of her slightly, he located the very crux of her desire, working his magic on her.

Leesa could barely sit still as he worked his power, as the heat converged into something wild and frenetic and finally burst into something white-hot and delicious. She threw her head back and cried out softly, as Lonzell crooned in her ear, taking her to a place in her thoughts where she was certain no decent woman should go, but it was too late, she was already there.

When her body quieted, Lonzell lowered her to the ground. Then he lay flat on the bench and helped her to straddle his head. "I'm going to taste you again," he said as he lowered her to his open mouth.

Leesa was once again caught up in the frenzy of sensation, but this time she wanted Lonzell to feel what he was doing to her. Without warning she leaned her body over his and took him into her mouth.

Lonzell's whole body shook with sure pleasure; he moaned against her as her mouth took him to a place of no return. Nothing had ever felt so good.

Leesa released him only to take him in her hot hands. She kissed and stroked his most sensitive parts before covering his hard iron again.

Lonzell basked in her sweet nectar as she drove him almost over the cliff. When he couldn't take any more, Lonzell eased his body up to the back of the bar that was on the weight bench and moaned, "Stop, baby, before it's all over for me."

Leesa stopped as he had asked. With her back to his chest she whispered breathlessly, "I want to feel you inside me again."

Lonzell turned her so he could devour her mouth. In one

movement, he had Leesa flat on the bench. She opened her mouth and welcomed his probing tongue. Lonzell reached for the duffel bag under the bench for a condom, lips never leaving Leesa's.

Shifting slightly, Leesa raised one knee so that she cradled him between her thighs. She felt his arousal and moved once, experimentally, against him. He released her lips and opened his eyes. Leesa's heart jolted at his expression. His face was taut, his light brown eyes singed her with raw male hunger.

"Put your legs on my shoulders," he said in a voice that didn't sound like his. Leesa did as he asked, just before he protected them. With lips, tongue, and teeth, he teased her to distraction. Just when she thought he was finished, he sucked one engorged nipple deep into his mouth. At the same time he entered her wet, aching core.

Leesa felt the fine sheen of perspiration on his skin, heard the telltale roughness in his voice. He gently probed his iron masculinity into her again and again.

"Oh, baby. Ooh, baby. That's it. Yes, ooh, yes," Lonzell whispered over and over in her ear.

"Oh, Lonnie, oh baby, you make me feel sooo good. Oh, baby, don't stop," Leesa cried, wrapping her legs around his neck.

Lonzell lost it then; he didn't realize just how much he'd missed her calling him Lonnie, until he heard her sweet voice in the heat of passion. "Open your eyes, Leesa," he said as he pushed deeper and deeper into her.

Leesa's eyes fluttered open to find Lonzell looking at her.

"I love you, Leesa. I always have, and always will," he stated over and over again.

Leesa wouldn't fight it anymore. "And I love you," she cried out as he sent her into ecstasy.

She stiffened and her tiny internal tremors precipitated his own. Lonzell gave a hoarse growl of possession and release into a bottomless pit. "You're mine, Leesa. Mine," he said in her ear.

"And you're mine."

• • •

Leesa was smiling to herself, as she remembered how Lonzell had gotten her to sleep in his bed. As she came down the stairs, the doorbell rang. Thinking it might be Lonzell because he had taken his car to be serviced, she opened the door.

"You forgot . . ." was all she was able to get out. The smile left her face as she looked at the woman who had given the man she was in love with life. None other than Ida Jean Jenkins.

"Hello, Ms. Jenkins."

"What the hell are you doing at my son's house?" Ida Jean barked as she pushed past Leesa.

I'm not in the mood for her shit this morning, Leesa said to herself as she closed the door. Turning to face Ida Jean, she said, "Good to see you again, Ms. Jenkins. How have y—"

"I asked you a question, gal! What are you doing here?" Ida Jean said, cutting Leesa off.

"You know, Ms. Jenkins, I don't know what you think I've done to you, but I'll be the bigger person here and say I'm sorry," Leesa said, folding her arms over her breasts.

Ida Jean looked down her nose at Leesa before speaking. "Sorry? I'll say! I know how your kind works."

"My kind!" Leesa said sarcastically. "Tell me, Ms. Jenkins, what is my kind?"

"I know your type, always running up and throwing your bodies at men with money. Then you sleep with them. Some of you even make them believe they are the fathers of your bastard children. Well, you're not going to do it to my baby."

Nobody was going to talk bad about her child. "Let me tell you something. I never forced myself on any man. What happened between Lonzell and me was love, not some fly-by-night roll in the hay. What we shared was love."

Ida Jean gasped as she brought her left hand up to her throat. "Let me tell you something, little trick, my son would never love someone like you. Sleep with, yes; love—never."

Leesa felt like a bull ready to charge the woman standing there in all red. But she wouldn't stoop to her level. Taking a deep breath, Leesa said, "Ms. Jenkins, I'm sorry you feel that way about me and your son. It saddens me to think you think so little of your own son. But I'm not going to stand here and let you disrespect me. Lonzell will be back soon. If you have any more questions about me being here, I suggest you take it up with him."

"You little black bitch, who the hell do you think you are talking to? You are just like your mother; you think you are Miss All That. Well, I'm here to tell you, you are nothing but trash, and you always will be."

My mother? What does my mother have to do with this? "You know, Ida Jean," she said, walking up to her, "I don't have to think who I am. I'm Leesa Elizabeth Fairchild, born to an African American mother and a Blackfoot Indian father who loved me unconditionally, and I'm the mother of Miles Xavier Jenkins. *And* I am not taking any more of your crap. *That's* who I am."

"Why, you—" Ida Jean barked as her right hand came across Leesa's face fast and hard.

Leesa let out a painful cry as tears filled her eyes.

"As long as you are black, don't you *ever* talk to me like that again," Ida Jean said, rubbing her stinging hand. "Do I make myself clear?"

Leesa looked at the woman who was the grandmother of her child and said, "Yes, you made it very clear. But remember this: Don't ever touch me again or I won't be responsible for my actions."

Ida Jean held her head back and laughed before saying, "I see you still got that smart mouth. Maybe one slap wasn't enough." With that said, Ida Jean raised her hand again to slap Leesa.

Leesa caught Ida Jean's hand before it could make contact with her face. "I warned you, Ms. High-yellow Witch, not to touch me again," shouted Leesa as her own hand came across Ida Jean's cheek.

"You little whore, you—" was all Ida Jean said as she fell to the floor.

"Get up!" Leesa screamed over the woman.

"Please, please don't hit me again. I'm sorry for whatever I did to you, but please don't hit me again," Ida Jean cried.

"What the hell is going on in here?" barked Lonzell as he ran over to his mother.

"Lonzell, it's not what—" Leesa began.

"What, Leesa? It's not what? That you're beating the hell out of my mother?" he snarled as he helped his mother up.

Ida Jean wrapped her arms around Lonzell as she whimpered, "I-I'm all right, son. I didn't mean any harm. I just came to say hello and tell you I was back from my trip, and . . . and . . . she attacked me," she cried.

"That's a lie!" Leesa cried. "I did no such thing. She slapped me—"

"Liar," Ida Jean said.

"Shut up!" said Lonzell to both of them. "Listen to yourselves. You sound like two crazy women out in the streets." Looking at them he shook his head. "Mother, can you excuse us for a moment?" Lonzell said as he sat her on the love seat.

"I-I'm so sorry, son. I didn't m-mean t-to—"

"It's okay, Mother, we'll talk later," Lonzell said as he kissed her on the forehead and touched her very red cheek.

Leesa watched the tender care Lonzell showed toward his mother and knew she had won again. It was always about her. All through high school it was about what his mother would say about them dating. Now, they had a child together, and she was *still* winning.

"Leesa," Lonzell said, cutting into her thoughts. "Let's go into the kitchen."

Leesa followed him. Once there, she muttered, "I know you don't believe her?"

"Have you seen her face, Leesa? What the hell do you expect me to believe?" he said, hitting the countertop. "What happened? I wasn't gone that long."

Leesa didn't want to cry—she wouldn't—but it was too late. The tears had a mind of their own. "I . . . I . . ." She stopped, wiped her eyes, and took a deep breath. "I expect you to be open about this. I expect you to see what she is trying to do. I expect you to see fingerprints on my face too.

I expect you—" She paused. "You know what?" Leesa said, holding her hands up. "I expect you to do nothing. We're out of here. Catch me if you can."

Lonzell didn't move from the sink as he listened to Leesa get her and Miles' things and walk out the door.

CHAPTER 7

LONZELL looked out the window from the attic of the house he'd grown up in. When he was a boy, the attic was his favorite place because it was the one place he could think.

He looked at his Rolex. If this were his weekend to pick Miles up, he would already be there by now. It had been three weeks since he had seen Leesa. He had talked to Miles every day. She must have gotten caller ID because Miles always answered the phone.

Lonzell let out a deep sigh and turned from the window. He looked around the attic. It looked like his mother had been packing things in boxes. "What is all this stuff?" he said to the open room as he walked to the boxes that were open. Lonzell picked up a few of the papers and looked through them one at a time.

After looking through almost all of them, Lonzell was just about to put them all back when the last sheet caught his eye. It was a copy of a cashier's check made in the amount of two thousand dollars with his name on it.

The blood rushed to his head and caused him to sway. "What the . . ." he said, pulling out more copies of cashier's checks, all with the same amount. Lonzell couldn't believe what he was seeing. There, right in his own house, were the cashier's checks to Leesa with his name on them. Who was playing this sick game? Who would be so cruel? He knew the answer, but why? Why had his own mother kept his child from him?

Leesa had been right all along. It was his mother. He had to talk to Leesa. He prayed she would forgive him.

Leesa was reading Francis Ray's latest book when a knock on the door startled her. Looking at the small crystal clock on her nightstand, she frowned and uttered, "Who could that be at nine-thirty?" Throwing the pale yellow sheet off her warm body, Leesa slid out of the bed as she reached for her powder blue robe. There was another knock. "Jeez!" she mumbled. "Keep your pants on."

When Leesa finally made it to the door and looked through the peephole she had to do a double take, because there on the other side was Lonzell. She put her hand on the doorknob only to jerk it away as if it were hot. As Leesa looked through the peephole again her emotions took over. First there was love. Even after all that had happened between them, she still loved him very much. All she wanted to do was open the door and leap into his arms, but then fear popped its big head up, and that made Leesa wonder why he had come by so late. Was he going to try to take her son? No. He wouldn't. He couldn't.

Before Leesa realized what was happening, anger took over her body. And it was anger that made her open the front door. "What are you doing here?" she said through the locked screen door. "Do you know what time it is? Just because we have a child together doesn't mean you can pop over anytime you—"

"I'm sorry," Lonzell said in a husky voice, cutting Leesa off.

Leesa took a good look at him. Something wasn't right. He looked hurt—not just bodily hurt; but emotionally hurt. She could tell from the light on the porch that he had been crying—but why? *Open the door and find out!* her brain yelled.

"May I come in? Please," he asked, looking at her with glossy eyes.

Leesa's heart ached for him. Her foggy eyes began to sting from the tears. She had no idea where they came from. And to make matters worse, she didn't know why. *That's a lie. You know darn good and well why you are feeling this way. You love him! Don't you?* "Yes," Leesa said, answering Lonzell and her mind at the same time. She unlocked the screen door and stepped back to let him pass. Leesa noticed he had a box.

"Thank you," Lonzell said, taking a seat on the sofa.

Leesa closed and locked the door before she took a seat in the matching chair. "Lonzell, what's wrong?" she asked, looking into his pain-filled eyes.

Taking a deep breath and letting it out slowly, Lonzell leaned forward, resting his arms on his thighs and entwining his long fingers together. Looking down he uttered, "Where do I start?"

"The beginning is always a good place," she said softly.

Lonzell looked over at Leesa and knew that he loved her very much and that he could never love another woman the way he loved her. Not only was she a loving and caring person, but she was also the mother of his child. His son. For as long as he could remember, she had been pulling for him. Even when he had hurt her, she was still pulling for him.

He gave her a small smile and said, "You have always been there for me."

Before she could say anything he went on. "I hurt you again. I'm sorry. I guess it's true, you always hurt the one you love."

Leesa didn't say anything as she got up and sat next to him.

Lonzell turned his left hand palm-side-up and looked at her.

Leesa placed her small right hand into his large one; they laced their fingers together. Neither spoke but they knew the broken link in their lives had just been welded back together. Nothing and no one would break it again.

They sat for a few more moments just enjoying each other before Leesa asked, "Are you going to tell me what's in the box?"

"The night w-we first made love, I told you no matter

what, I'll be there—well, I wasn't and I'm sorry," he said as his voice broke.

"L-Lonzell, please let's not—"

"No, I-I have to tell you this. You have a right to know why I wasn't there."

Leesa didn't know what was going on, but he was scaring her.

"Lonzell, what's wrong? What did you do?"

He shook his head. "That's just it; I did nothing—not a damn thing."

Leesa laughed nervously. "Lonzell, what are you talking about? You did, you took care of all the medical bills. Sure, I don't know why you sent them to my P.O. box on campus. I sent you the address to my apartment."

Lonzell's head snapped up. "What—when did you send me your address?" he asked, taking two big envelopes out of the box.

"Right after I moved."

"I found you, but . . ."

"But what? Why didn't you let me know?" Shocked, she asked again, "Why?"

"Because I saw you hugging some guy outside your apartment and since I hadn't heard from you—"

"You were there that day?" That had to be it because that was the only time James had hugged her in public. "You saw me hugging James? If you would have come up to me that day you would have learned that James is gay and he was thinking about having a sex change."

Lonzell looked at her with tears in his eyes. "I saw the pictures of you two together."

"What pictures?"

Lonzell took a small stack of pictures out of his back pocket and gave them to Leesa.

Leesa looked at the pictures. Sure enough, there she and James were, eating out, at the park, and in a few that were taken outside her apartment. "You had—"

"My mother sent those to me over in Korea. I didn't believe her, so I took a thirty-day leave and went to Florida to see for myself . . ."

"You saw James and me hugging." Leesa finished what she knew he was going to say.

Lonzell nodded in agreement.

"If you had gotten my letter, you would have known about James. He was and still is a very good friend. He was there when I had no one."

"Where did you send the letters?"

"To your mother's house. Why?"

"Leesa, there's a whole lot of stuff I found."

"What are you talking about?"

For the answer, Lonzell opened the first envelope and poured the contents on the table.

Leesa looked at the papers that were spread out on her table. "W-what is all this?" she said, picking up one of the bundles.

"I found this in the attic. I can't believe my mother did this to us."

Hot. The bundle felt like fire to Leesa. She dropped it before she stood and walked away from the sofa. "Sh . . . she did this? But why? What did I ever do to her?" Leesa cried.

To see the tears in her eyes cut him deep to the heart. It hurt him to know his mother was the cause of her tears—and the cause of all their problems. Along with his mistrusting her. "I don't know, but I plan to get to the bottom of this. She had no right to keep my son from me," Lonzell hissed as he took the rubber band off the bundle Leesa had put down. "I tried to put them in order. As far as I can tell, you started getting money from my *mother* in early April, then the two thousand a month started in December." Lonzell closed his eyes tight to stop the burning. "Miles' birthday is December what?"

"The twentieth."

"That explains why it was so much more."

Leesa turned to face him. "I thought you were taking care of his birthday and Christmas all in one."

"Did you get a card?"

"No. Not at first, but later on I did. Did you get your Father's Day cards?"

Lonzell picked up the other envelopes. "I have them now," he said.

Bringing her hands to her face, she wiped her tears. "I don't understand this. How could you *not* have known about Miles? I wrote you. I sent you pictures."

He then took out the pictures and letters. "I know you did. Here they are too."

"She read my letters to you. Oh God, no wonder she hates me," Leesa uttered.

"You have to believe me, I didn't know. After I left you, I went home, but you never called; when I left for Korea, I never heard from you. My mother also said you never called."

Lonzell stood and walked to her, not caring that papers, cards, and letters went everywhere, he held her hands. "Baby, I've wanted you for years. I just didn't know where to find you. And as far as Miles is concerned, I want him too," he said, holding her face in his hands, tears in his eyes. He touched her forehead with his. "I love you and I love our son."

"I love you too," she said, unable to stop the tears.

Lonzell was so overwhelmed that she still loved him, he let his own tears fall freely.

They held each other as if there were no tomorrow.

Lonzell pulled her back just enough so that his mouth could find hers. Leesa raised her head to meet his kiss.

His mouth closed over hers with his lips parted and his tongue demanding that she open to him, and Leesa gave him what he asked for. Heat swelled up in them. It went on forever, building in intensity, stoking fires that were burning high. He tore his mouth from hers, making her groan, but she soon sighed with delight as he pushed her robe open and her gown aside and kissed her breasts, his teeth worrying the nipples gently.

When his mouth moved down between her breasts, Leesa lost all her oxygen. She wanted him just as much as he wanted her. She opened his shirt and rubbed tentatively against his masculine nipples, feeling him convulse at her touch.

The violent passion of his touch shook her from her moorings, making her cling to him, making her arch toward him. Groaning, he kissed his way back up to her mouth as he picked her up.

The vibrant beat of his heart thudding against hers made him feel strong as an ox . . . weak as a puppy. But he didn't want to hurry any of it. He wanted to revel in it all, because being with Leesa was the only true lovemaking he'd ever known.

"Which room?" he asked against her mouth.

"First door on the left."

Without hesitation he carried her to her bedroom. Once inside, he closed the door with his foot. "Are you sure?" he asked in a hoarse voice.

"Yes, but you must keep it down; remember, Miles is only two doors down."

He nodded. Laying her on the bed, he pulled his shirt over his head and began to unbuckle his pants. Unclothed, he stretched out beside her.

His fingers slid into her thick, satiny hair, clasping her head as his mouth slanted over hers. "I love the way you taste and smell," Lonzell said as he inhaled her scent.

"Oh, Lonzell."

"You're the most beautiful thing I've ever seen," he said, his voice gruff and hard. His hands slid up under the delicate silk of her gown, moving to cup her breasts.

She gasped as his heat seared her, his large palms rubbing over her distended nipples. She moaned helplessly, her hips arching as she instinctively tried to get closer to him. The fire in his eyes scorched her. "That's it, baby, tell me what you want."

Leesa was almost beyond speech, beyond thought, and certainly far beyond reason.

Lonzell planted hot, wet kisses all down Leesa's body again and again. He ran his tongue over her outer thighs before letting it touch the hard bud at her center. Once he had her almost over the edge, he stopped and covered his member before he entered her with one thrust. He drove deeper and deeper into her again and again, taking her right to the tip of ecstasy before he pulled his iron member from her wet, sizzling cove and replaced it with his scorching mouth. Again, his tongue sent her back to the end of the cliff, only to stop before she went over. Lonzell kissed her long and hard as he pushed back into her rich garden. He laced their fingers together, bringing them over their heads. Lonzell didn't stop this time; Leesa wrapped her thighs tighter around his back as she rode out the wave of her climax. Lonzell was only a second behind her as he let out a loud roar, as he released his seed.

CHAPTER 8

LEESA listened to their heartbeats as she tried to slow her breathing. Never in a million years had anything felt so good. Her body still shook as Lonzell kissed her swollen lips and whispered how much he loved her.

They were still joined when they heard a knock on the door and it opened.

"Mommy?"

Leesa didn't know where the strength came from but she was able to push Lonzell off her and on the floor with a thump.

"Yes, sweetheart?" she said, looking for something to put on. Thank heavens her room was dark and Miles was still rubbing his eyes. "Mommy's here," she said breathlessly.

"I heard something, and I'm scared," he whined.

Damn! Were we that loud? "It was nothing, sweetheart. Mommy will take you back to your room and stay with you until you go back to sleep," she said, putting on the first shirt she felt in the pile that lay on the floor and walking to her son.

"Can we call my daddy to come over?" he asked, taking Leesa's hand.

No, sweetheart, we can't call your daddy to come over because he's already here, her mind yelled sarcastically. "Tell you what. I'll call your daddy later and make sure he's here when you wake up. Okay?" Leesa hated to lie but she could not tell him the truth.

"Okay," Miles said, getting into his bed.

Leesa let out a small sigh as she covered Miles up, sat on the side of the bed, and sang him a song: Leesa didn't have to sing very long; Miles was fast asleep before she was finished with the first part. She eased off the bed and kissed his cheek before going back to her room.

Lonzell was in bed when she walked back into her room. "Can I get you to lock that door?" he said.

Leesa smiled while locking the door. "I'm sorry. I just didn't want Miles to see us. I didn't mean to knock you on the floor," she said, taking off the shirt that she realized was his. "Did I hurt you?" Leesa asked, climbing back into bed.

Pulling her into his arms, he answered, "Come here, let me show you."

Leesa laughed as she straddled him, "Oh! Are you happy to see me, big boy?" she cooed in her best Mae West voice.

Lonzell filled his hands with her breasts and uttered, "Very."

Leesa ran her fingers over his nipples, making them hard. "I'm happy that you're happy," she purred, raising her body and then taking him into her hot core.

"I wouldn't have it any other way," Lonzell said in a hoarse voice, pulling her face down to his and covering her mouth with his as they worked on keeping each other happy.

Leesa and Lonzell had made love twice that morning, once in bed and then again in the shower, by the time Miles walked into the kitchen. He gave Leesa a hug and was about to ask her a question when he realized they weren't alone. Lonzell sat dressed in the black jeans, red shirt, and black Lugz boots he had worn last night as he sipped on a cup of hot coffee.

"Daddy, Daddy," Miles cried, running to Lonzell.

Lonzell set the cup down and pushed it away from him just in case Miles' little hand hit the table. He didn't want to burn the child. "Hey, buddy," he said, picking him up and kissing his forehead before giving him a hug.

Miles hugged him back. "You smell like Mommy, Daddy."

Leesa turned from the stove where she was cooking grits and looked at Lonzell with wide eyes.

Lonzell smiled at her over Miles' shoulder, giving her a wink.

Leesa smiled back. She couldn't help it. She loved him very much. She turned the burner off and covered the pot before she said, "Well, sweetheart, I gave your daddy a hug this morning. That's why he smells like Mommy."

It was the truth. They *had* hugged earlier, among other things. Just thinking about the other things made her nipples grow hard under the celery green tank top that was tucked neatly into a pair of stonewashed jean shorts.

"Daddy, last night I heard a loud noise," Miles said.

"Really," Lonzell said, looking at Leesa.

"W-what kind of noise, sweetheart?" she asked nervously, taking a seat in one of the padded wrought-iron chairs.

"It was a bear."

"A bear," Leesa said.

"Uh-huh. Two," Miles said, holding up two little fingers.

"Two!" Leesa and Lonzell said in unison.

He nodded. "A big and a little one."

Leesa listened as their son told them how loud the big bear was and how not so loud the little bear was, but all she wanted to do was have the floor open up and take her. Their child had heard them making love. Leesa was ready to be sent to "Mommy school"—on Mars.

"That's why your mommy called me, she said you had a bad dream," Lonzell said, tapping into her thoughts. *Dream! Yes, a dream,* her mind said.

"Don't worry, Miles, your mommy and I won't let anything happen to you. Right, Mommy?" he said with a smile in his voice.

"That's right, sweetheart. Nothing at all," she said, touching Miles' face. "I'm sure you won't have *that* dream anymore," she said, looking at Lonzell.

He only smiled and winked at her again as she finished their breakfast.

They spent the next forty-five minutes in the kitchen. Then Miles asked, "Why Daddy can't stay with us?"

Lonzell's jaw tightened as he placed the fork down on his plate. He had a bad taste in his mouth. If it hadn't been for his mother, they *would* be living together—as a real family. Like last night, when Miles woke up, he should have been the one tucking his son in, not hiding like some thief. The reason why he was there came back this morning to haunt him like a nightmare.

"Daddy," Miles chimed, bringing him out of his melancholy mood.

"Yes, son," he said, looking at the child—his own flesh and blood. He had missed so much, but not anymore.

"Why can't Mommy and me move our house in your house?"

"Sweetheart, we did go to Daddy's house, remember?" Leesa said. She was already doing God-forbidden sin with Lonzell and she refused to add shacking up to the list. No, if Lonzell loved her as much as he said he did, by golly, he could marry her first.

"No, I mean let's stay all the time. Like Ray-Ray, he and his mommy are moving to stay with his new daddy," Miles said, folding his arms over his chest.

Lonzell and Leesa didn't say anything so Miles went on.

"I won't be bad anymore. And I'll clean my room and eat my carrots," he said, making a face. "Some of them."

Lonzell was the first to speak. "Come here, buddy."

Miles hopped out of the chair and climbed up in Lonzell's lap.

"You haven't done anything wrong. Y-you're a good kid. And you can come to my house anytime you want," Lonzell said, fighting back the unshed tears that stung his eyes like onions.

"But I want to stay all the time," Miles said, with his little hands on Lonzell's cheeks.

Leesa's heart was breaking—not for her or Lonzell, but for their child. He didn't understand all this. She couldn't let him feel as if he were the reason his parents didn't live together.

"Tell you what, sweetheart. The holidays are coming up and we can go to Daddy's." Okay, okay, so she was adding shacking up to her list, but she would walk through fire with gasoline underwear on to remove the sadness from her child's big brown eyes.

"Yeah, let's start there and we can see what the new year will bring us," Lonzell chimed in.

CHAPTER 9

IDA Jean Jenkins was in her step aerobics class when her cell phone rang. Not slowing down, she hit the SEND button on the phone upon the third ring. "Hello," she said, breathless.

"Hello, Mother."

"Lonzell?"

"Yes, Mother, who else would call you and say, 'Hello, Mother'?" he asked sarcastically.

"Don't you use that tone with me, young man," she said just as sharply.

"I need to talk to you, Mother; I'm at the house. Say, in an hour?" he voiced, not caring where she was.

"Is something wrong, son?"

Don't call me your son! he wanted to scream, but instead he said, "Nothing I can't handle. I'll see you in an hour."

Ida Jean held the phone a little longer before she flipped it closed. She didn't like the way Lonzell sounded. His voice was gruff, like he had been crying. Which didn't make any sense to her. Why would he be crying? Narrowing her eyes like a snake, Ida Jean muttered, "This smells like Leesa Fairchild. That gal don't know who she's messing with." She stopped her workout and headed for the shower room. "I guess I'll just have to show her."

Lonzell sat in a chair watching the television. Before he left Leesa and Miles this morning, Leesa had given him a box of videotapes of Miles. They were dated back to his first day in the world. She also had taken all of Miles' pictures and made them into slides. Lonzell watched as the years of his child's life went by. How could a mother be so cruel?

Ida Jean pulled her black Jaguar into the driveway fifty minutes later. Killing the motor, she stepped out of the car, dressed in an apricot-colored, double-breasted DKNY suit. "Lonzell!" Ida Jean called as she walked into the house.

Lonzell didn't answer when he heard his mother's voice. He couldn't. The picture on the screen had all his attention. He wanted to go to the next shot, but his thumb had a mind of its own and wouldn't touch the button to bring up the next picture.

"There you are," his mother said, walking down the three steps that led into the den. "When you called, you sounded so . . . gauche. And when you didn't answer, that really gave me a fright."

"Hello, Mother," Lonzell said, never getting out of the thick padded chair or looking at her.

"Well, that's no way to greet your mother," she hissed, standing in front of him with her hands on her hips.

Lonzell ignored her remark, but asked, "Mother, do you know that child on the screen?"

For the first time since she walked into the room, Ida Jean noticed the picture her son was glaring at. She looked at the child with the big brown eyes and shook her head. "No. I've never seen him before. Why? Is he one of the children of the less-fortunate groups that we donate to?"

"No," he said dryly, looking at her for the first time. "What about this one?"

The hum of the slide projector was the only noise in the room as Lonzell pushed the remote control button.

He continued pushing the button until he saw his mother gasp and bring her hand to her mouth. "So, you have seen this one?" he asked, turning to look back at the screen. "Now, how did I know *that* would be the picture you would recognize?"

"W-whatever do you mean?" Ida Jean asked nervously, touching the pearls around her neck.

"What do I mean? What kind of crap is that, Mother? Do you or do you not know this child?" Not waiting for her to answer he went on. "Let's see if you know his mother," Lonzell barked, coming to his feet and picking up another remote. This time it was a home movie.

"Leesa," Ida Jean whispered, but not low enough.

"Yes, Mother, Leesa and *my* son! My son. How dare you do this, Mother? How dare you keep my son from me?" Lonzell yelled as he pointed from the movie to himself.

Ida Jean's shoulders shook as she cried. She had known he would find out one day, but never in a million years did she think it would be this soon, and this way. She had been very careful. She had pulled money from her own personal account to make sure the child was taken care of. Ida Jean continued to cry, wondering if Lonzell had found the boxes.

As if on cue, Lonzell bent down and pulled the box from under the chair he had been sitting in just moments before. "What's all of this? What were you thinking, Mother? Did you plan to let my child grow up without ever knowing his father? Did you want him to grow up like I did?" he asked, slinging the empty box across the room.

"N-no, son—"

"Don't call me your son. What mother would do that to her son?" he barked.

"P-please. Let me explain," she cried. "I-I was only trying to protect you. I know women like her. They will do or say anything to get their hands on men like you. I-I didn't want her to ruin our good name. And—"

"Good name! What the hell is that all about, Mother? There's nothing good about me having your last name—I should have had my father's last name. You can do better than that. Face it, Mother, you thought Leesa was like you," he said in a cold voice.

That last remark earned him a slap across the face, but he caught Ida Jean's hand in mid-air.

"Don't even *think* about it, Mother!" he roared, pushing her hand away from his face.

Ida Jean looked at the man she had given life to and realized she couldn't kiss it and make it better this time. Only an act of God would soften his heart toward her again.

"Don't worry about coming to Virginia to see me . . . ever again." His voice was laced with venom. "Keep the keys, because the lock will be changed," he said, walking away.

Ida Jean fell to the floor and cried . . . she had lost her son.

CHAPTER 10

LEESA couldn't believe it was already Thanksgiving. She had a lot to be thankful for. She was in good health. Everyone whom she loved was in good health and her best friend, Tara, would be moving to Washington first of the year. When she went to see Lonzell she could see Tara too. Things couldn't be better—well, they could if she and Lonzell were married. Or if he was talking to his mother. She had tried over the last few weeks to get him to talk to Ida Jean, but it was like beating a dead horse. Lonzell was so bullheaded, and she was becoming blue in the face talking to him about him talking to his mother.

Leesa was proud of herself. She hadn't moved in with Lonzell—Lord knows she wanted to be in his arms every night and wake up there too—but she couldn't. He was already getting the milk without buying the cow; even if he wasn't getting it every day, he still was getting it. Leesa was glad they were having Thanksgiving dinner at her home instead of Lonzell's. She felt more at ease in her own small kitchen. She smiled as she thought about Lonzell looking at her like she had another head growing out the side of her neck when she told him they were having duck in lieu of the traditional turkey.

"Something smells good," Lonzell said, walking into the kitchen just as Leesa pulled the duck out of the oven. "Here, let me get that," he said, taking the pan from her and placing it on the cooling plate on the white countertop.

"Thank you. Now I don't feel like a Hebrew slave over a hot stove."

"I'm glad you talked me into having duck because everybody is having turkey."

"Yeah, I know. Besides, Big Mama Shirley will send some turkey down here later."

"Did you make a sweet potato pie?" he asked. His warm breath caressed the back of her neck as he leaned his body into hers as he got the china plates she couldn't reach without the stool that was in the far corner of the room.

Leesa's nipples tightened as she felt his manhood brush against her bottom. She turned to face him. "Lonzell, please," she murmured.

"I must be nuts," he moaned, "to start this when I know we can't finish it, not with Miles watching a movie right down the hall, but Leesa, I want you so much. I can't get enough of you."

She touched his chest. Her hands drifted up and down the firm muscles of his stomach. It had been over a week and she wanted him to make love to her now, but she wouldn't give in. "That's right, so back up so I can pass," she stated, pushing him back so she could get by. "Let's eat."

"Mm . . . mmm. This is good," Lonzell moaned as he ate his third slice of sweet potato pie. He had already eaten himself full of duck, rice-and-cornbread dressing, candied yams, cranberry sauce and rolls. Not to mention the two large glasses of sweet tea.

"Thank you, but I'm trying to see where you are putting all this food." Leesa laughed.

Pushing back from the table, Lonzell patted his stomach. "I'll work out before I go to bed. Besides, I haven't eaten this way in years. You really put your foot in the food."

"Mommy didn't put her foot in the food, Daddy," Miles chimed in before looking under the table to make sure Leesa had both feet.

Lonzell and Leesa both laughed.

"No, son, your mommy—"

The two adults looked at each other as someone knocked on the front door.

"I'll get it," Leesa said, sliding from her chair. "Tell Miles what you meant by that statement." She raised her eyebrows at Lonzell before she went to get the door.

Leesa didn't bother to look through the peephole because she was sure it was somebody needing to borrow eggs or sugar. She opened the door and was shocked to see Ida Jean standing there. The last time she'd seen her was the day they had had the knock-down-drag-out fight at Lonzell's. The woman had aged.

"I know I'm the last person you want to see, but could I please speak to my son?" Ida Jean asked meekly.

Leesa unlocked the screen door and pushed it open. "Please come in and have a seat. I'll get Lonzell for you."

"Thank you."

"Would you like something to drink?" Leesa asked, walking toward the kitchen.

"Tea, if you have any."

Leesa smiled. "Tea, I've got."

Ida Jean looked around the small but cozy house. There were pictures of Miles in different stages of his life, but there was one that made her heart skip a beat. The picture had to have been taken at Christmastime because of the background. The child was standing and his little legs were so bowlegged, you would have thought they would break. That was the same way Lonzell had looked when he was at that age.

God! What had she really done?

Leesa was pouring Ida Jean a glass of tea when Lonzell asked, "Who was at the door?"

"Where's Miles?" she asked, ignoring his question.

"In his room playing with his train set. So, who was at the door?" he asked again.

Leesa picked up the glass and said, "Your mother, and she's still here."

Lonzell came to his feet. "What? I'll take care of her. Don't worry, she won't bother you again."

"No, you won't," she said, stopping him in his tracks.

"What?" he asked in disbelief.

"Lonzell, she is your mother. I know she isn't crazy about me, but that's her issue, not mine or yours. Talk to your mother, *and* be nice," Leesa warned as she handed him the tea. "She's waiting for you."

"How can you say that when she treated you the way she did?"

"I can't be petty about what happened in the past. *We* have a child to raise. Miles has always been a happy child and I plan to keep his life that way. What would I be saying if I can't get along with his grandmother? Lonzell, let it go," she said, walking toward Miles' room.

Lonzell stood there. He didn't care what Leesa thought. He wanted to be bitter about what Ida Jean had done to him, and he wanted her to be just as mad, but she wasn't. Lonzell realized that was why he loved her so. Letting out a deep sigh, he headed for Miles' room too.

Leesa was playing with Miles when Lonzell walked into the room. Even with her back to him she could feel him in the room. She turned and looked up at him. "What's wrong?"

"I want you to come with me. If she has anything to say, she can say it in front of you. I don't want any more secrets between us," he answered, reaching for her hand.

Leesa didn't disappoint him; she placed her hand in his and he helped her stand.

"Miles, sweetheart, you play right here and Mommy will be right back, okay?"

Miles watched the trains go around the track and nodded.

Ida Jean was holding a picture of Miles when they entered the living room. She looked at them, then back at the picture and stated, "He looks just like you when you were a baby. Thought if I said I didn't know who he was you would believe me. I see I was wrong and I'm sorry." She took the tea from Lonzell.

Lonzell didn't say anything.

"I guess all the hate I felt for Ruth Brown ate away at me for over thirty years."

"Why did you hate my mother?" Leesa asked, looking ticked.

"I was fourteen years old when my parents and I moved here," Ida Jean said, looking out into the open room as if she were seeing her life roll before her eyes. "I was the new

kid in school and nobody wanted me at their lunch table—
that is until Ruth Brown asked me to sit at her table.

"She was very nice and we became fast friends. And
before I knew it we were spending all our time together. I
guess you could say we were best friends before Daniel—or
Running Wolf—Fairchild transferred to our school. He was
part Indian with long black hair. He was to die for." Ida Jean
took a sip of the tea before she went on. "He liked Ruth right
away, but I couldn't understand why. I was—"

"Prettier," Lonzell voiced as he and Leesa took a seat.

"Yes. I was," she rushed on to say, "but Ruth was pretty
in other ways and that's why she was so well liked. All
through high school I tried to get Daniel to notice me, but
he had eyes only for Ruth. They were married right after
graduation." Ida Jean looked over at Leesa, who was watching her.

"I knew I could never be the wife Ruth was, she believed
in simple things. I had big dreams and I was going to blow
this small town. And I did; that's when I met your father,"
she said, now looking at Lonzell. "He was tall, dark, and
gorgeous. I fell for him hard and fast, so fast I didn't think
to ask if he was married until after I was carrying you. That's
when I found out he had a wife and two other children. I
was hurt and ashamed, and I came back to Lovebug to have
you."

Ida Jean went on to tell them all about the things she'd
tried to do to get Daniel and how it all backfired on her.

"Let me make sure I'm understanding this correctly.
You hated my mother because she, quote–unquote, took your
boyfriend, who didn't want you anyway, *and*, he just happened to be my father."

"Yes!" Ida Jean cried. "I'm so sorry. Please forgive me."

"What kind of sick person are you?" Leesa asked, standing to her feet. "Is that why you didn't tell Lonzell about
Miles? Is that why you *gave* me the wrong address and phone
number for Lonzell? You hated my mother so much that you
would let her grandchild suffer? Well, lady, he's your grandchild too."

Leesa walked towards Ida Jean. To keep from strangling
the woman, Leesa had to clench her fists so hard that her

nails bit into her skin. "Why did you send the money if you didn't believe Miles was Lonzell's?"

Ida Jean placed the glass on the end table. "I did the same thing Lonzell's father's mother did to me. She helped take care of Lonzell, just in case I ever came back to say Jeff didn't take care of his child."

Lonzell looked at his mother as if he didn't know her. He never knew she had taken money from his father's family. "What! *Jeff* was never a father to me—I don't even know the man," Lonzell snarled in disbelief. "You took money from his family. Why?"

"Because they owed it to you. That's why," she shouted.

Lonzell shook his head. "I knew you could be low, Mother, but I didn't think you could go snake-belly low. Once *again* I underestimated you."

"Lonzell, Leesa," she said as tears ran freely. "I know I did something you don't understand, and I'm sorry. That's why I'm here today asking for your forgiveness. Please, can we try to—"

"No. No, we can't try anything today, Ms. Jenkins. Today is Thanksgiving Day, not Forgiveness Day, and I'm in no mood to forgive you right 'bout now. What I should do is slap the taste out of your mouth and throw you out of my house, but I'll let Lonzell do that," Leesa said as she put some distance between them. "Not to disrespect you, but you have big-ass issues. Granted, we all have issues, but you need to get some help for yours. Look at the pain you have caused your son—and grandchild. It's going to take some time to forgive you for what you tried to do to my child. He didn't do anything to you."

"Oh, Lonzell." Ida Jean reached for him.

He backed out of her reach. "Don't touch me. I just want you to leave because I'm not in the mood to forgive you, either," Lonzell said, walking to stand by Leesa.

Leesa watched as Ida Jean put her head down and walked out the door. The warmth of Lonzell's embrace made her realize his mother could never again tear them apart.

Leesa touched the diamond teardrop necklace that Lonzell had given her for Christmas as she looked at their son playing with his toys, half-listening to her best friend on the portable phone. It would be hard, but she had to go on with her life. She couldn't keep this up. True, she loved Lonzell, but doing all this sleeping together outside of marriage wasn't for her. After the game, she was going to tell him. She was sure he would be calling in a few because the game just went off. Leesa hated to do it over the phone, but it would be better for them both that way.

"Leesa!" Tara said, tapping into her thoughts.

"I'm not going to see Lonzell after today." She whispered so Miles couldn't hear her.

"Y-you can't do that," Tara said a little too fast.

Leesa frowned, "What do you mean, I can't do that? Yes, I can. I have a child to think about. What am I saying to him? It's okay for Mommy and Daddy to live together without being married? No, I don't think so, Tara. This time it's all about me."

Tara knew she had to think fast or the plans she and Lonzell had hatched up were going to blow up in their face. "Okay. I understand what you are saying, but how do you know Lonzell doesn't want the same things that you do? Did you tell me you loved him? Did you not say he was the only man you will ever love?"

"Yes and yes, but if he wanted the same things I wanted, I wouldn't be having this conversation with you right now," Leesa said, looking at Miles pat his jeans pocket.

"Just think about it, Leesa."

Knock, knock.

"Hey, Tara, someone is at the door."

"Okay, call me later."

"I will," Leesa said, walking toward the door. She found it funny that Miles didn't run to the door like he always did, but she didn't put too much thought to it.

"Just a minute," she said when the person knocked again.

"Mommy, the door," Miles called out, never taking his eyes off the cars he was playing with.

Leesa opened the door and was surprised to find a man dressed in an Air Force uniform on her front steps. "Yes?"

"Leesa Fairchild?" the man asked.

"Yes, I'm Leesa Fairchild. What's wrong? Has something happened to Lonzell Jenkins?" she asked, frightened.

"I have a telegram for you," he replied, handing her the letter. "Please sign here."

With shaky hands Leesa signed the paper on the clipboard.

"Thank you, ma'am." The man nodded and walked off.

Leesa was about to close the door, but stopped when she saw her neighbors standing in their yards looking at her. She gasped when she realized the handwriting was Lonzell's. Leesa ripped the letter open and started to read it. Tears filled her eyes as she read it again.

> *I'm not dead. So, please read on. I love you so very much. I couldn't have found a better way to ask you to marry me but in front of God and all the folks in Lovebug, because this is where I fell in love with you. And this is where I wanted to ask you to marry me too.*
>
> *So, if you will meet me outside I'll be more than happy to ask you to be my wife. I love you, Leesa, and I want to spend the rest of my life showing you just how much.*

Leesa wiped her eyes before she turned to Miles. "Sweetheart, come with Mommy, we're going outside."

"Oh boy!" Miles jumped up and ran to her.

Leesa and Miles walked out of the house to find Lonzell standing in the midst of the onlookers.

A noise overhead made Leesa look up, and she about passed out as a plane pulled a banner, with the words *I Love You, Leesa. Will you marry me?* across the sky. She looked at Lonzell as he placed a small mic on his shirt.

"This is my friend Hank Jones," he said, giving the tall handsome man a shoulder hug. "I met him in basic training and he owes me a favor. Hank said he would help a brotha out once the game went off. So, here we are." Lonzell walked back to Leesa and Miles.

He got down on one knee, and spoke into the mic. "I love you and I can't live without you. I wanted to ask you the day before Thanksgiving, but things got out of hand. Then I wanted to ask you on Miles' birthday, but that was his day. Then again at Christmas, but that was the first time

Miles got to meet his grandmother and I didn't want to take anything away from his day. So, this was the next best thing. I'm asking you now, Leesa Fairchild, will you marry me?"

"Yes."

People began to clap and shout.

"Now, Daddy?" Miles asked, looking up at his parents.

"Yes, son, now." Lonzell stood, picking Miles up.

"Oh boy!" Miles yelled as he took the small green velvet box out of his jeans pocket and gave it to his father.

Lonzell took the ring out of the box and reached for Leesa's left hand, then slid the three-carat, pear-shaped diamond and platinum ring on her third finger. The crowd went wild.

Leesa looked at the ring, which sparkled. "I guess you caught me."

He pulled her into his arms and whispered, "You always said, catch me if you can."

"That you did," she said, wrapping her arms tightly around his neck.

Six months later in Aruba

Leesa looked at herself in the mirror and smiled. She was now Mrs. Leesa Fairchild Jenkins. They had married earlier today and only had time to give Miles a few kisses and hugs before leaving him with his grandmother and making a mad dash to the airport.

Leesa had forgiven Ida Jean a few months back. She and Lonzell had come to realize life was too short to hold a grudge. She let a small smile tug at her lips as she thought back to Lonzell being in Lovebug all that time and she didn't know. Yeah, he had planned everything right down to getting her best friend and their son to help him. She still couldn't believe Miles had the ring under his pillow. No wonder he told her he could make his own bed. Lonzell must have given it to him the day he flew back to Virginia.

Lonzell said they would go sight-seeing tomorrow, but if he liked her outfit tonight, sight-seeing would be out of the question. And she knew he would.

"Leesa, what are you doing in there?" Lonzell called from the bedroom.

"I'm coming out now. Keep your eyes closed," she said turning off the light and walking right in front of him. "Open your eyes, baby."

Lonzell opened his eyes, and his mouth fell open too. There standing in front of him was Leesa with nothing else on but an air force hat.

"I understand this is what all the wives of ex–air force men will be wearing for their husbands next year. Do you like my hat?" she asked as she slowly turned around so he could see all sides.

"Leesa, untie my hands," Lonzell said huskily. "I'll be more than happy to show you just how much I like the hat, and everything in between."

"Really?" she asked as she straddled him on the chair and kissed his nipples while stroking his manhood in her right hand.

Lonzell's breathing was fast and heavy as he tried to get his hands loose.

Leesa continued to drive him out of his mind until she knew he wouldn't last much longer. She then reached under the hat and pulled a small package out. Once she had the condom firmly on his iron member, she let him slide slowly into her hot, wet cove. Then Leesa untied his hands.

Lonzell grabbed her hips as she rode them into a beautiful sunset.

Later, as their breathing returned to normal, Leesa asked, "Do you think I can have another hat?"

"You keep this up, you can have anything you want," he answered, cupping her right breast.

"Really?"

"Really."

"I think Miles needs someone to play with."

"Well, we can start right now. Let me get rid of this condom, and I'll be more than happy to see what I can do," Lonzell said with a lazy grin pulling at his lips.

"No, let me." Leesa stood and lowered her head to him as her mouth and teeth pulled the protection off of him. "Now, where were we?" she said as her warmth covered him again.

PROMISES AND VOWS

FELICIA MASON

PROLOGUE

JEROME Gregory stared down at his sleeping wife. Long lashes concealed her expressive brown eyes. Her skin, he knew, was as soft as it looked. She was as beautiful as the day they'd met.

But they'd let outside forces, namely their individual careers, take over their marriage. Material possessions they had in abundance, but they'd lost something far more valuable while chasing *things*.

Elise shifted position, exposing a long expanse of leg that ended with delicate toenails painted in fire-engine red. Jerome sucked in his breath.

He'd planned just to look, since by right he shouldn't be here. They'd agreed on at least that much. His condo was ready for him to move into. But here and now, looking at Elise, he knew he couldn't walk away without touching her at least one more time.

The love they'd shared for three years couldn't be over. Not when Jerome's heart beat double-time when he heard her voice. Not when his day was made brighter just by her smile.

Thinking about all they were throwing away and regretting that he hadn't been able to keep their love alive, Jerome leaned forward. He traced a finger up and along the smooth curve of her thigh.

Elise moaned in her sleep.

All of the blood in his body rushed to one spot. Jerome's

erection throbbed. He ached with the need and want of her. It had been so long for them.

Elise turned over, the sheet tangling in her legs; one full breast escaped the confines of the silky pajama top she wore.

Recognizing the top as part of a matching set they'd been given, Jerome's mouth went completely dry. Carefully, he eased onto the edge of the large bed they'd shared. Just one taste, one nibble of the forbidden fruit and then he'd leave. He'd go back to the place where he belonged.

He extended an unsteady hand to the tip of her breast. He paused, took a deep breath, then licked the edge of his finger before returning it to hover over her. Like a starving man, he stared at the morsel he desired, and then he stroked her. Gently, evenly he traced his finger around her nipple. It hardened and puckered for him.

Elise whimpered. His gaze flew to her face. She still slept, though, oblivious to his middle-of-the-night sensual foray. Her legs chafed at the sheet that confined her. Jerome waited. When she settled again, he leaned forward. This time his mouth closed over the now-erect nipple available to him.

He suckled her for a moment; then, knowing he should leave before she awakened and before he got carried away, he eased from the bed and left the room they once shared.

A moment later, Elise opened her eyes and stared into the darkness of the bedroom.

CHAPTER 1

"JEROME, we have a problem."

With the headset attached to her ear, Elise freely roamed the space in front of her desk. This was the last thing she had time for today. A mountain of paperwork overflowed on her desk.

"Just one problem?" Jerome said. "The last time you lit into me. . . ."

"Listen, will you?" Elise ran a hand through loose-hanging hair, the full-length weave the last concession she'd made to try to save her marriage. She'd thought if she looked a little more like a Creole beauty, then maybe . . .

"What's the problem?" Jerome asked. She could hear the frustration in his voice. It matched her own.

"Your Aunt Josephine just called."

"And?"

Elise put a hand on her hip and stopped pacing. "And she's at the airport."

"What airport?"

"The New Orleans airport, *darling*." Elise knew the emphasis on the last word was like a knife twisting in an open wound. He hadn't been her darling for some time. "She wants you to come get her."

"What's she doing in New Orleans?"

"She said she got a bad vibe and wanted to check on us."

If she hadn't been expecting the expletive from Jerome,

Elise would have laughed. She'd met Auntie Joe exactly one month before her wedding day. The older woman took one look at Elise, proclaimed the upcoming union a happy and joyous one that would last many, many years, then packed her roots and potions and gris-gris bags to head to the place she called home in the backcountry of Louisiana.

Being from Atlanta, Elise didn't put much stock in any of the voodoo mumbo-jumbo that permeated New Orleans or Jerome's family. On the best of days it amused her. If it made Auntie Joe happy that she could pronounce them made for each other, it didn't bother Elise one bit. On days like today, though, there was nothing funny about anything, particularly the estrangement from her husband.

Elise and Jerome might have been made for each other three years ago when Auntie Joe gave her blessing and they'd exchanged the promises and vows that were supposed to last a lifetime. Now, however, was a different story altogether.

"Elise, what are we going to do?"

She stared into space for a moment. The woman was *his* aunt. It was his problem.

They sure as heck couldn't let Auntie Joe know that not only were they separated, but that Jerome was moving out. All of his stuff was packed up in boxes in the guest room where he'd been living for the last two months while he waited to close on his condo.

Elise sighed. "I don't know, Jerome. That's why I called you."

For several seconds, silence crackled on the phone line between them. Once upon a time they lovingly looked to each other for mutual support and problem solving. It had been a long time since either admitted that the other could help with a problem.

"Did she say anything? You know, like what hotel she might be staying at?"

She rolled her eyes. "Jerome, get real."

He knew as well as she did that Auntie Joe fully expected to take up temporary residence in the guest room at their house, the room they'd put her in when she'd come to visit once before. Problem was, they hadn't even told their best friends that they were sleeping separate and headed toward a divorce. News like that could give Auntie Joe a heart attack. Granted, it would be a Fred Sanford "big one"—but Auntie Joe would insist upon staying until they resolved their differences. And that, Elise and Jerome both knew, was impossible. The divide was too great between them.

"You're right," he said. "No hotel. Elise, we can do this thing. All we have to do is pretend to be lovey-dovey, the way she remembers us. She'll stay for a week, then, satisfied that all is well, she'll pack up her bags and head back home."

"And if she doesn't?"

She heard his sigh through the phone line. "Work with me, Elise. Work with me."

Knowing there were few, if any, other options on such short notice, Elise acquiesced. "All right. What do you want me to do?"

"I'll swing by the airport, pick her up and then stall for some time. I'll take her to Café Du Monde for beignets or take her out to the cemetery to see Mama. Do you think you can get enough of my clothes and things back in your closet and scattered around the house so it looks like I live there?"

Elise rubbed her temple. She had a bad feeling about this. "Jerome, there has to be another way."

"What, then? What? You said she's already at the airport."

Her back against the wall and knowing it, Elise nodded, then said, "Yes, I can get some of your stuff out. Any particular items you want?"

"You decide. What airline did she come in on?"

A light flashed on her telephone console. "Just a sec," she told him. "I need to take a call." Not waiting to hear his response, she answered her secretary's alert. "Yes, Yvette?"

"Jonathan Slocum on line two for you."

Elise grinned. "Excellent. I'll be right there." She turned back to Jerome's call and gave him the flight information.

"I'll try to give you two hours." Elise raised a brow at his clipped tone.

They clicked off, and Elise stood with hands on hips in the middle of her real estate agency office. Before she could get her thoughts together about Jerome, her office line buzzed again.

"Thanks, Yvette," Elise said as she settled into her chair.

Auntie Joe or not, Elise had no intention of letting what could potentially be the year's biggest commission slip out of her hands. She put a smile on her face and in her voice.

"Mr. Slocum, so nice to hear from you. I have a couple of properties that I think might be just what you're looking for."

Thirty minutes later, Elise got off the line with Slocum, grabbed her bag and told her secretary she'd be out of pocket for a couple of hours. "Block off my morning, though," she said. "I'll be taking Mr. Slocum out to a plantation house. Just rearrange any conflicts and put them in the computer. I'll check for updates."

"Pager or cell phone?" Yvette asked.

"Pager," Elise said. "But call me on the cell if there's an emergency."

With very little time to spare, Elise raced home. She kicked off her shoes at the front door and ran down the hall to the guest suite. They'd chosen this house because they liked the open floor plan in the front of the T-shaped home. The back was traditional New Orleans style, with all the rooms opening to a garden courtyard. Galleries ran the length of the back side. In happier times, they'd dined alfresco and danced in the moonlight there.

Standing in the bedroom doorway, Elise sighed. Jerome had so much stuff! There was no way she could get all of this put back before he and Auntie Joe arrived. If it were any other time she'd call her best friend. Under normal circumstances, Nina would hop to her aid. The two of them could turn this place around in no time.

But not even Nina knew about the extent of the trouble between Elise and Jerome, so she couldn't very well ask her to help move Jerome's stuff back into her bedroom. Two weeks before her best friend's wedding was definitely not the time to dump her personal troubles on Nina.

A quick glance at her wristwatch didn't bode well. After the time spent talking to Slocum, and then sitting in traffic on Interstate 10, Elise now had less than an hour to work magic on the house. Praying that Jerome had gotten tied up in the same traffic she had, Elise dashed to his closet.

Suits and shirts and shoes. Ties and belts. She raced between the guest room and the master bedroom. She didn't bother to hang anything. She just dumped loads of Jerome's stuff on the floor in her closet and ran back for more.

She scooped T-shirts and shorts and socks from his drawers. Armloads of whites overflowed in her arms as she ran down the hall. She dumped that load, grabbed a laundry basket and dashed back to Jerome's room. After snatching up a stray sock here and there on the hallway floor, she quickly moved to his bathroom. Deodorant, aftershave, toothpaste, combs, mouthwash. All of that she swept into the laundry basket.

An open bottle of Drakkar Noir crashed to the floor. Elise swore.

The cologne splattered, but the bottle didn't break. She grabbed a towel from the rack and tried to wipe up the spilled scent. Spying the top, she made fast work of sealing the bottle, then dropped it in the laundry basket with his other toiletries.

A sharp tug on the vanity drawer pulled it free. The drawer was jammed with all sorts of whatnot: toenail clippers, a hand buffer, more combs, doo-rags.

"God, Jerome. You have more junk than me."

Elise carried the laundry basket into his bedroom and set it on a chair. She took a careful look around the room. All of his stuff was in big moving boxes, carefully labeled: BOOKS, CDs, BED/BATH LINENS, COLLEGE, GYM CLOTHES. Elise paused and peered closer at one box.

Labeled PHOTOS/MEMENTOS, that box drew her. She opened the flaps. On top was a photo from their wedding day. The sterling silver frame, a gift to Jerome from Elise, was engraved: "I'll always love you."

Unexpected tears welled in Elise's eyes. She'd lived her entire life trying to prove to her family that she could rise above the limitations they put on her. She'd proved them all wrong. She'd graduated from high school without any babies hindering her progress. She'd gone to college despite being the poorest student on campus. She'd graduated, moved out of the projects and hadn't looked back since.

Now, though, all the predictions they'd made had come true: *"You can't keep a man like that."*

"Girl, you just a passing thang for him. With those big hips and that dark skin, he just wanna taste of something different. He gonna wake up one day and go looking for one of them light, bright, damn near white society girls. And where dat gonna leave you?"

"Alone," Elise said. She'd done something about the wide hips; a constant regimen at the gym solved that problem. Jerome had married more than her brown-skinned features and her figure. He'd married a total woman, one he no longer wanted.

The pain of her failure as a wife cut her.

But anger replaced the tears. It took two to make a marriage. Despite the sentiment engraved on the frame, there was a mission at hand. She set the photograph aside so she wouldn't forget to position it in a conspicuous place. She closed the box and carried it to her bedroom.

Twenty minutes later, she heard Jerome call out. "Elise, honey. I'm home."

Elise jerked upright. She'd been draping a sheet over the boxes she'd managed to push to a back wall. Jerome hadn't called her "honey" in ages.

"I'm back here," she called. "I'll be there in just a sec."

She surveyed her handiwork. The boxes marked BOOKS and CDS she left out. They could claim those were headed to a thrift store. All the others she'd shifted so they looked like a wall tier—or at least a modern interpretation of one. With carefully arranged sheets, and a few knickknacks on top, the setup might fool a casual observer.

"Elise?"

"Coming, Auntie Joe."

A minute later she was enveloped in the arms and ample bosom of the woman nearest and dearest to Jerome. Auntie Joe had practically raised him. Her long dark hair was streaked with gray and plaited in two strands that were coiled around her head. Sometimes she wore it in a bun, but Elise thought this style made Auntie Joe look rather regal. Her half-glasses hung from a decorated chain at her neck. And she was, as always, clothed in one of the housedresses she favored, this one a pastel plaid with pockets. Comfortable walking shoes of the lace-up variety were on her feet. The older woman held Elise out at arm's length.

"You're looking good, child. Looking good."

"So do you, Auntie Joe. It's good to see you."

Auntie Joe glanced between Elise and Jerome. "Well," she said. "Aren't you gonna kiss your wife hello?"

Aghast, they stared at each other and then Auntie Joe. The big woman smiled and waved a hand. "No need to get shy around me. I know how you two are. The last time I was here you couldn't keep your hands off each other." She smiled, looking for all the world like a benevolent Buddha granting wishes.

Jerome turned to Elise. "Hey, hon," he said. To Elise, the words rang hollow. He leaned forward to place a kiss on her lips. At the last moment, Elise turned her head so the greeting landed just off the corner of her mouth.

Jerome cleared his throat and stuck his hands in his pockets.

Elise turned a too-bright smile on Auntie Joe.

The older woman narrowed her eyes at them.

"Auntie Joe, I was just getting your room ready for you. Would you like to take a nap?"

Auntie Joe reared back. The snug housedress stretched across her ample bosom. "Nap? Do I look like I need a nap? First this one is driving me all over the city like I've never been here before. Now you're talking about a nap. No, child. I don't need a nap. I want to visit a while with my favorite nephew and niece."

"A while?" Elise echoed.

Jerome pulled Elise to him and grinned. "Well, we want you to enjoy your visit."

Angling free of the embrace, as casually as she could, Elise said, "Auntie Joe, I put some coffee on in the kitchen for you and I was just changing the sheets in your room. Let me go finish that." With a trying-to-be-subtle jerk of her head, Elise nailed her husband. "Jerome, why don't you get

Auntie Joe some coffee, then help me with her bags?"

"That sounds like a great idea," he boomed. Grabbing his aunt's arm at the elbow, he steered her toward the great room. "Your call took us by surprise," he said.

"Um-hmm," Auntie Joe replied. But her gaze was on the hastily retreating Elise.

"What were you trying to do back there?" Jerome asked the moment he walked into his bedroom. "She's gonna guess something's up if you keep pulling away from me."

Elise was tugging the top sheet up on the bed. Jerome went to the other side and together they quickly finished making the bed.

Jerome nodded toward the newly constructed wall unit. "That's creative."

Elise didn't address the compliment. "You took my Nikki Giovanni and Maya Angelou books."

"They were signed to me."

"Hmph," was all she said in return. She fluffed pillows with unnecessary force, then reached for the pull on the bed-side table drawer. "Where's the remote?"

Jerome dove onto the bed, rolled over and quickly barred her way.

"Jerome, what are you doing? You messed up the bed."

He ignored her sharp tone, instead concentrating on avoiding a bigger problem. If Elise saw what he had in that drawer . . .

"Uh, it looks like you got everything," he said, blocking her access to the nightstand. "I'll get the remote control. You go entertain Auntie Joe."

With hands on hips, she eyed him. "We have got to set up some ground rules here. Did she happen to say how long 'a while' is?"

Jerome looked at his wife. Even angry, she was beau-tiful. This estrangement was killing him. As far as Jerome was concerned, the best thing that could have happened was Auntie Joe showing up. Her visit bought him some time. Not a lot. But maybe enough to try one more time to win Elise back.

"No," he said. "She didn't. My guess is she might stay until Nina and Ricky's wedding."

Elise visibly paled. "Jerome, that's two weeks. We can't pretend to be madly in love for two weeks."

Her pager went off before he had a chance to respond. Jerome scowled. More than once he'd been tempted to throw that thing into Lake Pontchartrain.

"Sorry," she said as she plucked the device from the waistband of her skirt. He watched while the all-too-familiar scene played out before him: Elise checking the number, then reading the digital message, using one manicured nail to advance the scroll function.

He waited to see who she'd put first: him or her clients.

"It's the office," she said. "I need to return this call."

The outcome was always the same. But Jerome was gonna get his two cents' worth in this time.

It irritated him that he was always her second choice, after work, after her precious clients. He was grateful that Auntie Joe's visit would force them together, but he was tired of the games with Elise. Maybe it was time to just declare this marriage over. If Auntie Joe was here, she already suspected as much.

"Elise, I can walk out there right now and tell Auntie Joe the truth."

She grabbed his hand. "No. You can't."

He leveled a questioning look at her, surprised at her intensity. Wasn't she the one who until now had been pushing to cut their losses and call it quits? "Why not? She's family. They're all going to know soon enough."

Elise shook her head. He could see her considering and discarding her options. Jerome would have given anything to know what thoughts were racing through her mind.

"We can't. Not yet," she said. "Especially not Auntie Joe. I don't want her to think I . . ." She paused. "She'll be . . . she'll be so disappointed in us."

Jerome's mouth puckered. She'd been about to say something else, something important, but as usual she'd edited out the truth about what she was really feeling.

"So let's prove to her that her vibe was wrong," he said. "If we turn on the charm, she'll see that we're still happy together and then she'll pack up and go home."

"You think?"

She didn't at all look convinced.

Jerome couldn't blame her. He wasn't sure if even *he* was buying that line. It was all but impossible to pull a fast one on Auntie Joe. But right now, it was all he had. He nodded.

Elise sighed. "All right. But we have to talk about how we're going to pull this off." She indicated the pager. "I have to finish up some things at the office. But tonight . . ."

Jerome nodded. "You better get out there before she gets suspicious."

With one more uncertain look at him, Elise shrugged. She smoothed out the comforter that Jerome had wrinkled, then went to tend to Auntie Joe.

Jerome heaved a sigh of relief. He tiptoed to the door, made sure Elise was gone, then closed the door and went back to the nightstand and opened the drawer. The remote was there all right, but so were all of the love letters Elise had ever sent him.

And on top of the letters was a snapshot, one of three very sexy photos of Elise. Shot by one of her girlfriends, she'd given them to him for his birthday the first year they were married. The poses were pure seduction. His favorite was a back shot. Elise sat on her knees on a pallet of red satin. A long strand of pearls draped down the middle of her bare back. She looked over her shoulder, straight at the camera—straight at him. Her mouth parted just so and her full lips beckoned his kiss.

He always got hard just looking at that image.

He was lusting after his own wife.

"Wife for now," he said.

Their estrangement had happened so gradually that neither really noticed. Or if they had noticed, neither had had time to deal with the fact that they didn't talk to each other, they didn't laugh together anymore. They barely did anything together except call the same address home.

Being honest with himself, Jerome had to admit he was as much at fault as she was for neglecting their relationship. He'd spent too many nights making work his priority rather than Elise. Too many days spent chasing stories and directing his staff at the magazine and not enough time cherishing his bride.

Jerome's fervent prayer—to be granted one more chance to make it right with Elise—seemed to have been answered. And just in the nick of time, he thought. He was supposed to move out of the house on Saturday. Now he had a reprieve.

He glanced up toward the ceiling. "Thanks for sending Auntie Joe."

With a final look at the photograph, he slipped it and the other two snapshots as well as the letters into his inside suit jacket pocket.

Again surveying Elise's quick turnaround on the bedroom, he nodded. The guest room was ready for its special guest.

And tonight he'd spend the night where he belonged. In bed with his wife.

CHAPTER 2.

THAT night Elise stood at the foot of the bed contemplating what to do.

The bed was big enough for them to sleep comfortably without ever coming in contact with each other. Of course, that had never happened and Elise knew her body. It had been humming for Jerome since a week ago when he'd crept into her room in the middle of the night. At first she'd thought it was a dream, but when Jerome's mouth closed over her, she'd known it was all too real.

First he'd teased her with his finger; then his mouth had closed over her breast and it was all she could do not to moan out loud. Heat washed over her and her body moistened for him. She wanted him to stroke her harder, to take her to that place where she forgot everything but his name and the touch of his hand, his mouth, his body. She wanted to open herself to him. But all too soon, he'd pulled away. And she'd spent the rest of the night in frustrated agony.

Then, like now, she ached for him.

Would it be wrong to have sex with the man who was almost her ex?

Elise shook her head. She wasn't up to moral and ethical dilemmas, particularly not when an even thornier, hornier one was staring her in the eye.

She and Jerome hadn't shared a bed in more than six weeks. It had been longer still since they'd made love. Jerome's sex drive was high. Had he been getting what he needed physically somewhere else?

That thought sent a chill down her spine.

Elise didn't want to imagine him making love to another woman. But the fact was, he probably was. He'd wasted no time announcing that he'd found a place. She'd seen his open appointment book on the kitchen counter, spotted the address and checked out his little love nest. He was all ready to cozy up to his new squeeze. She could just imagine what the woman looked like. Probably like all his old girlfriends: She'd be tall and slim with skin the color of honey, hazel eyes and a head full of long, wavy hair. In other words, she'd be everything Elise wasn't.

Then why'd he come to you last week?

"I don't know."

"Don't know what?" Jerome asked as he walked into the bedroom.

Elise whirled around, clutching her chest. "You scared me."

Jerome stopped in his tracks. She watched as his gaze took in everything about her, from her bare legs on up.

Before getting lost in thoughts of Jerome and his potential girlfriends she'd been trying to figure out what to wear to bed—a negligee or a comfy cotton sleepshirt. The cotton was winning in the mental battle; but, still undecided after coming out of the shower, she'd dried and powdered herself and slipped into a short silk wrapper.

She saw and recognized the desire in his eyes. The look was one that never failed to make heat pool in Elise's midsection. "I . . ." Her mouth was suddenly dry. "I . . ."

Her own gaze traveled the lean, hard length of him. Jerome had obviously been putting in time at the gym. It showed. Muscles bunched in his arms and the hard ridges of his pecs. And that flat stomach appealed on all sorts of levels. He'd changed from work clothes to a white T-shirt and jeans. His feet were bare.

She tried to tamp down her desire. But she wanted him. And it was clear from the bulge in his jeans that he wanted her.

She licked her lips and willed her vocal cords to work. "Jerome, we . . ."

He closed the gap between them.

The next moment, his lips covered hers.

The kiss was like coming home after a long journey to a distant land. She drank from him, then lifted her arms and draped them around his neck. Jerome pulled her closer. His mouth molded hers. She gave back as much as she got and then some.

His hands stroked down, cupping her behind, pulling her even closer to his erection. He shifted, letting her feel him. Elise rocked up against him and moaned his name.

A knock sounded on the open door, followed by, "Excuse me, children."

Elise and Jerome jumped apart as though they were schoolchildren caught doing nasty things in the coat closet.

"Uh, Auntie Joe . . ." Jerome tried to position himself behind Elise. She, busy blushing and tugging on the end of her robe, kept scampering away.

"Hi, Auntie Joe. We were just . . ." Elise waved one hand while clutching her short robe together with the other. "I mean, we were . . ."

Auntie Joe chuckled. "You were just a-doin' what comes natural," she said. "I didn't mean to disturb you."

Jerome went to the other side of the bed. Elise nervously perched herself on the edge.

"Is there something you need?" she asked. "Bath oil? More towels?"

"No, child. I just came to give you this. A little something from me to you."

The rectangular box was about a foot long and wrapped in what looked like blue-and-green calico with a raffia bow on the top short end. Elise accepted the gift and glanced over her shoulder at Jerome. "Thank you," she murmured.

"Tomorrow's Friday," Jerome said. "I can probably get out of the office early if there's something you'd like to do."

"No. I'm not here to put you out. Don't change your schedules on my account. I have plenty to do and lots of people to see while I'm in the city," Auntie Joe replied.

Jerome walked over to the nightstand and picked up a

set of keys. "If you need to go anywhere, the Lexus is at your disposal."

"I know how to get around on the buses."

Jerome pressed the keys into her hand. "We wouldn't hear of it, right, Elise?"

Elise put the gift box on the nightstand and joined them. "That's right, Auntie Joe."

"But you just have one car, no?"

Jerome touched his brow, clearly embarrassed. "Uh, no. We have several."

"A Lexus, huh?" Auntie Joe said with a grin. "I'll be sitting pretty."

Jerome leaned forward and kissed his aunt on the cheek, then took Elise's hand in his. Her gaze shot up at him, then, remembering the role they were supposed to be playing, she smiled at him, placed her open hand on his chest and leaned into his body. She heard his quick intake of breath.

"We want your stay with us to be as pleasant as possible," she said.

Auntie Joe looked at them and smiled. "Seeing you two together is what makes me happy." Suddenly the older woman frowned and leaned forward. "Where be your wedding rings?"

"Uh . . ." Jerome started.

"I take the set off when I bathe," Elise smoothly replied.

Leveling a gaze at them, "Hmm," was all Auntie Joe said.

Elise smiled sweetly. Jerome pressed a kiss on top of her head. "Well, we'll see you in the morning."

Apparently taking the hint, Auntie Joe looked at them, looked at their bed, then said, "Good night." She pulled the door closed behind her as she left.

Elise snatched her hand off Jerome and put some space between them.

"This isn't going to work."

"What's not going to work?"

Elise waved a hand, encompassing the bedroom, but her gaze eventually landed on the king-size bed. "This charade."

She went to her jewelry chest and pulled out the diamond solitaire and band of her wedding set. She jammed the rings on her finger.

"Elise," he said, slowly approaching her. "I promise I won't do anything you don't want me to do."

Her brow furrowed. "You're playing your word games with me," she accused.

"I'd gladly sleep on the floor," he said. "As a matter of fact, I see you made a pretty nice pallet for me in the closet."

Sincerely contrite, Elise rushed to the closet. "I'm so sorry. I meant to come back and get everything up. I was in such a hurry this afternoon trying to—"

His hand on her wrist silenced her. She looked up at him.

"I know, Elise. I was just messing with you. I got everything put up and away. It looks like we share a bathroom and closet." He didn't say it, but Elise saw in his eyes and felt in the gentle caress on her arm that he'd added "and a bed" to that list.

His fingers trailed down her rings and he stroked the soft skin of her hand. "It's nice to see you wearing these again. Even if it's just for show."

Elise licked dry lips and tried to ignore the sparks of sensation shooting through her at his gentle touch. Jerome wasn't playing fair. But did she really want him to? It would take next to nothing to press her body against his, telling him without words that she wanted his touch. Craved it, actually. She cleared her throat and with some effort tried to clear her mind. "You said you'd sleep on the floor?" She couldn't keep the hopeful note out of her voice.

"I could," he said, folding his arms across his chest. "But it seems pretty silly. Both of us have to work tomorrow. The bed is big enough to accommodate two. Besides, what if Auntie Joe knocks again? It wouldn't do to have her see me on the floor."

Auntie Joe disturbing them again seemed a remote possibility as far as Elise was concerned. After seeing the two of them locked together like sex-starved newlyweds, Auntie Joe would assume they planned to make love all night.

Elise sighed. She definitely remembered *those* nights.

Uncertain, she looked over at the large comfortable bed.

They'd bought the bedding and the wrought-iron filigree headboard right after they bought the house. Her old queen-size bed had been relegated to the guest room, and his went to a thrift shop.

They could be adult about this. If he thought it could work, she did too.

"All right, Jerome," she said. "If we're going to be separated, we need to be separated. That means no . . . you know," she said, wagging a finger.

He grinned. "Even if we both want . . . you know?" he said, mimicking her finger motion.

"It's different for a woman," she said.

"How so?"

"Women need. . . ." She stopped, shook her head and started again. "I need an emotional connection, Jerome. We know our bodies want it, but I need more than a physical release. And I'm sure you're getting what you need out there somewhere." She said the last part as if it didn't hurt. She'd failed in the matrimony department. So if he knew she was already aware of his need for female companionship, so much the better.

His gaze met hers and he reached for her hand. "There's no other woman for me, Elise."

He said the words with such conviction that she wanted to believe him. But wouldn't he say that to convince her to have one more tussle beneath the sheets—for old times' sake?

She pulled her hand away from him, then got up and walked into their big dressing room. A moment later she emerged wearing a soft blue cotton T-shirt that came to her knees. She didn't look at him at all as she climbed into bed on her side and turned out the bedside lamp.

"Good night, Jerome."

His grunt could have been a word, but Elise doubted it.

A few minutes later, she felt him get into bed. As he pulled the covers up around his shoulder he seemed a mile away.

"What did Auntie Joe give us?"

Elise sat up. "Oh, I forgot." She clicked on her lamp and reached for the package. She pretended not to notice when he scooted closer as she unwrapped the fabric and ribbon.

"It smells good, whatever it is," she said.

A moment later, a thick aromatic candle was revealed. "Umm, smell that," she said, holding it out to Jerome.

He took a sniff, then closed his eyes. "It's like . . . I don't know."

Elise flipped the sheet aside, opened the nightstand and rifled around for some matches. Finding them, she lit the candle and placed it on the bedside table.

"That smells wonderful. She remembered we liked candles."

Jerome didn't say anything. She turned toward him. "Something wrong?"

He smiled, but it seemed forced. "No."

"All right, then," she said, fluffing up a pillow. "Good night."

For a long time they lay there, both still and stiff, pretending to be enjoying the scent of the candle.

"You won't forget to blow it out?" she said eventually.

"I won't forget."

"All right. Well, good . . . Oh, I said that."

"Yes. You did."

Elise turned several times, trying to get comfortable and failing miserably. After a while, she found a position.

Jerome watched the flame burn. His body still ached with the want of Elise. He knew just how hot she'd burn in his arms. She was just a few feet away, yet the invisible divide that separated them was much greater.

As he watched the flame and Elise, he wondered what potion Auntie Joe had used to make the aromatherapy candle. He knew his aunt, and he knew she'd go to any length if she felt they needed a boost from whatever powers she possessed.

When he was certain she'd finally drifted to sleep, he blew out the candle and settled down. It was going to be a long, hard night.

He knew he wasn't going to get any sleep, not with a soft and perfumed Elise next to him. So instead of paying attention to the part of him that mightily objected to being ignored, he thought about what she'd said.

I need an emotional connection, Jerome. . . . I need more than a physical release.

She'd provided him with the information he needed to seduce her. But like Elise, Jerome too wanted more than the relief he knew he'd find sheltered within her lithe body. He wanted the camaraderie they'd shared in the early part of their relationship. He wanted the laughter and the conversation and the times when no words needed to be spoken at all. He wanted back all of the things that made Elise different from the women he'd dated before he met her.

In essence, Jerome wanted an emotional connection with his wife.

He glanced over at her. She was hugging the edge of the bed in her effort not to touch him.

On a weary sigh, he closed his eyes and tried to get some rest.

Elise woke the next morning to a thick erection pressed into her buttocks. She moaned her satisfaction, then wiggled in closer, enjoying the feel of it, anticipating the moment when . . .

Her eyes flew open.

She and Jerome were spooned together in the middle of the bed.

"Jerome!"

"Hmm?"

He nuzzled her neck and wrapped an arm around her waist, effectively trapping her within his warm embrace. His large hand molded around a breast and gently kneaded the pliant flesh. Recognizing the touch, her nipple hardened and puckered against the thin cotton of her sleepshirt.

Elise stopped struggling and allowed herself a moment of sweet ecstasy. She placed her hand on top of his and slowly guided it down, across her rib cage and stomach. And then lower.

Her breath caught when he touched her at the juncture of her thighs.

He murmured near her ear. "Elise, if we don't stop now it's going to be too late."

She closed her eyes, remembering all the times they'd come together in the morning, making love before dawn. "I know," she whispered. But she didn't move.

"Elise?"

He was asking permission, but Elise wasn't interested in words. She shifted and took his hand, guiding it straight to the spot that ached for only him.

She heard his breath come out in a shaky gasp and Elise knew he wanted her as much as she wanted him. She was ready for him, but Jerome had always been a man with a slow hand. It was maddening and oh, so delicious.

He didn't disappoint her either.

He moved down the bed and positioned himself between her legs. Her knee bent allowing him access. His hands caressed the soft curve of her thigh, the indentation at her knee. Then he moved to her inner thigh, stroking her, slow and easy, up and down until Elise whimpered his name. She'd always thought it would be wonderful to have Jerome pet her like this for hours on end, but it had been so long and Elise craved another, more intimate touch.

"Please. More."

She heard his soft chuckle at her plea, and a moment later his mouth replaced his hands. Elise's hips bucked off the bed and she cried out his name as tremors of release wracked her body. She clutched at the sheets and moaned, riding the waves of her orgasm.

But a few moments later instead of the comforting weight of his body on hers, she felt him move away from her, and her moan became a groan. She realized just what she'd done—what she'd not only allowed him to do, but begged him to do. His erection had been a morning thing, and she'd turned the moment into something else.

He hadn't really wanted her, but he wasn't about to reject a gift so freely offered.

She got up and escaped to the bathroom.

As she showered and dressed for work, Elise's thoughts kept straying to that moment in the bedroom. She was ever so grateful that in remodeling the house, they'd paid lots of attention to the master suite. Jerome had a small shower he could use, so she could hide out in here as long as she needed to.

"Too bad we didn't build a door to outside from here," she muttered.

She eventually had to leave the safety of her bathroom, though. She knew that. She just didn't want to.

If she'd been embarrassed to face Jerome, she found herself equally as embarrassed to walk into her kitchen and see a full breakfast waiting, courtesy of Auntie Joe. Elise bit back a groan. As a guest, Auntie Joe shouldn't have had to make her own breakfast. Elise was apparently not only a lousy wife but a poor hostess as well.

The woman greeted her with a wink and a broad smile. "Good morning, *chérie*."

Elise kissed her on the cheek. "Auntie Joe, you shouldn't have. I have an early meeting with a client."

Despite the wonderful smells of crisp bacon at the stove and cinnamon from the oven, there was no way she'd be able to sit through a cozy breakfast under the all-too-knowing eyes of Jerome's aunt.

Auntie Joe just chuckled. Today's housedress was a blue floral print. "You know I cook whenever I'm in a kitchen." She held out a plate of biscuits dripping with butter. "You sure I can't tempt you?"

Elise licked her lips. "Well, maybe just a little."

Auntie Joe offered her a small bread plate and Elise reached for a biscuit.

"Ah, good morning, ladies," Jerome said as he walked into the kitchen.

Elise couldn't meet his eyes. What would he think of her? She'd come apart at just his touch, and he, Mr. Cool, hadn't been affected in the least. She reached for a paper towel and quickly wrapped the biscuit in it. "I'll just take this to go. I'll call you, Auntie Joe. Have a good day."

When the door closed behind her, Auntie Joe slowly turned to face Jerome. Her eyes narrowed and with slow, deliberate steps she advanced on her nephew, hands on ample hips.

"A blind man can see things ain't right around here. So,

you plan to tell me what's wrong between you and Elise or do I have to beat it out of you?"

Throughout the day as she drove dot-com millionaire Jonathan Slocum out to Vacherie and back, Elise's mind kept straying back to the night she had spent with Jerome. With Jerome next to her in bed she had found it almost impossible to fall asleep. When she finally did, it was to thoughts of *what if*. For example, what if they made love again?

It wasn't until she'd awakened nestled in his arms that she realized that that had been the first good night's sleep she'd had in weeks. Despite her doubts about their relationship, a satisfied smile crept along her mouth.

Back at her office, Elise checked her Palm Pilot. She and Jerome were supposed to have dinner with their best friends that night. As best man and matron of honor for the upcoming wedding, Elise and Jerome had decided to put forth a united front for Nina and Ricky. The farce would have been difficult enough to pull off without adding Auntie Joe into the mix.

"Call Nina," Elise said to her voice-activated cell phone.

The line rang three times, then Nina's voice said, "You've reached my machine. You know the drill." *Be-eep*.

"Hey girl. I know we're supposed to get together tonight. But Jerome's Aunt Josephine showed up. I don't want to leave her at the house—"

"Hello! Hello, Elise. Hold up."

Elise heard the crackle and loud-pitched whine of the answering machine as Nina turned it off. When she got back on the line, she was out of breath.

"Elise, you there?"

"I'm here. What are you doing?"

"Sweatin' to the oldies, girl. Richard is working me. I've got five more pounds to go for that dress to look the way I want it to."

Elise smiled. She well remembered the ten pounds she'd sweated off before her own wedding.

"What were you saying?"

Elise explained about the surprise visit.

"Is this *the* Auntie Joe, the high priestess?"

Closing her eyes, Elise expelled a long-suffering sigh. "I wish you wouldn't call her that."

"Girl, you have lived here for three and a half years. You need to stop denying what's all around you."

They'd had this particular conversation many times. Elise put no stock in voodoo mumbo-jumbo—unless it helped sell a house to a client who wanted to know what spirits also may have been inhabiting a property. Nina, who was born and raised in New Orleans, left nothing to chance.

"Bring her along. It'll be great," Nina said, a smile in her voice. "I'll call the restaurant and add another person to the reservation."

As it turned out, though, Auntie Joe had already made plans to visit some friends that night. That left Elise and Jerome together bickering in their bedroom.

"I don't have time for this, Jerome. You've already made me late."

"I've made *you* late? You're the one who's changed clothes three times."

They glared at each other across the dressing room they shared.

The phone rang, interrupting what would undoubtedly grow into a full-scale argument. They both turned toward the telephone. With a glance at Elise, Jerome, who was closer, punched the speakerphone button. "This is Jerome."

"You answer the phone like you're at the office," came the voice floating around them. "You need to lighten up, my brother. We leave that stuff at the magazine. All work's no good for the blood pressure."

"That's right," said a female voice, also on the line. "You two are supposed to be our rocks right now."

Elise and Jerome glanced at each other. A guilty flush made Elise turn away. Jerome bowed his head and rubbed his eyes.

Elise sat at her vanity and began to put on her jewelry. She clipped a large pearl-inset earring on one ear and tilted her head to attach the other. The thick waves in her shoulder-length weave swayed, giving Jerome a clear view of her neck. He stared at her reflection, then took a seat in the cane-back chair near his shoe tiers.

"Hello. Is anybody there?" the male voice on the phone said.

The female voice giggled. "Maybe they were getting a little early evening action and we interrupted."

Elise's head shot up. With the exception of that night when Jerome had slipped into her room while he thought she was sleeping—and, of course, this morning—there'd been none of *that* going on between them.

"We're here," Jerome said. Their gazes connected for a moment. This time, it was Jerome who looked away first. "We were just getting dressed."

"Come on, y'all," Nina whined. "Don't be late. Our dinner reservations are for seven. Don't make us lose our table."

Jerome looked at Elise, who was reaching for a strand of pearls. She lifted them to her neck. Jerome got up. "We'll be there," he assured their friends. He took the pearls from her hands.

"Jerome, what are you doing?"

"Shh," he said, as he positioned the ends of the strand.

Their gazes connected in the mirror. Some of the old fire smoldered between them. Without a word, Elise lifted her hair. Jerome bent to the task of clasping the pearls at her neck. He took his time about it. His skin lightly caressed the fine hair at her nape. He leaned forward, lower, watching her watch him. When she didn't object, he placed a kiss at the back of her neck.

"Jerome. Don't."

Sighing, he stuffed his hands in the pockets of his slacks and stepped away from her.

A giggle sounded. "I told you we were interrupting them."

Jerome sighed and closed his eyes. "Good-bye, Nina."

"Bye, Jerome," the woman on the phone singsonged. "Elise, girl, make it a quickie. If we lose that table . . ."

The rest of the admonition was cut off when Jerome disconnected the line.

Elise and Jerome looked at each other.

"We need to tell them," Jerome said.

"I know. I just don't want to spoil their day. It's just two more weeks until the wedding. We can tell them after they get back from their honeymoon."

Elise remembered that they'd barely seen any of the island on her own honeymoon because they'd spent most of their time wrapped up in the bliss of hot sex and new love.

It had been a while since they loved each other the way they did then. No one guessed, though. To all of their friends, particularly Nina Tippens and Ricky Shoregood, they kept up the facade of loving couple. The masks they wore outside easily shielded the gulf that was the reality of their lives together at home.

"About this morning . . ." Elise began.

"You look great," Jerome said over her.

Elise flushed. "I . . . Jerome. This isn't right."

He walked around her, taking in the curves of her body. "Everything looks right to me."

"Jerome, stop it," she snapped. Then, on a softer, gentler note, she added, "Please." She shook her head, trying to make sense of things. "What happened this morning was a mistake. I shouldn't have let you . . . We shouldn't have . . ." She flushed again and looked away. "I shouldn't have encouraged you."

When he didn't say or do anything, Elise glanced up. "We're going to be late for dinner."

For a long moment, Jerome stared at her. "What happened to us, Elise?"

Elise looked at her husband. He was still as gorgeous as he was the day they'd met. But now, he was just as much a stranger to her as he was that very first day. "I don't know, Jerome. But isn't it time we just cut our losses?"

CHAPTER 3

"I disagree," Jerome said. "There's a lot still good about us."

She faced him, arms folded across her midsection. "I don't know you anymore, Jerome. We're not the same people we were back then. We have different goals."

"All relationships go through rocky periods. We're just having one."

Elise closed her eyes. "Jerome, this is difficult enough. I have a lot going on at work and I . . ."

"Elise, look at us. Look around this place. We have everything, more than we can possibly use. We have money in the bank, art on the walls, three luxury vehicles in the garage. There's more to life than working to buy more stuff."

She rounded on him. "That's easy for you to say, Mr. Never Wanted for Anything. Everybody didn't grow up the way you did. All your life you've had things I couldn't even dream about back in those projects. You don't know what it's like to have nothing. Nothing!" Her eyes flashed with all the anger and hurt that rolled through her. "So don't you lecture me on what's enough. You don't know the definition of the word."

Snatching up her handbag from the vanity, Elise walked out of the bedroom, her head held high.

Inside, though, she was in a million pieces, each one a dagger crucifying her already wounded spirit. The old taunts haunted her.

Ghetto girl, you can't keep a man like that.

Look at her, who she think she is? Done got herself some college and think she better than everybody else.

You'll be back, Elise. We gon' put some of this government cheese in the freezer for you so you have sumthin' to eat when you move back to Perry Homes.

The memory of the day she'd left Atlanta for good was the one that propelled her, motivated her to work like a dog, putting in the hours, learning all she could about real estate. Along the way, she stockpiled money and possessions as if they were all going to be snatched away at any moment.

But now, now those hateful predictions from her so-called friends were coming true. Jerome Gregory was a golden boy; his Creole mother's roots dated back to old New Orleans. That he'd fallen in love with her—had chosen *her!*—over all the other women who'd been chasing him for years had always been a source of amazement for Elise. At five foot four, Elise could hardly claim to be statuesque. She was far from dark-skinned, but neither could she pass the paper bag test of the old families of New Orleans, families whose mixed blood included French, Native American and African.

She told herself her very difference from all the other women he knew was what initially attracted Jerome to her. She was from somewhere else and she brought a different perspective to his world. Those were the things Elise wanted to believe were true. And when she stopped believing those things in this place where skin tone and eye color and hair quality meant so much to those who were in affluent black society, that was when she began to "improve" herself.

So she'd further toned her body with exercise, inserted contacts to lighten her brown eyes and sat for hours in the hair salon getting a full weave integrated into her former short bob. She could swing it and flip it with the best of them. But a marriage needed more to sustain it than physical features.

A good marriage needed shared interests and goals to survive.

Honesty, trust, compassion and fidelity. Those things were equally as important as physical attraction.

The fact of it was they were good in bed. Had been from

the very first. And now, that was all that remained—at least as far as Jerome was concerned.

Standing in the hallway, breathing heavily, Elise counted up all her failures.

First, Jerome, then what? Her home?

She loved this house, but if she tried to swing the mortgage payments by herself, the money she had would quickly be eaten up. What would be next? Her furniture and clothes? She shopped at the best boutiques, but she'd have to sell her clothes to make ends meet. Before long, she'd be back, back in the projects where she started.

Where she belonged?

Elise's face contorted at that thought. Tears streaked down the carefully applied makeup she'd just spent thirty minutes putting on. Elise dashed into the powder room, sat down on the commode and gave in to the tears she'd been holding back for so long.

Outside the half bath, Jerome put his head on the door. He hadn't planned for them to end up in yet another argument. He wasn't even sure what this one was about. The one thing he did know was that the sound of her crying tore at his heart.

"Elise. Elise, please don't cry. I'm sorry."

"Go away, Jerome."

He placed an open palm on the door. "Elise, please come out."

"Go to dinner. Tell Nina I have a headache."

He heard the medicine cabinet door open and close and then water running. "Elise, a good meal will do you good and Nina always makes you laugh."

Elise opened the door, a frown marring her face. "I'm not in the mood to laugh, Jerome."

He reached for her hands, then pulled back when she took a small step away from him.

"I'm not going to be able to keep up this farce with Auntie Joe," she said. "I can barely keep it up now, let alone through a dinner with Miss Perception and Mr. Sensitivity."

Jerome smiled at the nicknames for Nina and Ricky. This time, he did take her hand. When she didn't immediately pull back, he claimed that small moment as a victory.

"We'll keep the evening short. I'll pack a bag and spend the night at a hotel downtown. We can come up with something to tell Auntie Joe later."

Jerome wanted her to say that that wasn't necessary, that they could and would work through their problems. But Elise didn't say anything at all. She turned big brown eyes up at him. The tears that still glistened there made him want to cry.

"Let's not fight," he said, softly. "We'll go to dinner, put on a show for Nina and Ricky, then come home. It'll be over before you know it."

What he didn't tell her was the plan he'd come up with to woo his wife. Without out-and-out saying that they were separated, he'd explained to Auntie Joe that they were a little stressed right now.

She'd simply said, "Um-hmm," and then told him that he needed to do what he did in the beginning.

At first, Jerome wasn't sure what she meant. When he'd actually asked her for clarification, she'd simply said, "You know what you have to do. Look within, Jerome. Look within."

It had taken him all day to figure it out. His mind had been elsewhere in every meeting at the magazine. Jerome was half afraid to go into the office Monday morning for fear that he'd approved some major expenditure or in-depth project during the forward planning meeting. If he had, he'd deal with that later. The most important thing to him now was winning Elise's heart all over again. Despite Auntie Joe's assurances that she could prepare a special love potion, Jerome didn't want to win Elise back via voodoo. He wanted her one hundred percent the old-fashioned way: head over heels in love.

And so, tonight, he'd launch his campaign.

"You've been awfully quiet tonight, Elise. Are you trying to make sure you don't slip up and spill some details about my shower?"

Elise smiled as she pushed some bread pudding around on her dessert plate. Dinner had been strained, at least for Elise. So she just let Nina carry the conversation. Details about the wedding went on and on. That was good because it kept Elise from having to say much.

The one thing Nina knew very little about, though, was the shower her matron-of-honor was hosting.

The bridal shower was next Saturday. Sparing no expense for her best friend, Elise had hired a caterer to handle the food and a decorator to transform her great room into a sultry pasha's tent. But Nina didn't know that, and wouldn't until the day of the shower.

"Don't say a word, Elise," Ricky told her. "I've been enjoying seeing her suffer."

Nina playfully jabbed Ricky with her elbow. "Hush, now."

"She's been on the case like a detective," Ricky reported. "Careful what you say, Elise."

Elise chuckled. Several of the guests had been trying to figure out what she had up her sleeves. She couldn't say because word would get back to Nina. The shower invitations simply told guests to "wear casual, loose-fitting clothes."

"I saw one of those invitations. I am not going to be doing aerobics at my bridal shower," Nina told her in no uncertain terms.

"You'll do whatever I have planned," Elise said.

"That's telling her," Ricky interjected with a laugh.

Jerome leaned toward Ricky. "A little advice from the best man," he said. "Don't egg them on."

Elise looked at Jerome, but didn't say anything.

"Elise, please. Just a hint, a little one. You're killing me."

"You'll love every minute of it."

"I better," Nina said. "I don't plan to do this again."

Jerome and Elise shared a quick guilty glance, then he reached for his water goblet and she took an even greater interest in pushing her bread pudding around.

They both missed the knowing look that passed between Nina and Ricky.

"So," Nina said loudly, snapping Elise and Jerome out of their distracted thoughts. As she looked up, Elise finally sampled the dessert she'd been playing with. "Tell me about

Auntie Joe. Is she going to be doing readings or blessings while she's at your house?"

Elise choked on the bread pudding.

Jerome patted her on the back and held a glass of water for her. It took a moment for Elise to catch her breath.

"Okay?" Jerome asked.

She nodded. "What in the world would make you think that?"

A conspiratorial smile broke across Nina's round face. "I told my mom. She just about went nuts. She said back in the day, Miss Josephine was one of New Orleans' most sought-after voodoo priestesses."

Elise rolled her eyes.

"Don't scoff. She has some powerful mojo working."

Jerome bit back a smile. "Nina, you know Elise doesn't cotton to that."

Nina waved a dismissing hand at him. "And you were supposed to acclimate her to our way of doing things."

He looked at his wife. "Elise is her own woman."

Something in his voice, maybe the admiring tone, made Elise look at him. Love shone bright in his eyes. She blinked, not trusting what she was seeing. When she looked again, he'd turned away and she didn't know if what she'd seen was real or not.

Nina reached for her hand. "Elise, Jerome. We'd like you to do something for us."

Elise had a sinking feeling she knew what was coming.

"Name it and it's yours," Jerome said.

Elise cringed at his magnanimity.

"Well, it's nothing so dramatic as your firstborn son or anything."

"That's good to hear," Elise muttered under her breath.

Jerome cut a glance at her but remained quiet.

"You ask them, Ricky," Nina said. She was practically bouncing up and down in her chair. "I'm too nervous."

"Baby, if you don't calm down you're gonna have to walk down the aisle pumped full of Xanax."

"Hush up and ask them."

With a patient sigh, Ricky turned to Elise and Jerome,

but his expression belied the light tone he was taking. Nina clasped his hand in hers.

"You know we're incorporating some of the old traditions in the wedding," Ricky said. When they nodded, he continued, "We'd like you to get Auntie Joe to bless us."

"It's a traditional job of the best man and maid of honor," Nina said.

"Well, I'm a matron of honor so that excludes—"

"You're it," Nina said.

Jerome's eyebrows furrowed. "I've never heard of this tradition."

Nina and Ricky exchanged a quick look.

"Uh, it's pretty easy," Nina said. "All you have to do is petition her on our behalf. She'll have you do some things and then, if she's sure we're supposed to be together, she'll give her blessing."

A chill ran up Elise's arms. Unbidden, a memory flickered through her consciousness. *Aunt Anva's prediction.*

She rubbed her bare arms trying to dispel the chill.

"What 'things' would we have to do?" Jerome said.

Ricky shrugged. "Whatever she says."

Jerome turned to his wife. "Elise?"

She shook her head, expelling a low, harsh breath. "I don't think so." She'd had a brush with that woo-woo stuff a long time ago, and it had freaked out her so much she had no intention of ever getting near it again.

Many people still adhered to the old ways. They believed strongly in the powers of the women reputed to be the city's most mysterious voodoo queens. Elise had heard the tales of Auntie Joe's spells and potions. Mostly terrified of ever having to cross paths with the woman, Elise had insisted that her own wedding be held in Jamaica, far away from the things she didn't understand. Her family members complained about the expense of flying to Jamaica for a wedding that could just as well have been held in New Orleans or Atlanta. Their grumbling stopped when Jerome's parents chartered a plane.

Elise had tried to run, but Auntie Joe had found her anyway—and had given her blessing to the union. Elise didn't like or feel comfortable with intangibles. As a child she'd had dreams and visions that left her shaken, even a little frightened. So she'd repressed that part of herself and tried to steer clear of all things mystical including "seances" in college in the dormitory that the other girls thought were fun. Later, after moving to Louisiana, the ban also included New Orleans–style voodoo.

It had crossed Elise's mind a time or two that the reason her marriage was in trouble now was that she and Jerome had defied the old ways. The path to ensure a long, happy union, according to practitioners of the old way, was to get the blessing of the obeah woman. Auntie Joe had held that particular position for more than fifty years, even though she'd officially retired to the country.

"Jerome, I don't think it's such a good idea."

"Please, Elise," Nina begged. "We want everything to be just right."

Elise sighed. She wanted everything to be perfect for Nina, too, but this was just too much.

"Nina, don't pressure her," Ricky said. "You know Elise doesn't feel comfortable with this."

Under the table, Jerome took Elise's hand and squeezed it. She cast unsure eyes at him. But more than anything the message of encouragement he sent under the table reassured her. It was a way they'd communicated in the early days, when one or the other needed a little boost.

To pull off the charade they were putting on for Nina and Ricky, Elise knew she'd have to do this.

Resigning herself to getting it over as quickly as possible, she took a deep breath. "I am not spending the night in any graveyards."

Nina and Ricky laughed. "No, we wouldn't ask you to do that."

"Just stand in the gap for us with Auntie Joe and get her blessing."

Elise nodded. Jerome squeezed her hand again. Ricky seemed to breathe a sigh of relief.

Nina jumped up and hugged Elise. "Thank you, so much. You won't regret it."

Elise sure hoped that was true.

When they arrived back at their house, Elise and Jerome sat in the car talking.

"The work of a best man and a matron of honor is never done. It won't be that bad," he promised.

"That's not what I'm worried about," Elise said with a glance toward the Lexus that meant Auntie Joe was home.

"What then?"

"We'll never fool her," Elise said. "I'm not a good enough actress and she has an unfair advantage."

"So you admit that some of the voodoo religion is real?"

Elise had never told him about her Aunt Anva and she didn't plan to share the story tonight either. "I admit that this whole voodoo thing gives me the creeps."

"I'll be there to hold your hand," he said.

She was silent for a moment. Then she murmured, "Thank you. I'd like that."

Auntie Joe heard the car pull up. Her work was almost done.

She hummed as she cleansed the house, performing the purification rituals that would rid the home of the bad energy she'd sensed from the moment she walked in.

"It's not too late, my children," she said. "It's not too late."

With great care and the prayers of several strong women, she'd prepared what was needed to mend the rift between her two favorite children. After glancing back to make sure the coast was still clear, she went into the master bedroom. She slipped the gris-gris bags under the pillows on Jerome and Elise's bed. They were filled with herbs, flower petals and some of her special potions.

"Tonight," she said with a knowing smile. "The magic will return."

She silently moved down the hall and into her room.

CHAPTER 4

"You may as well come in," Elise said. "If we're going to maintain this fiction we have to do it right."

"I'm not trying to pressure you, Elise."

"I know that. Besides," she said, pulling out the keys to her Jaguar, "I made a stop today and got something to help us."

She popped the trunk and Jerome peered at the big box. "An air mattress?"

"The salesman at the sporting goods store assured me it's very comfy."

"Uh, this is for you, right?"

She didn't even dignify that with a response. She also left Jerome to carry his new bed into the house.

When she didn't see Auntie Joe in the kitchen or watching television, Elise went to her bedroom and knocked on the open door.

"Auntie Joe, we're back from dinner. How was your evening?"

She was propped up in bed holding her stomach. "Oh, child. I'm so glad y'all are back. I didn't know what to do."

Elise rushed to her side. "What's wrong? Are you ill?" Elise's hands fluttered around Auntie Joe. "Jerome! Come quick. Jerome!

"You look kind of pale," Elise said. She looked around for the canvas tote bag Auntie Joe always carried. "Is there something I can get for you? Jerome!"

"Yeah?" he said, popping his head in the door.

Elise whirled around. "Auntie Joe. She's sick."

"Sick?" Jerome was at her side in an instant. He put his hand on her forehead, checked her pulse. "Is it your heart? Blood pressure? Do you have diabetes?"

Auntie Joe shook her head. "I'm feeling a little tired, children. Run down in the stomach. Do you think you could run a small errand for me?"

Jerome looked alarmed. To his knowledge Auntie Joe had never been ill a day in her life. "I can call Dr. Morrisette. I'm sure he'll make a house call just for you."

"Don't need a doctor, *chér*. Just a little bit of a healing root. I thought I had some with me, but I'm just plumb out. I called my friend Eliza Mae Botet. She has some but she don't drive, you know."

"Miss Eliza Mae," Jerome said. "She lives down in the Quarter, right? Just give me the address and I'll swing over there."

"Elise, she asked about you, too. Said she hasn't seen y'all in a while. Why don't you go together and say hello?"

"All right, Auntie Joe," Elise said. "We will. Are you sure you're going to be all right here until we get back?"

Auntie Joe held her stomach and moaned a bit. "I'm sure. Maybe a cup of sassafras tea."

Elise jumped up. "I'll get it for you, then we'll go get your root."

A few minutes later, with a cup of tea at her bedside, Auntie Joe assured them she'd be all right until they got back. With hugs and kisses all around, she shooed them out the door. When she was sure they were out of the house, she flung the sheets aside and hopped out of bed. She reached for the telephone and dialed her friend's number.

"Eliza Mae? They fell for it. They're on their way. Make it good now."

The term "cottage," loosely used in New Orleans to describe small, one-story structures sometimes of indeterminate age, was a stretch when it came to Eliza Mae Botet's place. The short, squat house could have been a nineteenth-century relic or it could have been built in the mid-twentieth century. Its blue shuttered windows desperately needed a coat or two or three of paint. There was no sign, no placard saying that one of the city's most respected voodoo priestesses operated under the roof. No flowers in overflowing containers greeted visitors or distracted from the austerity of the place.

"What do you think so far?" Jerome asked.

Elise glanced at the small house. "I'd say she knows she's sitting on a gold mine. This is prime real estate."

Jerome looked for a bell. Seeing none, he rapped on the door.

A moment later, a tall Creole woman opened the door. "Yes?" Her lush curves were covered in a form-fitting red sheath dress.

Elise and Jerome glanced at each other. "We're looking for Miss Eliza Mae. She's expecting us," Jerome said.

The woman nodded. "Right this way," she said, opening the door wide to let them in.

The foyer was surprisingly cool. And, typical of most houses in the French Quarter, the ramshackle exterior hid from view the treasures inside. The woman guided them into a parlor on the left.

"Make yourself comfortable," she said. "Miss Eliza Mae will make herself known to you shortly."

Elise cast a wary gaze up at Jerome. He reached for her hand and clasped it in his large warm one as they entered the parlor. Since this Eliza Mae was apparently one of Auntie Joe's voodoo friends, Elise was expecting beaded curtains, a crystal ball and maybe a skull or two with puffs of incense smoke drifting out of the eye and nose sockets.

What they encountered instead was a room appointed with antiques glowing with the patina of many years, richly upholstered sofas, good oil paintings of old New Orleans and fresh-cut flowers.

"It looks like *Architectural Digest* just did a photo shoot here," Elise whispered.

A deep chuckle sounded from behind them. "That's because they did. But it was two years ago."

Elise and Jerome whirled around at the voice. The woman was seated in a wing chair. Had she been there when they first walked in?

Jerome squeezed Elise's hand, apparently sensing her nervousness.

"Hello, Miss Eliza Mae," Jerome said. "It's been a while. This is my wife, Elise."

"You don't remember me, do you?"

Since she was clearly talking to Elise, Elise shook her head.

"I was at your wedding. In Jamaica."

"You were? I don't remember."

Eliza Mae just smiled. "Lots of people there. Very pretty ceremony with good energy."

The couple shared a glance, but didn't say anything.

"Have a seat. Carmen will bring tea for you and coffee for Jerome."

Elise eyed the woman called Eliza Mae. She was fairly certain she'd never seen her before. There weren't *that* many people at her wedding that she'd forget someone who sounded like and bore a striking resemblance to the late, great Barbara Jordan.

Jerome guided Elise to a sofa and they sat down. The seer rose and came forward. She stood in front of them, close enough that they had to peer up at her.

"You present a united front, but cracks show through the veneer."

Jerome cleared his throat. "Miss Eliza Mae, we came here for some roots for Auntie Joe."

The woman looked at him, then stared at Elise, looking for all the world as if she could see clear to the heart of her. Elise didn't like the feeling at all.

"I know what you came for," Eliza Mae said. "But I'm gonna give you what you need."

The older woman held out her hand. Elise glanced at Jerome, then up at the priestess.

"I don't bite."

At Jerome's imperceptible nod, Elise placed her hand in the woman's.

Warmth instantly surrounded her. Like a shield of protection and . . . Elise struggled to grasp the feeling Eliza Mae's work-worn hand evoked in her. Then, suddenly, she knew. At peace and at ease was what she felt, along with the warmth of being well and truly loved—three things she hadn't experienced in a long time.

"It can be like that again," Eliza Mae said. She released Elise's hand and took a seat in the chair facing them. Elise, feeling empty and bereft again, stared at her hand.

The woman who'd greeted them at the door slipped in with a coffee and tea service. After pouring for all three, she quietly left the room.

"So, Josephine tells me you are the head man in charge at *New Orleans Today* and that you, namesake," she said, addressing Elise, "are selling houses faster than people can write contracts."

"Yes," Jerome said, answering for both of them. He glanced at Elise, who sat erect on the sofa.

"So how come you haven't done a story on me? Even those folks at *Architectural Digest* found out about the treasure I have here."

"Your home *is* beautiful," Elise said. She reached into her small clutch purse, plucked out a business card and held it toward the woman. "If you ever think about selling, or maybe purchasing a second home . . ."

"Some things in life are more important and more precious than the busyness we label work."

Elise just sat there, her arm extended over the coffee table. Eliza Mae not only didn't take the proffered card, she rose. Elise placed the card on the table.

The priestess went to a curio cabinet and pulled out a small jewel-encrusted chest. She opened it and removed something, then returned to stand before Elise and Jerome.

"What you seek hasn't been lost," she said.

Elise primly clasped her hands together on top of her purse. Despite that brief moment when she'd felt *something*, all she was hearing and seeing now was a waste of time. They'd come here to get some root for Auntie Joe, not to be subjected to cryptic talk and bayou voodoo.

"Give me your hands," Eliza Mae said.

Jerome stood and held his hand out. Reluctantly, Elise followed suit, but only after a small nudge from Jerome. Eliza Mae placed something in each of their hands, then closed their fists before either could see what the other got. Clasping their hands together she bowed her head, mumbled what could have been a prayer, a curse or an incantation, and then told them to go in peace. Without another word, she was gone.

"Of all the . . ."

Jerome placed a finger over Elise's mouth. "Not here."

Shaking her head, she reached for her bag and then opened her fist. A small piece of paper lay there. On it was printed a single word: *Remember*.

At the door, the Creole woman handed them a brown paper sack. "For Miss Josephine," she said.

"That was weird," Elise said when they were safely back in Jerome's BMW.

Settling into the soft leather, she faced him as he navigated the narrow streets of the French Quarter to head back to the Interstate.

"I finally figured out the secret of this New Orleans voodoo thing."

Sparing a glance from the road and revelers in the street, he smiled. "What's that?"

"Talk in riddles, then mumble so people think you're putting a hex on them."

He laughed. "That could be a part of it. A lot of folks put great stock in the wisdom of their priestess."

"What wisdom? I didn't hear any wisdom." She paused for a moment, then said, "That's not true. I did feel something."

"What?"

"Energy," she said. "Peace."

Jerome took her hand. He squeezed it. They shared a smile and drove the rest of the way home in companionable silence.

They found Auntie Joe propped up in bed with a bowl of popcorn watching a rerun of *The Jeffersons*.

"I see you're feeling better," Jerome said.

"*Oui*, child. I had a bowel movement and things got right as rain."

Elise hid a smile behind her hand. "Here's your root from Miss Eliza Mae." She passed the paper sack to the bedridden woman.

Accepting the bag, Auntie Joe peered into it, then pulled out something that looked a whole lot like a hunk of sugarcane. "Did you have a nice visit with Eliza Mae?"

Jerome, busy propping pillows up, didn't see the sly look Auntie Joe sent his way. But Elise did. And she wondered if they'd been set up.

"It was very quick," she said. "We just exchanged a few pleasantries."

Auntie Joe frowned. "Hmm. Well, I'm gonna take a little bit of this, then call it a night. You should, too. It's almost midnight."

"Are you sure you have everything you need?" Jerome asked her.

"Stop hovering, boy. I said I'm fine. You all go on now. I'm gonna finish watching George Jefferson on the TV, then I'm gonna take these old bones on to sleep."

Jerome didn't look comfortable leaving her.

"I'm fine," she said. "Really. As a matter of fact, tomorrow night I'm gonna cook you two a special dinner just to show you."

"Auntie Joe, you don't have to do that," Elise said.

"I want to, so I will."

Elise smiled. "Yes, ma'am."

After saying their good nights, Elise and Jerome went to their bedroom.

"Was it just me or was she acting very strange?" Elise said.

Jerome shrugged out of his sport jacket. "Who knows? I wish she'd see a doctor, though. She probably has high blood pressure and doesn't know it. Maybe I should call Dr. Morrisette anyway." He headed toward the closet and dressing room.

At her vanity, Elise took off her jewelry. Her mind elsewhere, she didn't answer Jerome. She instead wracked her brain trying to remember if Eliza Mae Botet had been present for their wedding.

Elise opened her tiny clutch and pulled out the slip of paper the woman pressed into her hand.

Remember.

Unfortunately, that was about all she'd been doing

lately; remembering the pain and the fear of growing up in one of Atlanta's most notorious public housing projects. Remembering the ugly words hurled at her by women who called themselves her friends.

Remember the joy, Elise.

She whipped around. "Did you say something?"

"Huh?" Jerome's muffled voice drifted from the dressing room.

Shaking her head at her fancy, Elise turned back to stare at her reflection. There were good times to remember. Joy. Shared laughter. All of those memories infused her with warmth . . . and with hope. They could have that again.

A smile tilted the corners of her mouth.

Standing, she slipped out of her clothes and shoes and went to the closet. The sight that greeted her made her laugh out loud.

Jerome was tussling with a large piece of flexible blue plastic. The plastic was winning.

"What are you doing?"

"Making my bed," he said, his tone laced with surly frustration. He smoothed the material out, only to have it bunch up again and hit him in the forehead.

She laughed again.

He glanced up at her and laughed, too. "It's gonna take me until morning to figure out how this thing is supposed to work."

"The box said 'easy inflation'." Elise watched him, a small smile on her face.

She remembered shared responsibility. Shared rapture. She remembered their first Christmas together, an anniversary spent on a return trip to Jamaica. She missed the togetherness, the wholeness she felt when they were together. In essence, she realized, she missed Jerome's companionship.

"What did your little piece of paper say?"

"Huh?" The grunt barely qualified as a word. "You know what, Elise? This is supposed to have an air pump with it." He searched the box, but came up empty.

He'd taken her at her word about sleeping separate. Now though, she couldn't remember why that had seemed so important.

Right now, she wanted and needed to feel his arms around her. She yearned for his touch, the feel of his hard body pressed close to her soft one.

"Jerome."

He glanced up. She stood there in a black lacy bra and panties. The scalloped edge of thigh-high stockings graced the smooth skin of her thighs. She took a step forward, toward him. He rose, a question mixed with speculation in his eyes.

She held out a hand. "Hold me."

In the next moment, his arms enfolded her. They stood in the dressing room holding each other tight until slowly, inevitably, the embrace subtly changed.

His hand traced the outline of her face. Her finger caressed the curve of his ear.

He tilted his head to the left, hers went to the right. And in the middle, their lips met.

The kiss was soft and easy, a sweet but light confection very much like the first taste of cotton candy. Before long, the desire for more would overwhelm, but in the first few moments as their mouths became reacquainted, she reveled in the texture of his mouth, the sweetness of the kiss.

"I've missed you," she murmured against his mouth.

"I've missed you, too."

They couldn't get enough of each other. The kisses grew demanding, urgent. Her skin felt hot to the touch, her body thrummed with the awareness of a need that only Jerome could fulfill.

Eventually, reluctantly he pulled away from her.

"Shower," she said.

He nodded. She waited, hoping he'd ask to join her, praying he wouldn't and that he'd just step behind her into the space built specifically for two to share.

The memory of hot sex in the shower while warm water beat down all around them made Elise weak in the knees. She'd wrapped her legs around his waist and they'd rocked the tiles until they ended up on the floor outside the double shower stall fulfilling the need that consumed them both.

The memory seared Elise. She knew she was damp, ready for him. If only he'd make a move.

Ask me, she silently cried. *Join me.*

But Jerome didn't say anything. He simply stared into her eyes. Then, without a word, he pulled her close for a soul-shattering kiss. There was no gentleness in it, no lightness or frivolity. This kiss defined passion and hunger. He invaded her mouth and Elise willingly let him conquer. She was his woman. Now and for always.

"Go," he said, the single word sounding harsh. She undid her bra and stood before him. Her full dark breasts jutted out proudly, twin fruit willingly offered.

"Elise. Please."

With a saucy smile over her shoulder, she flounced into the bathroom.

She stayed in the shower a long time, expecting him to join her. When the water grew tepid she realized he wasn't coming.

She tried to suppress the disappointment that raced through her as surely as desire had not too long ago.

By the time she emerged from the shower, Jerome was stretched out on his uninflated air mattress.

"Jerome?"

He didn't respond.

She peered over him. Surely he couldn't have fallen asleep that fast. She stared down at him for a while. He'd wanted her. She knew it. But apparently he hadn't wanted her enough, even though she'd practically thrown herself at him—again.

Blinking back hot tears of humiliation, she tiptoed around him and went to her big lonely bed.

From where he lay, still wide awake, Jerome thought about Elise and the gift he'd declined. A part of him raged at the stupidity of turning down so fine an offer. Another part of him, however, recognized that he'd done the right thing.

Sex was always good between them. He wanted it, badly. But he wanted the greater prize even more.

He turned on his pallet on the floor, his thoughts on the slips of paper Miss Eliza Mae had given them. While she showered, Jerome saw Elise's on her vanity table top and picked it up.

They'd been given specific messages to help them heal the breach that was their relationship. Of that he was certain. How and why else would Miss Eliza Mae have said the things she said?

He'd already declared himself more than up for the challenge of winning back Elise's heart. Was she secretly doing the same? Was she there in bed recalling all the good times they'd shared, or dwelling on the bad?

Elise's note from Auntie Joe's priestess friend told her to *Remember*. But his said *Wait*.

And so he would.

Even if it meant turning aside her blatant invitation for the physical release he so craved.

CHAPTER 5

THE next morning, Elise was gone when Jerome awakened. She'd been not too long gone, though, because the scent of her perfume lingered, teasing his senses.

Groaning at the thought of his sacrifice last night, Jerome put his hands under his head and contemplated the ceiling of their dressing room. Never in a million years would he have guessed that he'd wind up sleeping on the floor in his own house. But his worthy cause demanded it. So he was game.

Dressing quickly, he sought out Auntie Joe.

"How do you feel this morning?" he asked, giving her a peck on the cheek.

"Just fine, child. Just fine. A touch of Eliza Mae's root magic and I'm just fine."

She pressed a cup of chicory coffee in his hands. Leaning against the kitchen counter, he assessed his aunt. "I know what you two are up to."

"Beg pardon?"

Jerome took a sip of coffee to hide his grin. He watched her fiddle with the griddle, then liberally add salt and black pepper to the bowl of whatever she was preparing. "You can stop playing innocent. I know what you're up to," he said again. From his pocket he pulled two small calico bags. He tossed them onto the counter near her.

Auntie Joe spared barely a glance at them, but her lips pursed.

"Elise found these," he said. Well, that was what he surmised. They had been at the foot of the bed, where he couldn't miss them. He hadn't planted any gris-gris bags and he knew Elise hadn't. That left just one guilty party.

"And?"

"And we can work out our differences unaided."

She turned, wiped her hands on the apron she'd fashioned from a bath towel. "Is that why you were all ready to leave? I saw the boxes, Jerome. Lots of them."

It took him a moment to comprehend that Auntie Joe was truly upset. Then it dawned on him. She'd called him by name—Jerome.

He stood up and carefully placed the cup on the counter. In his thirty-four years, he couldn't recall her ever calling him by his name—unless he was truly in trouble with her. Always, the endearment remained "child" or *chérie.*

"We're making progress on our relationship," he said carefully. Then, realizing he'd never lied to his aunt and didn't plan to start now, he sighed. "Yes, I was moving out."

Her breath caught. "You are divorced already?"

Jerome moved from the counter to the table. "No."

"But?"

"No, but for a while, it was looking like that's where we were headed."

She shook her head. "This 'for a while' and 'were,' what does that mean?"

He cast her a stricken look. "It means I was supposed to move out today. I already have a place over on St. Charles."

She clutched her heart and murmured a few words in a mixture of French and Yoruba. Then, unrolling the makeshift apron from her waist, she said, "Come, there is much work to be done."

He clasped her arms. "No, Auntie Joe. I love Elise with all my heart and soul. We've had some problems, but I've never stopped loving her. Thank you for the work you've already done, but let me handle it from here. Please."

Stern and disapproving, she folded large arms across her ample bosom. "Elise was up before seven, dressed and out the door to go to her job. On Saturday. Is that what you two do all the time, just work, work, work?"

Jerome rubbed his temple. She'd hit on a sore spot. "We're very ambitious people, Auntie Joe."

"What is ambition when there is no one to share the rewards with, huh? Tell me that."

"You don't understand," he said. "Elise has set herself some incredible sales goals. The weekends are when a lot of people look at houses. And my new position as managing editor at the magazine means—"

"It means neither of you care about what's most important!"

He stepped back. She hadn't raised her voice at him since he was in short pants. In the face of her anger, Jerome didn't know what to do or say.

She waved a hand. "This 'place' of yours. The one on St. Charles Avenue. I want to see it. Now."

"Auntie Joe."

"Now, Jerome."

"Yes, ma'am."

Unable to reach Jerome or Auntie Joe after closing up the property where she'd hosted an open house all day, Elise decided to just head home. She was tired, her feet hurt and she wanted nothing more than a nice, long soak in the Jacuzzi. Auntie Joe had promised to make them dinner, so she didn't even have to worry about that.

But before the bath and before the meal, she had a few errands to run. She needed prizes for the games the guests would play at Nina's shower.

Elise grinned. Everything was set for the party next Saturday. She rubbed her hands together, anticipating Nina's surprise and delight. Elise knew her friend would love every minute of the shower.

By the time Elise got home from the mall and a couple of specialty gift shops, the sun was setting.

"What a day," she said as she maneuvered herself and an armload of packages in the front door. "Jerome? Auntie Joe?"

No answer came to her summons.

She kicked off her shoes, then deposited the bags on a bench. A spot of color on the floor caught her eye.

"What in the world?" She peered at the floor. Rose petals in pale pink and vibrant red trailed from the door and led through the house. Elise deposited her purse and keys on the bench.

"Jerome?"

She picked up several of the petals. Rubbing the soft texture between her fingers, she inhaled the rose essence and followed the trail. "Jerome, what are you up to?"

The flower trail led to the loggia overlooking the garden. Candles burned all around, on tall pedestals and along the short wall. The flames from votives set along the brick walkway flickered like fairies in the night. The heady scent of flowers in bloom wrapped the garden in a sweet cocoon of fragrance. And the steady stream from the center fountain lulled like a summer lullaby in the growing evening.

In the middle of it all, at a beautiful table set for two, stood Jerome.

"Would you have dinner with me, Elise?"

Her heart tripped. Taking a hesitant step forward, Elise looked around. "It's beautiful." He closed the distance between them, then took her hand and drew her into the midst of the courtyard. "You did all this for me?"

"For us," he said. "Would you honor me with the pleasure of your company this evening?"

She smiled and nodded. "Where's Auntie Joe?"

"Out with Miss Eliza Mae."

He helped her into her seat, then opened a bottle of wine and poured for them.

Rose petals lay scattered across a table set with bone china they never used.

A self-conscious chuckle emitted from Elise.

"What?" he asked.

Her smile grew broader. "You're not going to believe this, but I'm nervous. It feels like a first date."

"It is. Maybe if I'm lucky, I'll get to kiss my date at the end of the evening."

Elise blushed furiously.

Putting the glass aside, Jerome reached for her hand. Lifting it, he pressed a kiss to her palm.

"Stop being silly," she said. But she regretted the words as quickly as they came out.

Jerome sighed. He let her hand go and picked up a plate to serve her.

Elise's heart ached. Every time he made an effort, her insecurities popped up and she said something stupid or hurtful. "Jerome, I didn't mean . . ."

Shaking his head, he waved away her explanation and apology. She reached for his hand. "Jerome, I didn't mean that the way it came out. I . . ." She paused, trying to make sure she got this right. "You were supposed to leave today. Instead, here we are in my favorite place in the world, this beautiful garden on a gorgeous night, and it's like we're starting over."

"Is that so wrong?"

She cast baleful eyes at him. "This is wonderful," she said. "But there are still things between us. Things that can't be solved with good food, fine wine and a candlelit garden."

"I didn't think we could solve all of our problems in one night," he said. "But one night is a beginning."

That much was true. Not sure how she felt, she decided to ease her way around their thornier issues, including one of the big ones: conflicting career goals. Right now, just by having dinner together, they were dealing with another: lack of communication.

"I've missed talking to you," she said. "Remember when we'd just sit on the floor and talk for hours?"

He nodded. "What happened to that?"

Her shoulders slumped. "Life got in the way. Maybe we grew up. Maybe . . ."

"Maybe we let our jobs and our possessions take the place of the really important things."

Elise sucked in her breath. She hadn't really wanted to deal with this tonight, spoiling the evening. A moment later, though, she realized that had been the problem. They'd spent months not finding the time to talk about their relationship. It had gotten so bad that their most in-depth conversation consisted of who was driving which vehicle.

"My career is important to me, Jerome. And you, you've worked hard to get where you are at the magazine. You want to throw all of that away? You want me to walk away from the business I've built up?"

"We're more than the positions we hold, Elise."

She harrumphed. "Now you're talking mumbo-jumbo like your voodoo relatives. By the way, did you see what I found under the pillows this morning?"

"I already talked to Auntie Joe about it. She said it won't happen again."

They ate in silence for a while, the relaxed novelty of the evening gone, replaced by the tiny barbs that cut deeper than any knife.

"Elise."

She glanced up.

"I do still love you. Very much," he said. "We can work this out. Whatever you want me to do, I'll do it."

She put her fork down and placed her napkin on the plate. "That's just it, Jerome. I don't want you to *do* anything. I just . . ." She shook her head.

He reached for her hand. "Talk to me, Elise. This is our time. It's just us here. You don't have to be afraid of anything."

How could she tell him that the thing she feared most was that he'd leave her and she'd be all alone, alone and unable to handle the weight of knowing her relatives and the girls she grew up with had been right all along?

"It's not you," she finally told him. "It's me. Maybe I need to see somebody for some therapy."

"We can go together," he said. "Marriage counseling is an option. We can find someone who . . ."

Leaning forward, she placed a finger over his lips. "Let's just enjoy the rest of the evening, all right?"

He captured her wrist and guided her finger into his mouth.

Elise's eyes widened. He licked the underside, then closed his lips around her finger. She squirmed in her seat as need and want and fear and hunger all coalesced.

She snatched her hand away.

"Are you finished?"

When he nodded, Elise rose and reached for their plates.

"I'll do them," Jerome said.

For a moment she paused, unsure. Then she dropped her hands to her sides. "Well, I guess it's good night, then. Thanks for dinner."

He stared at her, his gaze intent and unwavering.

Elise licked her lips and glanced to the side, both gestures unconscious. "What?"

Rising, he reached for her arms and slid his hands up and over her bare skin. "I was still hoping for a good-night kiss."

"Jerome, I . . ."

He leaned forward.

"Jerome . . ." Her words, whether protest or plea, were cut off when his lips covered hers.

The kiss was light and sweet, easy like the summer evening. Just the sort of kiss that might follow a candlelit romantic dinner shared by two people getting to know each other. And then it changed, growing bolder and stronger, like the expectant air before a fierce summer storm. The heat built around them, crackling and growing into something more, something sensual and demanding.

It had been so long and it felt so good.

"What were you going to say?" he murmured against her mouth.

"That I'd like very much for you to kiss me."

She felt his smile and smiled in return.

Elise's arms inched up his shirt until she clutched at him, trying to get closer to the heaven she was feeling in his embrace. She unfastened the buttons on his white shirt, then slipped a hand inside, rubbing along the ridged outline of his undershirt.

Jerome deepened the embrace, slanting his mouth over hers. Elise moaned and wrapped her arms around his neck. She ran her hands over his hair, drawing him closer and closer still.

Jerome's hands cupped her rear, pulling her to the erection that ran full and hard against the fabric of his slacks.

Elise moaned.

His kisses left her mouth and ventured down her neck.

He nibbled at her neck and took his time exploring the sensitive rim of her ear.

Elise shuddered in his arms. "Jerome . . . Yes."

The sound of her voice stayed him. With shaking hands he pulled her arms from his neck and tried to put a little breathing space between them. The outline of her full breasts and erect nipples distracted him. He held his hands over her breasts, hands cupped but just barely touching.

Jerome's entire body ached. He was on fire for her, yet he knew they couldn't do this. Not now.

Wait, Miss Eliza Mae's word had said.

Make it worth the effort, Auntie Joe had advised him.

He knew a way he could do both. A small smile tipped the corner of his mouth as he thought about the pleasure that he could give Elise. He loved this woman with all his being. The problems they had could be overcome—if Elise could remember what it was like before and if he could remind her of what they'd shared.

All he had to do was make her remember what it could be like between them. All *he* had to do was remember not to get too carried away.

Elise leaned forward so her breasts pressed against the hands he still held just so.

She'd wanted him before, then changed her mind. She wanted him now, and Jerome had no intention of letting this opportunity slip away. If Elise ended it again just when he was ready to take it to another level, at least she'd go away with something to think about, something to remember.

His edged his thumbs around the nipples he could clearly see through the light fabric of her blouse and the lacy-edged brassiere. Around and around, he drew light circles until her breath came in short, panting gasps.

"Jerome, I . . ."

He silenced her with a kiss, then set about an earnest seduction of her mouth. He rimmed her teeth with his tongue, then kissed the edges of her mouth, the dance a mating that would mirror a horizontal one. With one hand he cupped her closer to him, while the other caressed her neck.

"Oh, my," Elise said.

"You're beautiful, Elise."

Her eyes were wide, her mouth swollen. She gazed at him and lifted a hand to his face. She traced his mouth with her finger and then kissed him again. The kiss, like the night, was filled with promise and passion. Jerome nibbled at her neck, edging her blouse away.

Elise always wore sexy underwear, and tonight that played to his advantage. He traced the edges of the bra, knowing her skin would be sensitive. And when she swayed against him, he bent his head and captured one of the gifts she presented.

Sensations washed over Elise. She ran her hand over his head, drawing him closer, encouraging him to go deeper. When his mouth closed over her, she moaned again and lowered her hand to the erection jutting against his slacks. Closing her hand around him, she traced a path up and down.

He made a sound, a cross between a moan and a strangled cry. Then he caught her hand and brought it up to his mouth. He kissed the open palm, then darted his tongue between each of her fingers. When he found her mouth again, she lifted a leg to wrap around him.

Jerome's breathing was heavy. The last thing he wanted to do was let her go, but if he didn't stop now. . . . Her hands splayed across his chest and her mouth found *his* nipple.

Well, maybe just another moment.

With a shaky breath and showing more bravado than he felt, Jerome took a step back, and then another. His ragged and labored breathing attested to the barely controlled battle raging within him. He wanted her. How he wanted her.

"Jerome?"

He turned toward the table and lifted their dinner plates in trembling hands—anything to keep his hands occupied and off his wife.

"Thank you for dinner, Elise."

To Elise, his words sounded cold, almost distracted; definitely not passionate. Confused and left high and dry, she stood there for a moment. She had no idea what to say to him.

This was the second night in a row that he'd rejected her.

Didn't he find her attractive anymore? She worked out

four times a week to keep her body toned and limber. The erection he'd pressed to her belied the theory that he was no longer turned on by her.

It had to be a girlfriend, she surmised, someone he was thinking about while holding her in his arms. It seemed unlikely. He'd even said he still loved her. Elise realized with a start that loving someone and being *in love* were two completely different things. He didn't have to be in love with her to want to have sex. And Jerome had always had a more than healthy sex drive. He wasn't getting any at home, which left just one other option.

Elise's eyes narrowed. She thought about the condo he'd bought. Though much smaller than this house, it was plenty enough for two, a perfect little love nest.

She turned away, started to take her hurt feelings and wounded pride inside. Then, with growing anger propelling her, she whirled around.

"Why, Jerome? Just tell me that."

He was still standing there holding two china plates as if he were a busboy who'd forgotten how to get back to the kitchen. "Why what?"

"Why don't you want me? We haven't made love in ages. And here," she said, her hand encompassing the loggia and the garden, "here where it's beautiful and romantic and we shared a nice meal and a good bottle of wine and it was getting hot and sexy between us, you just shut things down and shut me out."

He put down the dishes, unmindful of the clatter they made, and he advanced upon her, slowly approaching like a lion stalking his mate. "If you think I don't want you, you need to think again, Elise. Look around you," he said, waving a hand toward the garden, the candles that now burned low, the flower petals strewn about and the soothing sweet melody from the water in the fountain. "Do you think I spent all afternoon setting this up because I don't want you? The only thing I want right now is to rip all your clothes off and to make sweet, hot, explosive love to you. Right here. Right now with your legs wrapped tight around me."

Elise's eyes widened a moment before her gaze dipped to the evidence of his hard arousal.

He shook his head and took a deep breath as if he were waging a war with himself, trying to hold on. "I've been playing with fire all night, Elise. I've been trying to be the gentleman. Trying to woo you body and soul, to make it like it used to be between us. But let me tell you one thing, woman. All that's on my mind at this very moment is what it would be like to sink so deep into you that I don't know where I start and where you begin. I want all these rose petals to be the mattress we lay on."

Elise's breath came in short unsteady pants. Her eyes locked with his.

He reached for one of the cut roses in a tall vase.

Ever so slowly, he traced the velvet softness of the rose against the silky texture of her skin. In the moonlight, she stood still, the rise and fall of her chest and the intensity of her gaze on his letting him know she was tuned in to every word, every nuance, every touch. "I want to shower your body with rose petals, then discover each and every inch of you with my mouth. Elise, I want you so bad that I ache with the need of you."

"Jerome . . ."

"Shh," he said, silencing her with the rose at her mouth. A heartbeat later, his mouth replaced the flower. "When you go to sleep tonight, I want you to remember one thing."

"What's that?"

"This," he said.

And then his mouth closed over hers. There was nothing gentle in the kiss, nothing tentative. All the pent-up sexual tension that he'd been holding back was focused on the touch of his lips and the thrust of his tongue that mimicked what his lower body was doing to her. Pleasure ricocheted throughout Elise. It had never been like this between them, so hot that she figured this must be what it felt like when a volcano erupted.

Then his tongue swept through her mouth and his hand squeezed her behind. All coherent thoughts fled her mind. His erect penis probed her, insistently pushing against his slacks. They rocked together making the same motion that his mouth did.

"Ahh. Jerome . . . I . . . !"

He slanted his mouth across her, silencing the words. The kiss went on and on and on until Elise thought she'd die of the hunger or melt in a puddle at his feet.

And then, abruptly, he stepped away. He picked up the dishes in remarkably steady hands and carried them to the kitchen, leaving her staring after him. Dazed, she reached an unsteady hand out to the chair for support.

Weak in the knees didn't begin to describe how she felt.

Elise didn't see Jerome again that night. As a matter of fact, she was certain he hadn't spent the night at the house. No evidence existed that he'd slept on the floor in the dressing room or even on a sofa in the great room. But he was there when Auntie Joe returned from Mass, there pretending that all was well between them.

"So, how do you usually spend a quiet Sunday afternoon?" Auntie Joe said. She'd already ragged on them both about not going to church.

Elise's spirit couldn't rise to the bait. Every now and then she'd sneak a peek at Jerome. She simply tucked her feet under her on the sofa and turned the page of the novel she was pretending to read. Jerome, who sat across from her with the Sunday *Times-Picayune* spread out around him, would have to carry the conversation.

"This is about it," he said.

Auntie Joe leveled a hard glance between them. "Hmm."

Jerome folded up the sports section. "There is something we'd like to ask you, though."

That "we" got Elise's attention. She couldn't think of a single thing that they needed to ask Auntie Joe.

"As you know," Jerome began, "our friends Ricky Shoregood and Nina Tippens are getting married."

Elise groaned. She'd forgotten all about Nina's plea for a blessing from Auntie Joe. After finding those voodoo bags in her bed, Elise wasn't of a mind to be dealing with that foolishness.

"What do they want?" Auntie Joe asked. "A reading?"

"No," he said, stretching out the word. "We're the best man and matron of honor. They want us to get you to offer a blessing to their union."

Auntie Joe nodded. "Standing in the gap. Old custom. Not a lot of practitioners follow it still."

Elise made a production of turning the next page of her book. She almost ripped a leaf out of the hardcover.

Jerome and Auntie Joe looked her way, but neither said anything. "Will you do it?" Jerome asked.

"No. I cannot."

"Why not?" Elise said, snapping her novel shut. "You sure didn't hesitate—"

With a look toward Jerome, she cut off the torrent of disrespectful words. "I apologize, Auntie Joe. Excuse me, please." She got up to leave, stepping over Jerome's newspaper.

"Elise." This time it was Auntie Joe's voice that stayed her.

She paused, but she didn't turn around.

"It's not that I don't want to," Auntie Joe explained. "I can't. The tradition requires that the couple, usually a best man and maid of honor, be united."

"We fit that," Jerome said carefully.

Auntie Joe emitted a mirthless bark of laughter. "Not by any stretch of the imagination, and mine is great. You don't fool me, though you have tried. I knew before I arrived that all was not well here. You may say you care for your friends. They look to you, but what do you have to offer them? Nothing," she said, answering her own question.

"That's not true," Jerome said.

"Not true? You get an apartment so you can live separate from your wife. She puts too much makeup on to cover the dark circles under her eyes from sleepless nights. It took me three hours—three hours—to cleanse this house."

Elise looked stunned. "You told her about the condo?"

"You haven't been sleeping?" Jerome asked. He could only hope he knew why.

"I thought we agreed . . ."

"Well, that's the thanks I get . . ."

The questions and accusations crossed each other. Auntie Joe rolled her eyes.

"This is why I cannot give my blessing. Listen to you."

While Jerome attempted to placate his aunt, Elise

thought about her best friend. Nina had been a trouper during the preparation for Elise's wedding. The least Elise could do in return was fulfill this one request.

"This is the only thing Nina's asked of me," Elise said, her voice barely above a whisper.

She didn't like the idea of participating in any voodoo, real or imagined. And she didn't even want to know what Auntie Joe meant about "cleansing" her house. But Nina and Ricky wanted this. They wanted it so badly they could barely get the question out at dinner the other night.

Personally, Elise couldn't understand what the fuss was all about. But it was very important to her friend. And for right now at least, Nina's happiness was her priority.

Slowly she turned toward Auntie Joe and Jerome.

"What do we have to do?"

"I knew this was going to be something I didn't want to do," she said several hours later.

Dressed in jeans and sneakers, she and Jerome stood on the bank of the Mississippi River. It was a quarter to midnight.

"Hand me the bottle so I can uncork it," Jerome said.

Elise looked over her shoulder and to the right and left. "We are going to get arrested out here. Isn't this illegal?"

"Just hand me the champagne. Did you bring the glass?"

Realizing that the sooner they got this ritual over, the faster they could get back to the security of their home, Elise passed him both items.

Following Auntie Joe's instructions, they offered champagne first to the earth, then the sky. After each sipping from the same place on the glass and saying both their names and Nina's and Ricky's, they poured the rest of the libation into the river.

"You know, this is why the city has such a problem with high water," Elise said. "It's all that alcohol people are dumping into the river."

"Shh," Jerome hushed her. "Hold the flashlight over here so I can read the next part."

It took another forty-five minutes to complete all of

Auntie Joe's directives, primarily because everything was done in sets of three.

The last, a prayer and a love poem, though in French, were hauntingly beautiful. Jerome supplied the translation as he read. Now Elise felt oddly at ease. She watched the river flow as Jerome gathered all of the items they'd brought with them.

He held out a hand to help her up. She dusted off her jeans, but their hands remained clasped together as they walked to the car. When he would have opened the door for her, Elise blocked his way.

"You know I don't put much stock in any of this hocus-pocus," she said. "But this was nice. I'm glad we spent this time together."

"Me, too." He kissed her then. Before it turned into something more, he opened the door for her.

As he started the engine, he faced her. "You know, this is our second date." Then he squeezed her hand.

He dropped her off at the house, then went on to his condo. Auntie Joe knew the truth, so there was no need carrying on the charade for her. Besides, they both could use a decent night's sleep.

But it wasn't until Elise was in her very big bed all by herself that she remembered. This time, though, negative memories of her days in Atlanta didn't haunt her. She instead remembered what Jerome had said in the car as they'd left the river. *This is our second date.*

A smile curved her mouth. She and Jerome had slept together for the first time after their third date.

CHAPTER 6

TODAY, Elise's energy ran high.

If they got back in the same bed before the wedding, maybe there was still hope. And it sure seemed like they followed a direct path there. She was glad they were getting to know each other again. Dinner alfresco had been lovely, but something about the river had called to her. Doing those rituals there, even on behalf of someone else, seemed to draw them closer.

Not, of course, that she'd ever admit such to Auntie Joe.

After a closing with a young couple, Elise went back to the office. Her cell phone trilled before she got to her desk.

She adjusted the volume on the hands-free control at her waist, then spoke into a barely there mouthpiece. "Good afternoon, this is Elise Gregory."

"Hey, girl."

"Nina, what's up?"

Elise grabbed a Slinky that she kept handy, then settled into her swivel chair facing the busy street her office overlooked.

"That's what I was calling to find out. So how'd it go with Auntie Joe?"

Elise frowned. "Nina, this whole hocus-pocus, voodoo thing . . ."

"Oh, my God," Nina cut in on a wail. "Elise, please tell me you didn't do something that's gonna jinx my wedding."

A long-suffering sigh was Elise's reply.

"Elise, please tell me everything's okay."

"Everything's okay," Elise parroted. She put the Slinky aside and sat back with her eyes closed. "I just don't get why you New Orleans folks are so caught up in this stuff."

"Elise, I'm the bride. You're supposed to humor me, remember?"

She smiled. "Yeah, I remember."

"So, what did she make you do?"

"Well, there were rocks and pennies and flowers and champagne and chanting at the river."

"Really?"

"Yes, really. We could have been arrested."

"Nah, the cops know people do rituals there all the time. It just depends on where you go. So what else happened?"

"That's it."

"No potions, not even a gris-gris bag?"

The shops in the French Quarter carried the little bags filled with charms or amulets. Tourists took them home feeling like they'd participated in a bit of New Orleans–style voodoo. Elise feared she'd been exposed to the real thing and was none too happy about it.

Elise quickly filled Nina in on what she'd found while making her bed.

"Maybe the ones you found were for us," Nina suggested.

Seeing no way to let Nina know she knew for certain they weren't, Elise just let that slide. "So, are you happy now? You got your blessing."

"Oh, that wasn't it," Nina said. "That was just the first part."

Elise rolled her eyes. "Lovely. Just how many parts are in this ritual?"

"I think three," Nina said. Then she said, "Hey, Elise?"

She immediately recognized the cajoling tone in Nina's voice and knew what was coming. "No."

"But Elise," Nina whined, petulance coming through the phone line loud and clear, "the bride is supposed to know what kind of shower she's getting."

"Forget it. You'll find out Saturday."

"This is so wrong."

Elise grinned. Keeping the theme a secret from Nina had been the best idea she'd had in a while. It was killing Nina not to know. And Elise was enjoying every minute of it.

A second later, the happy grin faded a bit. She swiveled the chair around and reached for the Slinky again. Elise had one secret from Nina that she very much wanted to share. Nina was her sounding board, her best friend and the one person who would understand and could maybe offer some advice on what to do with Jerome. Nina'd also know what to make of Auntie Joe and that Eliza Mae woman.

Well, Elise amended to herself, not so much what to do *with* Jerome, but what to do *about* their current state of affairs. Nina and Jerome grew up together. Nina had introduced Elise to Jerome. She'd know what to suggest to break through their current marital impasse.

But Elise also knew that now was not the time to dump all that negativity Nina's way, particularly since Nina showed signs of coming unhinged over something as silly as a voodoo blessing. Two weeks before her own wedding, the ever-efficient Elise was a basket case of nerves and last-minute details. Nina had seen her through it, though, and she was bound and determined to do the same thing for her friend.

"Well, will you at least tell me the color themes?"

Elise smiled again. "Nope."

"I hate you."

"Love you, too. Gotta go, my other line is flashing."

"Don't forget to tell me what happens tonight with Auntie Joe," Nina got in before they disconnected.

Tonight? Elise wondered as she punched up the line. After taking the business call, Elise tried to work, but her mind was elsewhere—mainly on Jerome.

No doubt about it, he still found her desirable and he'd been deliberately wooing her over the weekend. Elise's breath quickened and heat pooled in her midsection as she remembered the soft strokes from his bold hand and from that rose. She found it on her pillow the next morning. Leaning back in her chair, she closed her eyes, an absent hand fondling the same breast Jerome had suckled that night when he'd come to her room. Her fingers couldn't replicate the rough, gentle play of Jerome's mouth, the moist lapping of his tongue or the feel of his weight over her.

Elise moaned.

Her pager beeped.

Heaving a sigh of sexual frustration, she reached for the device.

"Like Pavlov's dog," she muttered.

That thought brought her up short. *Was* she a slave to her job? Granted, it took a lot of time and energy to sell houses. She was on call 24/7 and just like her platinum American Express card, she never left home without her pager, cell phone and Palm Pilot.

A frown marred her features as a whisper of understanding zipped through her. Her pager went off again, and the thought disappeared before it fully developed in her mind. As she pushed the button to read the message, the random thought flickered through her awareness a second, more coherent, time.

Remember when you let nothing come between you and Jerome?

Thoughtful, Elise turned her full attention to the incoming message. It was from one of her clients. It could wait. Suddenly, though, seeing Jerome and solving their differences couldn't.

Snatching up her handbag and car keys, she headed toward her office door.

"Yvette, I'll be out for a while. If Jonathan Slocum calls, would you leave a message for me on voice mail? I'll check it while I'm out."

"Got it," the office secretary said.

Outside, Elise's silver Jaguar gleamed in the spot where she parked every day. It took less than fifteen minutes for Elise to navigate the streets of New Orleans to get to the building where *New Orleans Today* had its offices.

She'd never barged in on Jerome during the day. They had an agreement on that; they respected each other's work and work space. As she pulled into a visitor parking spot, she saw Jerome come out of the building. Her hand hovered over the horn, ready to toot a greeting. But he had someone with him. A woman. The lighthearted buoyancy that had been propelling Elise's day so far vanished as quickly as the smile on her face.

Jerome pulled the woman to him for a quick hug and then wrapped his arm around her waist as they came across the pathway leading to the parking lot.

Even from where she sat, her hands gripping the steering wheel like a vise, Elise recognized the almond-shaped eyes and dazzling smile of Cassandra Blakely. Elise couldn't help but recognize her; the anchorwoman's face was plastered on billboards all over the city.

It didn't take much to be envious of the lanky, light-skinned beauty. She'd served a term as Miss Louisiana before graduating from journalism school. She'd eventually come home to New Orleans in a blaze of glory and publicity ads.

The woman said something that made Jerome throw his head back and laugh.

Hurt and jealousy ripped through Elise. He hadn't laughed like that with her in a long, long time.

A moment later, the woman draped her arms around Jerome's neck. Elise would have given anything to hear their conversation. But she had a pretty good idea about how it might be going:

First, Jerome would explain how he'd played his wife that weekend, and then he'd coax Cassandra to their new hideaway for a little afternoon delight. It would be just a matter of time, he probably promised, before they built or bought a considerably larger place.

Elise's heart twisted. Seeing with her own eyes that the suspicions she'd harbored indeed had merit didn't ease the pain one bit.

She watched as Jerome and Cassandra moved on, then stopped at a red Mercedes convertible. Cassandra leaned into him. At the car, they stood hip-to-hip. Jerome made not one move to put any distance between them. As a matter of fact, he seemed to be enjoying the attention.

They shared a few more words, then Jerome put his hands at her waist and pulled the anchorwoman closer, planting a kiss on her lips.

Elise closed her eyes, willing the image to disappear,

but it was already burned into her brain, a hot brand scorching what remained of her tattered self-esteem.

All their days had been leading to this one—the moment when Elise had to face the harsh reality that her marriage was, indeed, over. Jerome hadn't been seducing her in an effort to win her back. He'd instead been playing with her, toying with her emotions and her need for intimacy.

Her friends in Atlanta had been right. She couldn't keep a man like Jerome. He should have been with someone like Cassandra all along.

With tears clouding her eyes, Elise waited until the Mercedes-Benz pulled away and Jerome walked back into the building before starting her car. She peeled out of the parking lot on a screech of rubber and in a torrent of tears.

"I'm not going."

They stared at each other across the breakfast bar in the kitchen.

"You have to go," Jerome said. "We promised Nina and Ricky."

"Well, this is a promise I'm breaking."

"Elise, why are we arguing about this? You agreed yesterday that you'd do this. We spent an hour at the river last night."

"Yeah, another hour of my life wasted on you."

He grabbed her arm. "What are you talking about? I thought we were cool, that we'd made a connection."

Hurt, anger and humiliation blazed in her eyes. "You made a connection all right. You could have at least waited until we were divorced. You didn't have to rub my face in it."

He threw his hands into the air. "What are you talking about?"

"I saw you, Jerome. I saw you and your little reporter girlfriend."

"My what?"

"Don't stand there looking all innocent, Jerome. I saw you. I saw you with her. Your behind is busted, brother."

He looked so confused that for a moment Elise faltered. Then she remembered his laughter and his exuberance with the anchorwoman. The image of that kiss blazed across her mind.

"Get the hell out of my house."

He opened his mouth, then snapped it shut. "Fine, Elise. Fine."

Elise's pager went off. She reached for it. But Jerome got to it first, snatching it off the counter. "You think I have a girlfriend. Well, I'm sick of competing with *your* little black beeping lover." He slammed the still chirping pager into the trash and stormed out the back door. The door rebounded against the wall so hard that the glass shattered.

Stunned, Elise just stood there.

When she finally moved, it was toward the trash can. She peered in, staring at her pager as if the thing had suddenly sprouted wings and horns.

The rest of the week was a nightmare. Elise called in sick two days and spent the others in such a daze that she went home early. Auntie Joe offered no solace, though she did try to comfort Elise. And a couple of times, Elise heard Auntie Joe on the telephone yelling at someone, presumably Jerome.

Promising she'd be back, Auntie Joe packed her bags and disappeared on Wednesday.

Nina spent an evening at the house trying to get the story out of Elise. But the pain of her abject failure was too much to share, the hurt too raw.

Despite her best efforts to banish from memory the image of Jerome and Cassandra Blakely together, her mind refused to let it go. In morbid fascination, Elise watched the news every night, staring at Cassandra's smiling face and wondering if the TV woman truly loved Jerome. Two media power brokers together made a whole lot more sense than a magazine editor and a real estate agent.

Elise punched the power button on the remote and threw the thing onto the table.

It was Thursday night and the latest round of the pity party had begun. A few tears leaked, and then more came. Elise yanked open the drawer where she kept flatware, grabbed a tablespoon and turned toward the refrigerator.

The front doorbell rang as she reached into the freezer for some rocky road.

The ice cream carton was empty, though. Just like her life. She tossed the carton in the trash, then decided to ignore the front door. She padded to her bedroom, but the person at the door wasn't giving up easily.

"All right, all right," Elise muttered.

She dragged her weary body, her bare feet and her ratty robe to the door.

"Goodness," Nina said a moment later. "You look a fright, girl."

Elise just turned around and headed back down the hall.

"I brought something for you," Nina sing-songed.

Elise whirled around. "If Jerome's out there . . ."

Nina shut the door and pulled her hand from behind her back to reveal a plastic grocery bag. With a flourish, she presented a half-gallon of rocky road ice cream.

A hint of a smile ghosted at Elise's mouth. "You are the woman," she said on a sniffle.

The sniffle launched a twitching of the nose and soon a tear fell, followed by another.

"Don't go getting all emotional about my shower," Nina said. "See, that guilt wouldn't be eating at you if you'da been a real sisterfriend and come up off the theme."

Elise laughed in spite of herself. "You'll find out Saturday."

"Hmph," Nina said. She put her arms around Nina's shoulders. "You ready to talk, now? What's wrong, girl?"

"Nothing."

"Uh-huh. That's what you've been saying all week. But your time is up. Come on." Nina grabbed her arm and dragged Elise into the garden room. She made her sit, then went to the kitchen for spoons.

"Ta da!" she said a moment later, holding high two dessert spoons.

Seeing Nina there brought all the pain, the insecurities and the fear about the future bubbling to the surface. Elise's face crumpled and she let out a wail.

Nina rushed to her side and put her arms around Elise. Ten minutes later, Elise's eyes were dry but still red and puffy. The two women sat cross-legged on the rattan sofa in the garden room, the ice cream between them.

"Talk to me, Elise."

"I didn't want to bring you down so close to your wedding."

"That's what friends are for."

Elise snorted.

Leaning forward, Nina took her hands. "Two heads are better than one."

Elise started to say something smart-alecky about the cliched proverbs, but she didn't have the energy. She had a burden that needed to be lifted and maybe Nina could help.

"Jerome and I are separated. He's having an affair with that TV woman, Cassandra Blakely."

Nina's eyes widened. "I knew you guys were separated, but Cassandra? You mean his old girlfriend?"

CHAPTER 7

ELISE blanched and almost choked on a spoon full of rocky road. "His what?"

"Uh-oh," Nina said.

Putting the ice cream and their spoons to the side, Elise grabbed Nina's hand. "Please tell me I didn't hear what I think you just said."

"Elise, it's ancient history."

She fell back on the sofa, an arm over her face. "Oh, God. It's true."

"Come on, Elise. Jerome's not having an affair with Cassandra. They were over a long time ago."

Elise sat up, took as calming a breath as she could manage and faced her friend. "Talk. And I mean all the details."

"There's not much to tell. A long time ago, a *very* long time ago," she added hastily, "Jerome and Cassandra were an item."

"How long were they an item?"

Nina winced. "Three years."

Elise closed her eyes. "They were together as long as we've been married."

"Elise, it was like ten or twelve years ago. They were at Xavier, we all were."

"Go on."

Nina didn't look at all pleased to be bearing this news. "He probably never mentioned her to you because there was nothing to mention."

Folding her arms, Elise's gaze pierced her friend's. "Get on with it."

Nina sighed, heavily. "They got together junior year. By senior year they were exclusive." Nina rattled off the facts like shotgun fire. "The engagement—"

Elise let out an anguished wail. "They were engaged?"

"—lasted for about eight months. They broke it off when Cassandra got a job at some small TV station in Ohio. Jerome didn't want to move there."

"Then what?"

"Then nothing," Nina said. "We all kind of lost contact with her."

"Until she decided to come home to New Orleans. I see Jerome didn't waste any time getting reacquainted." Elise punched one of the pillows on the sofa, then sat back in a huff. "I knew I didn't like her the minute that first billboard went up."

"Jerome is not having an affair with Cassandra."

"What makes you so sure?"

"I know Jerome."

"Yeah right, that's why he's living in a condo in the Garden District."

Nina's mouth dropped open. "He moved out?" She shook her head. "I knew you guys were in trouble, but I didn't think it was that bad."

Elise slowly sat up. "What do you mean you knew we were in trouble?"

Nina reached for the ice cream. "Here. Want some more?"

"No, I don't want any more," Elise said as she stood up and faced her friend. "I want you to tell me what you meant."

Nina wrung her hands. "Don't be mad, Elise. We did it for you."

"We? Who is 'we' and what did you do?"

Nina had the grace to cringe. "Me and Ricky. We set up the whole thing. We called Auntie Joe. We asked her to intervene."

"You what?"

"I know you don't believe in voodoo or anything," Nina said, talking quickly, "but we thought since Jerome is so close to Auntie Joe that maybe the three of you could talk out your problems, you know, like a marriage counselor. It was obvious things weren't going well between you guys. And it was killing me that you were so unhappy."

Elise tossed her hands up. "I don't believe this."

"Don't be mad, Elise. Please."

"That whole thing at the riverside. What was that about?"

"A binding ritual to get the two of you back together."

"Uh-huh," Elise said, folding her arms. "And what was tonight's supposed to be?"

Wincing, Nina said, "A candlelight service in the chapel where you renewed your vows."

Elise just grunted.

"He's not having an affair with Cassandra," Nina said. "I know Jerome. There's got to be some other explanation. Did you ask him?"

"I told him I saw him with her."

Nina looked up. "And?"

"And he didn't deny it. He didn't even deftly change the subject."

"Where exactly is he?"

"He's probably out with Cassandra." She stretched the name out and pasted a big fake smile on her face the way the television reporters did.

Nina put the top back on the ice cream and went to the kitchen to tuck it into the freezer. "I doubt that, Elise," she said when she returned.

"You know that whole thing about happily-ever-after that we read in books and see in the movies?" Nina nodded. "Well, I know you're getting married next week, but don't believe the hype."

"Where are you going?"

"Come on," Elise said. "I know you won't believe this unless you see it for yourself."

A minute later, Elise went into her bedroom. She marched straight to the huge closet. Everything male was gone. A stack of shoe boxes sat empty sentinel over the large area that had been filled with Jerome's suits, shirts, ties and shoes.

"Uh, what's up with that?" Nina said, waving a hand at the empty space.

"This way, please," Elise said, as if she were showing a house to a prospective buyer.

All across the house they went, to the other side. Elise knocked on the closed door, just in case. Nina looked at her as if she'd lost her mind.

"Come on."

They entered the guest suite. "Auntie Joe has been in here the last few days. But this is where Jerome lived until he closed on his place. Those," she said, pointing to a few remaining boxes, "are his belongings."

Elise went to the walk-in closet and flung its French doors wide. More packed boxes and bags were jammed in there.

"What's going on here?" Nina asked.

"I could ask the same question," Jerome said from the bedroom door.

The women jumped as if they'd been the victims of a voodoo doll pricking.

"Jerome!"

"Excuse me," Elise said. She tried to brush by him, but Jerome wasn't having it.

"What's going on?" he said as he shifted to fully block the door.

"Uh, hi, Jerome," Nina said. "We were just, uh . . ." Helplessly, Nina glanced between her two friends. "I think I'll be going," she said. She ducked under Jerome's arm. He let her pass without a word.

"I'll let myself out," Nina called as she made haste down the hall and out of the line of fire.

"I came to get my stuff. What were you doing in my closet?"

"Does it matter?"

He stepped forward. She stepped back. "Yes. It matters. What were you looking for?"

A lot of things, Elise wanted to rage at him. *Lost dreams and hopes, the happiness we used to know.* But she said none of those things.

"Sit down, Elise," he said, his expression firm. "We're going to talk about this once and for all."

"Jerome, I have a headache." That was the truth. Her head had been pounding from the moment she found out about him and Cassandra. She tried to go around him, but he halted her with an outstretched arm.

"Don't you care about our relationship?"

Fire flashed in her eyes. "I'm not the one who walked away. I didn't pack up all my belongings and go buy an apartment."

Jerome cocked his head. "Sit down, Elise."

She glared at him, but she sat on the edge of his bed. Jerome dragged a chair from under the window and parked it a few feet in front of her.

"Let's start at the beginning," he said.

"All right. Let's. Why don't you tell me about your relationship with Cassandra Blakely? I understand you two were engaged. Funny, you never mentioned that."

He sighed. "Cassandra is ancient history, Elise."

"Yeah, Nina used those words, too."

"So why don't you believe her or me?"

Elise leaned forward. "You haven't given me a reason to believe, Jerome."

"I thought I gave you several reasons the other night."

"*That*," she said with a curt nod, "was nothing more than a physiological response. Making out isn't the same as making a relationship."

He reached for her hands, but she pulled away. Jerome sucked his teeth. "Okay, Elise, we'll play this your way. Do you know when things started falling apart between us? You probably don't because you were so wrapped up in work. Things fell apart when we got our so-called dream jobs."

"Don't you blame my career . . ."

Ignoring her interjection, he stood up and walked to the window. "All my life, I've wanted to be in this position, managing editor of a terrific publication. And now that the dream is a reality, all I get is twelve- and fourteen-hour days. When I do have some downtime and I plan something for us to do together, you know what happens? I have to compete with your pager and your cell phone. I work long days, too, Elise. But when I come home, I'm home. You never go home, Elise. You never come home to me."

"Well, guess what, Jerome High-and-Mighty, you're not the only one who has dreams. It's taken me a long time to get where I am. And I'm not about to give it up for . . ."

"Us," he finished. Facing her, Jerome nodded, resigned. "I'd hoped that it wouldn't end like this."

He went to his closet, pulled out a box.

Panic shot through Elise. "What are you doing? Where are you going?"

"I told you. I came to get some more of my stuff."

"You're going to her, aren't you? Aren't you? Well, go, dammit. See if I care."

Jerome brushed by her. "Good night, Elise. I'll get the rest of this later."

"Don't bother. It'll all be outside at the curb."

He faced her then and Elise recoiled. Anger marred his features, lines of tension throbbed at his temples. Elise had never seen him like this, barely in control.

"You will not," he said, pointing a finger directly in her face. "You will not pull a *Waiting to Exhale* on me. Sell my stuff or burn my cars and you'll be sorry you ever tangled with me."

Eyes wide, Elise stared up at him.

"Do you understand me, Elise?"

All the anger, the frustration, the jealousy and the hurt she felt roiled within her, making her careless, not at all mindful of the harsh words that cut like a knife. "Get out. And don't ever come back."

A few moments later, Elise heard the front door slam.

Mourning all she'd lost, she crumpled onto the floor hugging her midsection and crying silent tears.

The ringing phone woke her sometime later. Disoriented, it took Elise a moment to realize she wasn't in her bed. At some point in the night, she must have crawled up and onto the bed in the guest room, because that was where she lay. Getting her bearings, she reached for the telephone.

"Hello."

"There is much work to be done, child. Get washed and dressed. I will be there in twenty minutes."

The line went dead before Elise had a chance to tell Auntie Joe that she wasn't seeing visitors and wasn't in the mood for company, particularly not any voodoo priestess company.

As she replaced the receiver, all the ugly words from the previous night came back to her. Elise moaned as if in physical pain.

Tomorrow she was supposed to play cheerful hostess for Nina's wedding shower. Elise, however, felt anything and everything but cheerful. As a matter of fact, six feet under sounded like a good place to be about now.

She pushed herself from the bed, took a final look at the room where Jerome had been living, then pulled the door closed. Until he'd mentioned it, the thought hadn't crossed her mind to burn his belongings. While it held some appeal, that wasn't Elise's style.

She was a fighter and a scrambler. She knew how to survive in tough times. In her thirty-one years she'd seen enough to know the routine.

Instead of heading to her bedroom and the shower, she detoured to the kitchen, where she brewed a strong pot of coffee.

She was standing at the counter drinking her second cup when the front doorbell chimed.

"Surely that old woman didn't really come here."

But when she opened the door a few moments later, it was indeed Auntie Joe standing there, a large bag in her hand.

"Beignets and croissants. I didn't know which you might prefer."

"I thought you people knew everything," Elise muttered.

"Ugliness does not become you," Auntie Joe said. "Are you going to let me in?"

Elise waved a hand as if she didn't care one way or the other and simply walked away from the open door.

"He loves you, you know."

"Uh-huh. So much that he couldn't wait to get out of here last night and run to his girlfriend."

"You unjustly accuse him."

Elise whirled around. "Why is everybody on his side? Doesn't anybody see my side of this?"

Auntie Joe navigated her way to the kitchen. "Your 'side' as you call it leaves no room for explanations from a pure heart. You have been judge and jury."

"I'm going to get a shower."

Auntie Joe nodded. "You do that. I will begin the cleansing ceremony."

Elise rolled her eyes and went to her bedroom.

Fifteen minutes later she felt much better; she also felt guilty for being rude to Auntie Joe.

"I'm sorry," she said when she entered the kitchen again. Auntie Joe sat at the table, three candles lit in front of her.

"Come. Sit, my child. We shall begin the work."

"Auntie Joe, I can respect your religious and cultural traditions. I just don't believe in those things."

"Do you believe that love heals?"

Elise thought about her own situation. "I did. Until last night."

"Do you believe that the heart knows things the head will never understand?"

Elise sighed. "I really have a lot to do today. The party planners will be arriving to set up the house and I do have to get to work sometime today."

Auntie Joe pulled something from the pocket of her housedress. "Anva wanted you to have this."

"I beg your pardon?" Elise watched as the older woman stretched her arm out, then slowly opened her hand. A small locket lay nestled there on her palm.

"What is it?"

"I think you know."

Elise did know. That was why she didn't move to touch the locket. It was identical to one she used to wear as a child. Hers had been stolen, ripped from her neck one day in the courtyard of the projects where she lived.

"Where did you get that?"

"Take it, child. Open it."

Elise's gaze met Auntie Joe's. She didn't read any malice or malignance in her eyes. Instead she saw, or thought she saw, a welcoming warmth, coupled with sincere care and concern.

Slowly Elise reached for the locket. She turned it over. "Open it."

At Auntie Joe's prodding, she glanced up. Then, with deliberate care, she moved her thumb over the clasp.

The locket sprang open.

And Elise remembered.

She felt the light weight of the locket in her hand and sensed the comforting presence of Auntie Joe, but Elise's mind was in another place, another time. She closed her eyes and remembered so much. . . .

"One day, my child, you will meet a man. He will capture your heart and his photograph is one you can wear close to your heart."

Great-Aunt Anva slipped the locket into young Elise's hands, then fingered the locket she wore suspended from a gold chain around her own neck.

"Is your true love's picture in there?"

Anva nodded. "Look." She opened the locket and let the eight-year-old girl peer at the tiny but clear image of an unsmiling man.

"That's an old-fashioned picture," Elise said. "There's no color."

"It was taken a long time ago, when I could have chosen a different path. You, Elise, you have the chance for great happiness. Do not let it slip away."

Elise didn't understand what the old woman was saying. And she never got the chance to ask. Anva died that night, sitting in her rocking chair, holding the locket that carried the image of her long-ago beloved.

In her kitchen, the adult Elise opened her eyes. The light scent from the burning candles soothed the ragged edges of her nerves and her soul.

"She came back to me," Elise told Auntie Joe. "In a dream, she came back twenty years later on the eve of my wedding."

"And what advice did she give you, child?"

"She told me to cherish my beloved." Elise stared at the

miniature photograph in Anva's locket. "Where did you get this, Auntie Joe?"

"From Eliza Mae. Anva was her mother."

It all made sense now, Elise thought. Even Miss Eliza Mae calling her "namesake" made sense, as did her prompting for Elise to *remember*.

Elise squinted at the picture, then held it up closer to the flame of one of the burning candles. "Impossible."

"What is it?"

Elise sat there for a moment, staring at the nearly 100-year-old photograph as if trying to divine the secrets of the ages, wondering how what she was seeing could possibly be real.

"Child?" Auntie Joe prompted.

She finally turned awestruck eyes to Auntie Joe. "He looks like Jerome."

CHAPTER 8

"BEFORE your guests arrive, burn this in a glass ashtray." Elise accepted what looked like a fistful of dried weeds. "It will help clear the negative energy that has been generated here. Then, give this to the bride. She must sleep with it under her pillow every night until the wedding."

"Is this really for Nina or is this another of your ..." Elise stopped a moment before the word *tricks* slipped out. "... One of your marital aids for me and Jerome?"

To the older woman's credit and Elise's relief, Auntie Joe smiled. "It is for your friend. All brides should have sweet dreams."

The small sachet was fragrant with herbs. "Anything else?"

"That will be all. For now," Auntie Joe said.

After Auntie Joe left, Elise realized her great-aunt's words had remained with her all these years, even though she'd been a mere child when she'd last talked to the woman. All of her life she'd run from her true heritage. Since she was actually related to Miss Eliza Mae, the blood of voodoo priestesses ran in her veins.

A new sense of purpose heartened her spirit.

Jerome was worth fighting for, and she wasn't going to let any old TV anchorlady, former beauty queen or not, ruin what was ordained by destiny. She also knew there were some things she'd have to change about herself.

"Cherish your beloved," she said, turning the words over

and over, listening to the sound they made in the empty kitchen. "Cherish your beloved."

Friday was one of those days. But Elise had other priorities. Somehow she managed to placate Jonathan Slocum, who wanted to buy a house that wasn't for sale, and get some backlogged paperwork done. At four-thirty she called it quits. About to stuff work in her briefcase, she paused.

She neatly stacked it all on her desk and walked out the door. She got home in time to let the party organizer set up.

Now, Saturday, she was trying not to feel guilty about the work she'd left behind.

"Get a grip," she told herself. "There's more to life than work."

Cherish your beloved.

She wanted to. She just couldn't reach him. She'd swung by his new place, but didn't see his car.

So here she was late Saturday afternoon, ready to entertain guests when all she really wanted to do was see Jerome.

The party was supposed to start at six. Elise showered and changed into shirt and slacks. She checked on the caterer who'd set up shop in the kitchen, then went to answer the first summons at the door.

Within half an hour the house was filled with twenty of Nina's closest friends and co-workers. Upon arrival, each woman signed the guest book, dropped off her gift and was diverted down the side hall to the spare bedroom being used as the preparation room. Nina's orders were to show up at seven o'clock and not a moment earlier.

She rang the door chime at six forty-five.

Elise opened the door and put hands on hips. "And what are you doing here?"

Nina, dressed in a short skirt and twinset with strappy high-heeled sandals, pouted. "Come on, Elise. It's close enough to seven. Let me in. I see all the cars, so I know everybody's here."

Closing the door behind her, Elise stepped out into the balmy night. "Nope. You have fifteen minutes. You can sit in the car, drive around the block or stand out here and talk to me."

"All right, tell me what happened with Jerome."

Elise cocked her head at her friend. "We are not going there. This is *your* night, Nina."

"Come on, Elise," Nina whined, trying to get past her to the door. "This is so wrong."

"Patience is a virtue," Elise said.

Nina stomped to the edge of the walkway. "I've had about as much virtue as I can stand. Do you know Ricky won't even tell me where we're going on our honeymoon? All he'll say is, 'You're gonna love it.' Well, half of loving something is being able to anticipate it."

Elise chuckled. "I know where he's taking you."

Nina whirled around. "Oh, don't even say that. Do you? Where, Elise? Tell me, please."

Elise just grinned.

"Hawaii? Jamaica? It's someplace tropical, right? Or maybe Paris. Ooh, Paris would be awesome. Is it Paris?"

"Wherever it is, you'll be with Ricky, so you'll have a great time." Elise couldn't help thinking about her own Jamaican honeymoon. That week with Jerome was heaven on an island paradise created for lovers.

They'd been so in love.

She'd never believed it was possible to love someone as much as she loved Jerome then. They complemented each other, in temperament, in ambition. Light to dark, yin to yang.

"You're my world, Jerome," she'd told him.

"And you are the reason I breathe each day."

That day on the beach as the sun set, they reaffirmed the vows they'd just taken, committing their lives and destinies to each other.

Nina touched her arm. "Hey, girl. You all right?"

Elise blinked. It took another moment to shake out of the memories. *Remember, child, cherish your beloved.*

Remember.

She did. And now, probably too late, she realized the intrinsic value of what she was losing. She fingered the diamond and the large gold band on her ring finger. She'd put her wedding set back on right after talking with Auntie Joe.

"I'm fine," she told Nina, adding a smile to reassure her

friend. Elise glanced at her watch. "It's five to, I think it'll be all right if you go in now."

"Yes!" Nina charged toward the front door.

"Hold up, sister. There's a condition."

Nina turned around. "I don't think I'm gonna like this. You *do* know that bridal showers aren't supposed to be torture."

Elise smiled as she pulled something from the pocket of her slacks.

"Come here."

Nina took the three steps that put her beside Elise. "What is that?" Then, when she recognized the blindfold in Elise's hand, she said, "You are not serious, I know."

"It's the only way you get in."

On a huff, Nina turned so Elise could put the blindfold on. "Can you see?" Elise asked.

"Like I'm really gonna tell you."

Chuckling, Elise took Nina's hand and guided her into the house. When Elise made a left instead of a right, Nina protested.

"Hey, where are we going? The living room's the other way."

"You'll see," Elise said. "Oops, I forgot, you can't see anything."

"I don't know how I got to be friends with such an evil woman," Nina muttered.

Elise guided Nina into the bedroom where attendants from the party planning group waited. "Nina, there are two people here, both female. They are going to give you something comfortable to wear."

Nina looked toward Elise's voice and then jumped when she felt hands tugging at her clothes. "I'm not having fun yet."

"Don't worry, you will." Elise quickly changed her own clothes, donning a flowing silk shift and balloon genie pants. When Nina was similarly attired, Elise took her hand again.

"Thanks, guys," Elise told the attendants. Pressing a finger to her lips to remind them to keep quiet, she nodded and pointed toward the door. They slipped out with Nina none the wiser.

"I don't know what you're up to," Nina said, "but I love the feel of this silk. Can I keep this?"

"Maybe. Come on, bride-to-be. It's time."

Elise led Nina to the living room.

"Ooh, something smells good," Nina said. "Is that incense or aromatherapy oil?"

Someone giggled.

"Shh."

"Who was that?" Nina said. "That sounded like Tanisha's little laugh."

"Stop right here," Elise told Nina. She turned Nina a bit so she faced her audience. "To the court, may I present Nina Tippens, the guest of honor. All rise."

Soft rustling issued forth. Nina reached for the blindfold. "I can take this thing off now?"

"Yes, Nina. Take it off."

Before the words were out of Elise's mouth, Nina ripped the blindfold from her eyes. "Oh. Oh, my God. Oh. Oh, my God." Then she burst into tears.

CHAPTER 9

FOR a moment, no one said a word. Elise, the guests and the party planners looked on in stunned horror. Then all of a sudden, everyone talked at once and Nina found herself surrounded by almost two dozen women.

"Nina, honey, I'm sorry. I thought you'd like it," Elise said as she rubbed her friend's back, trying to comfort her.

"I do!" Nina wailed. "It's beautiful."

A heartbeat later, laughter rippled around the room. "Girl, you are a trip," someone said.

"You had us worried," another said.

"Somebody give that girl a tissue."

The party coordinator heaved a sigh of relief.

"It's just pre-wedding nerves," said Nina's mother, Wanda. "She's all right, right, baby?"

Nina nodded, accepting a tissue someone pressed into her hand. With Elise and her mother at her side, she stepped closer to get a good look around. Elise's great room had been transformed into a sultan's tent for a pampered harem. The high ceiling offered enough room for a tent with purple and gold silk gathers to flow around the women. The furniture normally in the room had been moved or draped with lush fabric in royal hues of red, gold, blue and purple. Large pillows for seating were scattered all over. In the far corner of the tent, two tables were covered with fabric.

"Oh, Elise. It's beautiful. It's a dream come true. Thank you."

"You deserve it, Nina. And, my friend, the best is yet to come."

The two women hugged and Elise found her own eyes misting. That she was able to do this for her best friend filled her with joy. Someone handed her some tissues and Elise dabbed at her own eyes before passing more of them to Nina, who noisily blew her nose.

Shaking her head, Nina looked around again. "I don't think it can get any better than this."

Elise led Nina to a pasha's chair. Her shower gifts, stacked on both sides of the chair, surrounded her.

Elise made her way to the center of the tent. "Ladies, thank you for coming tonight as we celebrate the soon-to-be nuptials of our friend and sister."

The women clapped for Nina, who was still sniffling and wiping her eyes. "I tell you, this was worth all that secrecy. Y'all knew and didn't say a word."

"No, we didn't," said Tanisha, Nina's cousin and a bridesmaid. "The invitation just said wear comfortable loose clothes."

"Chile, I thought we were gonna be doing some aerobics up in here," Ella Rae Tippens said around munches on a jumbo shrimp.

Several people laughed.

"So did I, Aunt Ella Rae," Nina said.

"No exercise for this shower," Elise told her guests. "Tonight is a night of pampering, ladies. We'll play some games, too. And at eight-thirty or so, we'll be served dinner."

"Umph, you go, Miss Nina. I can tell you, my wedding shower wasn't nothing like this."

Elise chuckled. "In the meantime, help yourself to more hors d'oeuvres and then get comfortable for a bit of entertainment."

The women let Nina go to a table laden with gourmet delicacies and a selection of white, rosé and blush wines. After everyone was settled with food and wine, Elise clapped her hands twice, then sat on a cushion near Nina to nibble from her own plate. Middle Eastern music flowed in around them; a moment later, three belly dancers entered the tent.

Cheers went up as the dancers performed. Then it was

time for the guests to learn the sensual moves.

After the belly dance lessons, the women played a few traditional bridal shower games. Elise slipped out to check on dinner.

"Is everything ready?" she asked the caterer who'd turned her kitchen into a place she didn't recognize.

"All set."

Elise looked around. "Well, where are they?"

The caterer smiled. "Everything's under control. Go enjoy your party. It's a hit." He winked at her.

Laughing, Elise went back to the tent. A few minutes later, chimes sounded. Elise smiled. "Ladies, please take your seats. Dinner is served."

The fabric tent flaps parted and four barefoot and barechested men entered. They ranged from light as honey to dark as molasses—a little something for every woman's taste.

Catcalls and whistles went up all across the room as the men distributed first plates and napkins, then delectable finger foods, lingering to serve each woman with a smile.

"Elise, where in the world did you find these gods?"

Plucking a juicy green grape from a small cluster, Elise grinned. "I aim to please," she said.

Nina leaned over. "Girl, this is the bomb. I cannot believe you did this."

"I'm glad you're having fun."

Elise thought about the time, the planning and the money that had gone into making this shower happen for her friend. Unbidden, the advice from her great-aunt came to mind: *Cherish your beloved.*

The bite of guilt lanced through her. She'd put more effort into coordinating this bridal shower than she'd put into saving her marriage. That was what Jerome had been talking about. That was what Anva had warned her against. That was what she realized now—too late.

She'd expended more creative energy for her girlfriend than she had for the man to whom she'd made promises and vows.

Tears welled in her eyes.

She quickly scrambled up before anyone noticed. Grateful that they were all distracted by the sexy waiters, Elise slipped away to her bedroom, hoping to regroup and reapply her makeup so her guests would see her everything-is-wonderful-in-my-world face.

She sat on the edge of her bed staring at her wedding set. The rings she and Jerome exchanged on their wedding day represented an unbroken circle of love, a promise of a lifetime together. But the lifetime had lasted just three years.

"Hey, girl."

Elise looked up to see Nina standing in the doorway. She tried to smile, but the motion, like her spirit, was half-hearted. Nina came in and sat next to Elise, hugging her shoulder.

"What's got you down, sisterfriend?"

Elise wiped at her eyes and shook her head. "Nothing. You're supposed to be out there getting a massage by one of those waiters."

"Aunt Ella Rae and Yvette jumped up first when they announced that. I've never seen my mama's sister move that fast. The brother with the blue pants said they'd give massages to anyone who wanted one, and she was up off that pillow like somebody lit a flame under her behind."

That got a smile from Elise.

"Come on, talk to me," Nina urged.

"There's nothing to say. You're getting married, and I'm getting divorced."

"Stop saying that. The two of you can work things out. Who was the one telling me to be strong and proactive and to fight for my man when Ricky was acting all crazy with that flight attendant he met?"

Nina waggled her ring finger in front of Elise's nose. "I'm the one with the ring *and* the man. Not her. If you love him, fight for him."

"But Cassandra Blakely . . ."

Nina's sigh echoed through the bedroom. "I told you, she's not a factor. That's ancient history stuff, Stonehenge, the pyramids, Peaches and Herb."

Elise smiled, but she also took a deep breath. "I don't know where to even begin."

Nina tipped Elise's chin up. "Do you still love him?"

Elise nodded.

"Well, that's where you start."

A knock on the open door drew their attention. "Excuse me, y'all," Tanisha said. "Jerome's at the front door."

Elise jumped up. "Jerome's here?"

Tanisha nodded. "He said he didn't want to disturb the party."

Elise looked back at Nina, who nodded.

"Go, girl."

She needed no more prompting. Elise was out the door and headed to the front of the house. "Where'd Jerome go?" she asked when she didn't see him.

One of the women headed into the powder room answered. "Said he'd be outside. He was mumbling something about too much estrogen in the house."

Elise snatched open the front portal. Sure enough, there he was.

Her heart beat triple-time and her palms grew clammy even as her mouth went dry. After three years of marriage and their current estrangement, he still made her go weak in the knees.

"Jerome?"

He turned around. His gaze took in all of her. Belatedly Elise remembered the harem girl outfit she wore. Backlit from the bright lights in the foyer and beyond, the silky gauze probably highlighted every curve of her body. From the look in Jerome's eyes it was true.

But before she could use the seductive garment to her advantage, his gaze connected with hers and the warmth she'd sensed in his presence vanished, replaced by a look she couldn't read.

"Hello, Elise. I just dropped by to pick up some more things. I'd forgotten this was Nina's party night."

She reached for his hand. "Jerome, we need to talk."

"What's that?" he said pointing to her ring finger.

"Something very important to me that I shouldn't have relegated to a drawer."

He looked unsure, but a peace settled over Elise. Whether it was Anva's spirit, Auntie Joe's conjuring or just the realization that this was it, she didn't know. All that mattered was trying to mend the rift between them.

Something about her was different. Jerome sensed the change in her. Had Auntie Joe indeed put a spell on her?

Seeing Elise in that harem outfit not only fired Jerome's blood, it gave him an idea.

They needed to work out their differences on neutral territory. The house wouldn't do, neither would his condo.

He couldn't re-create the beach where they'd been on their honeymoon, but maybe he could do something else romantic. Miss Eliza Mae had said he was supposed to wait. But the time for waiting was over.

Jerome was a man of action, and the time for that was right now.

He didn't necessarily want an Elise who came to him as a result of voodoo magic. But at this point he'd take her any way he could get her. Unfortunately, the determination he saw in her eyes was more than likely a resolution she'd come up with regarding their separation. Equitable distribution of property, how to split up the gym membership, who'd get which CDs and that sort of thing. The future looked awfully bleak after a restless night.

"Hey, Jerome," Tanisha said, poking her head out the door. "What's happening?"

Jerome barely took his eyes off his wife. "Hi, Tanisha. Enjoying the shower?"

"It's terrific. Elise really outdid herself. I'm glad, too," Tanisha said on a giggle. "That Marcus has some wonder-working power in those hands of his."

Jerome's head snapped up. "Marcus, who's Marcus?"

Tanisha smiled in a way that left no question as to what she thought about the man. "He's one of the guys who—"

"He's one of the waiters," Elise cut in. "I had a caterer do the food."

Tanisha smirked and winked at Jerome. "Yeah, that's right. He's a waiter. He's waiting on Christa right now. You should hear her moaning, begging for more. Your turn is next, Elise."

With that, Tanisha gave a "ta-ta" three-finger wave to

Jerome and Elise and scampered back toward the shower festivities.

"What's going on in there?"

Elise folded her arms. "Do you really care?"

Before Jerome could answer, a tall, muscle-bound man appeared behind her. He placed his hands at Elise's waist. "Your turn," he said near her ear. "Hey, man," he greeted Jerome with a nod.

"I . . ." Elise looked everywhere except at Jerome. "It's not what it looks like."

"This one is my woman, Jerome said. "Go find your own. There're plenty to choose from in there."

With a shrug, the waiter turned and went back in the house.

Elise gazed at her husband, wonder and curiosity in her eyes. "Your woman? But I thought . . ."

Jerome shushed her with a kiss. "That's just something to let you know that we have some unfinished business. Unfinished by about forty or fifty years together."

A smile blossomed on Elise's face. She wrapped her arms around his shoulders. "What are you saying?"

He stole another quick kiss. "I'm saying we have some things to discuss, but I know you have a house full of women. And judging by this costume and that bare-chested guy, it involves strippers."

Elise laughed. "No, not quite."

Jerome ran a hand from the middle of her back down, over and around her rear. "I want more than sex with you, Elise. You're my world."

"Hey, Elise," someone from the door called. "Miss Ella Rae is asking for you and the caterer said he needs you to sign something."

"You need to get back to your guests."

"Um-hmm." But neither of them moved.

"Elise?"

"I'm coming," she called over her shoulder.

Jerome squeezed her rear as a sly naughty smile curved his mouth. "Not yet, you aren't. But you will when I finish with you."

Elise's smile was slow and broad. "I'll hold you to that."

CHAPTER 10

THE next morning, Elise and Nina were sprawled across pillows in the harem tent. After bidding farewell to all the guests, the two friends opened several bottles of wine and proceeded to empty them as they talked about life, love and men.

Rubbing her eyes, Elise squinted. "What time is it?"

"Too early."

The doorbell rang.

"Make it go away," Nina moaned.

Elise slowly made her way up and to the front door. "All right, already. I'm coming."

She opened the door to see Jerome.

"What in the world was going on here last night, an orgy?"

"Jerome, honey, not so loud," Nina said, as she tried to sit up.

Stepping over several pillows and empty wineglasses, he made his way to Nina and gave her a hand up.

Muttering her thanks, Nina moved around him. "Gotta pee."

Jerome stood in the middle of the tent looking at the remains of the so-called bridal shower. There were supposed to be crepe-paper streamers and balloons, maybe some leftover cake. That was what the church fellowship hall looked like after his sister's bridal shower. This place looked like a pleasure palace.

"Elise?"

He turned around, but she wasn't there.

Jerome went to the kitchen. Unlike the great room, it was spotless, cleaner than even they usually kept it. He started a pot of coffee for the two women, who looked like they could use it.

The refrigerator was stocked with carefully labeled left-overs.

"They sure ate well," he said.

He closed the refrigerator and went in search of Elise.

The shower in her bedroom was running; so was the shower in the guest suite. Shaking his head, he went back to Elise's bedroom.

Quickly making up his mind to follow his plan, he went to the big closet they used to share. He pulled out an over-night bag, then quickly packed a few items. He found her matching cosmetics case and left it open on top of the dress-ing room bureau. He sniffed a couple of her perfume bottles and put the one he liked best in the case. Then, methodically, he added what he thought she'd need for a couple of days away. From her jewelry case, he selected three pieces, all gifts he'd given her, then folded them in a handkerchief he pulled from his pocket and tucked them in the case.

The shower went off. Glancing up, Jerome zipped up the cosmetic bag, secured the locks on the clothes bag and slipped out. When he came back, Elise was standing in front of the mirror, staring down at her vanity top.

"What's wrong?"

She jumped and clutched her chest. "Jerome, you scared me."

"Sorry," he said. But he wasn't really. The towel she had draped across her body slipped, giving him a delectable view of the soft curve of her back.

She faced him, gathering the towel closer to her breasts, forgetting, to Jerome's advantage, the image he got in the mirror.

"We need to talk. And we can't do it here."

"Elise, do you have some . . ." Nina walked into the bed-room. "Oh, I'm sorry, y'all."

"It's okay," he said, but his gaze never left his wife.

Nina looked between them and cleared her throat. "I'll just let myself out. Elise, I'll call you later. The shower was fabulous. Thanks again. 'Bye, Jerome."

Before they knew it, they were alone: Elise standing in nothing but a towel and Jerome, hands in pockets, wishing he could take the towel away.

Elise bit her lip. "I-I'm going to get dressed."

"Okay," he said, but he didn't move.

When he didn't say anything else, Elise slipped into the dressing room, grateful for the chance to be out of his line of sight.

"I'll be in the kitchen," he said.

"All right."

A few minutes later, Elise, dressed in shorts and a cropped cotton top, joined him.

He poured her a cup of coffee and eased an omelette out of the skillet and onto a plate. "Perfect timing," he said.

"Jerome, what are you doing?"

Wheat toast popped up from the toaster on the counter.

"Making you breakfast. Sit." He moved to the table and held a chair for her. Fresh-squeezed orange juice was already there.

"Why are you doing this?"

"Because I don't have a choice."

As she chewed she mulled over his words. "This is good. Thanks."

"I've missed having breakfast with you."

Elise smiled, but little joy showed in her face. "It has been a long time." She watched him for a moment. No movements were wasted as he cracked eggs in the skillet, added cheese and a few vegetables. A few minutes later, he was sitting at the table with her.

The breakfast they shared was quiet, neither one willing to break the silence. Elise poured more juice for him and for herself.

"They were waiters," she said.

Jerome looked up.

"The guy you saw last night, he and the others were waiters. Nina has always liked the *Arabian Nights* story so I tried to re-create a little of it for her. We had belly dancers, too." She grinned. "You should have seen some of those women trying out the moves. Miss Ella Rae had everyone laughing, and Nina's mother said she was about to throw a hip out."

He smiled as she talked, enjoying the sound of her voice and just being in her company.

"After serving dinner, the waiters gave back massages to anyone who wanted one. That's what that guy meant, Jerome. I don't have a boyfriend," she said just to clarify.

He met her gaze. "I'm glad." A moment passed, and then he said, "And I don't have a girlfriend."

She pushed a bit of omelette around her plate. "You don't?"

"No. But I do have a wife. One I'd truly like to call wife again."

"You would?"

He nodded. "Cassandra and I dated in college. But we eventually went our separate ways."

"I saw you together at the magazine. I came by Monday to surprise you. I got the surprise, though. You kissed her."

He nodded again. "The same way you kiss Ricky."

Elise opened her mouth to protest, then realized maybe he was right. Had she misread that situation?

"She's getting married," Jerome said. "That's what she was telling me when you saw us."

"Getting married?"

"To her soul mate."

Elise was quiet for a while. Her gaze eventually connected with his. "I'm sorry, Jerome. I'm sorry I put everything in my life in front of you."

"And I'm sorry I let running a magazine take precedence over our relationship."

"I'm cutting back at the real estate agency. I even left work on my desk yesterday. It was very hard to do," she admitted.

He brought her hand to his mouth and kissed it. "We can't change overnight," he said. "But we can change together."

Elise took a deep breath. She wasn't sure how Jerome might take what she had to say next. But she needed to say it, she had to at least ask. They had too much to lose. "Jerome?"

"Um-hmm."

"Before, when we were talking, you mentioned . . . well, you mentioned a marriage counselor. I think that would be good for us. Plus," she said, hating to admit this part but realizing it was necessary, "I have some insecurity issues I think a counselor could help with."

He let her hand go and cleared the table. When he returned, he had a sticky cinnamon bun on a small plate and two forks in his hand.

He'd almost not stopped for the treat. But if he had any chance of winning her back, he had to pull out all the emotional stops. He was playing to win.

"I think all good counselors encourage couples to relive positive moments in their lives." He placed the plate on the table before her.

Elise smiled. "Our first date. A cinnamon bun at the mall after the movie."

"I hoped you'd remember."

She nodded. He sat down, cut a bit with the edge of a fork and fed her the sweet. She did likewise, feeding him a piece of the bun.

After two more bites, she shook her head. He put his fork down and met her gaze.

"I think a marriage counselor will be good for us. But Elise, I have something very important to ask you," he said.

"I have something I want to ask you, too."

"You first," he said.

"No, you go ahead."

"Will you marry me?" they said at the same time.

They both started laughing.

Jerome slipped from his chair and got on one knee on the kitchen floor. "I already packed your bags while you were in the shower. I was planning to whisk you away today and give this to you at a bed-and-breakfast I reserved for us."

Tears glistened in Elise's eyes. "Give me what?"

He pulled a small jeweler's box from his pocket. He opened it. A diamond anniversary ring sparkled.

"Oh, Jerome."

"Will you marry me again?" Jerome asked.

"Yes."

And then she kissed him. Slowly at first. Then with a greater hunger, this one predicated not merely on lust but grounded in the love they shared.

Elise joined him on her knees on the floor, wrapping her arms around his neck. The kiss between them grew demanding, urgent. She tugged at his shirt and he slipped a hand beneath the cropped top she wore.

"I've missed you, Elise."

"Not as much as I've missed you. I love you, Jerome Gregory. I really do."

They nibbled and sampled and tasted the sweetness that had been denied for too long. Knowing they'd never make it to the bedroom, Jerome rose and brought Elise up with him. He backed her against the counter. She unzipped his pants and he pulled down her shorts. Their loving was fast and furious. Later, there would be time for gentle words and play and tender lovemaking. Right now, they had to ease the hunger.

She cried out his name when he came to her. With her legs wrapped around him, they loved hard and fast. Both moaning and straining to get closer, then closer still.

When they finished, Jerome lifted her in his arms and carried her to the bedroom, their bedroom.

He carefully deposited Elise on the mattress. Then, sitting next to her, he undressed her, slowly. His mouth kissed each new part of her that was revealed to him. She arched her hips and cried out.

"Easy," he murmured. "We have all the time in the world."

When she lay before him naked, Jerome's breath caught. "You are so beautiful."

She reached for him. "Jerome . . ."

He caught her hands in his and raised them above her head. "I want to look at you," he said. "It's like seeing a rainbow after a storm, or discovering flowers in a barren field. You're my world, Elise."

"Show me," she said.

He grinned. "I love a challenge almost as much as I love you."

"I'm hearing a lot of talk," Elise said, her tone sassy.

"Hmm." He got up from the bed.

Elise shot up. "Where are you going?"

"I forgot something."

"What?"

But he was already out of the bedroom. She sat up in the middle of the bed. "Jerome?"

He returned a moment later, a straw basket in his hand. A large pink bow graced the handle.

"What is that?"

He stood there for a moment at the side of the bed, just staring at his wife. That's when Elise remembered she was stark naked. She lifted a hand to shield her breasts.

"Uh-uh," Jerome said. He placed the basket on the floor and shed his own clothes. "You're too beautiful to cover yourself. Let me see you."

"Only if you'll let *me* see *you*. I've missed you, Jerome."

He sat on the edge of the bed and drew her close. "Lie back."

There was a question in her eyes, but she didn't say anything as she settled back on the bed.

"Now," he directed. "Close your eyes."

When she did, he smiled and reached for the large basket. A moment later, fragrant rose petals drifted all over Elise.

"Jerome, you didn't."

"I told you what I wanted to do."

She smiled. "Yes, you did."

When all but her face was covered in pink, red and white petals, he did exactly what he'd told her he wanted to do. At the first touch of his mouth, Elise moaned. Heat raced through her; every nerve ending was taut, straining for the release that would soon come. But not soon enough. At the second touch of his mouth she arched her hips toward his.

"Jerome, now. Please."

"Easy now. I've got a long way to go before I taste every inch of you. I plan to enjoy this feast."

"You're gonna kill me!"

"Then we'll go together," he said. With nothing but time, he took sweet care loving every single part of her. His mouth dallied as he licked and nipped and kissed his way across her breasts, her navel and the juncture of her thighs. Elise lifted herself to him, ready for the hard, thick feel of him. But Jerome took a detour just when she thought she'd fall apart.

He scooted down on the bed and introduced himself first to her toes, then slowly, deliciously worked his way up her body.

And when every rose petal was off of her and on the bed, he settled between her legs. Elise, a mass of sensation, was beyond words, beyond enchantment.

"Now, please."

"Look at me, Elise."

She opened her eyes and saw in his a reflection of the love she felt for her husband.

"Forever, Elise, that's how long I'll love you."

"Forever," she said. And then he slid home. With a moan of pure ecstasy Elise welcomed him. She wrapped her legs around his and held him tight. For a moment, they just lay together, neither moving, both savoring the feel and warmth of the other. And then her hips began to rock as she reveled in the hardness of him, filling her to her core. His thrusts became more urgent and she cried out his name.

This is where she belonged, where she wanted to be. Always. Forever. Loving Jerome and having him love her. Her heart soared even as she felt the first tremors of her body about to take its own flight.

She clenched herself around him, and a moment later Elise shattered into a million brilliant stars as wave after wave of tremors wracked her body. He licked her breasts, murmuring sweet words of passion. And when she finally stilled, Jerome brought her to the brink again and again, before seeking his own release.

Much later, when their breathing and their bodies had returned to normal, Jerome pulled her closer to him and whispered sweet words in her ear. Then he loved her again.

• • •

The morning of Nina and Ricky's wedding dawned sunny and warm. Nina, a radiant bride, joined Ricky at the altar, where they exchanged vows that would bind them forever in love.

At the end of the service, Nina's mother shooed everyone out of the chapel. The guests all thought photos were being taken of the bridal party. In truth, another ceremony was about to take place.

Elise and Jerome stood before the priest, with Nina and Ricky standing nearby as witnesses. Auntie Joe was there. So was Miss Eliza Mae.

"Do you, Jerome, promise to love, honor and cherish this woman as long as you both shall live?"

"I do," he said.

"And do you, Elise, promise to—"

"I do," she said, cutting off the priest's words.

"You're supposed to wait until he finishes," Nina whispered.

Auntie Joe and Miss Eliza Mae chuckled.

But Elise remained focused only on her husband. "I love you, Jerome. Through good times and bad. For always."

The priest smiled and nodded toward Jerome. "You may salute your wife."

Jerome cupped her face in his hands. His whispered "I love you" made her heart soar. And the kiss they shared sealed a promise of love to last a lifetime.

KIDNAPPED!

KAYLA PERRIN

For M.H.,
for inspiring this story

CHAPTER 1

BETTER lover than him, his ass!

Jamal Simpson dropped his cigarette butt to the concrete beside the outdoor table where he sat, then ground it out with the heel of his Dr. Martens. He didn't often smoke, just did so to calm his nerves from time to time, but not even a fix of nicotine was doing him any good today. Neither had the two draft beers he'd downed on an empty stomach, he realized, looking at the second empty mug. If he were smart, he would have eaten something as he drank, but he was too on edge to keep anything heavy down. Instead of feeling a buzz or even the beginnings of numbness as he'd hoped, he felt even more queasy than when he'd first arrived. He had to admit, none of his vices had made the situation any better. How could anything make things better right now, when his mind kept replaying the conversation he'd had with Nia last night?

The sound of female laughter made Jamal look up. Three beautiful women in bikinis with hip wraps strolled past his table. It was a sight that would normally lift his spirits, but today the sight only made his gut twist—every beautiful woman made him think of Nia. The sun was shining brightly this June day, and the sky was clear for as far as the eye could see. Tourists crowded the beach strip, enjoying the perfect weather.

And here he was, sitting with a frown.

Nia. Damn her, the cause for his foul mood. Their re-

lationship was over—had been over for a good year—and
he would have done well to remember that yesterday. He
shouldn't have gone to see her before what was supposed to
be the most important day of her life. He should have left
well enough alone and let her walk down the aisle without
any question from him. Which is exactly what he'd planned
on doing . . . but when had he ever stuck to anyone's plans,
much less his own?

The problem was, no matter how many times he'd told
himself to leave well enough alone in the last couple weeks
before Nia's wedding, something had nagged at him, making
him restless at nights. After days of little sleep, he'd finally
realized what was wrong: He needed to know that Nia was
really going to be happy. Sure, their relationship was over,
and they certainly didn't have a future, but he still cared
about her and always would. So for his own peace of mind,
he had to know she was happy before she walked down any
aisle. He didn't want her to make a mistake about something
as important as marriage, especially on account of him.

Nia said he had too much of an ego, and maybe she was
right, but considering she had been in love with him for so
long, Jamal couldn't help thinking that perhaps her engagement to this John guy was a rebound thing. Right up until
the day Nia had hooked up with John, she'd been asking
Jamal to give their relationship another chance. So yeah, he
had his doubts about whether her feelings for John-boy were
true. If Jamal was wrong, fine, but he'd just wanted to know
for sure.

So, despite not having spoken in months, it was that very
thought that had him showing up on Nia's doorstep the previous evening. Forget the fact that the last time they'd spoken, she'd told him she was tired of his games and to stay
out of her life forever.

"Hey, Nia," Jamal had casually said when she opened
the door last night. To his credit he didn't flinch, not even
as her mouth dropped open in shock.

"What are you doing here?" she'd asked, the note of
horror in her voice not escaping him.

"I wanted to see you." He'd heard from a friend that she
was staying at her parents' house until the wedding, and he'd

waited around until he saw them drive off. He certainly didn't need the aggravation that would come from dealing with her mother and father. "To see how you're doing."

Nia stared at him good and hard for several seconds. "To see how I'm doing?"

"Yeah, you know."

"No, I don't know."

"You're about to get married, and—"

"And what?"

"And . . ." Jamal shrugged. "And I wanted to make sure you're okay. Happy."

"Really?"

"Yeah, really."

"Well, isn't that special? Call me crazy, but I don't see how my marriage is of any concern to you."

"C'mon, Nia," Jamal responded, a hint of playfulness in his voice, as though they were the best of buddies. "Why wouldn't I be concerned? We're friends, aren't we?"

"Friends?" The word spilled from her lips like spoiled milk. She paused to stare at him incredulously, then continued. "What a surprise. And here I was, under the impression that we were nothing to each other anymore."

Ouch. Nia's words stung—words he'd once said to her. But she was wrong. He'd only told her that to make it easier for her to move on with her life. As long as she thought they had a chance, she continued to cling to him, and Jamal knew a future wasn't in the cards for them. But he still cared about her and always would. Just because they didn't have that forever kind of love didn't mean he wanted anything less than complete happiness for her.

"Look, Nia," Jamal said, his tone now softer. "I'll be straight and tell you why I'm here. We meant a lot to each other once, and no matter what I may have said in anger in the past, I'll always want the best for you." He paused. "But John? I don't know. He doesn't exactly seem like he's the man to make all your dreams come true."

Nia planted a hand firmly on her hip and scowled at him. "Is that so?"

"No offense, Nia, but let's face it—John is old enough to be your father. He might have lots of money and be able to buy you everything your heart desires . . ." His eyes ventured to the huge rock on her finger. "But what about your other needs?"

Nia's eyes instantly bulged. "Ex*cuse* me?"

Jamal's voice deepened as he said, "Nia, I know you."

"I know you didn't just go there . . ."

"He's older. There's no way he can be in the kind of shape a younger guy—"

"How dare you?" Nia was so livid, Jamal almost expected to see steam coming from her ears. "How dare you come to my place on the eve of my wedding and talk to me about this?"

Jamal knew he was venturing into territory that was none of his business, but he couldn't stop himself. One thing about Nia—she was always passionate, and that was something he'd loved about her. Even her anger had turned him on. Because after their crazy fights, they'd always had the best sex. His groin tightened with the memory of how he and Nia had been in bed. Was she as excited with John? Jamal couldn't picture it. And he certainly couldn't imagine another man satisfying Nia sexually the way he had.

"Answer the question, Nia," Jamal pressed. "Tell me he takes care of you in every way, and I'll wish you all the best, then leave."

Nia merely stared at him, her ragged breaths causing her full breasts to rise and fall enticingly, but she didn't answer the question.

"That's what I thought," Jamal said, feeling a bit smug. He knew there was no way John-boy could ever please Nia the way he had.

"Not so fast." Nia's tone was like a pinprick in Jamal's ego. She blew out a weary breath that said he'd asked for it. "Since you must know."

Jamal's throat went dry.

Looking him squarely in the eyes, Nia had replied as coolly as a cucumber, "John is an *amazing* lover. Much better than anyone I've ever had. You know what they say about older men being more experienced." Her lips curled in a sly smile. "Well, it's true. Sorry if that disappoints you."

Sorry if that disappoints me? Jamal had repeated mentally, but had been unable to find a voice for the words. And before he could, Nia had closed the door and left him standing on her doorstep, stunned.

Jamal shuddered from a sudden chill that the memory brought. He reached for his pack of cigarettes on the table, but dropped his hand inches short of retrieving it. Another cigarette wasn't going to make him forget her words. Words that burned him—burned him because she might as well have come right out and said that John was a better lover than he was. Nia had been a virgin when they'd gotten involved during her junior year of college, and after their breakup two years later, he knew she hadn't been with anyone else. Hell, for the past year she'd tried and tried to win him back, right up until the day that John the choirboy had walked into the restaurant her father owned and she'd seated him at a table for dinner.

At least that was what Jamal had heard.

At first, he had missed her calls, missed her appearances at the auto shop where he worked, but when he had learned that she was seeing someone else, he had been determined to forget about her once and for all. They couldn't be together. He'd known that even as he'd lusted after her and tried to pretend it was something else. Ultimately, when she'd started talking about her dreams of getting married and having children, Jamal had known that he'd had to end the relationship. Him as father material? Not in this lifetime.

The final straw had been when she'd told him that she'd talked her father into hiring him on as a manager at the restaurant—complete with on-the-job training *and* her father's blessing. Well, Jamal didn't believe that. He wasn't going to fit into that prim and proper world, and he sure as hell knew he was never going to earn her father's approval. For a while, he'd convinced himself that Nia could accept him for who he was—a mechanic with only a high-school education—but her going behind his back and getting him a job had proven to him that Nia, the good girl he'd fallen for, could never have a life with a guy who'd been considered a bad boy his whole life. It was a fantasy, and he'd put an end to it. So, he'd pushed her away and moved on. It was best that way.

But even though he'd forced her out of his life, he still thought about her all the time. It was the sex, he was sure. There was something about the way Nia gave herself to him that made the act much more pleasurable with her than it had been with anyone else. Still, he did his best to forget her, because they didn't have a future—and as much as any healthy guy might wish it, you certainly couldn't build a relationship on sex alone. And Jamal wasn't dumb enough to believe a happily-ever-after was in the cards for them.

So when he'd heard that she was engaged, though he'd been surprised at how quickly it had happened, he had accepted that it was for the best. He couldn't give her what she needed or deserved, and her family sure as hell would be happier with him permanently out of the picture.

So, he'd stayed away from her—until last night. Last night, he'd finally given in to the urge to see for himself that she was happy.

He hadn't expected her to diss his performance in bed!

"Sir, can I get you anything else?"

The waitress's voice shocked Jamal back to the present, and he looked around, almost surprised to find that he was at a crowded outdoor bar on the Fort Lauderdale beach strip.

"No," Jamal said. Standing, he reached into his back pocket and withdrew his wallet. "How much for the beer?"

"Only three dollars. It's two for the price of one during happy hour."

Happy hour, his ass. Jamal handed the waitress a five, then headed toward the road and his parked motorcycle.

Any minute, Nia would be tying the knot. The church was on Sunrise Boulevard in Fort Lauderdale, not too far from where he was now. He had a mind to drive by and see her before the ceremony, tell her that he knew she was lying about John being a better lover. He knew what she'd say— she'd tell him to get over his ego, but this wasn't about ego. This was something he *knew*.

Jamal climbed onto his motorcycle and revved the engine. A second later, he was merging into the busy Saturday afternoon beach traffic.

He should have made a left at the first street he came to, then doubled back to Los Olas Boulevard to head for

I-95, which would take him south to his North Miami home. But something made him continue north, then turn left onto Sunrise Boulevard, heading west.

Toward the church where Nia was getting married.

Nia Copeland stepped out of the limousine and halted on the sidewalk. She blew out a long, weary breath as she looked up at the beautiful old church. Though her family lived in North Miami and attended church there, her father had grown up in Fort Lauderdale, and it was his dream for her to be married at the church where he and her mother had married thirty-one years earlier. Indeed, her parents had taken care of most of the wedding plans, so much so that all she really had to do today was show up.

Nia's eyes lingered on the church's tall steeple as another slow breath oozed out of her. *I'm really going to do this,* she thought.

"Nia?"

Nia abruptly turned at the sound of her older sister's voice. Seeing the concern in Christine's eyes, Nia gave her a bright smile.

"Is that the best you can do?" Christine asked. "This is your wedding day, Nia. You're supposed to be happy."

"I *am* happy," Nia protested, knowing full well that her weird mood didn't match her words. "Why wouldn't I be happy?"

"I don't know," Christine replied. "You seem . . ."

At the sound of a motorcycle, Nia's head flew in that direction. Her stomach actually did a little nosedive when she saw that it wasn't Jamal. Silently, she chastised herself for the feeling. Of course she was glad it wasn't Jamal. She never wanted to see him again.

Nia faced her sister. "I am happy. Just a little nervous, that's all."

Christine approached Nia and started to fuss with her veil. "Of course you're nervous. You want everything to be perfect—and it will be. The day couldn't be more beautiful. Nice and sunny, with just the hint of a breeze. Look around you. Everything is so lush, so vibrant. And the scent of hibiscus is heavenly."

"Yes, I guess."

"Oh, sweetie. Don't you worry your pretty little head about a thing. Mom and Dad hired the best wedding planner in South Florida, so I highly doubt anything will go wrong. I know it didn't help that that jerk Jamal showed up last night, but don't let him get to you. I don't know what his problem is, anyway." Christine folded her arms over her chest and gave a satisfied smile. "Perfect. You look so beautiful, hon." She wrapped an arm around Nia's shoulders and gave them a gentle squeeze. "Forget about Jamal and think about John. Today, you become Mrs. John Whalen, sis. Till death do you part."

Don't remind me, Nia almost said, then was horrified. Good Lord, where had that thought come from? What was wrong with her? John was a good man, and she was minutes away from becoming his wife.

As if in answer to her unspoken question, Christine said, "You feel a little tense, but hey, it's perfectly natural for people to get cold feet before they say 'I do.' I had cold feet when I married Howard."

"*You?*"

"You'd never know it, huh? But when I was walking down the aisle, I suddenly wanted to turn around and run from the church."

"I never knew."

"For a moment, I was deathly afraid that I was making a mistake." Christine gave her another squeeze. "I'm telling you this so you realize that what you're feeling right now is common."

Nia held her head high and squared her shoulders. Her sister's words gave her comfort. If Christine had had second thoughts about marrying Howard, the poster-child dream man, then she could relax.

"The bridesmaids are here?" Nia asked.

"Of course. Everyone is in the church. They're just waiting for today's star." Christine paused, then asked, "Are you ready to shine?"

"Ready." Nia spoke confidently.

Christine went behind Nia and began gathering up her dress. Nia clutched her bouquet to her chest and tried to imagine John in the church, standing at the front, anticipating her appearance. She knew he loved her. He would do everything in his power to make her happy.

Nia started for the steps. The loud sound of a motorcycle engine made her stop and turn. It was a Harley, and this one didn't whiz by. It pulled up behind the limo.

The next instant, her heart went berserk.

Jamal!

In two seconds flat, Jamal had the bike parked and was striding toward her. "Nia."

She stood, frozen. Lord help her, what was it about Jamal? Wearing form-fitting black jeans, a black tank top that displayed his beautifully sculpted muscles, and dark sunglasses, he looked damn fine. He looked much the same way he had the very first day she'd seen him in high school— like the bad boy who'd stolen her heart. She'd admired him from afar, having no idea that she'd end up dating the sexy bad boy only a few years later.

"I'll handle this, Nia," Christine said, clearly irked. She marched toward Jamal. "Jamal, I have no clue what you're up to, but go home. You have no right to be here."

Jamal ignored her. "Nia, I need to talk to you."

"Go inside, Nia," Christine instructed, quickly blocking Jamal's path.

Nia didn't move.

"Please, Ni Ni."

Ni Ni. Nia's heart melted at the sound of her old nickname on Jamal's lips.

"I just want a minute of your time," he said. "Before you walk down the aisle." He stepped to the right, but Christine matched his movements, holding a hand to his chest. Jamal stopped. "At least give me that."

"We . . ." Nia felt a moment of weakness, which made no sense at all. "There's nothing more to say, Jamal."

"Go home, Jamal." Christine took hold of his arm and tried to turn him around, but Jamal easily shook out of her grip. He continued toward Nia, walking briskly. As she watched him, Nia momentarily imagined Jamal as her bad boy prince coming to save her from making the biggest mis-

take of her life. Coming to save her because he couldn't live
without her.

Because he still loved her.

Jamal stopped mere inches before her. He pinned her
with an intense gaze. "Tell me you didn't mean what you
said yesterday."

The bad boy prince image fizzled. Nia narrowed her eyes
as she stared at him. "What's wrong with you, Jamal? Have
you been drinking?"

"Tell me you didn't mean it."

"Mean what? That I'm marrying John? Of course I
meant that."

Jamal's eyes bored into hers. "Not that. When you
said—"

"I'm going for help," Christine announced, and scurried
to the church's steps.

Jamal's eyes followed Christine's movements, and for a
second, he seemed concerned. Facing Nia once more, he
spoke quickly. "When you said that you've never had a better
lover than John, you were lying, right?"

This was why he'd come here? Again, Nia's heart fell.
She couldn't allow Jamal to continue hurting her, least of all
on her wedding day. "Jamal, you're tripping. You need to
get over yourself." Nia gathered the skirt of her gown and
whirled on her heel toward the church.

"Wrong answer," Nia heard from behind her, a moment
before Jamal's strong arms encircled her waist.

She let out a startled cry. "Jamal!" He swept her into
his arms, and she cried out louder. "What the hell do you
think you're doing?"

"You're coming with me!"

"Are you insane?" Ignoring her, Jamal hustled with her
to his motorcycle. "This is my wedding day!"

"You're not marrying that loser. Not until I prove to
myself what I know to be true."

Nia's heart thumped—hard. What was he saying?

He placed her on the bike. "Get on. And stay on. If you
even think about running from me, I'll chase you into the
church and object to your wedding."

"On what grounds?"

"On the grounds that John-boy can't please you in bed—at least not the way I did last night."

"What? We weren't together last night."

"But John-boy doesn't know that." Jamal got onto the bike in front of her. "By the time I get through with him and the whole church, you'll never be able to show your face in South Florida again."

Nia's heart sank. She knew well enough not to test Jamal; he didn't bluff. He was the kind of guy who didn't care what others thought about him. He'd do whatever necessary to suit his purposes.

Christine appeared at the church's entrance with their father, their cousin Marvin, and the wedding planner. Jamal was revving the engine when John appeared a moment later.

"Wrap your arms around me, Ni Ni."

Lord help her, this was nuts. How was this happening?

"Nia!" Christine cried. "What are you doing?"

"Hold me tight," Jamal said.

Wrapping her arms around Jamal, Nia took one last look at the startled expression on John's face as he charged down the stairs. But he wasn't fast enough for Jamal, who whizzed the Harley into traffic at a speed that said the man loved living on the edge.

Nia screamed from the momentary shock, then clutched him tighter. To protect her face from the wind, she planted her cheek against Jamal's back and got a good whiff of the alluring musky scent that was uniquely his.

From the corner of one eye, she could see her family—and her future husband—running along the sidewalk.

But it was to no avail.

There was no way they'd catch up with her and Jamal.

CHAPTER 2

JAMAL'S heart pounded from an adrenaline overload. Christ, what had he done? All he'd planned to do when he'd taken a detour by the church was get a confession out of Nia that she'd been lying yesterday.

He hadn't planned on kidnapping her!

And even though he knew he should regret it—Nia's old man would have his hide over this stunt—strangely, he didn't. The feel of Nia's arms wrapped around his waist, her body pressed to his back, made his latest stunt worth it.

Even if only temporarily.

She'd go back to John, he was sure about that, but not before he gave her something to remember him by when John-boy tried to please her at night.

"Jamal, you need to stop," Nia said above the motorcycle's roar and the sounds of other traffic on the road.

Jamal angled his head over his shoulder. "I will. Soon."

"This is ridiculous," Nia protested. "My dress . . . it's gotta be ruined. You have to stop right now."

"Not until we're far enough away."

They were heading south on I-95. Jamal hadn't thought much beyond hightailing it from the church. Hell, he hadn't thought much, period. Now, the best he could figure to do was keep driving until he ran out of road.

I-95 would take them to Key Biscayne, but why go to Key Biscayne when they could go as far south as possible?

At least that way, Nia would be less likely to call her father and have him come rescue her.

Besides, the turnpike would be a less populated road—if by any chance Nia's old man had called the cops. Her father wouldn't expect him to head to Key West, not with Nia dressed in her wedding gown. He'd probably assume Jamal would stop at a nearby hotel, or even take Nia to his North Miami home.

Yeah, they'd head to Key West. There, he'd have time to deal with Nia without any outside interference. One night, then he'd bring her back tomorrow.

Jamal signaled and entered the right lane. They were approaching the Dolphin expressway and he'd have to head west to hit the turnpike before going farther south.

"Jamal—"

"Just hold on, Ni Ni. It won't be long."

Jamal hit the gas, accelerating his motorcycle through traffic. Nia held on tightly, her face still pressed against his back. He could imagine her with her eyes tightly shut, though he didn't think she was afraid. She trusted his driving skills. And when they'd been a couple, she'd always loved to ride with him on his Harley.

Jamal's gaze went to his gas gauge. He would need more fuel if he planned on getting to Key West. And perhaps it was a good plan to stop now, give both of them a chance to stretch their legs. They had a long ride ahead of them.

But he wasn't going to stop yet. Not until he hit the turnpike.

The farther away he could get before they stopped, the better.

Twenty minutes later, Jamal pulled off the highway and into a service station along the turnpike. The moment he parked his bike, Nia got off and tore into him.

"My dress!" She held up the edges of the skirt, a mix of horror and anger passing over her face. "Jamal, look at this dirt. It's ruined. Do you know how much this dress cost?" She huffed her frustration. "I can't believe this. Where are you taking me, anyway? Do you know how crazy this is? You took me from the church on my *wedding* day. What on earth were you thinking?"

"You want something to drink?" Jamal asked calmly, deliberately ignoring her other questions.

Nia glared at him, dropping her dress as she did. "No, I don't want something to drink. I *want* to go home."

"I'll grab you a Coke."

"Oh, now you're deaf, too?"

"Going home right now isn't an option, Nia. But don't get yourself all bent out of shape. I won't be keeping you forever. We have a couple things to deal with first, then I'll get you home."

She cocked her head to the side, her eyes flashing fire at him. "A couple things to deal with?"

"Yes," Jamal replied simply.

"What on earth could we have to deal with on my wedding day?" Nia's voice hinged on hysterical. When Jamal didn't answer her, she threw her hands in the air, then began to pace. "This is a nightmare. I hope John doesn't think I had anything to do with you pulling this stunt."

"Now why would he think that? You two are happily in love, aren't you?"

Nia's expression was enough to kill him, but she didn't confirm or deny his words.

"Don't worry. I'm sure he won't hold it against you. Your family has always said I'm crazy."

Nia didn't say a word. A tall white man exited a car that had pulled up at the pump behind them. Smiling, the man approached Jamal and extended a hand to him. "Hey, congratulations."

Jamal shook the man's hand. "Thanks."

As the man walked back to his car, Nia rolled her eyes. "Oh, this is just wonderful," she whispered in a lethal tone. "People think we just got married. Isn't that a joke?"

Jamal ignored Nia as he gassed up, partly because he didn't know what else to say to her. He knew her snide comment was in reference to the fact that she'd always hoped they would get married. But that was something he'd known wasn't in the cards for him from the start.

When he was finished getting gas, Jamal asked, "Shall I get you a Coke, or something else?"

Nia crossed her arms over her chest. "Whatever."

"If you have to use the bathroom, now's the time. We'll be on the road for a while."

"Fine." But her tone said the exact opposite.

Jamal headed for the inside of the gas station, and Nia fell into step beside him. Rather, she stomped. A woman passing them offered her congratulations, and when Nia huffed, Jamal put an arm around her shoulder and pulled her close. "C'mon, Nia. You have to admit this is kind of funny."

She gave him an elbow in the ribs as Jamal reached for the door with his free hand.

"Ow."

"You deserve a lot more than that!"

With one hand on the door handle, Jamal curled his other hand around Nia's upper arm. "Maybe I do, but don't do anything cute, like sneaking off to use the phone."

Nia jerked away from him and yanked the door open, then marched into the store. After a quick look around, she headed in the direction of the rest rooms.

Jamal watched her tramp off, a smile touching his lips. Oh yeah, she was still feisty. That was one thing he'd always loved about her. She hauled herself and her dress into the rest room with as much misery as anyone could. Yet the sight still tickled him. Shaking his head, he finally turned and made his way to the counter.

The middle-aged cashier gave him a bright smile. "Hi there."

"Hi."

"So you tied the knot, huh? Oooh, there's nothing I love more than a wedding," the woman crooned. "Congratulations."

"Thanks," Jamal replied nonchalantly. "I'm gonna grab a couple Cokes. Add those to the bill."

"Sure thing." The cashier started to ring up the purchase. "That's pretty untraditional, riding away on a Harley instead of in a limo, but I have to say I find that very romantic."

"It was one of those spur-of-the-moment things. And it's a bit uncomfortable, mostly for her."

"But imagine the story she'll be able to tell your grand-kids." The cashier sighed happily. "Your wife is one lucky lady."

"Thanks." Jamal gave the woman a tight smile. "Take care."

Jamal went to the refrigerated display case and grabbed the sodas, then went back outside to wait for Nia. No doubt it was taking her extra long in the rest room because of that gown she was wearing. She had so many layers of netting to her skirt, she looked like a real-life Cinderella. But it was hardly practical for their drive.

Not that she'd planned on riding a Harley to Key West in it. . . .

He had his soda opened and his head tilted back when Nia appeared at the door. Jamal immediately stood straight, watching her as she strode toward him. Something caught in his throat. With her hair disheveled beneath her crown-like veil, and the spaghetti straps of her dress hanging off her slender shoulders, she looked particularly enticing. Like a mouth-watering vision right out of a man's fantasy. Because he could easily picture her wearing white garters and one of those sexy corsets beneath the layers of netting on her full skirt—and the thought turned him on.

He threw his head back and downed half the soda in one gulp.

Nia moved beside him, resting a hip on the motorcycle. Jamal wondered if she knew just how delicious she looked with that low-cut dress of hers and ample cleavage spilling out of the form-fitting bodice.

"Here's your Coke." Jamal passed Nia the soda.

She snatched it from his hand, opened it, then downed a liberal sip, all the while scowling at him. When she was finished, she said, "Honestly, Jamal. If we're going much farther, I'm going to need to change. My dress is already in bad enough shape, but probably savable at this point. Besides, wherever we're going, I'm going to need clothes. I can't very well walk around in this dress all the time."

Jamal shrugged. She had a good point. But he certainly wasn't in the mood to stop and shop for any clothes. "What are you wearing underneath that thing?"

"*Excuse* me?"

"I'm sure you have a bra and underwear on. That'll do. I don't plan on keeping you long."

Nia gaped at him. "What do you mean that'll do?"

"You don't have anything I haven't seen before." His tone was matter-of-fact.

He saw something spark in Nia's eyes, something familiar, and blood pumped his groin. Damn, she was thinking about how they used to be together. He could feel it. And if what he was feeling wasn't one-sided, just the suggestion that she'd be getting naked with him later already had her hot and wet—just the way he liked her.

"Have you completely lost your mind?" Nia gawked at him. "This is my wedding day. What don't you get about that? Whatever you've seen of me before, you are certainly not entitled to see again."

Say it like you mean it, Jamal almost said. Instead, he merely chuckled. The spark of fire in her eyes told him everything he needed to know. She was thinking about him sexually, and from there it wouldn't be long before she was moaning in his arms. Man, he wanted her. He needed another taste of what it was like to love her. They both needed it. He didn't give a damn what she said—he knew John-boy couldn't satisfy her every need. Call it instinct . . .

"Get that hot and bothered look off your face." Nia's words were like a douse of cold water. "You're crazy. I always knew that . . . But fine, we'll play this out your way. But know this: When you bring me home, I *am* marrying John. And if my dress gets completely ruined, you're going to have to buy me a new one."

"If you're so worried about the dress, you could always take it off now. People have certainly done crazier things in South Florida." But Jamal smiled to make his words jovial, even if the idea of her wearing a thong and bra while riding behind him was giving him a hard-on.

Nia snorted and turned away. Jamal watched her throw her head back as she finished her soda. She tossed the empty container into the nearby trash can, then faced him again. "Exactly what are your plans?"

"I figured we could talk," Jamal replied, getting serious

once again. In reality, he wanted to know that she was truly going to be happy with John. And if he was saving her from making a mistake, he'd never regret doing something as crazy as kidnapping her.

"What could we possibly have to talk about? Our relationship is over. In the past. *Forever*. In case you've forgotten, that's exactly the way you wanted it."

Jamal didn't know what to say. She was right, of course, but now that he'd gone as far as kidnapping her, he knew he had to see this plan to its fruition.

He'd felt an inexplicable wrenching in his gut when he saw her outside the church in her sexy white gown, realizing that she was truly going to get married. At that moment, the idea of her walking down the aisle to give herself to another man was almost incomprehensible. Something he couldn't let her do. Not before he knew she'd really be happy.

The bad thing was, once she'd put her arms around him and pressed her face against his back the way she used to when she rode with him, it hadn't taken long for Jamal's thoughts to turn to sex.

All the while they'd been together, he was thinking about making love to her; even now, as they stood here at a gas station. One last roll in the hay with someone who'd once been his girl? Was that so wrong to want?

He blew out a ragged breath.

"What's wrong?" Nia asked.

"Nothing." Shit, everything. His thoughts now were downright crazy. He didn't know if she'd run right back to Johnny-boy the moment he let her go, but he sure as hell knew what he wanted to do between now and then.

He wanted to give Nia a night she'd never forget, and something to remember him by when she snuggled up with Johnny-boy at night.

Call it ego, but if Nia ended up in his arms one last time, never again would she question who was the better lover.

CHAPTER 3

As was prone to happen daily in Florida during the summer, the skies opened up and it began to rain. The sun still shone, and the rain was light, but it was enough to cause Nia concern. She definitely didn't want to continue driving if the weather got worse, certainly not dressed as she was with no protection from the elements. The problem was, though it was sunny right now, the weather could change for the worse without a moment's notice.

"Jamal, it's starting to rain," Nia said. "We can't continue driving."

He didn't respond, and Nia wondered if he was hellbent on not stopping. How far would be far enough away for him? Cuba? But minutes later, he slowed down and exited US-1. Nia breathed a sigh of relief.

It seemed like days later, but they'd really only been on the road a couple of hours by the time Jamal pulled the Harley into the parking lot of a Best Western hotel. And while minutes earlier it had been drizzling, the sky was once again dry. Jamal got off the bike nonetheless, clearly satisfied with their location.

They were in Key Largo. Knowing Jamal and how he thought, he'd probably wanted to head to Key West. Thank God for the few drops of rain, because the drive had been long enough for Nia and she was happy for the break.

But they were at a hotel. Alone. Nia's heart pounded like a drum as she got off the motorcycle and watched Jamal walk to the hotel lobby. His golden skin glistened with a mix of sweat and raindrops. Goodness, he was still damn fine. Literally a six-foot golden brown Adonis. She looked away, but her gaze went to a couple entering one of the units several feet away. She and Jamal would be doing that shortly. She exhaled a shaky breath. Though she'd known that ultimately Jamal would take her to a place they couldn't be found, the idea of spending the night with him in a hotel room was suddenly discomfiting.

How could she spend any time alone with him, when the two of them had a history of not being able to keep their hands off each other?

Not that they'd been intimate in a year, so Nia shouldn't be worried about that. Yet she was. She'd seen the fiery look in Jamal's eyes back at the gas station, a look that had always come before sex in the past. And as much as she hated herself for it, she'd felt a flush of heat at that intimate look. But perhaps it was just the familiarity she had responded to, her body reacting in that basic way it invariably had. She'd always found Jamal irresistible, and almost impossible to deny when it came to sex. Not that she'd wanted to deny him. Their lovemaking had consistently been of the out-of-this-world variety in its intensity and pleasure.

The loud sound of chirping drew Nia's attention to the palm trees. She searched the leaves for what she knew she'd find, then caught sight of a few green palm parrots. A smile touched her lips despite the emotions warring inside her. She didn't know what it was about palm parrots, but seeing them always boosted her spirits.

Returning her gaze to the lobby door, the smile quickly faded. "Jamal, what are you up to?" she asked, but the only answer came from the chirping birds.

Sighing, Nia thought about her words last night, how they had gotten her into this mess. She had known that Jamal wouldn't get any sleep after telling him that John had been her best lover. But she certainly hadn't expected him to show up and confront her about it moments before she was to walk down the aisle.

Brother, the man had an ego the size of Montana. Which was exactly why she'd assumed he'd leave her alone after what she'd said. Yeah, she'd been lying when she'd told him John was a better lover, but it was something she had to do to protect herself from him. Her relationship with Jamal was over. And after the heartbreak she'd suffered because of him, there was no way she could allow him to hurt her ever again.

And she wanted a life with John. John was safe. John was stable. John loved her and wouldn't hurt her. Jamal didn't have to know that she hadn't slept with him yet. Tonight would have been their first time—their wedding night—something she had suggested and John had agreed to.

Personally, Nia couldn't imagine sex with John being better than with Jamal, not considering how explosive it had always been with her bad boy lover. But maybe she was wrong; maybe John would know exactly how to please her. At the very least, she knew she couldn't expect fireworks the first night. And that was okay. They had a lifetime to work toward that.

Nia moaned softly. She hoped John wasn't angry with her for Jamal's stunt. She looked over, looking for a pay phone. She needed to call him, make him understand.

Her shoulders drooped when she didn't see one. She looked over her surroundings. The place was pretty secluded. Palm trees encircled the hotel's perimeter, and through one of the building's walkways, she could see a marina and some boats. Despite the fact that she'd lived in South Florida all her life, she had never been to Key Largo. Whenever her family had headed south, they'd ended up in Key West.

A breeze swirled around her, making Nia's veil flutter about her face. Frustrated, she reached up and removed the headpiece from her hair. How ridiculous she must have looked, riding around like this. Once again, her eyes went to her gown, to the dirty edges. She could never wear this dress again.

"Congratulations."

Nia whirled around to see an elderly woman smiling brightly at her. She forced a smile and replied, "Thanks."

Good grief, this was really a nightmare. And she had no clue when it was going to end.

Her feet were killing her from the ride, and no longer

able to bear wearing her sexy heels, she bent to slip them off. As she slid off the second shoe, she saw Jamal exit the lobby and stride toward her. Slowly, she stood to meet him, pulling one of her gown's straps back onto her shoulder as she did.

Jamal's eyes took in her every movement, lingering on her hand as it held the strap, then going lower to her chest. Heat coursed through her body, sending a zap to the apex of her thighs. Damn it. What was wrong with her? Why was she even feeling anything remotely sexual for Jamal at a time like this, when the man had taken her against her will and ruined her wedding day?

"Jamal, I have no clue what is going through your mind, but this is a bad idea. For whatever reason, you wanted to ruin my wedding day, and you have. So we should—"

"Is that what you think today was about? Ruining your wedding?"

"You took me from the church minutes before I was supposed to walk down the aisle."

"Like I said, there are some things we need to discuss."

"What things?"

"Not right now, Nia."

She rolled her eyes. "Fine."

"Don't worry. It will be soon," Jamal continued. "Now that we have a place to settle for the night. By the way, the clerk gave us the honeymoon suite. She saw you in that gown from the window and figured we were honeymooning."

"Gee, how wonderful." Nia flashed him a plastic smile. "I don't get to use the honeymoon suite John and I had reserved, but here I am in Key Largo and lucking out to get one with you." She paused, then said, "Don't expect me to be happy about it, except for the fact that the room is hopefully big enough for you and I to never have to see each other."

"Ah, Ni Ni. You try too hard."

She felt a spurt of anger, mixed with a hint of passion. "Try too hard to what?"

The edges of Jamal's lips curled upward in the slightest of grins. "I'll tell you in the room."

Nia wanted to knock the smug look off his face. Damn him and his crazy antics!

Without so much as another glance at her, Jamal turned and headed for the hotel. It wasn't a high-rise, but rather built as a cluster of two-story cottages. It was definitely private, nestled away at the end of a small road. It was a wonder they'd found this place.

When Jamal was halfway up the set of stairs, he paused and faced her. "You coming?"

Nia looked around hopelessly, not liking this one bit. She could head into the lobby area and ask to use the phone, call John or her father and let them know where she was. By now, everyone must be either worried sick or livid.

As if Jamal sensed what was on her mind, he said, "One night, Ni Ni. Then you can go back to John-boy."

Nia shot a lethal glare his way, but Jamal didn't even so much as flinch. Shaking her head with resignation, Nia huffed and stomped toward him. This was going to be the longest, most miserable night of her life.

If Nia had come here of her own free will, she would have been delighted with the accommodations. The place was indeed like a home away from home, with two levels. The living room was immediately to the left of stairs that led up to the second level, and behind the full living room was a kitchen.

"This is nice," she heard herself say as she stepped into the unit. She was glad to sink her toes into the plush carpet.

"Yeah, it'll do."

Do for what? Nia wanted to ask but didn't dare. Especially since Jamal was at the base of the stairs, ready to head up. It didn't take a rocket scientist to figure out that the bedroom had to be up there—a place she wasn't prepared to go with him.

"It's been a long day," Jamal said. "If you want to take a shower and get some rest, that's cool."

"You bet I do. It's a good thing there's a bathroom down here." She wandered farther into the living room. "And I'm sure this is a sofa bed."

"I was thinking more along the lines of a hot bath. I know how much you like to take those."

Nia stared at Jamal incredulously. "Let's not pretend this was a planned outing, nor that I'm supposed to get comfortable with you here."

"Oh, come on, Ni Ni. Don't make us out to be enemies, not after how close we once were."

Nia didn't know whether to throw a shoe at Jamal or ask him what his game was. She had no idea what he really wanted, and that scared her. And damned if she wasn't annoyed with herself for thinking that him kidnapping her had something to do with the fact that deep in his heart he still loved her. He'd had plenty of opportunity to tell her so if that were the case; indeed, the best time to have professed his love would have been at the church as he'd scooped her into his arms.

But he'd said nothing, nothing except to ask her if she was serious about John being the better lover.

She was a moron, and she'd do well to remember just how much Jamal had hurt her, rather than venturing off into la-la dreamland.

"You know, Jamal, I wish you'd get to the point of whatever it is that you want."

"I will. As soon as we both relax for a bit."

Nia plopped herself on the wicker sofa. God, the man was incorrigible! He'd ruined her wedding day, most likely over his huge ego, and he was going to take his sweet old time holding her here as if she didn't have a life to get back to.

"Why are you doing this?" Nia asked.

"I told you."

"You haven't told me anything that makes sense."

"Like I said, we'll talk." Jamal paused. "You want to head upstairs? Take a hot bath?"

Nia gave him a look that said he was as foreign to her as the Chinese language, but she knew it wouldn't do any good. Jamal was stubborn; once he set his mind to something, no one could talk him out of whatever he'd planned to do. Frustrated, she looked away from him—and saw the phone to the right of the sofa.

A quick swallow, and she returned her gaze to Jamal. "Like I said," she slowly began, "I can take a shower down here. If you'd like to take a bath, go ahead."

"You're sure?"

"Oh yes. Definitely."

Jamal traced Nia's eye line and knew exactly what was going through that pretty little head of hers. "Don't even think of it," he said, walking to the living room phone in three quick strides. He unplugged it from the wall and wrapped the cord securely around it.

Nia gave him an exasperated look. "Jamal, this isn't funny."

He placed the phone on the nearby chair. "Do you see me laughing?"

"I need to call my family. At least let them know I'm okay."

"Maybe later."

"Maybe later? You've already got me in the middle of nowhere—"

It wasn't a good idea. He was sure of it. He didn't want any interruptions, not tonight. "Let me think about it."

"What—are you trying to figure out what your ransom demand should be?"

Jamal frowned at her. "Don't be silly."

"I'm not the one being silly. I mean, I honestly have no idea what to think anymore."

"I . . . I'm not a kidnapper."

"You're not?"

"No, damn it. You know I needed to talk to you."

"Yeah, so you keep saying." Nia paused. "You've already ruined my wedding day. What harm will come of me calling my family? I don't have to say where I am, only that I'm okay. Please, at least give me that."

Turning, Jamal thought about Nia's words. It wasn't an unreasonable request. Besides, even though he'd taken her from the church, he didn't consider himself a kidnapper. If she truly wanted to leave, he'd take her home tonight.

"All right," Jamal agreed. "I'm sure there's another phone upstairs. You can use that one." Nia jumped to her feet and hurried past him, toward the stairs. Before she reached them, Jamal said, "Nia."

She faced him. "Yeah?"

"If you really want me to take you home, let me know. I spoiled your day, and the truth is, I don't really know why. All I know is that I felt the need to talk to you, before you married someone else."

Nia gave him an odd look, a look that said she was trying to figure him out, but couldn't. "What are you saying?"

Jamal shrugged. "I don't know. I only know that I want you to be happy."

The look of disappointment in her eyes caused his heart to take a nosedive to his stomach. He looked away.

But seconds later, when Jamal didn't hear Nia climbing the stairs, he turned once again and found her still standing there, still staring at him.

He didn't think, just started toward her. He could almost feel Nia's heart beating . . . or was that his own? What was it about the five-foot-five beauty that had him thinking of getting her naked every time he laid his eyes on her?

Before he knew it, he had cupped one of her cheeks in his palm. His thumb softly stroked her caramel-colored skin. "You believe me, don't you? That I didn't do this to hurt you?"

For several seconds, Nia didn't respond. But something stirred in the depths of her dark eyes, something that made a surge of heat spread through his body. Damned if he wasn't suddenly tempted to gather her in his arms and feel those soft lips of hers beneath his once again.

One last time. That's what he wanted, wasn't it?

Nia swallowed, her gaze going to the floor. "I'm not sure what to believe, Jamal. I have no clue why you've brought me here, and where you're concerned, I certainly don't want to jump to any conclusions."

"I lied when I said we were nothing to each other." At his words, Nia's eyes flew to his once more. "That much will always be a lie. You will always mean something to me, Ni Ni. Always."

Jamal looked over her face, his gaze finally settling on

Nia's full lips. They were parted, as if she expected him to kiss her. Hell, he wanted to. But where would a kiss lead?

There was no such thing as a simple kiss with Nia. He'd want her upstairs and naked in seconds flat if he dared to do any more than he was doing now. There was no such thing as simple with Nia, period, which had always been their problem.

"Jamal . . ."

He wasn't ready to start something he couldn't finish. He dropped his hand and took a step backward. "Go on upstairs," he said with difficulty. "Make your phone call. I just ask that you please . . . give us tonight."

Nia exhaled audibly, and he could imagine what thoughts were whirling around in her head. She was wondering what on earth was wrong with him.

To tell the truth, so was he.

CHAPTER 4

"I'm fine," Nia assured Christine for the second time. She sat on the king-size bed with her legs pulled up to her chest, an arm resting on the netting of her skirt. "Honestly. A little tired and frustrated, but otherwise okay. Please let Mom and Dad know I'm fine as well, because I'm sure they're worried—"

"Of course they're worried!" Christine exclaimed. "We all are. In fact, Howard and I are heading to their place right now. Why don't you call there in a few minutes so we can all talk to you?"

"No," Nia quickly replied. "I'm not ready to talk to them."

"Not even your fiancé? You know he's there, too."

Nia closed her eyes, then opened them. "I . . . I'll talk to him later."

"Later?" Christine asked, her tone saying she thought Nia had lost her mind. "What is going on, Nia?"

"Nothing. I just don't want to call him until I'm back. But if you can let him know I'm okay—"

"He is totally worried," Christine explained. "Sure, it's good to hear from you, but if you don't give me a message to give to him, he's gonna be crushed. He's going to know that you don't want to talk to him, and he's going to wonder why. And quite frankly, I'm wondering why, too."

"Not now, Christine. Please try and understand. I'll talk to you later. To all of you later. But please, let everyone know I'm okay. I'll be back tomorrow for sure."

"D-did you plan this?" Christine sputtered.

"Of course not!"

"Then forgive me for saying that I'm having a hard time understanding why you're not crying bloody murder right about now. Or is Jamal standing right there? God, of course. Look, can you try and tell me where you are? I'll send someone right away."

"Christine." Nia spoke firmly. "Listen to me. No, Jamal isn't standing over me. No, he's not forcing me to say anything."

"Then tell me where you are. Howard and I will come to get you."

"No. I'll be fine. Jamal—he wants to . . . talk. And at this point, considering everything, I may as well hear what he has to say."

"I don't believe this," Christine muttered. "You have gone and lost your mind."

Disappointment swirled in Nia's stomach. All her life, her parents and her sister had made her feel as though she couldn't make her own decisions. They'd never liked Jamal, partly because he did blue-collar work, and partly because of his bad boy reputation. Forget the fact that he'd been good to her. Her parents and sister hadn't even shed a token tear for her when she'd been depressed over their breakup. And all Christine had been able to say was that Nia would "get over it" and find someone truly worthy of her.

John had been a friend of her father's, and the moment he'd shown an interest in her, her father had instantly encouraged her to get to know him. Ultimately, Nia had started dating John, not to please her father, but for herself. He was a nice man, a true gentleman, and someone she enjoyed getting to know over their numerous dinners. And it was a plus that he helped take her mind off of Jamal.

When John had proposed, there had been no real reason to say no. After her relationship with Jamal ended, she certainly hadn't wanted the kind of love that swept you off your feet but landed you flat on your butt ever again. And John, dear sweet John, loved her, and would always take care of her. He wouldn't push her away, then come running back, only to push her away again. He was a man, a man who knew what he wanted, one who was secure.

So, yes, Nia had fallen for John, but only after she'd been pushed toward him by her family. Now, she was tired of their "gentle" persuasion. If she didn't want to do something, she shouldn't have to—and she sure as hell shouldn't be subject to the third degree from them for whatever decision she made.

"Christine, I appreciate your concern, but now isn't the best time to get into anything. I'm going to deal with Jamal once and for all, then I'll be back home. Please, tell everyone I'm all right and that I'll talk to them soon."

"Sure." Christine's tone was clipped. "I hope—"

"Good-bye." Nia quickly hung up. A second later, she covered her face with her hands.

Lord help her, she hoped she knew what she was doing.

She hoped she didn't live to regret not telling her family exactly where to find her.

When, several minutes later, Nia was still alone upstairs, she wondered if Jamal had fallen asleep on the sofa, or if he was giving her time alone.

Her lips curled in a sad smile. He wasn't pressuring her, wasn't making sure she kept her word. To know that he still trusted her lifted her heart, as did the knowledge that he truly didn't want to keep her against her will. Jamal had a decent side, even if no one else—not even him—saw it.

She lay back on the bed, restless. As much as she'd dreaded being here with him tonight, the truth was, if they were going to spend time alone, they might as well do whatever talking Jamal wanted to and get it over with. There were so many unresolved issues between them, something Nia had always known, and it seemed Jamal had finally realized the same thing. She wasn't against dealing with them before they both went on with their lives.

Of course, Jamal had picked the worst possible time to come to that realization.

Nia sighed. She should be more than mildly upset that she wasn't with John right now at their wedding reception. Yet she wasn't. And she had to wonder why.

It had been a long day, and she was both wired and tired. She did need to unwind. Jamal had suggested a hot bath. Rising from the bed, Nia stretched, then made her way to the back of the bedroom and the adjoining bathroom.

Her pulse raced when she saw the tub. It was red, heart-shaped, and could fit two comfortably. It was the kind of tub she'd seen in magazines when she was looking at places to honeymoon. There were several Jacuzzi jets, and Nia could easily imagine the tub filled with thick, scented bubbles.

She sank down to the tub's edge and reached for the faucets. She turned both on, adjusting the temperature until it was right for her. Her eyes surveyed the vanity area and she was happy to see a small bottle of shampoo. That would work for some bubbles. She'd been in Jacuzzi tubs before and knew that the powerful jets would give her the maximum bubbles.

As she stood Nia's foot got caught in the netting of her dress. Annoyed, she quickly reached for the side zipper and yanked it down. It was about time she got out of this cumbersome dress, anyway.

With the dress loosened around her body, she let it fall to the floor and stepped out of it. The crinoline was so stiff, the dress practically stood up on its own.

A fairy-tale dress for a fairy-tale day. Only this fairy-tale had ended with her being kidnapped by her once bad boy prince.

Once. Not anymore. Jamal would never be anything to her anymore, and Nia would be best off remembering that.

She retrieved the shampoo and poured it into the tub, then started up the jets. The water began to foam, filling with bubbles. She stripped out of her thong and bra and eased her way into the warm tub.

Seconds later, her body adjusted to the water, she lay back, resting her head in the tub's groove. Jamal was right; this felt divine. Just what she needed after quite an eventful day.

Nia closed her eyes. A satisfied moan slipped from her lips. But seconds later, when she heard the door click open, she bolted upright, throwing a hand across her breasts at the same time that her eyes flew open.

Her heart pounded a mile a minute as she took in Jamal's muscular form. Casually, he extended a hand and braced himself against the door's frame, all the while his onyx eyes never leaving her own.

Several seconds passed with neither saying anything. Once her breathing calmed, Nia spoke. "The door was closed for a reason, Jamal." As though his appearance hadn't rattled her, she settled back once again. Indeed, she hadn't needed to cover herself. She was deep enough in the tub, and there were enough bubbles to hide her nakedness.

"Sorry," he said, the word sounding like a mockery on his lips.

He took a step toward her, and Nia's heart went wild. Her head began to swim, and she gulped in a quick breath in an effort to assuage the dizziness. Maybe the water was too hot. Or maybe it was Jamal's heated gaze that suddenly had her feeling faint.

"You called your family?"

"Yeah."

Jamal slowly sauntered toward her. "And what did you say? What did they say?"

Nia eyed him warily, wondering what he was going to do. Over her shoulder, she watched as he ventured to the small window and peered outside. "My sister said they were all worried—naturally—but she was relieved to hear from me."

Jamal turned from the window and walked to the tub. He eased down onto its edge, his body near her head. "What about John? What did he have to say?"

"Uh . . ." Nia couldn't help noticing the way Jamal's jeans clung to his strong thighs. "Nothing."

Jamal lifted the washcloth from the side of the tub and dipped it into the water beside her. When he withdrew it, he squeezed, creating a waterfall of steam and bubbles.

He asked, "What do you mean John said nothing? He didn't want to talk to you? Don't tell me—he was off at the wedding reception without you, dancing to 'I Will Survive.' Lean forward."

"I didn't talk to John because . . ." Nia was glad Jamal couldn't see her eyes. "Because I didn't call him."

"Didn't call him?" Jamal's curiosity was piqued. "Why not?"

"Because I had no idea what to say to him."

"You could have told him to come get you."

Nia whipped her head around to face Jamal. "Really? After you begged me to give you one night to talk?"

Jamal dipped the washcloth into the water once more, then said, "Lean forward."

Nia blew out a wary breath. "Jamal, what are you doing?"

"I want to wash your back."

"You haven't washed my back in . . . in over a year. This is crazy."

"I'm just trying to be helpful."

"This isn't . . ." Nia's voice trailed off when Jamal's hand touched her back. "This isn't helping."

"No?"

This was too painful. Much too painful. It reminded her of all she and Jamal had once shared. If this were like old times, he would be in the tub with her within a matter of minutes. But it wasn't old times. Their time together was over.

Nia inched forward, beyond Jamal's reach, then turned to face him. "What's your game?"

Jamal's expression was unreadable. "You want the truth?"

"Of course."

"I want you," Jamal said simply. "One last time before you walk down the aisle."

Jamal's tone left no room for playfulness, and Nia knew his every word was true. Lord help her, the man truly was crazy. Yet his admission left her breathless; and if the odd look on his face was any indication, he was as surprised by his words as she was.

Nia wanted to jump out of the tub and run from here, run from this hotel and not stop. But she was naked and had nothing practical to wear, so that was definitely not an option.

"I guess I just figured that out," Jamal added matter-of-factly.

"You're crazy." Confusion and anger fought for control of her heart.

"I don't think anyone would dispute that."

"I mean really crazy. As in you need to have a psychological examination."

"Oh, come on, Ni Ni. You know the only thing I'm really crazy for is this body of yours." Jamal trailed a finger down the length of her spine, stopping when he touched the water.

Nia flinched. But even as she did, she felt a tingle of desire.

"Damn, Nia. There's no way you and John can be as good together as we were."

"Get out of here."

"Nia—"

"I mean it, Jamal." She hoped he hadn't heard the quiver in her voice. "I don't understand this game you're playing, and quite frankly, I don't want to understand. All I know is that you need to get over your stupid ego. I've had a stressful enough day. Please, let me bathe in peace." When he didn't move, she slapped a hand against the water, causing it to splash in his face. "Go."

"Well, look at this. Now I'm all wet." Jamal stood and stripped out of his shirt. Nia stared at his beautiful pecs and washboard stomach, then promptly turned away.

"It's okay to look, Nia. It's okay to want me."

Every part of her fought for control, fought not to succumb to the overwhelming longing to steal another glimpse of his glorious body.

"What's it going to hurt, being together one last time before you marry Johnny-boy?"

"His name isn't Johnny-boy," Nia replied, whirling back around to glower at Jamal. But her eyes quickly fell to his fingers, which were resting on the zipper of his jeans. As he dragged it down, her heart went haywire. "What are you doing?"

"You have no clue how much I want you, do you?"

"Jamal . . ."

"I know, I'm crazy. Yeah, I guess I am. Crazy enough

to realize that I wouldn't be happy if you married the wrong man."

A lump of emotion clogged Nia's throat at Jamal's words. Somehow she was able to speak around it. "What is that supposed to mean?"

"You deserve to be happy, Nia. Truly happy. In every way."

"I was. I-I am."

"Really? Does John make you happy?"

"This is ridiculous. I wouldn't be marrying him if he didn't."

"Just a year ago, you were hoping to marry me."

Anger flared inside her at this game Jamal was playing, and brought the memory of his rejection crashing down on her with full force. "And you didn't want to marry me, remember? Why are you doing this? You made your choice. Now you have to live with it."

An emotion she couldn't read passed over his face. A second later, he sat on the edge of the tub once again. "All right. I hear you. But that's part of what made me go see you last night, Nia. This isn't about ego, but . . . when I say I want you to be happy, I mean that. And something about you and John as a couple doesn't sit well with me. I don't know . . . I'm not sure I believe he's the man you've been waiting for all your life."

"Go to hell," Nia spat out, angry with herself for the way her voice shook with emotion. She'd been doing what she could to hold herself together, but now, this was too much. Advice about her love life from the guy who'd caused her the worst heartache? How dense was he? She slid her bottom across the tub's floor, positioning herself as far from Jamal as she possibly could.

Jamal simply moved closer to her. Nia refused to look at him, even as his fingers grazed her cheek. "I just want you to be happy, Nia." His voice was incredibly gentle. He trailed his fingers down to the base of her neck, then lower, skimming the roundness of one of her breasts. "Doesn't this make you happy?" She kept her head turned away from him, even as her breathing grew more ragged. She didn't dare steal a glance in his direction.

His hand went lower still, with aching slowness, as if seeking permission. Nia lifted her eyes to his, their hot gazes locking, but still she didn't say a word. At last, his fingers closed around a nipple.

Nia's eyelids fluttered from the instant pleasure, but she forced them to stay open. How could her body do this to her, crave his touch so much even when her mind knew it was the wrong thing? She didn't understand herself anymore. All she knew was that she finally felt a release of the tension that had been building from the moment she'd gotten on the motorcycle with Jamal today.

"God, Ni Ni. I remember how it used to be. Sometimes, remembering the look of passion on your face haunts me at night. No one else has been able to give me what you gave me."

"And yet it wasn't good enough." Nia's words were simple, but laced with pain.

He brought his hand back to her face, where he ran a thumb across her lips. "No. That's not true. I know I had my share of problems, but my inadequacies are no reason for you to settle. Damn, Ni Ni. I want you. Right now."

Despite her mixed feelings, a sigh escaped her lips. It was a sigh that said she wanted him, too. A sigh that said she was powerless to deny him.

"John . . . he loves me."

"But you don't love him, do you, Ni Ni? At least not the way you should."

"Don't do this to me, Jamal."

"Okay. Let's not talk about John." Jamal gently palmed her face. "Kiss me, Ni Ni. Put me out of my misery."

Nia looked at him long and hard. Despite the warmth of the water, a shiver ran down her spine. She actually did see misery in Jamal's eyes, misery mixed with longing. But what did it mean? The man was an enigma, always guarding his emotions and his heart, which was why their relationship had fallen apart in the first place.

But thoughts of their failed relationship quickly fled her mind as Jamal's other hand framed her other cheek, as he lowered his head to hers. John had kissed her several times, yet not even one of his kisses set her skin on fire the way Jamal's simple touch did.

She moved toward him, and though she saw his face nearing, the moment of contact surprised her. Because though so much time had passed, nothing had changed. She still felt sparks when their lips touched.

As Jamal's tongue delved into her mouth, his hands slipped into her hair. He loosened the hairpins, letting her curls fall around her neck and shoulders. Then he was securing his arms beneath her own, wrapping them around her back. With one strong pull, he lifted her up, drawing her naked body to his.

A satisfied groan rumbled deep in his chest, as if he'd found and tasted heaven.

"One last fling, Ni Ni. One last fling before you go back to John."

Every protest that rose in her throat died on a series of moans as his hands brought pleasure to her body.

She couldn't lie to herself. She wanted this. She wanted this blinding passion that consumed her every time Jamal laid his hands on her. There was something about him that made her powerless to resist the fire between them, powerless to do anything but succumb to her body's desires. And though she'd never had another lover, Nia doubted any other man would ever make her feel this way.

One last fling. Jamal's words sounded in her mind, a gentle invitation to live life on the edge the way she once had with him. She'd felt a liberating thrill every day of her relationship with Jamal, as though the burden of her predictable life was lifted from her shoulders when she was with him. That was what she'd treasured most about her time with him, being able to live life on her own terms, and having someone support her dreams.

One last fling.

Reason tried to come up with an excuse to save her from doing something as reckless as falling into bed with Jamal again, but reason failed miserably.

One last fling with her one bad boy lover before she went back to the life she'd carved out for herself. A life she'd been led into by everyone else's will, not her own.

Lord knew, that life would come soon enough. But for now, she wanted a piece of the passion she would probably never have again.

Was that too much to ask for?

Nia's eyelids fluttered shut as she slipped her arms around Jamal's neck and held him close.

CHAPTER 5

NIA surrendered to Jamal's kiss. Her body exploded with wonderful sensations as he nipped and suckled at her lips. Shivers of desire danced down her spine.

"One last fling," Nia managed between ragged breaths. "We'll end this the way we should have, as friends."

"Yes. I regret that, the way we fought."

Nia regretted it, too. Even now, she wasn't sure Jamal understood. He'd thought she was trying to remake him, mold him into something she'd be proud of. In truth, she'd been trying to give him an opportunity he wouldn't normally have. He'd said many times that a guy like him didn't get the same kinds of opportunities that others did.

But she didn't want to think about that now. Right now, she wanted to concentrate on the one thing that had always been fantastic between them, the best part of their relationship. Because when they made love, they connected in a way that was beyond defining in words. In each other's arms, there were no fears, no questions, only love.

"You don't know how much I've missed you," Jamal murmured in her ear. "Missed this."

"I've missed this, too," Nia heard herself say. "So much."

"Do you fantasize about me at night? Do you fantasize and get yourself off?"

Nia mewled softly as she dug her fingers into his back. "Yes."

"Wrap your legs around me, Ni Ni."

Nia lifted one foot onto the tub's edge for balance, then wrapped her other leg around Jamal's waist. As she did, he lifted her higher, and she brought her other leg around him as well.

"I can't take this anymore," Jamal said, running his hot tongue along the side of her neck to her earlobe. "I need to get naked. I need to be inside you."

Smothering her mouth with his, Jamal carried her through the bathroom door and into the bedroom. His tongue played over hers, flicking against the roof of her mouth. With Nia securely in his arms, Jamal brought a knee on the bed and gently eased her down. When she was flat on her back, he tore his lips from hers and stood, dragging his jeans down over his lean hips.

Jamal's eyes never left her body as he stripped out of his clothes, and Nia's skin burned with a passion too long denied. She wasn't the most beautiful woman around, but Jamal's gaze never failed to make her feel as though she were supermodel material. And she felt comfortable with her nakedness in front of him, even though they hadn't been together in over a year. Even though their history was a rocky one. If she had a lick of sense left, she would have called John and had him come here as quickly as possible to pick her up and take her back to sanity.

But John . . . Oh, forget John.

Nia checked out Jamal's naked form. The man was an icon of male perfection, from his wide shoulders and brawny arms to his flat stomach and slim waist. Her eyes went lower. Jamal's erection was large and thick. Seeing the evidence of his desire for her sent a jolt of heat straight to her vagina.

"I am so horny for you," Jamal said, his voice as thick as melted chocolate. He started toward her, then stopped. "But I don't want to rush this." He wrapped a hand around his penis. "Spread your legs, Ni Ni. Touch yourself."

Nia had crossed her legs at the ankles as she'd watched Jamal get undressed, and now she slowly lifted one leg and moved it across the bed.

"Oh, Ni Ni." Jamal stroked his erection. "Touch it."

As she had every time she'd been with Jamal, Nia felt

a surge of sexual power—as if she literally had control over Jamal's very pleasure. She brought a hand to her vagina and ran a finger along the folds. "Like this?"

"Oh." A slow, hot breath oozed from Jamal's lips. "Are you wet? I need to know you want me."

Nia bit down hard on her bottom lip as she eased a finger inside her. "Yes. I'm wet."

Jamal got onto the bed on his knees, still stroking his arousal. "Let me feel it."

Nia withdrew her finger and Jamal instantly brought his hand down on her. As he fondled her, he groaned. "I love how wet you get. Tell me you get this way only for me."

"Only for you . . ."

Nia raised her hand to Jamal's lips, offering him her finger. He took it eagerly in his mouth.

"Oh, yeah. You are as sweet as you always were, baby. Lie back."

Nia lay back on the bed and closed her eyes. *This is crazy,* a voice in her mind said, the thought surprising her. *This is your wedding day, and Jamal isn't your groom.*

A wave of nostalgia washed over her, but it died the moment she felt Jamal's hot tongue on her body.

"Oh, sweetie," Nia moaned. She ran her hands over his close-cropped hair as Jamal lapped at her, every cell in her body tingling with the sweetest of feelings. Slipping his hands beneath her hips, he urged her even closer as his tongue picked up the pace, flicking over her nub, tracing her opening. And then his mouth covered her, and he suckled her with agonizing gentleness.

Moan after moan escaped Nia's lips, her breaths becoming more and more ragged. She lifted her head to watch him, the intensity of her pleasure increasing tenfold as she did. The sight of him loving her . . . there was nothing more intimate. And then her head flew back and her hips bucked as an orgasm hit her with delicious force. Jamal held her tighter, keeping up the pressure with his tongue.

"Please . . ." Nia managed breathlessly. "I need you inside me."

"One second," Jamal said. He scooped up his jeans from

the floor and pulled out a small foil package from one of the back pockets.

A condom . . . Nia felt a sting of disappointment. "Guess you always travel with one of those."

"I bought a few when we stopped at the service station." He shrugged. "I was hopeful."

"Oh." Nia suddenly felt better.

"You know what you do to me, Ni Ni." Jamal winked at her before opening the package and slipping the condom on. Then he slid his body over hers, settling between her legs. He brushed the tip of his penis against her opening at the same time that he flicked the tip of his tongue over her lips.

"Don't tease me," Nia said.

"You sure you want this?" Jamal asked, a hint of playfulness in his voice.

"Yes!" Nia locked her legs around Jamal's hips.

Jamal wasted no more time guiding himself inside her. A sound of complete satisfaction rumbled in his chest. "You are so tight," he whispered, his breath hot against her ear.

Nia arched her hips, urging him to go deeper, even though she felt slight pain as his erection stretched her. It had been so long since she'd last made love.

Jamal followed her lead, slowly easing himself deeper into her body, until he filled her completely. "Oh, Jamal . . . Oh, I've missed this."

"You feel so good. I almost forgot how good."

Jamal withdrew and then thrust deep inside her, and Nia cried out from the ecstasy. Jamal paused, staring into her eyes. Slowly, he withdrew, only to thrust deep once more. Nia tightened her arms around his neck as more pleasure filled her.

"Yes, that's it, Ni Ni. I need to know how much you want this."

"I want this, Jamal. More than anything."

Jamal's mouth found hers, and he kissed her with urgency.

As he increased the pace of their rhythm, Nia matched his every movement. How easily her body responded to his, just as it always had. How easily she felt completely comfortable in his arms.

She felt a sudden urge to cry.

How could she and Jamal connect so well between the sheets, but fail to make their relationship work on a day-to-day level? Damn her naïveté. Jamal was the bad boy who'd set her world on fire with passion, but it was a rocky world, one she wasn't accustomed to. Still, she'd been willing to give up everything—the approval of her family, which she had always tried to gain—for a life with him.

But all he'd truly seemed capable of giving her was an exclusive sexual relationship.

Burying her face in his neck, Nia pushed the negative thoughts to the back of her mind. She roamed her hands over the breadth of Jamal's slick back, over his butt, focusing on the solid feel of him. Her fingers traveled to the base of his neck, lightly skimming the length of the scar he'd gotten when his mother had once beat him with a belt. She fingered it gently, wishing that her touch had the power to take away all his pain and fears.

Because she knew pain and fear were at the root of his inability to love her the way she wanted. The way she needed. In Jamal's arms, she was sure of that.

That reality made her sad, and she didn't want to be sad. Not now, while she and Jamal were reconnecting.

"Kiss me," Nia whispered into his ear. If this was going to be her last time with Jamal, she needed it to feel right—to feel as if he loved her. As if their bond had been based on something other than the simple yet powerful desire to get naked together.

Jamal went still. His dark gaze met hers. He looked at her for what seemed like an eternity before slowly lowering his mouth to hers and giving her the gentlest, yet most passionate of kisses. The sweetest sensation washed over her, and in that moment, she did feel loved.

Together intimately, Jamal's body spoke the secrets of his heart. As did hers.

Jamal trailed his lips to her ear, breathing hotly against it as he once again picked up the pace.

Nia knew his body so well, knew he was about to climax. She closed her eyes and glided her fingers up and down his back. "Yes, Jamal," she whispered, nibbling on his earlobe. "Oh, sweetie."

"No, not yet." Startling Nia, Jamal rolled over onto his back in one quick motion. Nia now straddled him. "Yes, this is how I want you. I want to see your face as you come again."

Jamal's words were like an aphrodisiac, and as his hands gripped her hips, holding her down as he filled her, Nia felt herself beginning to lose control. Jamal lifted his head to capture one of her nipples, sending swirls of delicious sensations down to her core.

And then she was lost once again, lost on a wave of passion that carried her out to sea before bringing her back to the shore.

"That's it, Ni Ni." Jamal raked his fingers through her hair, then pulled her face to his. He kissed her, making her even more breathless.

They felt so good together, how could this be wrong?

Jamal's arms tightened on her body, and his urgent breaths indicated his own release was imminent. Nia ran her tongue along his jaw, nipping gently at his skin with her teeth. She gyrated her hips over him, feeling him wonderfully deep inside her. And then Jamal moaned loudly as he climaxed.

He was kissing her once more, kissing her with the passion only he could bring to her life.

Their slick bodies still locked together, Nia was well aware of one simple fact.

She'd never stopped loving Jamal.

She probably never would.

Jamal and Nia spent the rest of the evening naked, in bed, unable to get enough of each other. They made love until they were exhausted, until their bodies were spent from getting reacquainted in the most intimate way.

Now, Nia lay in the crook of Jamal's arm. Jamal listened to the steady sound of her breathing. He felt a mixture of both happiness and sadness at the sound—happiness at the fact that they were still comfortable together, but sadness at the reality that their lovemaking session hadn't made anything better. If anything, it had made things worse.

Because now, Jamal couldn't quite imagine going back to the way it had been before he'd kidnapped her—living without her in his life. Despite his earlier thoughts, making love with her today had actually made it harder to let her go.

But he had to let her go. She wasn't his. Not anymore. For tonight she was, but tomorrow would come and they'd still have the same insurmountable problems they'd had before. Sexually, they were dynamite together, but outside of the bed—Jamal held no illusions that their relationship would work on a day-to-day level.

He knew what he wanted, even if Nia would hate him for it. If she and John didn't work things out, he wouldn't mind continuing an exclusive sexual relationship with her. No other woman had ever made him feel the way Nia did. In fact, with the few other women he'd been with since his breakup with Nia, the sexual act had been empty, unfulfilling. He'd come to realize that he could connect only with Nia in that special way, and being able to have a piece of her would be better than having nothing.

But Jamal wasn't sure that Nia would go for such an arrangement.

Nia stirred, her soft breasts brushing against his side. Just like that, he was hard again. Damn, why couldn't he get enough of her?

Making a soft sound, she stirred again, then rolled over. Her round bottom settled against his leg. Even in sleep, she made him crazy with lust. She was so delicious, he wanted to take a bite of her caramel skin. Unable to stop himself, Jamal placed a hand on her beautiful butt, stroking the smooth flesh.

Jamal heard a smile in Nia's voice as she softly moaned. He ran his hand up her body and cupped her breast.

Nia turned then, wrapping an arm around him as she did. "You are *not* horny again, are you, Mr. Simpson?"

"Baby, I am always horny when you're around. I swear you put some kind of hex on me, so that I'll only be able to enjoy sex with you."

"Hmmm. I'd say it's the other way around."

Jamal's arm tightened around her. "So, are you admitting it? That John-boy doesn't please you in bed the way I do?"

"You really do have an ego the size of Texas, you know that?"

"I'm right, aren't I?" Jamal repeated the question when she didn't answer.

Nia blew out a quick breath. "I have a confession to make."

Jamal pulled his head back to look completely in her eyes. "What kind of confession?"

"About John. He and I . . . We haven't been together the way I let you think. Sexually. We haven't been intimate."

That got Jamal to sit up. He rested on an elbow as he stared at her. "You haven't?"

"No."

Jamal couldn't help chuckling with relief. He didn't know why it mattered so much, but it did. He was glad to know that Nia hadn't shared with John what she had shared with him.

"Don't get all excited," Nia quickly told him. "We were waiting until our wedding night. It was supposed to be . . . more special that way."

Jamal shot her a skeptical look.

"I didn't want sex clouding our relationship," Nia added, a tad defensively. "The way it did ours."

"Is that what you think?"

"Honestly?"

Jamal nodded.

"If it wasn't for the sex between us, I'm not sure we would have lasted as long as we did."

"Hmm," was all he said. He lay back on his pillow. Her words bothered him, though he couldn't outright deny them. Hadn't he said the same thing himself—that the basis of their relationship had been their sexual chemistry?

Jamal's thoughts were interrupted by the loud growling of Nia's stomach. She giggled with embarrassment.

"Yeah, it's been a long day without food." Jamal dragged a hand over his face. "I should order something."

"Maybe you should go out and pick up some food."

"Why—so you can plan your escape?" Jamal softened the words with a smile.

"No. I was thinking you could head out for food and pick up something for me to wear while you're at it. I can't very well go out in my wedding dress."

"I guess you're right." Jamal sat up, then swung his feet off the bed. "You want something in particular? Chinese? Pizza?"

Nia pulled the covers over her body. "Not really. Whatever's quick." Her stomach growled once more. "Yeah, I'm definitely famished. Even burgers will satisfy me."

"I'll see if there's a Wendy's around. No onions, cheese."

"Yes," Nia replied, the word sounding like a happy moan.

"I remember many things, Ni Ni."

Maybe he remembered too much. Like the hope she'd made him feel, hope that he'd finally have a normal, secure life. But he also remembered the pain at losing that hope when their relationship had fallen apart.

Melancholy gripped him as he slipped into his clothes. He was so used to burying any hope, it was painful to remember it. All his life, he'd had disappointment after disappointment. But if you expected the worst, nothing and no one could let you down.

He had expected more with Nia, only to realize that it was all a dream. He couldn't give her what she needed. And he'd never fit into her world.

That didn't change the one thing that was right with them: They communicated best when making love. Being with her again only made it more apparent how much he missed her in that way.

Maybe it was too much to wish for, but he didn't want to lose that.

CHAPTER 6

NIA threw the door open seconds after she heard the knock. The smell of burgers and fries made her salivate.

She reached for the paper bag Jamal held, saying, "I swear, nothing has ever smelled this good."

Jamal pulled the bag out of her reach, and when Nia gave him a surprised look, he lowered his head and softly kissed her lips. Warmth flooded her body at the same time that a stab of pain pierced her heart. She wished Jamal wouldn't do things like this—kiss her like he was in love with her, give her affectionate looks that said she was the only woman who would ever own his heart.

Jamal reached for the top of the towel that Nia had securely wrapped around herself. "I'm not sure what's more tempting right now," he said, his voice husky. "This food that my stomach craves, or you."

Nia swatted Jamal's hand away. "I don't know about you, but my energy is definitely depleted. I need dinner . . . before any more dessert."

Jamal gave her a sly smile. "True."

He passed Nia the bag; taking it, she hurried to the living room sofa. Before her butt hit the cushion, she had a burger withdrawn and partly unwrapped. She was about to sink her teeth into it, but then asked, "Are they both the same?"

"Mine has onions."

Nia checked out the burger, and realizing that this one

was indeed hers, dug in. She groaned happily as the delicious flavors exploded in her mouth.

Jamal settled beside her and began eating. When they were both finished, Nia gathered the garbage and disposed of it in the kitchen. On her way back into the living room, she couldn't help noticing the intense look Jamal gave her, even though he quickly looked away.

By the time she sat next to him once more, Jamal's eyes simmered with sexual desire, very different from the look she'd seen moments ago. She was suddenly aware that she was dressed only in a towel. It was hard enough to resist Jamal when she was fully clothed—not that she'd ever wanted to resist him—but tonight, the sex had a different meaning for them. This was one last fling, as Jamal had said, and each time they made love, she knew it was one time closer to being the last.

Nia pushed the irksome thought to the back of her mind. Strangely, even though she felt a measure of sadness, her body longed for Jamal's touch.

"You remembered to pick up some clothes for me?" Nia asked, proud that she'd mastered a nonchalant tone, considering the fact that her body was already thrumming with sexual awareness.

"I did." Jamal's lips curled in a small frown. "But you might not like what I found."

"What does that mean?"

"There wasn't much of a selection, so I wasn't able to shop for style. Sorry, Ni Ni."

"As long as I don't have to go out dressed in that wedding gown, that's all that matters." Nia stood. "All right. Let me see what you got."

Nia took a step toward the door and the plastic bag that had to hold the clothes, but Jamal wrapped his hand around her wrist. With one strong pull, she was on his lap. "Not so fast," he said slowly. For a moment, their breaths mingled—his mouth was so near to hers that they were almost kissing. "The clothes can wait, Ni Ni." He brushed his nose across her cheek. "Right now, I'm in the mood for dessert. And I can't think of anything better than this sweet body of yours."

Jamal gently suckled her bottom lip. "What about you, Ni Ni? Aren't you in the mood for dessert?"

Nia wanted to say no, that she couldn't play this game with him anymore because it was too painful, but instead she closed her eyes and lifted her head, allowing Jamal greater access to her neck. His hot tongue flicked over her skin, and the simple motion was potent enough to flood her body with glorious sensations. She could deny it all she wanted, but she was powerless to deny the chemistry between her and Jamal, which was the one reason she'd known she'd have to stay away from him. With Jamal, it was all or nothing. While the sex was amazing, she wanted more from him, more than he was able to give.

Yet right now, as his hands burned a sensuous path along her skin, her mind kept downplaying all the reasons she'd vowed to stay away from him.

One last fling.

When Jamal loosened the towel, she fleetingly thought of John, but not as the man she missed. She thought of him as the man she now felt sorry for, because the woman he'd been about to marry didn't love him enough to fight to get back to him.

Jamal's warm breath fanned her nipple, and even before he took it in his mouth, it puckered and hardened with anticipation. And when Jamal began to softly suckle her, Nia thought she would die of the pleasure. Lord help her, she wanted Jamal with a passion she couldn't control.

Jamal slipped a hand between her legs, stroking her nub. "Man, I love how you're always ready for me. Always so wet . . ."

Nia whimpered in reply.

Jamal lifted his slick finger, stroked it across her nipple, then took the nipple in his mouth once again. The pleasure from the act was so erotic, Nia almost came.

"Take your clothes off," she breathed against his ear. Easing her body off his, Nia reached for Jamal's jeans. She undid the button, but Jamal had to lift himself to pull down the zipper. With his jeans dragged over his hips, Nia reached for him. She moaned against his lips when she found him erect.

He was driving her crazy, and she wanted to give him a dose of his own medicine. She took him in her palm and began stroking his shaft. With her thumb, she fingered the moist tip.

"You're wet, too," she whispered. "Mmm . . . I love that."

"Ni Ni, I need you. Don't torture me."

"The way you've been torturing me?" She gave him a sly smile as she bent down before him, settling her body between his legs. "If it's good for the goose . . ."

Nia's voice trailed off as she brought her mouth down to his thighs. She kissed his warm flesh, flicked her tongue over the hairy surface. Her reward was his long rapturous moan. Feeling powerful, she moved her lips upward, trailing her tongue along his member. When she flicked it over the tip, Jamal moaned again, more intensely than the first time.

Nia was relentless with her mouth on his skin, her own body feeling such intense carnal pleasure simply because of how much he was enjoying it. Oh yes, she was loving every minute of his loss of control, and it was exactly what he deserved, considering what he did to her.

Jamal slipped his fingers into her hair and urged her upward. He brought her lips to his, delving his tongue into her mouth. Sucking, nipping, Jamal made her weak with every movement of his mouth and tongue.

"Straddle me, Ni Ni."

Nia did, and with one easy movement, Jamal guided himself into her body. Nia cried out from the pleasure. Wrapping her arms around Jamal, she pressed her face against his. As she mewled softly against his ear, he breathed raggedly into hers. Their bodies joined, they were one—the physical pleasure secondary to the emotional.

Nia's brain knew then what her heart had always known—she only enjoyed Jamal sexually to the extent she did because of what she felt for him in the depths of her heart.

It was her love for him that made their sexual connection so powerful.

She held him tighter as he thrust deep inside her. It felt right. It *was* right.

"Oh, Jamal," she murmured against his ear. She stopped herself before saying, *I love you.*

She'd loved him almost from the moment they'd started dating three years ago. And given the way she felt even now, she was certain she always would.

Nia clung to that, clung to the love she felt for Jamal. Because if this was their last night together, she wanted to be able to savor this one last fling with the man who would always have her heart.

CHAPTER 7

THE high Nia had felt in Jamal's arms during the night had sunk to a horrible low by the next morning. Resting her head on both hands as she watched him sleep, she was overcome with a deep sense of loss.

Last night with Jamal had been spectacular, but it had cost her so much. Perhaps too much.

Because of their time together, she could never go back to John. She knew that without doubt. But where did that leave her? Alone? Or did she have a future with Jamal?

Nia's stomach clenched at that thought. Despite how close she and Jamal had been for the past several hours, there had been no talk of love. It was still there, in her heart. But what about his? She didn't want to set herself up for failure. Given everything that she had already gone through with Jamal, Nia would be a fool to jump to any conclusions simply because they still connected in bed.

Damn him. How dare he come back into her life just when she thought she had it on track and pull the rug out from under her world? Of course, it would all be worth it if Jamal wanted a life with her, if he'd come to realize that he loved her and couldn't live without her.

Did he?

His sleeping form gave her no answers.

Nia sighed and rolled onto her back. She had a mind to wake Jamal up and get the answers she wanted, the answers she deserved. Because if he didn't want a future with her, then she couldn't spend another moment here with him.

Her opportunity to talk came approximately twenty minutes later, when Jamal reached for her and pulled her body close to his. It wasn't a gesture made in sleep, given the fact that he buried his face in the groove of her neck and started to kiss her.

Nia fought the pleasant emotions flooding her body. She would not let him seduce her, not this time. Now wasn't the time for sex. They'd had last night, a night where they pretended the rest of the world didn't exist. But with the morning came the need to face reality.

Nia turned in Jamal's arms until she was face-to-face with him. She wanted to blurt out what was on her mind, but she was afraid. The mood between them was almost too perfect to ruin.

Almost. Knowing that he loved her and wanted a life with her would make it perfect.

"Hey, you." Jamal smiled.

"Hey, yourself."

"How long have you been awake?"

"Long enough."

Jamal ran his fingers down to her butt. "This is nice, Ni Ni," he said softly. "Waking up with you like this."

Nia's heart ached at Jamal's words. *Then why don't you want it every day?*

Jamal leaned forward and kissed her lips, but Nia moved her head. He frowned at her, finally catching on that she wasn't in the mood.

"What is it?" he asked.

"Why did you kidnap me?"

A few seconds passed before he replied. "I told you. I didn't want to see you make a mistake."

"That's the only reason?"

"Isn't that one good enough?"

"So . . . you didn't have any other motive?"

Jamal cupped a butt cheek. "You mean other than me having my wicked way with you?"

"Not now, Jamal." She shifted her body away from his, pulling the cotton sheet up to her chest as she did. "I'm trying to be serious."

"All right," he said warily. "What's on your mind?"

Nia counted to five, gathering her courage, then spoke. "I want to know . . . your kidnapping me . . . that had nothing to do with you . . ." She stopped. Inhaled deeply. "Did your kidnapping me have anything to do with you realizing that you . . . that you still love me?"

It had taken all her courage to get the words out, only to be rewarded with silence. One agonizing second passed into the next.

The silence stretched.

Finally, a ragged breath. "Like I said, I didn't want you to make a mistake."

Nia's stomach was a ball of tightly mangled nerves. "Why did you think I was making a mistake?"

"Because of what we just shared."

She felt anger rise at his comment. As if she'd planned on sharing this with him! He had orchestrated it all. But she kept her cool and asked, "What exactly did we share?"

There was a pause. "I think it's fair to say that if you could still give yourself to me the way you did last night, then you shouldn't be marrying John, much less anyone else."

"Really?"

"That's my opinion. I don't think John-boy would be too happy to know what happened between us."

"You said yourself it was one last fling. That's the only reason I agreed to it."

Something flashed in Jamal's eyes. Fear? "So you're going back to John?"

"Will that bother you?"

"Hell, yes."

"Why?"

"Because you're not going to be happy."

"What's going to make me happy?" Nia challenged.

Their gazes met, held. Jamal didn't say a word, but Nia tried to read his emotions in his eyes.

"What are you afraid of?" Nia's words were merely a whisper.

"Nothing," Jamal answered quickly. Too quickly.

"Do you want me?"

"I want what's good between us."

"In other words," Nia began, "you want me to take ten steps backward with you." She paused. "When are you going to face your fears?"

"Don't do this."

"Me?" In one quick movement, Nia was sitting cross-legged on the bed, the blanket hiding her nakedness. "Damn you, Jamal. You've turned my whole world upside down, and you don't think I have a right to ask you a few questions?"

"I don't want to fight with you."

"No, you just want to f—" Nia blew out a frustrated breath.

Jamal sat up, leaning his head against the heart-shaped headboard. "It's not that simple. I didn't want you to get married with us still on bad terms. I guess I wanted closure. Positive closure."

"This doesn't feel positive. I . . .". Nia's voice trailed off. "I have so many more questions now," she finished quietly.

Jamal didn't say a word. His gaze was fixed on his hands, which rested on his lap—covering his penis.

Nia continued, "I know how afraid you are . . ."

"I don't want to talk about this."

"You said we had unresolved issues. This is what needs to be resolved between us."

"It didn't work, Nia." Jamal finally faced her then. "We're from two different worlds."

"But I'm good enough to have sex with when you're ready."

"You know that's not true. I don't know. I guess I still want you in my life."

"Sexually."

"Sex is the one area we always got along."

Nia had gone out on a limb, hoping Jamal would for once take a risk and face the things that held him back. When was she going to learn? She was still a fool, the consummate dreamer who couldn't discern reality from fiction. "I can't believe you."

"If there's going to be anything between us, maybe we need to concentrate on what's good, build from there."

Nia guffawed. "I'm not going backward with you. You either want me or you don't."

"You think it's that easy?" Jamal challenged.

"It should be. If you care about me. If you don't, then . . . I guess I'm the world's biggest idiot."

"Of course I care about you. I wouldn't be here if I didn't."

"But you don't love me."

There was a long pause. Then he said, "You got me a job working for your father."

Nia was surprised at Jamal's statement, because it was so out of the blue. But it had been the catalyst for the end of their relationship, and was clearly still an issue. "You still think I did that because I wanted to hurt you, not help you?"

"Work for your father?" His tone was incredulous. "You knew damn well I couldn't fit into his world. And he'd never like me, no matter how you dressed me up."

"You were the one saying how much you hated being a mechanic, that you wanted a different line of work."

"Yeah, well, I didn't need that."

"As far as I could tell, you didn't know what you needed. I don't see why you had to be so upset with me trying to help out."

"I would have found my own way, sooner or later. But that was for me to do, not you."

"You're still a mechanic."

"Yeah . . . But now I'm taking some business management courses." He shrugged. "In case one day I decide to, I don't know, open my own shop."

Forgetting she was upset, Nia's heart lifted a little. "Oh, that's great, Jamal."

"Acceptable, you mean?"

His words were like a vise around her heart. "Why do you have to do that? Say something like that?"

"Because I wanted you to accept me as I was, damn it. Not for what you saw I could be. In dress pants and ties, having dinner with the kinds of people your family considers important. That's what you wanted, Nia. And that wasn't me."

Jamal's words stopped Nia cold. How could he say that?

She'd always accepted him, despite what her family had said about him. "That's not true."

"Isn't it?"

"Of course not!"

"John-boy fit into your world. Your family loves him."

"I didn't want him. I wanted you. I love . . ." Nia nearly choked on the word. "I loved you."

Jamal was silent for a long while, and Nia fought the emotion that threatened to overwhelm her. The last thing she was going to do was let Jamal see her cry, not if he didn't want her.

"I told you from the beginning," Jamal said softly, "that I didn't think I'd be good at a relationship, at the whole marriage thing."

"So, what—you're never supposed to grow, change? You also said you'd never love me or anyone else, but that changed. Was I so wrong to hope that maybe one day we could settle down and get married? That's what people in love do."

"Like you and John."

"Go to hell," Nia spat out, then turned, swinging her legs over the side of the bed.

Jamal wrapped a hand around her wrist. "I wanted things to stay the same, Ni Ni."

Nia closed her eyes and shook her head, frustrated. "A woman is only going to be happy for so long, living with a man as his wife yet having none of the perks—"

"That's not what I mean," Jamal said, his voice so soft Nia almost didn't hear him.

Nia turned. "Then what do you mean?"

"Everything in my life always changed, Nia. First, my mother who was supposed to love me abandoned me. My grandmother could only deal with me for a few years before she shipped me off to an aunt."

Like so many times in the past, Nia felt the strongest urge to comfort him. Even though Jamal had told her about his past before, this was the first time he'd told her the story with any emotion. She'd been right about him; despite his tough exterior, he was sad and lonely on the inside. Perhaps he didn't even believe that he deserved love, given the fact that he'd never truly received it.

Nia moved closer to him. She reached for the side of his face and gently caressed it. "I understand you, Jamal. More than you know."

Jamal turned away from her touch, and the rejection hurt. But Nia pressed on, telling herself that Jamal wasn't rejecting her, he just didn't know how to truly accept what she was offering him. That had been his problem all along.

"I can't do this, Nia."

"Why not?"

"You . . . you deserve better, and I can't give you that. You deserve someone who's stable—"

"Don't tell me what I deserve." Nia was going to be damned if she'd let Jamal off the hook so easily. If he loved her, then he was going to have to fight for her, finally. It was about time he overcame his fears.

Jamal placed a hand over hers, taking it off his face. He looked at her with unwavering eyes. "Your family will never accept me. Especially after this stunt."

"I don't really care what my family wants. I can't live for them forever."

"And that's why you're working for your father's company instead of teaching, right?"

Nia's mouth opened, but she couldn't think of a thing to say. Instead, she swallowed painfully and looked away.

"Do you see now?" Jamal asked. "I only make things more difficult for you."

"I plan to go to teacher's college in the fall." Nia paused. "Because you made me realize that I had to live my life on my own terms, in my own way." Which made her think about John. She'd agreed to marry John because the one man she'd truly wanted had cut himself out of her life. There would never be another Jamal, and yes, she wanted a family. So, she'd decided to settle. But when it came to her other life's passion, teaching, she'd realized that all Jamal had told her about living her life for what she wanted was exactly what she had to do.

A smile spread across Jamal's face. "Really?"

"Yes."

"That's great, Ni Ni." He caressed her face.

Nia pulled back, away from his touch. "Don't touch me." Confusion flashed in his eyes. "You tell me I should go for what I really want, but what about you? What do you do? You hide behind your fears, as if that's okay."

"I am trying not to be selfish," Jamal replied, his expression saying he couldn't understand why she didn't see his point.

"And to hell with who you hurt in the process, right? How selfish is that?"

Nia scrambled off the bed and stormed from the room, fleeing down the stairs. She wasn't going to cry, not again. She'd shed too many tears over Jamal already and she'd be damned if she was going to let him get the better of her emotions now.

It was over. Deep in his heart, he might want her, but he was too afraid, too stubborn, or too hell-bent on living in misery to go for what he wanted.

And she couldn't deal with that. Not anymore.

The fact that she didn't hear Jamal coming down the stairs after her almost made her break down, but she held herself in check. She needed to get out of here.

How was she going to get home? And what the hell was she going to wear? She couldn't wear the wedding dress. If she had to hail a cab, she certainly didn't want to do so in that gown.

The bag! She rushed to the door and retrieved the plastic bag Jamal had brought in last night and took it to the sofa. Inside, she found a large T-shirt with the word "Florida" written on it, as well as a picture of dolphins. The bottom piece was a bathing suit wrap with waves of aqua.

Hardly fashionable, as Jamal had told her, but it was her only option.

Nia slipped into the clothes.

Sinking onto the sofa with a sigh, her eyes caught sight of the phone on the chair. Yes, the phone! Relief washed over her when she remembered that she could call someone to pick her up, rather than try to find a cab service without a phone book. It was Sunday morning, and all her family should be home.

Christine would come and get her.

Nia grabbed the phone from the armchair and unraveled the cord that Jamal had wrapped around it. She plugged it into the wall outlet.

Quickly, she punched in the digits to her sister's number. "Hey, Christine. It's me. I need a ride home. Can you come and get me?"

CHAPTER 8

"I don't want to talk about it," Nia said glumly as Christine headed out of the hotel's parking lot. To her surprise—and disappointment—Jamal hadn't argued with her when she'd told him that she'd called her sister. Instead, he'd merely shrugged, resigned to the inevitable. It was his last chance to put his heart on the line, and he hadn't taken it.

Well, at least Nia knew it was truly over. Even if the reality hurt.

Nia rested her head against the window, but even though she didn't look at her sister, she could sense Christine's eyes on her.

"Nice outfit," Christine commented.

"I know," Nia replied. "It was all I had to work with. And it was better than wearing that gown again."

"I'm sure." After a moment, Christine asked, "Did you . . . sleep with him?"

"Christine—"

"All right, fine." Christine sighed. "Can I ask you this: Why didn't you call John to come get you?"

"Because I can't face him right now."

"Oh, God. You *did* sleep with him."

"I didn't say that," Nia quickly pointed out, looking at Christine. But she felt her cheeks burn with the knowledge that she'd done exactly that and she quickly turned her gaze to the view along US-1. "I can't face John yet because . . . because I don't know what to say to him. This is all so . . .

bizarre. Besides, I've been doing some thinking."

"Uh-oh."

Nia's eyelids fluttered shut as she thought of the night she'd spent with Jamal. One last fling, he'd said. In the heat of the moment, it had seemed like a good idea. Yet it had left Nia unsatisfied. She wanted so much more, so much more than he could give her.

"John and I moved too fast," Nia went on.

"Damn Jamal."

"No, this isn't his fault." Nia faced her sister then, and Christine met her eyes for a moment. "I know you won't understand this, but what Jamal did . . . he helped me. Marriage is a very serious commitment, and if I can't marry John without any reservations, then I shouldn't be marrying him."

"You were set to marry him twenty-four hours ago!"

Christine hit the brakes as she came up on another car too quickly.

"Keep your eyes on the road, Christine."

Christine groaned. "What's changed in twenty-four hours? I'll tell you what's changed. Your ex pulled some crazy stunt, and that's got you reminiscing about the past. You've completely forgotten all the reasons why it didn't work in the first place. But you shouldn't forget, Nia. Jamal broke your heart once, and if you continue to live in this fantasy world where he's concerned—"

"Stop!" The tone of Nia's voice surprised even her. But she was sick of this, sick of everyone else thinking they had the right to criticize her feelings, just because she was the baby in the family.

"You and Howard may be happy working for Dad, and you know what? That's great. But that's *your* choice. I want something different for my life."

"Jamal?"

"Yes." Nia practically shouted the word. Too bad he wanted nothing to do with her. She had lied to herself for a year, but it was clear she wasn't over Jamal. She wasn't sure she ever would be.

"And I want my own life," she continued. "I want to do more than tutor kids a couple days a week. I want to be a teacher. That's my passion. Not dealing with the books for Dad's restaurants."

"You know Dad wants to keep the business in the family."

"Well." Nia threw her hands in the air. For a moment, she felt the familiar guilt creep into her brain, but she cut it off.

"That really isn't my problem, now, is it? I hate accounting. I hate numbers. I love children. I want to teach. I was born to teach. This is the gift the Lord gave me, and I intend to use it."

"What's gotten into you?" Christine asked.

If Nia hadn't been living in her own skin for all her life, she might wonder the same thing, too. She was always the one who agreed with her family's "wisdom," the one who did what she was told. She'd followed the path set out for her without question or protest. It wasn't a life she wanted to live anymore.

"I am trying to be me," Nia replied, her voice sounding weary. "I just want to be me."

Christine didn't say anything else, and to Nia's surprise, she realized she didn't care what her sister was thinking. Living for everyone else and by the standards set out by her father had only made her miserable.

She would have to talk to John, make him understand. She cared for him deeply, but she didn't love him. And she wanted love. And passion. Last night with Jamal had confirmed for her that she couldn't live her whole life with a man she felt less than 100 percent crazy about.

So where did that leave her?

Hell if she knew. The only man she loved like that, the only man she probably *would* love like that, was too afraid to give her his heart.

"He should be arrested." Nia's father paced back and forth along the living room floor.

"I'm okay," Nia stressed, looking up at her father from the sofa. "He didn't hurt me."

"His type . . . he comes from bad stock. I always knew he was trouble when you first started seeing him."

"Don't start that, Dad," Nia said. "That whole snob routine never looked good on you."

Her father shot her a horrified look. "What did you say?"

"There's only one reason you didn't like Jamal, and it had nothing to do with how he treated me. And how he treated me should have been your number-one priority."

Her father scowled, his eyes flashing fire, but he didn't say anything.

"I won't have him arrested. Like I told you, I'm fine."

John placed his arm across her shoulders and pulled her close. "It's okay now. All that matters is that you're back."

Nia stiffened in John's arms. When he placed his lips on her cheek, she turned her face.

She felt John's eyes boring into her, as though trying to figure her out. And she felt guilty. But she couldn't continue living a lie.

"I know," John said after a moment. "It's been a crazy twenty-four hours. But don't worry. We'll get married just as soon as we can."

"That's right, sweetheart," Nia's mother chimed from the armchair across the living room. "I've already spoken with the wedding planner about rescheduling at the earliest possible date."

Nia's heart stumbled. Her breathing became shallow. Once again, she felt her whole life slipping from her control. Over their mother's shoulder, Christine, who stood by the window with her arms crossed over her chest, gave Nia a disapproving look.

"No offense to anyone," Nia said, "but I am pretty tired right now. I don't really want to talk about the wedding."

"Of course you're tired." Her mother stood. "Milton, Christine, John. We should let Nia get some rest."

"Actually, I'd like to speak with John alone."

"Yes, naturally," her mother said. "Let's give them some time alone." Nia's mother, father, and sister began filing out of the living room. As Christine passed her, she made eye contact with her, as if to say, "Don't blow a good thing."

Nia waited until she no longer heard any footsteps in the distance before turning to John.

Giving her a soft smile, he took both of her hands in

his. "I want to ask what happened," John began slowly. "But it really doesn't matter. As long as we're still getting married, nothing matters."

John's eyes searched her face, as if in hopes of finding the answer he wanted. And Nia knew then that it was true, that the eyes were the windows to the soul, because John's face fell and he suddenly looked away.

"You don't want to marry me, do you?" He released her hands. "Not anymore."

Nia inhaled deeply, as deeply as she could considering there was a lump the size of a basketball lodged in her chest. "John, I care about you . . ."

"But you don't love me."

"I never wanted to hurt you. And I know this sounds horrible, but I think it's a good thing we didn't get married yesterday. Because the last thing I'd want to do is realize in six months that I made a mistake."

John was silent for a long while, and Nia didn't know what to do. Finally, she placed a gentle hand on his knee. "I know this won't make things better, but I'm sorry."

"You're in love with him?"

Pause. "Yes. I guess I always have been, but I thought I couldn't have him."

John's eyes met hers. "And he waited until our wedding day to decide he couldn't live without you?"

Nia didn't answer.

"Great," John said. "He still doesn't want you, does he? Man, I don't believe this. He doesn't want you, yet you still don't want me."

"You don't want me by default, John. Because the man I love doesn't love me back." God, it hurt for her to say that. Too much. "You want someone who loves you for you, whose being with you doesn't depend on if she isn't able to be with the one she really wants. You deserve that, John. Life is too short for anything else."

Resignation flashed in John's eyes. He couldn't deny the truth of what she was saying.

Nia gave him a rueful smile and stroked his cheek. "It's not you, John. You're a good man. But Jamal still has my heart. No matter how much I think right now that a life with you is what I want, in a few years, you'd be miserable with me. Because I'd be miserable. Please understand. And please forgive me."

"I love you, Nia. And I want you happy. Even if that's not with me."

Nia sucked in her tears as she wrapped her arms around John. He could have made this so much more difficult for her, but he hadn't. "Thank you," she said softly. "Thank you."

Telling the family wasn't as easy as telling John. But once the fireworks died down, Nia lay in her bed, exhausted. Despite how hard it had been to do what was in her heart, she felt relieved. She no longer carried the burden she'd been carrying for months where John was concerned.

But there was a different pain in her heart now. The pain of loneliness that came from knowing she'd laid it all on the line—but the man she wanted would probably never accept her love. She'd taken a risk, but she was still going to be lonely.

Sighing, Nia rolled over. What could she do? She didn't want to turn the clock back to Saturday afternoon when she'd been about to marry John. She didn't want a chance to live that moment over again. Because regardless, she knew now that marrying John would have been a mistake.

And just the way she knew she'd never love John the way she should, it wasn't going to help to fantasize that Jamal would ever come around to loving her the way she hoped—not if he didn't already.

That was the most frustrating part of all this. She *felt* that Jamal loved her. Had she been so wrong? Was he simply able to give himself to her while lovemaking in a way that made it *seem* like she had his heart? After being with him again, she knew it was impossible to deny that she was anything but hopelessly in love with him. Everything they shared physically came from what was in the depths of her heart and soul.

But here she was, still alone.

• • •

Jamal swung his feet off the bed, stubbing his toe against the buckle of a belt he had thrown on the floor. He let out a howl and started to curse—stopping only when he realized that it wasn't the physical pain that was bothering him as much as the ache in the center of his gut.

Was he a fool? Ever since Nia had left him yesterday, he'd been miserable. He'd told himself that if he just had a taste of her one last time, she could go on and marry John and he'd be content. Just one last fling. . . . Those had been his words, and now they haunted him.

He hadn't spoken with Nia, and he had no idea what was going on. The not knowing was driving him nuts. He could imagine that John was comforting her now, and that once he had his hands on her again, the man wouldn't let her go. That was what Jamal would do—if he were in John's shoes.

Yeah, he was pretty sure she and John had had a sweet reunion. It made sense.

Otherwise, wouldn't he have heard from her by now?

And though he tried to console himself with the thought that this was for the best, as he made his way to the bathroom he couldn't avoid the voice that said, *Jamal, you're a fool.*

CHAPTER 9

THE last person Jamal expected to see on his doorstep late the next evening was Christine. Her hands planted firmly on her hips, she greeted him with a scowl.

"Christine. What can I do for you?" Jamal didn't bother with the pleasantries. It was clear she wasn't here on a social call.

"I need to speak with you," she announced. "Preferably inside."

Jamal shrugged nonchalantly, though mentally he was preparing to defend himself against whatever Christine was going to say. She'd never approved of his relationship with her sister, and she most certainly wasn't happy with how he'd disrupted the wedding. Damn, he didn't need this now. He'd had a long day at work, with a couple of pissed-off customers. He didn't need Nia's pissed-off sister to top the day off.

When she was in the foyer of his apartment, Jamal closed the door. Then he faced her.

"Do you love my sister?" Christine asked, getting right down to business.

Jamal was startled by the question.

"You showed up minutes before she was going to get married, and you kidnapped her. Now, it would be one thing if you did that because you realized you were hopelessly in love with her. But if you ruined her wedding day—her life—

simply because you didn't want to see her happy with anyone else, then I'll never forgive you for that.

"Not that you care about my forgiveness," Christine went on. "But I'm hoping you care about Nia."

"Is she okay?" Jamal interjected.

"Physically, yes. Emotionally, no. You did something to her when you took her, Jamal. And she hasn't been the same. In many ways. She's called off the wedding."

"Postponed—"

"No, called off." Christine blew out a weary breath, her expression softening. "Listen, I came to see you because I think you should know. It's obvious my sister still loves you. And I hope to God you didn't ruin her wedding day in vain. I hope to God that in that heart of yours, you actually love her and will be man enough to step up to the plate. Because she's miserable, and I've finally realized that it doesn't matter what I want for her, nor what my parents want for her. If you're the one who makes her life complete, then you two should be together." She paused. "Anyway, it's late, and I have a husband to get home to. So, that's all. I just thought you should know the deal."

Whirling around, Christine left as quickly as she had come, closing the door behind her.

For a long while, Jamal stood in the foyer. He felt winded, like he'd done battle. Though he hadn't. He hadn't even said a word.

Yet Christine's words had pulled the rug out from under him and knocked him flat on his back.

He wasn't stupid enough to think that her visit meant she liked him. But she loved her sister. And since she'd actually come to tell him the news that Nia had called off the wedding, then it meant that Christine had finally come to accept that what was best for Nia mattered most—even if it was him.

She'd said that Nia had changed in a lot of ways. What had happened when she'd left him? She'd called off the wedding, that was all he knew. What had she told her family about her reasons, and how had they reacted?

Oh, to have been a fly on that wall. . . .

There was still a way to find out. Yet Jamal didn't move

into the living room to use the phone. His feet were rooted to the vinyl floor in the small foyer of his apartment.

He was afraid, he realized. Afraid of what Nia would say.

The next morning, Jamal was still afraid. All night, he'd tried to pinpoint his feelings, to get at the root of the fear. He wasn't sure he'd succeeded. He only knew that he couldn't go on letting the fear or anything else hold him back.

He needed to talk to Nia.

He pulled his Harley into her driveway, then killed the engine.

And sat there.

There was no movement. No angry mother or father running out to tell him to get off their property. The family's Mercedes was in the driveway, however, so Jamal was certain that at least one of Nia's parents was home.

It didn't matter. He hadn't come this far to have anyone send him away.

He got off his motorcycle and strolled up the driveway, then rang the doorbell.

Jamal didn't realize that he was holding his breath until the front door opened.

"Jamal." His name was an expression of surprise on Nia's lips.

Jamal swallowed. "Morning, Nia."

She eyed him with a guarded expression. "What are you doing here?"

"I wanted to talk to you," he replied softly.

Nia gave him an assessing look, then asked, "Why?"

Jamal had a sense of déjà vu. Nearly a week ago, he and Nia had stood here. So much had changed in that time.

Hearing noise in the background, he suggested, "Maybe we can go for a ride."

"On your Harley?"

"Yeah. Like we used to." He shrugged. "I figured we could find a spot to talk. Somewhere private."

Nia looked over her shoulder, then back at him. "I'm not sure that's the best thing, Jamal."

"We haven't talked since . . . since you came home." Jamal saw Nia's chest rise with a deep breath, and he knew she was uncomfortable with the topic.

"I know what you wanted, Jamal. It happened, and . . . I'm fine with it. One last fling."

The sadness he heard in her voice was like a punch in his stomach. How had he ever convinced himself that he could live without her? That she'd be better off without him? That thinking had led to a year of misery for both of them.

"There are some things we need to discuss," he said simply. "And I'd rather not do that here."

Nia gave a glum nod. "All right. I guess it can't hurt. Give me a minute."

Nia disappeared into the house, then returned about thirty seconds later. She looked so sad, and Jamal knew it was all his fault. Christine's words rang in his brain. If he'd had the gall to end her wedding and her potential happiness, he pretty much owed it to her to be true to his feelings.

But he didn't want to tell her that here. He wanted to take her to the spot on Hollywood beach that had been their special place.

Jamal passed Nia a helmet, then got onto the Harley. She climbed on behind him. The feel of her arms around his waist gave him pause. He closed his eyes and savored the feeling. A life without Nia holding him? Jamal didn't even want to picture it.

The drive took a little less than half an hour, all of it in silence. Jamal pulled his Harley into a parking spot along A1A on Hollywood beach, then parked it. He got off the bike, but Nia didn't move.

When he faced her, she simply looked at him, a question in her eyes.

Why here?

Jamal offered her a hand and helped her off. Then he led the way toward the ocean. Nia walked a couple steps behind him. He could feel her presence, even if he couldn't see her.

Jamal continued walking, until they got to the stretch of the beach they both knew so well, just behind one of the modern high-rises they'd once talked about living in. Stopping, he faced Nia.

Nia didn't look at him. Instead, she glanced around at the beach. The silence was so thick you could make sand castles from it. Because Jamal knew exactly what she was thinking, even though he couldn't see her eyes.

Finally, she whirled around to face him. "If this is your idea of going full circle—"

"Meaning?"

"Meaning it began here, so it has to end here?"

"Ni Ni," Jamal said, a hint of playfulness in his tone, "why do you have to be so pessimistic?"

She averted her eyes, then looked at him once more. "Why did you bring me here?"

"I told you, I wanted to talk."

"But why *here*? This is where we used to . . ." Nia's voice trailed off as she looked at the beautiful high-rise, and Jamal was certain he'd heard a little hitch in her voice.

"This is where we used to come to talk about our lives, what was right and what was wrong." Jamal stepped toward her and placed his hands on her shoulders. "Remember how we used to slip right between those two buildings there and make out?"

Nia shrugged away from Jamal's touch. "I'd rather not take this trip down memory lane."

Jamal couldn't help smiling. God, he loved her. He really did. He loved her passion, whether she was purring in his arms or telling him where to go.

"You once told me I was a coward," he finally said, his tone now serious. "You were right."

Nia's eyes registered surprise. "I'm listening."

Jamal blew out a weary breath. It wasn't easy expressing his feelings this way. He was so much better at non-verbal communication. But this needed to be said.

"I've had a lot of time to think over the past couple days. And I miss you, Nia."

"If you are going to suggest that we have a physically exclusive relationship once again—"

"Hear me out."

She eyed him warily, then finally replied, "All right."

"Yes, I miss the sex. I even convinced myself that the sex was the reason I'd kidnapped you. That if I could have you one last time, I could get you out of my system. I know now that was a lie.

"I'm in love with you, Nia." When she scowled at him, he held up a hand. "No, please listen. I was always in love with you. You know that."

"You said love wasn't enough."

"I was afraid. Nothing in my life ever lasted. No one ever loved me forever. It wasn't you I doubted. I guess I doubted my worth. Why would you love me forever when my own mother, my own family, couldn't wait to get me out of their hair?"

"My love is unconditional, Jamal."

"I know. And now I believe that. That's what I'm trying to tell you." Jamal reached for Nia's hand and gently pulled her close. "I don't want to live my life being afraid anymore. I don't know why we met, why we clicked the way we did. I only know that no other woman can make me feel the way you do. And when I'm old and lonely, am I going to regret letting you slip away when I had the chance to try and make a life with you? I damn well know I will."

Jamal raised both his hands to Nia's face, where he softly stroked her skin with his fingers. "I'm still afraid."

"Afraid of what?"

"The truth?"

"Of course."

Jamal closed his eyes as the old feelings of sadness over not being loved washed over him. But if there was one thing he knew, Nia was nothing like his mother. "What scares me the most is the thought that one day you'll wake up and realize that I'm not worthy of your love."

"Oh, Jamal." Nia's voice was laced with pain.

"That's always been my fear. But I only realized that last night. And then where would I be, after counting on having a life with you? It was a chance I didn't want to take."

"Oh, baby." Nia framed his cheek. "Do you know how much good you've done for me? Because of you, I had the strength to go for my dreams. And you know what I learned? That the world isn't going to fall apart if I do what I want. I can live my life on my terms, and my family won't die."

"I'm glad."

"And that includes you, Jamal. If my family loves me, they'll have to accept you."

"I can only hope."

"Howard's family didn't like Christine in the beginning. They thought she was a snob."

"Well . . . she is."

Nia chuckled. "I know. But my point is, she wasn't their first choice for Howard. Now they love her." She paused. "You may not be my family's first choice, but you're *my* choice. I'll be damned if I let you slip away, when I know they'll come around to loving you one day. And it's not like they hate you . . ."

"I know."

"And if they don't come around . . . that's their problem. But considering they've given me their blessing about pursuing teaching, I know how they'll respond."

Jamal inhaled deeply. He could only offer her arguments about why a life without him would be easier, but he knew that anything worthwhile in life didn't come easily.

"I don't want you to change," Nia went on. To Jamal's surprise, her eyes misted. "I love you just the way you are. *Because* you are the way you are. I want you to know that."

"I believe you, Nia. But more important, I finally believe that I can really have that kind of love. That I deserve it. I really didn't believe it before. But I've come to terms with my past, with everything that went wrong in my life. And it started with forgiving my mother.

"I don't want to live without you." Right there on the sand, he dropped to one knee. "So, Ni Ni, if you'll have me, I'd like to make it up to you for ruining your wedding day."

Nia brought a shaky hand to her mouth. "Jamal . . ."

"What do you say? Will you marry me?"

Nia sank onto the sand in front of him, wrapping her arms around his neck. "I say you didn't ruin my wedding day. You saved me, and I thank you for that."

"Marry me, Ni Ni. Make my life complete."

She started crying then.

"Hmm . . . Tears. I'm not sure this is a good thing."

"It's a wonderful thing," Nia said softly.

Jamal brushed a tear away. "Yeah, it is, isn't it?"

Nia nodded.

He kissed her. It wasn't a kiss like they'd shared a couple nights ago, all hot and full of passion. This kiss was full of hope. Full of the promise of a million tomorrows.

Yeah, it was a wonderful thing, Jamal thought, his heart full of real happiness for the first time in his life.

From the *Essence* and *Blackboard* bestselling author Francis Ray comes a powerful and touching novel about a man's struggle to come to grips with his violent past in order to find love in the present . . .

SOMEBODY'S KNOCKING
AT MY DOOR

FRANCIS RAY

Coming in May 2003

**Available in trade paperback from
St. Martin's/ Griffin**

SKAMY 11/02

AWARD-WINNING AUTHOR OF *A FAMILY REUNION*

BRENDA JACKSON

The Ties That Bind

A compelling, moving novel told with Brenda Jackson's trademark sensuality about strangers who became friends, and friends who became lovers.

It all started in college, in the turbulent sixties, when Randolph and Jenna became lovers. Randolph knew the moment he saw Jenna Haywood that he had to make her his. But the path to love is not an easy one. His wealthy Grandmother Julia disapproves of the match and unbeknownst to him, his brother's seemingly docile fiancée has a few plans of her own that she would like to set in motion. Betrayal and devastation lurk in unexpected places and test the bond they believed was unbreakable. As they struggle with love and passion, secrets and lies, the question is: Is love enough to help them see each other through the storms that await them ahead?

"[Brenda Jackson is] a writer before her time."

—Carl Weber

"Jackson turns up the heat."

—*Publishers Weekly* on *Fire and Desire*

AVAILABLE WHEREVER BOOKS ARE SOLD FROM
ST. MARTIN'S GRIFFIN